Diverse Voices

An Anthology of Short Stories and Poems

By the Heritage Writers Group of McDonough, Georgia

Diverse Voices
An Anthology of Short Stories and Poems
By the Heritage Writers Group of McDonough, Georgia
Copyright © 2016 by the Heritage Writers Group

For more about this book please visit http://heritagewritersga.weebly.com/

Michael McLarnon
188 Maddox Circle
Jackson, GA 30233

Ordering Information: Quantity sales. Special discounts are available on quantity purchases by corporations, associations, and others. For details, contact the publisher at the address below:

heritagewritersga@gmail.com
 ISBN 978-1-942042-04-4

1. Main category—[Fiction]
2. Other category—[Poetry]

First Edition
Printed in the United States

ACKNOWLEDGEMENTS

The Heritage Writers Group of McDonough, Georgia would like to thank the following people who helped in bringing this project to life.

Peggy Renfroe: Our founder and guiding light.

Michael McLarnon: President and Editor of this edition.

Sharon Davidson: Formatting and Printing.

Moira Fisher: Art Work and Cover Design.

R.S. Raniere: Back Cover material.

Cynthia Anne Cofell: Marketing.

And all the rest of the Heritage Writers Group who helped in editing and submitting material for the book.

DEDICATION

This book is dedicated to PJ Renfroe, founder and avid supporter of The Heritage Writers Group.

Peggy had a vision to gather a group of like-minded individuals who wanted to further their writing, culminating in the creation of The Heritage Writers Group.

Since its inception, she has worked continually to help aspiring authors refine their work through critiques, educational guidance and emotional support. Without her work, many local authors would still be struggling, not having seen their dream of being published.

Peggy, on behalf of The Heritage Writers Group, we wish to take this opportunity to thank you for your past and future guidance. We will always remember your mantra: Only God is perfect, the rest of us need editing.

SM Davidson

TABLE OF CONTENTS

THE PAINTED PORCH

By

Daniel Leckie

The house was in turmoil. Aunt Rebie and Mom and half-a-dozen young women moved about the house yelling, carrying, discussing, arguing while my little four-year-old sister, Ginger, and I watched, mystified.

Aunt Rebie's boarding house for young professional women was usually relatively sedate. Boarders did occasionally run up or down stairs, yelled things and left with young men but it was like distant artillery fire. This was all of that and more. One of the women was getting married and she wanted to have the ceremony in the parlor. It wasn't really big enough for a large group but she couldn't afford something bigger.

We stood in the parlor until they shooed us away. We stood in the hall until they complained. We were put into our room and we complained.

Ginger spoke to Mom, "Why do we have to do this?" The tomboy in her hated the brand new frilly white dress with full skirt and short puffy sleeves with socks and shoes to match. I wore my first long pants (total anathema to a five-year old) with white shirt and brown shoes and socks. I preferred bare feet.

"You look beautiful. Daniel, you'll be the ring bearer and you, Ginger, will be the flower girl. It'll be fun." We wanted out but we were told to "stay clean and stay here".

"Why can't we go outside?" Ginger asked me again, as though I knew.

"We can ask again." I saw Mom rushing up the hallway from the back of the house.

"Mom!"

"Not now." And she raced on by us.

"Aunt Rebie?"

"Ask your Mom." and she hustled by, her arms full of white gauzy stuff. It was obvious I would have to resort to extreme behavior. I saw Mom headed our way and stepped in front of her.

"Oof! Daniel! I almost knocked you down. Stay out of the way! Go to our room!" Our room was the first floor rcom Aunt Rebie provided our little family in return for Mom's help with everything.

"It's too hot in there!" Air conditioning had not yet penetrated to our part of the nineteen forties world so cooling meant opening all the windows and the front and back doors to coax a fickle breeze to blow through. The heat didn't bother us but it was a useful complaint at times because the adults never believed the heat didn't affect us.

"OK! You can go out on the porch but stay out of the way and STAY OUT OF THE BASEMENT!"

Mom made two mistakes here. First, she trusted us though she knew we could not be trusted but she was so harried and exhausted she took a chance. Secondly, she told us to stay away from the basement and she should have remembered we always interpreted "stay away" as "go there". Before the door slammed we were off the porch, headed for the basement.

When Aunt Rebie bought the house it came with a large, high-ceilinged basement divided into two rooms. The large frcnt room was filled with junk. Ginger and I always wanted to look around in there but the only working light was on the ceiling with a pull string. We were too short to reach the string.

9

But the rear room had a light switch and, during the day, there was plenty of light from the large opening in the back wall for the coal bin and the concrete steps for the coal delivery people.

Just a few days before, the coal people came and filled the coal bin. It was fun to watch!

"It's all smoky in here. Maybe we should leave." Ginger pursed her lips and narrowed her eyelids.

"It's just coal dust. It floats in the air. I can take care of that." I had seen one of the coal men put his thumb on the end of the hose and spray the air with water. I turned on the faucet. The hose started writhing like a snake spraying everything in the room.

"Catch it! Catch it!" I yelled as I tried to catch the moving end while Ginger just screamed as the hose wet us again and again. Finally I managed to step on it and work my feet up to the end and grabbed it.

"Okay, I got it!" I yelled to drenched Ginger, her back to me, her white cotton dress clinging to her body. Even in the morning heat she was shivering. I was too.

In a shivery voice she said, "Why didn't you turn the water off?" That hurt. She wasn't supposed to be smarter than me.

"Why didn't you?" I retorted.

"I couldn't get to the water thingy!" She sniffled. I turned off the water and hugged her.

"Let's go out and get some sun to warm up." We walked up the concrete steps, out through the coal chute opening in the back wall and a dozen steps into the late morning sun. After a few minutes we felt better. I looked at the tomatoes growing in Aunt Rebie's garden. They looked almost ripe enough to, suddenly...

"I'm king of the hill!" Behind me, Ginger shouted from the top of the coal pile.

"No you're not. Only boys can be king of the hill. It's a boys' game." I shouted back from the gravel drive.

"I don't care! I'm king of the hill and you're not! Yaaa!" She stuck her thumbs in her ears and stuck out her tongue at me. My first thought was to throw her down the coal hill but she's my sister! I love her. I decided to grab her, pick her up and carry her out then take her place.

"What are you doing? Leave me alone! Stop it!" She resisted me and tried to keep me from getting my arms around her. In the shifting rocks of coal we lost our balance. "Look out!" We tumbled down the pile, coal shifting and falling down behind us. We finished up on the concrete floor with lumps of coal around us, covered in coal dust.

"Ow!" We chorused, followed by more ows as we struggled to get up.

"I got coal dust in my eyes!" Ginger yelled then started to cry. I had dust in my eyes too but I managed to clear my vision enough to find the hose. This time I held the end before I turned on the faucet just a little. I rinsed my face and clothes then I took the hose and rinsed off Ginger's face and dress. There were still streaks of black all over us but we were more comfortable.

She looked at me. "You look terrible! You're all streaky." I looked down at myself. Then I looked at Ginger. Her dress, her face, her blonde hair was streaked with black.

"So are you."

"Mom's gonna kill us."

"She never does that. It's worse. She cries." Ginger nodded, sadly.

"Daniel! Ginger! It's time to come in. Where are you?"

We never paid attention the first time she called.

"Daniel Marvin Leckie and Ellen Virginia Leckie? You get back here now!"

"Whatta we do?" Misery draped her face. She began to shiver again. I froze. I couldn't think. What can we do? What can we do?

That meant Mom was mad. We couldn't go back when she was mad. She might actually punish us. Usually she just looked disappointed and cleaned up whatever mess we made and she would take away our toys or send us to our room without supper or, in this case, lunch. When she was mad she might take away our radio privilege. That would hurt. The radio was the only entertainment we had. We never wanted to miss the comedy, crime shows and Milton Berle!

"I got it! Let's go where she won't look."

"Where?" A glimmer of hope passed across her face.

"Let's go visit Mrs. Grimes!"

"Who?"

"The milk and cookies lady!"

"OH!" Her face brightened. Mrs. Grimes lived next door and whenever we visited her she helped us get into her porch swing and gave us milk and

12

cookies. Then she would sit with us and we'd swing. She would tell us tales. She was just next-door but she and Aunt Rebie had a pretend feud. It was something about Mrs. Grimes' pecan tree. It was on her property but Aunt Rebie gathered the pecans for her pies. We didn't believe it was a real feud because Aunt Rebie gave her a pie every week. We never told Mom about the milk and cookies so she never looked for us there.

We walked around the small brick wall that separated the two yards. We stopped at Mrs. Grimes' huge pecan tree. We loved to hug the tree. The roughness of the bark and the sense of power and permanency that seemed to flow from the tree always cheered us up.

This was when innocence betrayed us. We agreed that if we went far enough away no one would know we had ever been in the basement. Mrs. Grimes lived forty feet away. She had a nice long front porch with a chain-hung swing. Even though it was eighty degrees the calendar said it was fall. So we tried to step on as many dry leaves as possible. We loved the satisfying crunch they made. Then…

"Look!" Ginger exclaimed.

"Wow!" I said. The entire porch was shining white! It had been gray but now it was almost gleaming in the morning sun. We walked up the three steps to the porch, amazed at this wonder.

"It's so smooth!" I ran my hand along one of the columns and rubbed my cheek along it to feel the smooth warmth of it. Then I ran my hand along the wide banister and up and down each of the three other wide white columns. It all felt so good! Ginger did everything I did but was not as impressed. She quit.

"Look at the swing!" She yelled.

The porch steps were near the left end of the porch but there was enough room on that end for the swing, just big enough for two adults. This was the swing we shared with Mrs. Grimes. She would sit between as we grabbed cookies or brownies from the plate she held. Each of us had a huge glass of milk. Sometimes we spilled our milk. She was so nice about it. She kept a towel with her just to clean up. We loved her.

"Oof! Oof! Ouch!" Ginger huffed and puffed trying to get onto the swing but it kept moving away from her. Usually Mrs. Grimes was there to help us but she was still inside. I tried but we were too short to keep the swing from moving away as we tried to get on.

"Wait! Wait! I know. You stand behind and hold the swing for me and then I'll help you up." This worked. It was still a struggle because the swing was a little high for us so we had to scramble, sliding legs and arms across the seat to grab the back and pull ourselves up. After I got seated I pulled her left arm as she struggled and finally we were facing forward and managed to get the swing moving. Soon we heard Mrs. Grimes at her front door. Our mouths watered for milk and cookies. We heard the door latch and the whine of the screen door...

"AAAAGH!" Mrs. Grimes threw up her arms, scattering milk and cookies across the porch.

"What have you done? What are you doing? Why did you... This is awful! I spent hundreds to get this painted! I... I...   Come with me! Now!" She grabbed a hand of each of us and escorted us to our front porch. Then she calmed down. She let go of our hands and rang the doorbell. Mom opened the door. Aunt Rebie was right behind her.

"Look at these kids!"

"What happened?" They asked in chorus.

"I just had my front porch painted. It was all white! My mom and dad are coming next week and I wanted it to...to..." Then she started to laugh.

Aunt Rebie and Mom joined in. Mom turned to me. Why was it always me?

"What happened?"

"I don't know. We just went over to see Mrs. Grimes. We saw this beautiful porch and it all felt so smooth! And we got up on the swing all by ourselves! We didn't do anything wrong!"

"You went into the basement." Mom said, "Both of you played in the coal! Why would you play in the coal? Have you looked at yourselves? You completely ruined the brand new clothes we bought you! That'll never come out. Didn't you hear me calling you? You were supposed to stay on our porch. Go to our room. Get out of those clothes. Take a bath. We'll probably have to throw the clothes away. I don't know what we'll do about your parts in the wedding. We won't bring you a piece of the cake! Oh. I'm taking the radio away." We trudged down the hall, leaving little black footprints. We heard loud laughter before we reached our room.

They decided to have us help clean Mrs. Grimes porch. I did most of the cleaning while Ginger swung and had brownies and milk -- something about girls not doing that kind of work. When I was done it was still filthy. It was uncleanable. Somehow it got repainted. It was still smooth and pretty but Mom made sure our hands were clean before we visited Mrs. Grimes again. Oh! Mom brought us a big piece of the wedding cake after all.

REINCARNATION

By

Lorraine Sullivan

Pinocchio was not a rock,
but rather a "chip off the old block",
dressed in colorful clothes
with an expansive nose.
One day his creation earth did call
and into the black earth he did fall
where again he was born
And changed his name to John

THINGS THAT MAKE MY HEART SMILE

By

Moira Fisher

I love it when my heart is full of joy—it helps me soar through my day, puts air into my feet affording an easy ride as I navigate rough terrain, and it makes the corners of my mouth turn up instead of down. I purposely fill my mind with the things that make my heart smile to get me through the day like a red umbrella on a rainy day.

The sound of my grandson kissing the phone, and saying, "I kiss da phone, Grandma."

My mind reaches to a time before when he called me, "Grandpa," for several years. The annoyed voice of my granddaughter, "It's GrandMA!" When he is tired, slips and calls me, "Grandpa."

I rummage through the filing cabinet of my mind to find the place when he was a three-year-old and took my hand to lead me to his parent's bedroom. He hopped on the bed and asked me to lie with him. Reluctant, because the bed was smoothly made, I told him I would just lie on the covers, but he squirmed his way between the soft sheets. He reached for me, hugged me, kissed me, then rolled on his back and said, "Ah, I needed that!" I keep that luscious memory like a cupcake still warm with extra frosting trying to stay on top of the cake mound, yet slipping into the creases of the paper. And I savor it.

The look on my daughter's face as she strokes the baby comforter I made for her newborn.

The smell of my newborn grandbaby.

The company of fast friends, laughing over old news, repeated stories, fresh revelation, and forgetfulness. Warm, non-judgmental companionship reminiscent of slipping on memory foam slippers and a well-worn bathrobe.

Remembering the way our little daughter would walk about humming a tune. The happiness of childhood blossomed into womanhood, the skill now developed into composing songs.

Rainbows. All their predictable colors blending precisely reminds me of a walk with our granddaughter after an afternoon rain shower in Florida. "Someone had to paint that rainbow, Grandma," she said. I nodded, not wanting to break the holiness of that deep thought. I wondered if she was recalling a time in the past when this soul was still with her Maker. I looked at the tiny, shining face and knew that the presence of Heaven still lingered there. I relish and savor this mystery of life, of heaven, of memories, of holding her tiny hand in mine.

The smell of laundry hung on a clothes line with the sunshine radiating all of its pure life and love into the fabric.

The luxury of kicking my shoes off at the end of a long day, stepping into my plush carpet. Heading for the shower to allow the bubbles to wash away sadness and rubbing in the nourishing parts of a good day.

The faces of pansies as they push their way through snow. I admire the sheer resilience of these plants that last all the way through fall, endure the winter chill, and then raise their heads proudly to greet the spring.

A posy of sunshine in the form of yellow daffodils next to my kitchen sink. In the spring daffodils serve as a reminder that summer is on the way and my bones can relax and thaw out.

The smell of just-washed earth after an afternoon thunderstorm mixed with the busy sounds of birds finding dinner for their chicks.

Memories of my daughter sneaking up to me, hands behind her back, with yet another posy of freshly picked flowers. Tiny, chubby hands would hold that sweet bouquet and she would exclaim, "For you!" Sometimes they came from the neighbor's yard, but he did not mind, judging by the size of the bears he bought her for Christmas. Knowing that the next bunch she gives me will be grown in her own garden, placed in her guest bathroom and another vase filled with be on the nightstand. With the familiar exclamation from her daughter to me, "For you!"

The smell of a new shower curtain liner reminds me of freshly unwrapped dolls from my very distant childhood Christmases. Their freshly starched clothing and clear blinking eyes were delights I wanted to cherish. Snuggling and sniffing those baby dolls must have taken all my motherly instinct because when I reached adulthood I found myself lacking. I had no desire to have children. But once I sniffed the scent of my newborn baby's neck, I was head-over-heels in love. The fragrance lingers today and nothing makes my heart smile more than hugging her and burying my face in her hair so I can smell that fresh-from-heaven scent.

SATISFACTION

By

PJ Renfroe

Trying to satisfy some people

Is a bit like trying to

Put boots on a flea.

LOST IN LIFE

By

PJ Renfroe

There are many souls withdrawn from life to live for one hereafter

There are also those whose base desire is for ridicule and laughter

To tear apart another's heart to feed a raging ego

And never know that warm slow glow of being another's hero

TIME

By

PJ Renfroe

Time waits only for time

The bell tower in London rings out its chimes

Trees add a ring as the sparrows sing

There's a new day tomorrow.

OUT OF THE MOUTHS OF BABES

By

Moira Fisher

Many adults, feeling bombarded by children's endless chatter, simply tune them out. Yet, these small ones, so fresh from God's presence, do have a knack for telling it like it is. If we have ears to hear, we can receive astounding insight into the way things are.

Our daughter, Lisa, at around three years of age, called my briefcase, "the grief case" and referred to scrambled eggs as "strangled eggs," letting me know about my attitude toward work and my hurried state of mind.

There is usually a lot going on when you are a parent. The tantrums, the unending lessons on why we don't put those items in that orifice, interspersed with a steady stream of "no!" The constant surprises of finding an offspring doing something absurd. The sheer frustration of having yet another argument with a toddler whose feet are welded to the floor, is enough to bring a grown woman to her knees, which is not a bad place to be, all things considered. All the while, the ego is wanting to be seen as the Perfect Parent.

I still shudder as I recall the day I found myself wiping the nose of a perfect stranger's child. Mercifully, it was on a tissue and not my sleeve. Sleepless nights found me acting crazy. In the quest for sanity, it seemed appropriate to tune out the words that came out of that tiny mouth.

When my husband and I went out, armed with a diaper bag crammed with things we might need, dragging the elaborate stroller that I required instructions to unfold, we would look around at other couples with children and he would elbow me and whisper, "They look normal."

We travelled across the USA for almost five years with our home being a 40 x 8 foot travel trailer as we went from church to church with our message of love and forgiveness. I felt like I had washed our home on wheels too many times and it had shrunk.

One day when our daughter spoke, I listened. After traveling all night, I opened an overhead cabinet in our tiny kitchen creating a shower of empty plastic containers on my head.

Not choosing my words, I said, "That's the limit! I'm so tired of this."

Slinging the containers back onto their shelves haphazardly, I noticed the small, anxious face looking up at me. I froze in mid-fling, wanting to reach out and grab those words back and stuff them into the garbage disposal.

"I need space," I tried to explain, "maybe an apartment?"

The answer was crystal clear to me. Move to an apartment with an oversized couch, where books stayed on the shelves without having a bungee cord stretching along their titles, and where I didn't have to pack up all my child's school work before fixing a meal because the table doubled as her desk. Yet, this was the life I had chosen. Being with my husband as he traveled seemed like a better alternative to being stuck in a home not on wheels with our child. I preached to women in the morning meetings we held. I loved the messages I shared; pearls of wisdom cascading from my perfectly lined and glossed lips.

You might have heard someone called a Bible-thumper, but that day I was not prepared for a deeper pounding. My seven-year-old took a bloodstained sliver of the old wooden cross, filed it to a polished arrow, and stabbed me in the heart with it.

"Mom," she said, "how can God give you a different home if you are not grateful for the one you have? You should be thanking God that we are all together and not in separate prisons for preaching the gospel, like people are in other countries. Now if you change your attitude, we can pray and ask God for what you want."

The smug "I've-got-this" attitude crumbled around me, shot to smithereens by her words of wisdom, and I was brought face-to-face with who I really was—a big, bratty two-year-old dressed in heels. It took me just one deep breath and I made my attitude adjustment to one of gratitude.

We joined hands. I felt humbled. She asked me what we could agree on. Holding those tiny hands that day, we prayed for an apartment. We had three requests for our new home. It should be near a pool because we liked to swim, with a small garden to plant flowers and there should be a gym nearby we could attend together.

In less than three months, we received a totally unexpected gift of $10,000. My husband put a down payment on a brand new house with not one, but two pools in the subdivision, a generous garden to express our creativity with flowers, and located less than two miles from the gym.

I am glad that on that day, standing in the kitchen of my 40 x 8 foot home on wheels, I had ears to hear what the Spirit was saying through my little girl.

QUOTABLE QUOTE:

"God speaks to us every day only we don't know how to listen." ~ Mahatma Gandhi

SWEET GEORGIA BREEZE

By

Lorraine Sullivan

Peach satin fragrances
Slip through the air.
Sweet Southern juleps
With their mint fans
Tingle the fingers
Of the whispering leaves.
Powder puffs gently pat
The green leafy visages.
Unwrinkled velvet falls
On my receptive senses,
As a sweet Georgia breeze glides
So softly.

THE VISIT

by

C. J. F. Mobley

Snowflakes swirled in the bitter January winds before settling on the white blanket covering the frozen Youngstown, Ohio landscape. Blowing snow and low clouds obscured the tall, circumferential fence topped with silver razor wire. The red brick walls of the penitentiary rose in stark contrast to the dismal, gray milieu. Father Marcus Parnell pulled his coat collar closer to his neck as he trudged through the ankle-deep snow past towers and armed guards toward his car. Once inside his mobile sanctuary, he waited for the defroster to heat up, allowing ample time to contemplate his visit with the condemned murderer.

Nothing had gone as he expected. He had been so sure about his convictions, so positively certain he carried out God's will when he walked down death row to pray with Jefferson Michaels. Within moments, that clarity shattered; altered like the downy crystals dissolving into a frosty slush on his windshield.

Armed with his worn Bible and stalwart determination, the good priest stood ready to defend the incarcerated man who proclaimed his innocence even in the face of insurmountable evidence against him. Having met the condemned man only an hour before, the steady ground on which the priest's convictions rested began to quake. In all his life, Father Parnell had never met a person whose eyes alluded to an unspeakable evil residing within the soul. Even the hair on the nape of Parnell's neck stood at attention when he looked into the glacial eyes of the doomed killer. The priest knew in that instant the prisoner was guilty as charged. But, did that warrant another death?

Easing his car over the compacted snow to the parking lot exit Marcus drove mindlessly over frozen streets unsure of what he should do. Troubled as he was, he could not bring himself to drive back to the rectory nor did he wish to return to his church office. Twenty minutes later, he found himself parked in front of the home of his long-time friend and mentor, Pastor Dave Turner.

"I've been expecting you."

"You have?" Parnell asked somewhat surprised as Dave ushered him into the warmth of his home.

"Certainly. You are new to this business of saving souls."

Father Parnell nodded in understanding as he followed his host down a short hallway to the pastor's home office. Turner pointed to a burgundy leather chair after taking the priest's coat and hat.

"You look a little worse for wear. Would you like a drink or some hot tea, perhaps?" Turner asked.

"Oh, no. Nothing. Thanks."

Turner sat down behind his desk waiting for his young protégé to speak. Silence droned in the small office for several minutes before Turner finally spoke.

"It happens when you visit the prison."

"What happens?" Parnell looked at the warm eyes of his friend hoping his insecurities were not visible.

"You begin to question your faith," Pastor Dave nearly whispered.

"How did you know that?" Marcus gave Dave an incredulous look.

"I've been doing this much longer than you have, Marcus. We all have times when what was once crystal clear becomes opaque." Turner leaned his arms on his desk staring intently at the young priest seated across from him.

Shaking his head, Parnell let out an audible sigh. His encounter with Jefferson Michaels was nothing as he envisioned inside his head but he did not know how to explain the bitter disillusionment he felt inside.

"You have mixed feelings about your beliefs. What started out to be black and white is now gray and even the gray come in myriad shades," Turner continued when Marcus remained stoically silent.

Minutes ticked by before Parnell spoke. "I'm just...." Words to express his feelings did not come and he wasn't even sure of his feelings at the moment. Rising from his seat, he threw up his hands in utter frustration.

"Michaels claims he's not the murderer. If that is true, then an innocent man dies." Moving toward the window, Marcus peeked out at the landscape that lay frozen as his faith before him.

"But are his claims true?" Turner asked the younger man.

"No, I'm afraid not. There is much evidence against him."

"Is that what's bothering you? You think the evidence is wrong?" the pastor asked.

"His eyes. I've never seen...." His voice trailed off unsure of how to explain the hollowness he witnessed in the accused man. "He looked guilty," Parnell muttered as he turned to face his friend. "But there is no reason for him to die."

Turner nodded and then opened a drawer of his desk. "Here is something you might need to see." He removed a scrapbook of sorts. Quietly, he opened the binder and removed its contents. He carefully laid out photos and newspaper articles of each of Jefferson Michaels' victims which graphically detailed the murderer's hatred of women. Struggling to keep his eyes on the damning evidence was difficult for the young priest.

"Where did you get this?" Marcus demanded turning away from the graphic display.

"You are not the first man of the cloth to be summoned to the prison, Marcus. Your Michaels has been on death row for 15 years, much longer than you've worn vestments."

"I didn't want to believe it," Parnell whispered. "I could tell he was lying, but...but that doesn't mean he should die for his crimes. The Bible says, 'Thou shall not kill'."

"It also says an eye for an eye," Turner replied.

Parnell looked up at his friend, shock registered on his face. "Are you saying you support the death penalty?" he demanded angrily. For years he assumed that he and Dave shared similar views on the issue but suddenly realized that the topic had never arisen for discussion.

"Not necessarily," Turner responded calmly. "But how does one know which words are true?"

Marcus stared at his friend as if seeing him for the first time. The man that had been there for him when he was a troubled kid in grammar school now seemed like an alien being.

"The Bible is the inspired word of God", the young priest bellowed.

"No, son, it's the inspired word of man," Turner countered.

"How can you say that?" Parnell shouted angrily. "Those words," he pointed at the bible on Turner's desk, "are why we do this; why we live this life!"

"Oh, come on, Marcus!" Turner growled; his calm demeanor eroding as he rose from his own chair. "People interpret the Bible for their own purposes every day. You know that. Just look around. There are dozens of religions in this world. Even in Christianity itself there are churches on every corner, each labeled a different denomination and all claiming to know the truth! Even you and I hold different beliefs."

Father Parnell stood in stunned silence trying to process this side he'd never witnessed in his friend. The realization came that did not know Dave Turner as well as he thought. "But you've been my mentor; the person I've always turned to. You're the reason I became a priest."

Turner walked to Marcus, placing his strong hand on his shoulder. "I know how difficult your childhood was, Marcus. Very few boys that grow up in foster care turn to God, and almost none make the ministry their vocation. You are a rare person, Marcus."

"I know what it's like," Marcus uttered as unpleasant memories of his childhood skipped across his mind. "That's why I wanted to make a difference. So many kids end up in jail before they've even begun to live their lives. I could have been a statistic like the rest." He looked Dave Turner in the eyes. "You kept me from being a number."

"No, you chose not to follow the easy path." Dave's eyes shone with admiration at the younger man who overcame such difficult circumstances.

Marcus acknowledged Dave's praise with a nod of his head and then seated himself once more in the burgundy chair. Dave had done much for him in the past, but now he needed more guidance for the tough challenge he faced.

"Now I have a chance to help save this man's life, even if he has done bad things in his past. Can't you understand that?" He asked, silently pleaded with his mentor to understand his need to help Jefferson Michaels.

Dave nodded his head. "I do understand, but it is easy to be the bystander, Marcus, to make judgments that do not affect your life directly; much like the football fan yelling at the players on his television screen. It is always clear and easy when you can see the whole picture or when there will be little impact on your own life. Victims don't have that luxury. Neither do we. We cannot know or even fathom the mind of God. I don't question why Michaels ended up on death row."

Parnell looked intently at his friend. "Well what should I do? I promised to help him. He's scheduled to die next week. I can't let that happen if there is a way for me to stop it."

After what seemed an eternity, Dave Turner went to his desk. Opening a drawer, he removed his address book and quickly scribbled something onto a piece of paper. He hesitated a moment before handing the scrap to Father Parnell as if judging the wisdom of doing so.

30

"You should go see this man," Turner sighed as he held out the slip of paper toward Marcus.

"Why?"

"Let's just say he faced a similar experience a long time ago. Mind you, it won't be easy. Father McCloskey doesn't talk to many people these days."

"Did he take a vow of silence?"

"No." Dave hesitated before adding, "You might not like what you find out, Marcus." Pastor Dave did not expound and Father Parnell did not force the issue. He thanked his friend for his time, grabbed his coat, and headed back out into the harsh elements just as confused as when he arrived.

Father Parnell sat in his car contemplating the words of his friend. Was he truly on a fool's errand? This morning he awoke with concrete convictions, confident that he could help spare a man from certain death. All that seemed eons ago. In a few hours' time, a quiet shift in his fault line between truth, justice, and right or wrong now altered his perceptions. The very foundations of his beliefs appeared to be crumbling with his every move. Should he go see this priest as Dave suggested or simply walk away?

A small movement from Pastor Turner's front window caught his eye. Parnell waved, started his engine and drove away from the house.

"Okay, Google, …" he read the directions Dave provided into his mobile phone. Following the automated voice of the GPS, he made his way across town to Father McCloskey's home. The house was a dilapidated affair on an isolated corner in one of the more desperate areas of town. The entire street reeked of neglect but the ramshackle cottage standing before him seemed to sag under years of depressing inattention. Paint peeled from every board and

31

overgrown bushes obscured the front so that the door was barely visible from the street. He could not see the yard due to the layer of snow, but felt sure it fared no better. In fact, he wondered is the place was even occupied at all.

Parking his car on the cracked and crumbling drive, Parnell walked gingerly over the icy walkway to the drooping front porch. He eyed his dismal surroundings warily. Nothing stirred. Only the sounds of distant traffic floated through the frigid air.

Hoping the aged boards would support his weight, the priest made his way to the door. He knocked. The sound was a gunshot in the quiet snowfall, but no one was outside, no dogs barked in reply. The whole place had a deserted feeling to it as if all living things were hibernating from the icy afternoon. Why did Dave bothered to send me here?

As Parnell turned to leave, he heard the clinking of locks being opened. He turned back toward the door. It opened very slightly.

"What do you want?" The voice that emanated from a small opening was full of anger and the sliver of face even more so.

"Hello. I'm Father…"

"I can see that. I asked what do you want?"

"Dave said…Pastor Dave Turner said I should talk to you."

"Did he, now?"

"Yes, he did."

"I got nothing to talk about." He pushed the door closed.

"Please." Parnell asked through the wooden barrier. Frustrated at his abrupt dismissal, he pounded the door once more. Waiting several minutes in the freezing cold and hoping that the old priest would change his mind, Marcus again contemplated Dave's reasoning for sending him to this gloomy place. Just as he turned to leave a second time, the door opened.

"At least get warm." McCloskey frowned as he stood aside so that his visitor could enter.

"Thank you for seeing me," Marcus said as he wiped his feet on a faded, frayed rug just inside the door.

The old priest stopped and whirled around to face the younger man. "I didn't say I was seeing you. I said you could get warm. You've got 5 minutes to be on your way."

"But, I thought…"

"Well, there's your problem," Father McCloskey growled. "You think you can just barge in and make a nuisance of yourself until you get what you want."

"No, no. That is not…." Marcus shook his head for emphasis quite startled at the old man's behavior. "Okay, look. I have a problem and I'm looking for help. That's all." Father Parnell silently prayed the old priest would at least, listen to his questions.

Father McCloskey eyed Parnell cautiously. "Five minutes," he said over his shoulder as he continued down the short hallway without bothering to take his visitor's coat.

Once inside the small, shabby kitchen, he pointed Parnell to an old, round battered-looking table with a few mismatched chairs stationed about. Parnell selected the closest one, a rickety structure that held his weight but groaned in protest. McCloskey gave a quick glare before reaching for his kettle.

Marcus decided to make the best of his five minutes.

"I saw Jefferson Michaels today. I told him I would help him."

McCloskey gave no indication that he heard his guest. He filled the kettle then placed it on a burner before slowly lumbering to the table. "Your mistake," McCloskey finally responded.

"How can I help him? David said you…"

"You can help by letting him die," McCloskey growled.

Clearly affronted at the older man's suggestion, Marcus declared, "I am a man of God. I don't condone the death penalty and killing Michaels won't bring back his victims."

The old man stared at Marcus, his poker face revealing nothing of his thoughts as seconds then minutes ticked by before McCloskey spoke. "I believe your five minutes are up." Father McCloskey pushed his chair away from the table and rose. Ignoring the younger man's bewildered look, McCloskey moved to a drooping set of cabinets by the stove. He busied himself with the whistling kettle and making a cup of tea prior to walking out of the small, dingy kitchen completely ignoring his unwelcome visitor.

Stunned, Marcus did not move. "That's it?" Parnell shouted after the old man as he lumbered down the hallway. "You've nothing more to say?"

Marcus remained seated in the rickety chair waiting for some sign of acknowledgement. Realizing after several moments that he was wasting his time, he rose from his seat. Clearly, this man was of no help to anyone.

Marcus made his way to the dark, decaying living room, pausing at the front door. He stared once more into the empty eyes of the older, broken priest.

"I don't know how or why you ever became a priest, but I am certainly glad you no longer wear the vestments. You disgrace them."

Father Parnell turned to leave but a barking laughter stopped him. It was a mirthless sound that seemed to come from a pit of despair. He turned to face the ex-priest.

"Oh, that's rich," McCloskey gave a guttural sneer. "You with your self-appointed righteousness think you know all about God. Well, let me clue you in, boyo, you know nothing!"

"That's not true," protested Parnell.

"Do you have any idea who Jefferson Michaels truly is? Do you?" McCloskey demanded as his gnarled hands clutched the arms of his chair.

"I met with him today. I know...." but McCloskey interrupted.

"You know nothing as I stated before. You don't want to see a murderer killed but you don't know the victims or their families do you?" McCloskey leaned forward for emphasis.

Marcus fought back the retort he wished to hurl at McCloskey realizing only more venom would spew from the angry old priest if he engaged in an argument. It appeared to him that the old man needed to vent the pain and anger that were turning him into a rancorous fossil.

"You don't know the pain and agony they suffered at the hands of Michaels, a man you met once, who confirmed in your childish little mind that he killed those innocent women. Yet you stand there ready to condemn me while defending him." He let go of the armrests and plopped back in his sagging chair, his chest heaving in his anger.

"Killing Michaels won't bring back those victims. Vengeance is Mine, sayeth the Lord."

"Don't quote scriptures at me, you sanctimonious little punk."

Father McCloskey pushed himself up so quickly that Marcus was quite astonished at the old man's speed. McCloskey stood now, eyes blazing at the young man before him. "Jefferson Michaels' death is God's vengeance and you want to stand there and challenge his sentence like a petulant brat who didn't get picked for the kickball team at recess. How unfair," McCloskey mocked.

"How can you believe that's true? Where is your compassion?" Marcus questioned the old man.

"Compassion?" McCloskey shouted. "Where was Michaels' when his terrorized his victims?" he snarled at his visitor. "Truth? You want the truth, boy? The truth is Michaels raped and stabbed five women," Father McCloskey yelled at Marcus. "They suffered horribly as he took his time inflicting the most unimaginable pain on these girls. Have you read the papers? Better yet, have you talked to these girls' parents? There was no compassion or mercy in what he did to them." The forceful enunciation of each word made Marcus feel as if the old man was trying to hammer their meaning into his brain.

"Well, no, but...." Parnell could only bray his shameful response.

"But nothing." McCloskey pointed a castigating finger at Marcus. "You care more about the perpetrator than the victims of the crime." McCloskey threw his hands up in disgust. "What I figured from the likes of you." He plopped back down in his threadbare recliner, his whole body emanating his revulsion of the young man standing in his living room.

"What good can come from talking to them?" Marcus asked quietly. "I can't possibly help the victims as I said before, but I can help one man that's sure to die."

McCloskey glowered at the younger man. "For the love of God, can you not empathize with the families of this man's victims? Can you just imagine what it must feel like to hear that the man that killed their child, sister, cousin, niece, or friend might not get executed for his crimes?"

Marcus stood in silence, unaccustomed to being berated about his convictions, yet the older man continued with his brazen rebuke.

"It is difficult enough to lose someone you love to accident or illness. Can you envision if a loved one was a victim of murder? What would that feel like to know that some piece of slime decided to take their life? Would you want the killer to spend his life in jail receiving three meals a day, health care, and watching television?"

"I don't have a family. I never knew my father and was orphaned when my mothed died of cancer." Marcus was surprised to hear is own voice. He rarely talked to anyone about his mother's illness which culminated in her death and his entry into a foster care nightmare when he was six years old. It had been devastating. It was Dave Turner who had always been there to help him as he transitioned from one foster home to another until he finally found a stable home.

"I see," McCloskey nodded as he stared at the young priest with no hint of compassion on his face.

Marcus became uncomfortable under the scrutinizing eyes which bore into his. The vitriolic ex-priest could offer him no insight on how to save a condemned man seeming to believe that saving his life was justice denied. After several moments of silence, he realized once again, that there was nothing for him in this wayward expedition, he turned to leave.

"Sorry to have wasted your time," Marcus said as his hand grasped the doorknob.

"I knew a man like you once. It was a lifetime ago." McCloskey's voice was only a whisper.

Marcus turned again to face the old man, his hand falling to his side. The old man stared off into times unknown to Marcus. Whatever memories were parading in the old priest's mind, Marcus wanted to know more about them. He waited silently for McCloskey to expound.

"A young priest, he was, ready to save the world on his own. Didn't matter that others tried the same tricks for millennia before him. He was special, he was. Knew all the answers." McCloskey nodded at his own words.

Minutes ticked by as the old man appeared lost in the past, remembering but clearly not wishing to something from long ago. He shook his head at some distant, painful memory before words came again.

"This arrogant upstart got a placement at a church in a town with a state prison. Of course, the death penalty was carried out there but he was going to put a stop to that nonsense. Killing the condemned was a sin he told everyone. Forgiveness was what Jesus preached so he did the same. Rallies, marches, demonstrations; he organized them all. Dozens flocked to the prison when an execution was scheduled. Their support fueled the charismatic priest.

"The priest, he was successful, too," McCloskey nodded his head at his own words. "Three stays of execution in five, sentences changed to life instead of death row."

McCloskey stared into Marcus' eyes. "Power like that, goes to a man's head."

Marcus got the message easily enough, but he had not done any of those things of which McCloskey spoke. He only wanted to prevent another life being lost.

"Our young priest figured he was doing the right thing; that God was behind all of these 'miracles' as he told reporters. He was only carrying out God's will."

McCloskey sat in silence for a few moments, but Marcus figured there was much more to the tale.

"Well, this misguided priest got involved with a man accused of killing a young girl. There were some questions about the evidence at the trial, but the jury convicted the man. The judge sentenced the criminal to death but our young priest got on his soap box again. One crucial piece of evidence from the first trial was inadmissible in court due to some improper search he touted. Of course the killer's lawyer loved the publicity the priest garnered. He raised so much doubt that the murderer got a new trial."

Marcus stood listening in silence as McCloskey sat lost in his thoughts. Minutes passed before McCloskey spoke again, but Marcus dared not interrupt.

"It took months for things to be decided, but the condemned man was let go. Without that key piece of evidence, the cops had nothing concrete. All the evidence the police had was circumstantial. He had no other arrests."

McCloskey eyed Marcus again. "Can you imagine how the victim's family members felt?"

Marcus shook his head, amazed that a young priest and a good lawyer were able to overturn a conviction.

"How excited the priest was when he was able to talk to the freed man; even invited him to come to mass on Sundays," McCloskey continued. "Oh, and our murdering ex-con did show up to church with his Bible in hand, a model of attrition. The priest basked in his conceit until three weeks later when a young woman was found strangled with a piece of clothes line."

Marcus gasped aloud. He knew where the story was heading now, suddenly annoyed at both Dave and McCloskey for trying to dissuade him of from helping a man they would condemn to death.

"She was a 21-year-old college student home for her mother's birthday celebration that weekend. She was raped, repeatedly over the course of hours before the killer strangled the life from her. Her family didn't know she was missing until a concerned roommate called on Tuesday to see when she was coming back to class. They had an exam. Do you know what that does to a family?" McCloskey asked his uninvited guest.

Marcus focused his eyes on McCloskey as the direct question hung momentarily in the space between them before snaking its way into his brain where it bounced around the gray matter. A shake of the head was all Marcus could manage by way of an answer. He had not considered the survivors only his anemic mantra that he could not help the victims. Those grieving survivors had not crossed his one-tracked mind. But he still felt an obligation to help the condemned man, Jefferson Michaels. He had given his word.

Additional chastisement and accusations were what he expected from the old man, not the bone crushing silence that seemed to stretch out between them like a well-worn rug to cover the ugly flaws of human nature, those unpleasant sins of pride, arrogance, and narcissism all of which, Marcus realized, he possessed in unmitigated bounds. He should consider the family members of Michaels' victims before rushing to his defense.

"The girl that was murdered was my cousin." Father McCloskey seemed to sag with this admission. "I've seen firsthand the slow destruction that comes; first to the individuals and then the family as a whole."

"I'm sorry for your loss," Marcus muttered but was startled at the sound of that mirthless laughter that came once more from the old man.

"I was that priest. I helped free a murderer, invited him into my sanctuary to fraternize with my congregation; not just my parishioners, but my own kin." McCloskey's voice was flat and hollow like that of a mechanical doll that speaks when a button is mashed or a string pulled, but his eyes were cold and empty as if no warmth had touched him in decades.

"But you could not have known he would kill again," Marcus offered as if to lessen the burden of guilt the priest still carried after all these years.

"Yes, I knew," McCloskey snapped, his whole demeanor shifting from self-despair to anger in a matter of seconds. "I bargained with God and He let me know real quick-like that I had no business messing with his plans, just like you have no business interfering with Jefferson Michaels' circumstances. He's going to hell and that is God's judgment."

"But the Bible says," Marcus was unable to finish his statement as McCloskey rose to his feet and shouted.

41

"You want scriptures? Is that what you need to make every decision?" McCloskey threw his hand up in disgust. "God, you'll make as poor a priest as I did." He collapsed into his recliner with an air of defeat.

Marcus could think of nothing to add to the conversation wanting nothing more than to remove himself from the suffocating hopelessness emanating from the still-grieving old priest. He turned to the door once again.

"Thank you for your time, Father."

The old priest looked at Marcus. "Don't spend your time trying to save the damned, son. Catch them before they get to that point, else you'll end up like me."

Nodding his head, Marcus opened the door and felt the bitter chill of the late afternoon. Before closing the door, he spoke to Father McCloskey. "Who was the man you freed from prison?"

"A man that's haunted me for ages," he said. "Name was Parnell. Robert Marcus Parnell."

LOVE IS

By

Cynthia Anne Cofell

Love is frilly, sometimes silly, Lopsided and flip floppy.
Love is uneasy, cheesy at times willie nillie and eye popping

Love is funny, uncertain, googly eyes and wishie washie.
Love is chocolatey, sweet, owie gooey delicious finger licking throat smacking.

Love spins, titters, rolls, dips and dives like dish washers.
Love is good times, sour times it grows, and flows like river watching.

Love is mercy, pretty things, longtime friends and holiday laughing.
Love is home, grandma's mommies and daddies black berries, red cherries and go shopping.

Love dances, hustles, wiggles then jiggles, like hip hopping.
Love is fire, desire, big hugs, over the rainbow lip locking.

Love is happy, up and down round and round non stopping.
Love whispers, remembers, forgives, thrills and chills heart pounding.

Love is fizzy fuzzy all over, warm and cuddly topsy turvy like road winding.
Loves gives, is patient, endures, secures a tickle a tasket, open minded.

Love shimmers, dazzles, glimmers and sparkles like blinding diamonds.
Love is spring time, flower buds, ocean waves, cool breeze and summer magic.
Love Is.

MONKEY BUSINESS

By

Moira Fisher

Over the years I have found that many aspects of my childhood in South Africa have proven interesting to people, but to me it was a normal way of life. People often ask if I had lions in my backyard, and I tell them that we only had monkeys.

My fondest memories involve my furry friends eating from the fruit bowl on top of our refrigerator.

I thought they were particularly cute. To my mother, however, they were most disagreeable and she would literally freak out.

We did not have air-conditioning so she would leave the doors and windows open to allow a breeze to cool the house. Since there were no screen doors, it was an open invitation to the monkeys. Red apples, golden mangoes, green and red grapes, orange papaya, glowed brightly in the fruit bowl—the fresh fruit fragrance wafting on the warm sub-tropical breeze. The yellow fingers of the bananas my Dad grew must have beckoned those wide-eyed creatures, and the refrigerator remained the perfect spot for their afternoon snack.

We had a long passageway leading from the bedrooms to the kitchen, and I would watch quietly as the little gray family came inside and settled on top of the refrigerator. I especially loved it when the mother introduced her babies to the fruit basket. She would hand each of her tiny handed flock a banana, take one herself and they would settle down to peel them, chattering happily. Sometimes the mother would stroke the head of one of her babies as it munched. As they were eating, I would hear my mother screeching at them from the bedroom side of the passageway. They would notice her and watch her curiously, chewing thoughtfully. It was not until she got to the kitchen that they would jump down and scurry out of the house, still clutching their bananas. My mother would be shouting and spluttering in anger, shooing them out of her house and chiding them to never come back.

When my mother would jut her head around the corner into the dining room, I would be pouring over my homework and would simply furrow my brow as if being roused from the scholarly corridors of the learned, unaware of her troubles. She would shrug and sigh and go back to her bed making. I would stifle a giggle, secretly cheering for the monkeys, knowing that they had picked the best bananas from the bunch.

&❧ &❧

On another occasion, we were enjoying scones and tea in the outdoor garden restaurant at the Botanical Gardens in Durban. This was not your average outdoor café, but one with starched white table cloths, heavy, polished silver, and fine china. Beautiful wrought iron furniture with plush cushions encourage patrons to linger and sip a second cup and maybe stop for lunch while savoring the sights and sounds of nature.

It was the custom of the monkeys to jump onto the table when the guests were done and eat their leftovers. I took great delight in watching them dine before the waiters shooed them away with the wave of a starched white napkin. I even dropped scones on purpose, so they could get an early snack from our table.

I felt that my chattering friends loved me too. As we were leaving, my mother warned me not to get too close to them. I trailed behind my family and walked up to a monkey who was sitting on the low stone wall that lined the pathway

45

to the parking lot. I planned to hug him, but before I had the chance, he bit me on my right hand, just above the thumb. I two-stepped to catch up with my parents with my bleeding hand behind me. My mother turned to see where I was and gasped as she saw the trail of blood. The whole family turned, their eyes fixed in horror.

The rest of the evening was a sort of blur with my father making excuses for the monkey.

"He probably thought you had food for him."

My mother fussed at me, "I warned you about those monkeys. They are wild animals."

On and on she droned about the naughtiness of monkeys as the nurse administered my tetanus shot. I don't remember if I needed stitches.

Over fifty years later, I still have the scar as a memory of my ongoing love for monkeys.

HE'S WITH YOU STILL

By

Delores L Staton

Written for a dear friend on the death of her fiancé May 2001

She turned briefly
Feeling a light breeze touch her shoulder
She looked after it;
Longing surfaced in her eyes,
Her body turned to question
Her mind closed down
The pain was real.

Sandra, lady of the beautiful countenance,
Lady of the laughing eyes
Bent with sorrow
Struggling to understand
Her body turned to question
Her mind closed down
The pain was real.

We, people of god look deep into our souls
For, in those depths, we find solace.
Relief and peace will be slow to come
Tranquility may require an eternity
Her body turned to question.
Her mind closed down.
The pain was real.

Sandra looked longingly after the breeze
As she stared, dimly, a light appeared
At first tentatively,
At first haltingly,
The light deepened.
Now, shimmering brilliantly
The breeze touched her shoulder gently
Her body turned to understanding
Her mind opened to clarity.

Sandra stood tall beside the pain
Sandra, lady of the beautiful countenance,
Lady of the laughing eyes, wept healing tears
Knelt before god

Embraced her pain
And unfolded fully before the light.

BLUE SNAKE RUNNING

By

PJ Renfroe

PROLOGUE - 2650BC

Jacob pushed the oar deep to push the small boat quickly and stealthy over the gently rolling aquamarine waters of the Nile. He used the guards' fires on the opposite shore to guide him toward his destination—a canal built to float supplies to a construction site.

Huddled beneath a cured crocodile skin, he stroked through strong current to reach a channel into the calmer, shallow water of a canal. Tall reeds growing along its edge shielded him from the guards.

Early evening light quickly changed to fuzzy gray as fog moved in shrouding his main objective—a 482-foot architectural marvel built on 13 acres of verdant soil, the Great Pyramid.

He turned the paddle to slice into the water as quietly as possible, rowing alongside the reeds. The glow from the guard's fires wavered slightly, and in the quiet, he heard a guard walking along the edge of the canal. He pushed the oar down into thick muck on the bottom and bent forward, holding it with all the power in his lean body, desperate to stop the boat's forward motion. The guard stood still, taking his good old time to relieve himself.

Jacob's muscles soon demanded relief. The boat rocked, something disturbed the water ahead, and he recognized the hollow grunts, heard the guard's startled gasp, saw his vague shadow against the light as he jumped back, and heard the scrunch of his sandals on rubble as he ran back to the fire.

Jacob's body relaxed, he pulled the oar free, and the boat began to float out from the reeds. When he lifted his head, he was face to face with a crocodile, probably the one that scared the guard. Evil, unblinking yellow eyes stared from the ugly prehistoric head revered by some as Sobek, the crocodile god. Jacob was not a part of that cult, and as far as he was concerned, the only crocodile of any merit was a dead one.

With cat-like curiosity, the croc nudged the reed boat with its ugly snout and raised its knobby head to stare at Jacob, who sat huddled beneath the cured croc skin, the head and great jaws resting on his head like a crown. He grasped a short handled spear, ready to repel the beast, while staring into those vicious eyes. Seconds seemed hours as time hung waiting. The crocodile blinked first, it slapped its narrow-ridged, knobby snout against the water, lifted its huge head as though in protest of some strange inexplicable danger, bellowed, almost in fright, and swam away.

Jacob breathed a sigh of relief. That had worked to his advantage. The guard would attribute any unusual movement to the crocodile. He disregarded stealth and moved quickly to his next destination, the deep shadow near a massive dock. He took time to scan the area to see if the croc had followed, but no unusual ripples marred the swirling water, and no yellow eyes stared back. He anchored the narrow craft against the bank and removed the leathery disguise. Crawling from the boat over the lip of the canal, he quietly threaded his way through piled up discarded stone, stopping only once to look back to fix the location of the boat in his mind.

It was common knowledge that the main construction of the outer shell of the pyramid was finished and the heavy workforce had left for parts unknown.

50

Only the coating and the capstone were yet to be completed. There appeared to be no guards in this area, and he wondered why.

Weaving his way through debris, he came to a wide, smooth trail. The swirling fog blinded him to anything more than several yards ahead, but he decided to take a chance and moved quickly over the trail's well-worn surface. Only minutes later, although he was expecting it, he was startled when the enormous structure loomed up in his path. Its stark splendor rose majestically through the mist piercing the indigo sky, its peak glittering with unworldly light.

Stymied only for a moment, awed by the massive structure, he remembered graphic warnings of the horrible things that would happen to anyone who dared breach the sanctity of the pyramid. Those spells reverberated through his mind. He hesitated, considered the superstition—knew he had no plan to enter the sanctuary of the Pharaoh. Some innate strength surged through him, filling his body with the courage to complete his quest.

Walking carefully around its massive base, he came to a great cedar ladder, which scaled the monolith like a squashed and disjointed giant centipede. He grasped the raw wood struts, smoothed by many hands, and stepped up on the first rung, leaning in close to make less of an outline against the fog-blurred sky. He murmured a prayer, and began to climb. The minute creaking sounds his reed sandals made on the rungs, normal night noises, the guards murmuring voices, and the minute creaking of the ladder were all that marred the quietness of night.

Moving quickly, he was a third of the way up when a grating noise fractured that eerie silence, and sent him scuttling into darker shadow beneath the ladder. He pressed his body against the top of a large stone, and waited. So far, the enveloping ground fog had masked his movements, but now, above it,

51

and once back on the ladder, he would be in the open. Looking over the edge of the stone, his vivid green eyes squinted to peer through the cloaking mist to locate any movement while his keen hearing searched for the source of the sound.

Although the night was cool, sweat saturated his thick brown hair and rolled down to drop salty needles into his eyes. The slightest move to wipe it away might reveal his position. When the sound came again, he recognized it as stone scraping against stone. There was a slight rumble and then spears of light shot upward through the mist! He jerked back from the edge, terrified by what he had seen, yet curiosity sent him sliding back to peer over the ledge again. Down below, a huge stone had moved outward seen only because bright light emanated from the hollow center of the stone! That light also revealed steps that curled down into the brightly lighted maw of the pyramid!

A ghostly figure climbed those spiral stairs carrying a lamp. When at waist level with the top of the last stone, he stopped, and slowly lifted his head, revealing beady black eyes that glittered in the light. Jacob squinted to see through the scraggily fog. It was as though he looked through a bridal veil. The man had a large hooked nose similar to the beak of a great bird. It dominated a long, gaunt, and weathered face. He turned and spoke to someone behind him, took the last few steps cautiously, climbed out and stood on an adjoining stone. The man was very tall, his back slightly stooped. Those piercing black eyes seemed able to see in the dark as they scanned the entire area, and then skipped upward and over the ladder where Jacob lay hidden in its shadow.

Jacob concentrated to meld his mind to become small as a beetle on the stone. Well-hidden as he was, the man could not see him, but he needed to block the man's inner sight of him. He prayed for release from fear, which could weaken his vision, for he knew that man! Yes, he definitely knew the

Pharaoh's chief scribe, Stomata, the keeper of the ancient books, the man from whom no secret was safe. Of all the people to encounter, this man was the absolute worst. However, Stomata appeared satisfied no dangers lurked, as he slid down beside the open block of stone, gave it a shove and the huge stone slid, almost silently, back into place. Then, he walked the fifty feet or so to the ladder and climbed down.

As Stomata stepped from the ladder to the hard packed earth and turned to leave, an uneasy feeling touched his mind. A mental sense more intense than an animal's keen nose, detected a trace of something alien on the ladder. It intrigued him. Similar to a hunter on the scent, Stomata tugged the hood of his gray work robe over his smooth head concealing his face in deep shadow, and sent tendrils of questing mind hooks sliding over the pyramid.   As they slid over the ladder a lump intrigued him. Something is there, but what is it? Hmm . . . a bit large for a beetle! A shocking thought skittered through his consciousness: *Could the intruder be a remnant of the Merer tribe? Only they have such a mindset. Ancient scholars recorded the Merers as descendants of an alien God! The last pharaoh was supposed to have killed them all. He feared their mind's eye, which could see into the soul and he could not control their thoughts. If this was a descendent and his eyes were green, he would be a fine specimen. However, no need to worry; he isn't here to steal. The Merers believe theft despoils the soul. So why is he here? I must know!*

It was now apparent to Jacob why no guards were in the inner circle. The moving stone was a secret of major proportions. Death would be the reward for anyone who saw that well-kept secret. He watched the glow of Stomata's lamp as it moved down the ladder through the thinning mist and disappeared, but he knew Stomata was aware someone was in the vicinity, and although he left, the man was alarmed. Jacob was not the only one now in danger. Should the Pharaoh learn his secret entrance had been become known, even Stomata

53

would not be safe. Cautious, Jacob waited precious minutes. When no alarm sounded and no long nosed dogs searched him out, he decided to continue his quest.

By judging the direction of the city in relation to the river, and where the moon would rise, he fixed the location of the moving stone in his memory for future reference. With fearful determination and the agility of an acrobat, he swung back onto the heavy ladder and scurried up to eventually step off on the very top of the pyramid.

After such a fast climb, his heart thundered in his chest. He slumped down with his back against the wall beneath where the capstone would eventually rest. He unwound a headband from his wrist, wrapped it around his forehead, and tied it loosely. The fog securely covered the landscape allowing only glowing spots where the guards and the city's fires intruded on the vast panorama.

Every day, he had faced danger just to survive, but this was extreme. It was necessary for him to get above the clamor of the multitude in order to contact the Counselors! He lifted his eyes to the sky, calmed his mind, and concentrated on chanting a mantra. His eyes closed, and he breathed deeply to slow his heaving chest. Soon, his soul soared into the night sky, leaving his body, the pyramid, and the world behind; transported to a balcony overlooking a city seemingly built on clouds.

Once before, he had been here, and been honored to stand on that same balcony overlooking a great white city, to observe a trial in progress. At that time, some of the judges wore white robes and others wore light brown with different color combinations of woven braid around one shoulder. They were arguing the case of a man from earth his sins spread out before them. This time one man only greeted him, and without preamble the big man, who wore a white woolen robe with no ornamentation, began to speak.

"Jacob, Stomata sensed your touch on the ladder, and his private guards plan to capture you on your return. Fortunately, he has no time to call enough men to ring the entire base of the pyramid. Even if he could, he would not, because he wants to catch you, but he does not want anyone else to know. He is fierce old devil intent on his own power, so he will not raise a major alarm.

"I know you are here to plead the cause of your brother. In order to free him, we must deal with the Grand Priestess Aleeze. Send the blue on the night breeze, give it its head, and send her soul to us. She has done great evil. Perhaps the others will take this example as a warning to be less iniquitous in their judgments. Eventually, Egypt will lose her glory and future generations of your family will become part of a different world. Your brother will be released in the morning, meet him in the courtyard."

"My family and I are grateful for your instructions."

He started to turn away, then turned back and said, "Stomata realized you must be a Merer, and possibly the last one alive, and he wants you! If he does not catch you, he will send searchers through the city and countryside. In order to save those who remain of your family, you must leave the city, and take your family out of Egypt immediately. Now, follow the shadows down the dark side of the Pyramid, and if you are very careful, you should get safely away."

"May I ask your name, Counselor?"

"I am Xarsante, Counselor to the Just."

The giant figure nodded, "I will always be here for you and your family." He slowly vanished as Jacob's soul slipped through the stream of space to return to his body on the pyramid. The shining white city seen from the balcony where Xarsante had stood, and the serene kind wisdom of the man, had erased all fear from Jacob's mind.

He sat still for a moment, centering his mind and reviewing what he knew of the layout of the temple. He imagined a path in his mind to the Grand Priestess's private quarters. That was not necessary; however, it would make it easier, so he closed his eyes and visualized the Priestess. He found her standing beside her wide sleeping platform. Three cats were mewing and circling around her feet.

Taking a deep breath, he called on the blue and sent it flying, snaking rapidly toward the temple. The temple cats detected danger and began mewing, clawing the air, trying to attack what they sensed but could not see and alarming the Grand Priestess. She sensed fear and rang for her guards. This was no asp, scorpion, rat, or beetle the cats could catch and destroy, and it was too quick for the priestess to form any kind of defense. The air crackled, blue lightning filled the room as the blue, quick as a snake and with a will of its own, circled the beautiful Priestess and performed its deadly job. The Priestess fell senseless to the floor. Her slaves screamed in agony and fell beside her, fearful for their own lives. Guards came running into her chamber, saw her lifeless body on the tiles, and began searching uselessly for an intruder.

Having completed Xarsante's instructions, Jacob removed the headband and began to slide silently down the stones on the dark side of the Pyramid, back to the dirt and survival, to face the evil and the good.

THE BEST PART OF WAKING UP

By

Eunice L. Sykes

There used to be a popular saying
It sounds something like this
The best part of waking up
Is a "certain coffee" in your cup.
For me, though, that's not quite true
We seemed to have missed a detail or two
What about just waking up?
What about a new day blessing to fill your cup?
To me, that's the best part of waking up!
What about opening your eyelids on this side of Glory?
Seeing the light of a new day, with nary a worry?
What about gazing at horizons you've never seen before?
What about movement in your limbs when your feet hit the floor?
To me, that's the best part of waking up!
What about a reasonable portion of health and strength?
What about being in your right mind once again?
What about a "thank you" meditation slipping from your lips?
Then you can think about what you're going to sip.
To me, that's the best part of waking up!
You see, I'm really not a coffee drinker…not so into it
For I realize waking up according to my mother's wit
Has to do with a "new-dawn-we've-never-seen-before" blessing
And gratitude for grace and mercy while I am dressing.
Still, I like a little coffee in my sugar, among all that cream.
It goes along with feeling like I'm someone's special queen.

So the next time you think of that jingle once again

Consider the dew on the roses, then say AMEN.

Now that's the best part of waking up!

And that, my friend, makes life itself good to the very last drop.

THREE CHILLING NIGHTS IN A CASTLE

By

Daniel Leckie

In the early sixties I served aboard the USS ENTERPRISE CVA (N) 65. More than five thousand men managed hundreds of jobs an aircraft carrier requires. A carrier takes a cruise as part of a fleet to show the flag, train the crew and pilots. On a cruise in the Mediterranean Sea I signed up for a Navy sponsored ski tour in the French Maritime Alps.

For these tours the Navy works out a discount and the sailors get to spend a small amount for what would be an expensive ski weekend for civilians.

I was the odd man in the group. I was added at the last moment. The others were all machinist mates from the ship. Machinist mates repairs most of the machinery the crew uses. You might think everyone knew everyone but, in fact, most of us were busy every day doing our jobs so there wasn't a lot of interaction.

I had never skied in my life but I was sure it would be fun and snow is soft, right? A Navy bus delivered us to a hotel in a village a few miles from the ski resort. The hotel lobby was modern and warm, with plate glass windows and comfortable chairs scattered around. It was a welcome change from the cold bus and the little hills of crispy snow skulking in the shadows.

We stood in a standard Navy line to sign in and get our room assignments. Beyond the check-in desk was a longer room with a collection of tables and chairs – the dining room. There were trays of snacks, sweets, water and wine on the tables. We had to pay for the wine.

After the snack, a beautiful young French girl with auburn hair and green eyes approached me. She wore a loose skirt and peasant blouse with a low-cut bodice. The French know how to please sailors.

She spoke, "Pardon, Monsieur. I must lead you to your room while there is still light."

The others stopped conversing and watched as we left together. No one was escorting any of them. We went out a side door then started up winding stone steps that curved to my left. A wind blew from behind me and up the tower. The top was hidden in darkness.

Since I was taller than her I was enjoying the view when she grabbed my arm.

"I appreciate your interest in my breasts, Monsieur but you must watch your step."

She pointed to my left. I was inches from a gaping black hole. This was a castle turret. There was a stonewall to our right but open space to my left. I could see a hint of the flagstone at the bottom. Did I mention there were no railings?

"Is this what everyone is getting?" I asked.

"No, Monsieur, only you. There were only the forty rooms. The leader said you would not mind."

I could guess why. They knew one another. I was tacked on to the tour at the last minute. None of them wanted the tower. Maybe it was her intoxicating perfume but I accepted the situation.

"What is your name?"

"Michelle, Monsieur."

"My name is Daniel." I put out my hand. She hesitated then shook it.

"Bonsoir, Monsieur Daniel."

"How far up do we go?"

"Almost there, Monsieur Daniel. Ah! Here is the door."

"We passed a few other doors. Why couldn't I get one of those?"

"They are uh, uh story…storerooms. You are unusual. I mean we don't put people out here unless we have no choice."

I heard a high-pitched sound. She worked a wrought iron lever and handle. It took some effort to move the heavy wood door. A cold wind blew into the room from behind us but the noise stopped. Michelle pushed a stone against the door to keep it open. She gestured for me to enter.

The room was shaped like a pie wedge. The door was the point and there was a large opening in the curved outer wall. The whole room was thick stone, like a prison cell. The cold wind continued to blow from the door to the window-like opening and out.

"Michelle, can we close the door? That's a cold wind blowing through."

"Sorry, Monsieur, we cannot close the door when we are in the room with a guest." She went to a four-drawer chest and picked up an oil lantern. She lighted it and gestured as she described the amenities.

"The bed is large and soft with two pillows. The covering is down and very, very warm. You are welcome to use the chest and the armoire is for dress clothes." Using two hands, she picked up a large bowl from the chest.

61

"This is for washing and teeth, Monsieur. I filled it tonight but you should fill it each night before you go to bed. We have no running water here." She leaned down and pulled another bowl from under the bed.

"This is for…for…"

"Night-time emergencies?"

"Yes, Monsieur. You should not mix them up." She blushed appealingly. Then she went on, "I am sorry, Monsieur Daniel. We have no electricity here. The lamp is the only light. You should, uh…"

"Not waste the oil?"

"Oui. She lowered her head then asked, "Do you have any questions?"

I pulled a few dollars from my pants.

"No Monsieur Daniel. I cannot take money. They should not have done this to you." There was no good response to that.

"I almost forgot. What time is breakfast?"

"Pastries and juices will be served at five a.m. every morning.

The bus leaves at six."

"Thank you."

"Dinner every night will be served from five to seven." She backed out of the room and curtseyed. I got my last view of her cleavage but the light was dim. I did a short tour of the room. She hadn't told me everything. My spirits dropped. The 'window' was a three-foot by six-foot hole in the wall. It looked like a window but one trip in the wrong place and I'd go right out and explode like a watermelon on the flagstone patio below. The tables and chairs

62

on the flagstone would not help me at all. I closed the door to stop the wind and I immediately heard this high-pitched noise. I had an ancient key to the iron lock but figured no one else would ever come up there so I never used it. I blocked the door open and went down to supper. It was more comfortable in the dining room.

Supper was a feast, French style. The long table I had seen was piled high and wide with vegetables, salads, water, dinnerware and magnificent French bread and butter. We competed for the French bread until we learned they replaced what we ate. Of the two days they served supper this first meal was the most sumptuous and the only time they served free, cold, milk. Most of us nibbled or skipped the vegetables. As they cleared them from the table they served each of us a small bowl of orange sherbet. We were mystified. Michelle was one of the servers. I asked her if that was all there was.

"Oh. Non, Monsieur Daniel, there are many courses. You will be happy."

We greeted the fish course with groans but some liked it. I ate more bread and butter.

The staff could see we weren't enjoying the fish course and quickly replaced the fish with sherbet. This time it was lime. Most of the diners started banging their sherbet bowls. "We want meat!" These sailors had had a few beers.

The cooks and servers were prepared. They scattered large platters of Steak, Chicken and Lamb. The French staff was dismayed that the lamb sat, untouched, while the steak and chicken were demolished. The servants served an assortment of steamed vegetables that mostly grew cold, untouched.

The meal was edgy. The French were used to their way of dining and we were completely unfamiliar with it. The food was fantastic but both sides finished

63

the meal with a little discomfort. Still, by nine p.m. everyone but me staggered off to bed a little bit drunk and probably full.

I stretched out my hand to feel the roughness of the stones and slid the hand along the wall to make sure I didn't fall off the other side. People of the Middle Ages didn't think of banisters and I had forgotten to take my lantern to dinner. I kept going until I hit the large, heavy door. I decided to skip the lantern. I got out of my shoes and got into bed still in my Navy dress blue uniform.

The bed was iceberg cold but it soon warmed under the heavy covers. Then it over-warmed, then heated, then seemed on fire. I threw the covers off and froze. I took off my blues and put on pajamas. Because of the giant hole in the wall the outside and inside temperatures were the same – twenty degrees or colder. I felt the cold wind blowing through the room so I shut the door. The wind was reduced because it blew under the door. This created the high-pitched keening that sounded like a banshee wanted to get in and welcome me. Between the wind and the banshee I chose the latter. I didn't get much sleep that night but, toward the morning, I began to adapt.

That first morning the machinists got up early, wolfed down croissants, butter and coffee and persuaded the bus drivers to take them up early. I got the same meal, alone.

Eventually, the bus came back for me.

I didn't have the money to spend any time at the resorts so I spent the day teaching myself how to ski. I was lucky. I had this little hill all to myself. I'm from Alabama. One inch of show causes a celebration and chaos. Here I was, in my Navy dungarees and work jacket, my boondocker boots buried in six inches of pristine reflected sunlight, the snow sometimes flashing like diamonds. It was cold but I didn't feel cold. I felt exhilarated! Maybe it was the evergreens but the air had a clean, clear smell. I looked out across the gentle slope with skiers trekking up and skiing down, a line of people at a small shack and little dots racing through the crowds. I followed their path back and up a slope to a nearly vertical dark pinnacle. The black dots started there. I walked closer and could see they were skiers, mostly little kids, leaping off the top and coming down the slope at bullet speed. As I watched, one of the kids fell and the skier behind him collided with him. The ball of coats and skis tumbled down the slope until the two separated as the slope leveled out. The two re-attached their skis and got back into line to ski again. I vowed to skip that experience.

Off to the side of the ski zone was a gentle slope about fifty yards long with unused, pillowy snow and a large area at the bottom to stop. Some nice person showed me how to attach the skis and I skied down this small slope. The skis popped off each time I fell at the bottom of the hill. I thought I had to put the skis on before I got up. It took both ski poles and several falls to learn how to get up without popping out of my skis. Then I struggled up the hill sort of slanting them so I wouldn't keep sliding back.

The day went well, if lonely. No one else ever appeared on my little slope. Too soon I noticed the low sun beyond the trees. I had forgotten lunch but I didn't know how to get it and no one tried to find me. I managed to get to the gentle slope most of the skiers were using. I tried skiing there but I kept running into people. When I slammed into a beautiful young blonde girl she laughed.

"Why don't you stop before running into people? Or did you mean to knock me down?" She smiled.

"Sorry. I don't know how to ski so it's knock people down or fall down. I usually run into people before I can think to fall down." She laughed again.

"Okay. I'll teach you how to stop and you won't run into people again. Stand beside me, facing down slope, like me." I managed that.

"Now, when you want to stop, you turn the right ski to your right and the left ski to your left. You see?" She demonstrated.

I tried but my legs splayed out and I fell on my face, my skis splayed out beside me. As I struggled to get up she laughed.

"Don't turn the skis quite so far. Try again."

After a few more tries she decided I had mastered the skill. She smiled, blew me a kiss, and went off to some guy luckier than me. This new skill worked well, when I remembered to use it. I saw fewer people skiing and began to worry about getting back to the hotel. I saw the Navy bus. I turned in my skis and returned to the hotel in time for supper. The dinner was small and simple. I was the only guest. All of the other sailors belonged to the same division on the ship and they decided to stay at the resort. The hotel staff gave up on the feast but was still friendly, adaptable to my tastes and excellent.

After supper I felt the tired aches from the day and slowly climbed the tower steps. I was going to just drop into bed when I realized my clothes were wet. I lit the lantern. I took everything off and, shivering, I draped the dungaree trousers over the windy ledge, the chambrey shirt over the back of the only chair in the room, hung the work jacket over an armoire door. I dropped the underwear in a corner of the floor. I found a large towel in a drawer. I debated drying or dying. I was too tired to stand on one foot and fell on the floor trying to get my underwear on. When I finally pulled myself under the heavy covers I slept without moving. A cat burglar could have taken everything in the room. In the grayness of early morn Michelle knocked at my still-open door.

"Pardon, monsieur, breakfast is ready and the bus driver will want to leave soon."

"Merci," I said and nodded.

Michelle left and I pulled myself out of the covers. It was too difficult to lift them.

I had four sets of socks and underwear, just in case. Donning a set made me feel better. I wanted to save my only clean pair of dungarees for the last day so I went to the window to get yesterday's dungarees. I lifted them from the window and they were frozen into the shape of a sharp angled 'U'. My icy shirt and work jacket could stand up. Yesterday's underwear was frozen but I had plenty of fresh underwear. I decided to wear the dry set or dungarees and hope another day of bright sun would dry out the frozen clothes.

Because I was the only person staying in the hotel the hotel driver took me to the resort right after breakfast. Since I didn't get lunch the previous day I ate extra and wrapped some croissants in linen napkins and stuffed them in my work jacket pockets. In the warm car my work jacket finished melting. The car was comfortable but, when I got out of the car, the driver grabbed a towel to dry my wet seat. My napkins and croissants were wet. I apologized and left the mess with the driver.

The second day was like the first. Skiers were skiing on the gentle slope and a stream of black dots was racing down the cliff beyond them. A line of skiers waited to get tickets to ride to the top of the cliff. The ski rental shack stood alone.

"Pardon, monsieur, do you need assistance?" The big man beside me looked menacing in the large silver fur that matched his hair but he seemed friendly.

"No. I'm just trying to figure out where the beginner's slope is. I thought I was on it yesterday but now I think I wasn't.

"Where were you yesterday?"

I pointed to the area beyond the skiers'. He looked then turned to me.

"There's nothing there. Am I looking in the right area, monsieur?" He pointed. I nodded.

"I am sorry, monsieur, but that is waste snow. That's not for skiers."

"Then where is the beginners' slope?" He pointed to the slope with the stream of skiers racing down.

"Monsieur, that is the beginners' slope."

"There aren't any others?" To me, a one hundred foot slope was too tall for beginners.

"Of course, monsieur, the adult slope is there." He pointed to a taller slope some distance away. Next he pointed to a mountain rising into the clouds. My heart sank.

"That is the slope for professional skiers. It is closed today."

"I was hoping for something smaller." He laughed.

"Monsieur, this is the children's' slope. It's as small as there is." The man with the silver hair shook his head and walked away.

I looked long at the ominous slope.

"Maybe it's not as bad as it looks." I said to no one. I rented skis and poles and got into line for it the chair lift.

"How many?" The ticket man looked at me.

"What?"

"Tickets, tickets! Sacre Bleu." He rolled his eyes and spat into the wet dirt outside his ticket booth. At least the one ticket was cheap. I walked through the ticket booth to the line for the top. I followed the guy in front of me, heart racing, legs trembling. When my turn came I stepped forward and presented my backside for the ski lift chair. An aluminum pole banged against my back, slid around me and moved on. Another pole did the same thing, then another…another…another…

People standing behind me began shouting things in French. I didn't know what was going on. Finally, A loud, clear voice shouted, in English, "Grab the pole, you idiot!" I looked around and saw no chairs, only a line of these poles. I grabbed one. It dragged me along for twenty feet or so.

"LET GO!" people shouted at me. I let go and fell to the slushy snow. Other people skied over me as the pole pulled them up the mountain. I rolled out of the way and saw what was happening. I managed to get my skis back on and grabbed the first pole I could. I was clumsy and managed to trip over my skis and fall again. The third time I grabbed tight and was pulled up the slope, sometimes hanging from the pole, until I got to the top. The pole pulled me in a curve to the left.

"LET GO! A crowd of people shouted at me. I looked ahead and saw a chasm yawning before me. I let go and fell to the ground. The line of poles continued out over forest that was several hundred feet below. It took several minutes to stop shaking. I got up and looked back at a line of children age five to teen. They walked to the edge of the cliff, stepped off and disappeared. I watched long enough to recognize some kids I had seen before.

69

"How hard can it be if children love it?" I realized I spoke out loud but no one seemed to notice. I felt my legs turn to rubber as I approached he edge. I looked down. I thought of three things – The bottom was a long way down; it was not snow, it was ice and I saw no other way to return to the gentle comfort of the base.

A brief lull urged me to take a closer look. I leaned my head over it. It still looked bad. I estimated it was a mile to the sparkling snow at the base, too far away to see detail.

"How hard can it be if little children love it?" I realized I was repeating. Was I losing my mind? I wasn't surprised. The skiers really did go like bullets. I felt the bony hand of Death on my shoulder. I saw his macabre smile as he looked with eyes both close and infinite. "This is the only way down," he said and laughed. I looked down again.

"Those kids are little, not much mass. I'm much bigger. If they fall, they get a little bruised. I'll get broken bones." I said to what I thought was Death.

"Look kid, don't be so glum. I'm really here to save you. Look over there." I looked and noticed the finger wasn't bony. Some Frenchman was pointing and smiling. I saw an elderly woman in a long black coat holding the hand of a girl in a little red riding hood. At first I thought it was an hallucination, like Death. But they walked into the woods and gradually sank from view. They were going downhill! I slapped my skis along the mushy snow and found a path that led through a thick forest of conifers. I saw the woman and the little girl walking in snowshoes. The woman was older than me and the girl looked to be about four. I started skiing slowly but the steep slope increased my speed. I yelled "Look out!" They must have been experienced because they stepped aside without looking back as I crashed into the trees bordering the first turn. By the time I got up they were well ahead. I skied after them and

70

crashed at the next turn. I was suffering minor bruises and scratches at each turn. I crashed every time. After several turns we came to the ski slope. It WAS ice. The woman and girl were there ahead of me. They removed their snowshoes, hunched a little and slid down slope across the path in their shoes!

I looked for other options. There were none. So it was me and the skis. I angled myself to cross and took off. It went smoothly until I hit the snow on the other side and fell on my face. I managed to make it to the bottom without falling again. Still, it was thrilling. I spent the rest of the day on the gentle slope.

When the graying skies signaled end of day I turned in my skis. The hotel driver had several towels on the seat. I thanked him for the ride. I was so tired I paid no attention to supper. The clothes I left to dry were frozen. The ones I was wearing were wet. I took them off to squeeze them dry. Shivering, I tried to squeeze out as much water as I could, bending over the stone window gap, freezing, blue and naked. I draped these clothes. At least I still had dry underwear and pajamas. The down comforter was warm. But I felt the cold when I got up. By the time I got to breakfast my frozen clothes were wet. It was the third day.

The third day was the last. We had to leave after lunch to get to the 'Big E' by evening. I grabbed some pastries and a half-quart of milk. The staff provided the milk for free because I was the only one who drank it. All of them felt the other sailors should not have treated me badly. The hotel driver added six towels on the passenger seat and four draped over the back. I was the second person to rent skis. I knew how to use the poles.

At the top I got in line. There were two three-foot girls in front of me. I watched as each one dropped from sight. I crept to the edge, leaned my head over and looked straight down.

I heard a lot of yelling by the French kids lined up behind me. I'm pretty sure the comments were rude, at least. I ignored them. Someone behind me poked me with a ski pole and I fell over the edge. It was like falling off the Empire State Building. I screamed and tried to stay upright. I couldn't tell but I think I screamed the whole way. I felt my face freeze and something was pelting it. My vision blurred. My left ski began to rise but I forced it back to the ice. My scream followed me as I skidded along the ice, wobbling and trying to gain control of my skis. I squatted to keep from falling over. The ski poles were useless. I've never gone so fast outside a vehicle. I concentrated on keeping my balance. I felt the slope level out. I had ice on my glasses. My throat was raw. I thought, "How do I stop? Oh yes, one ski left, one right."

I plunged face first into the snow and skid between the legs of a young woman. She fell backward onto me. I mumbled an apology from the snow. Faintly I heard her.

"Are you okay?" I lifted my face and felt the pains in my body parts. I moaned and grunted but I managed rise up. The voice came from a pale face with auburn hair and black eyes.

She grabbed my face and looked.

"Oh! You're bleeding." She pulled out a lacy handkerchief and wiped my face.

"It's nothing." She stood up and left.

I struggled to my feet as skiers skied around me. Several commented.

"Get out of the way stupid fool!"

I struggled to my feet and looked around. Kids and adults skied around me, shouting something in French. I looked up and saw a line of skiers coming at

72

me. Before I could dodge an adult skier knocked me over. Cursing, I think, in French, he untangled his skis, said "Stupid fool. Get out of the way," and skied off. Several tiny skiers dodged me and yelled things in French. I didn't think they were old enough for real curses but I got the point. I moved to my right. I turned in my skis and waited for transportation to the hotel.

The other 'guests' were laughing and yelling about the great time they had. I checked out before them and boarded the bus.

I sat at the back as the machinists shouted to one another about their exploits. I asked the leader where all of them were.

"Partying. You shoulda been there."

"I wasn't invited and I didn't know where it was."

"Right. Well, we didn't know you."

"Why didn't one of you take the turret so I could at least have a comfortable room?"

"Why should we? We don't know you."

"But you weren't using the rooms." The machinist rolled his eyes and joined the group conversation.

I wished I had brought a book.

ANGST

By

Delores L Staton

And he hurt me so
How was I to know
When we met last fall,
It wouldn't last at all.
Come, come and tell me now
Where it all went wrong.
Who's singing our song?
Can't cry no more
My soul's too sore
Ah, he hurt me so.

Country Cats Caught in the Cadi

By

Eunice L. Sykes

One of the most memorable moments about my deceased birth father was his quirky sense of humor. This trait was especially evident while he and I, along with my stepmom, were visiting the family compound to see his mother, Granny Miller--the only grandmother I ever knew--and oldest sister, Aunt Ollie. It was during this time that he and I shared one of the most poignant and humorous moments that I have experienced with him.

Granny's homestead in Hodges, South Carolina, had land as far as the eye could see. Situated at the front end of the property was a dusty and windy three-hundred-yard dirt driveway with a white picket fence on the left side and a well-manicured lawn on the right side. At the end of the drive, the lawn was adorned with neatly trimmed bushes that surrounded a white, two-story home with columns supporting a covered porch containing two welcoming rocking chairs and two side tables, just waiting for tired souls to sit a spell and sip an iced sweet tea. Family, friends, and associates have come to and gone from this welcoming place enjoying genuine southern hospitality, Miller style (no beers please).

Nevertheless, on my first trip to the homestead as an adult, I was unimpressed. The location was remote, with the nearest interstate about forty-five minutes away. The next house was a block or two down the road, across the road, or up the road. Now, I am not a city girl. I am not a country girl either. I'm a northern girl, specifically a Midwesterner, from a bustling, small steel manufacturing, blue collar, three shift town in West Virginia, near Pittsburgh, Pennsylvania. I'd never been to South Carolina, nor to any particular place south of the Mason Dixon line. Yet, here I was travelling on windy, country, dirt roads in sweltering heat, surrounded by little-to-no air conditioning, bugs and other critters (big and small), roaming the area as if they owned the place. They did. Dogs lie in the middle of the street, and stray cats meandered the grounds looking for their next meal. Folks from all walks of life visiting the compound moved carefully around whatever had stretched out on the concrete floor of the covered carport area, acknowledging the hallowed presence of all kinds of animal life living here and lazing around on those steamy afternoons. Aunt Ollie encouraged them by offering leftovers that were temporarily placed in an aluminum pie pan, once containing a sweet potato pie, that she kept on her kitchen counter near the stove. "Auntie" was like a lioness protecting her young, feeding and caring for any four legged creatures that might stop by for morsels. She welcomed them with such warm and loving gestures that these animals, in turn, made their "stop" home.

During a visit there about twenty-five years ago, my father, making his semiannual trek from Chicago to Hodges, slowly turned right off Miller Road and drove his clean-as-a-whistle, shiny, black Brougham Cadillac to the end of the driveway. After parking "the ride" in the carport on the left side, we cautiously stepped out and climbed the five wooden stairs leading to the kitchen entrance. There, Aunt Ollie welcomed us with hugs of joy and a delicious hot breakfast of grits, bacon, eggs, liver pie, buttered toast, coffee, and orange juice. After breakfast, we lingered at the table to discuss the latest events in the neighborhood and in the world.

About midafternoon, Dad and I decided to ride into town. When we approached the car, I noticed two cats, one black, one white, sunning in the back window of the cadi. Dad and I looked at each other recalling one cardinal rule: Raise the window when you park your vehicle, or risk having any and all kinds of four legged varmints, large and small, inside the car upon your return.

When those cats spotted us approaching the car, they scurried back and forth trying to escape. Both romped from the front to the back, from the back to the front, from left to right, from right to left, jumping up and down, racing past each other with wide eyes, tails flailing, whiskers sticking straight out. Startled, I looked at Dad, he looked at me, and together we howled with gut laughter. I held onto the door to keep from sliding onto the concrete. He was wobbling backward trying to steady himself as laughter overtook him. We both bowled over, laughing so hard as those two cats sought to escape our collective wrath.

After what seemed like an eternity—it was likely seconds—one cat, the black one, got it. He leaped out the front window and ran off in the direction of the fields behind the house, leaving his stunned left behind buddy, the white cat, to fend for his own nine lives. The white cat pranced in a confused, frightened state. Seconds later, he too escaped his hell and darted out the window landing on his belly before doing a U-turn and fleeing for the fields. What a sight! By this time, we were busting our sides laughing so hard. I was doubly tickled for I had never seen my dad so amused. Here we were, enjoying a rare, silly moment. I was thoroughly entertained by a sight unlike any I'd ever seen before: country cats caught in the cadi.

Have you ever been so amused that you couldn't stand up straight, your shoulders and chest heaving, your breath shortened, tears rolling down your cheeks, and your body going into spasms and jerking wildly all over the place? Imagine that scene on an otherwise lazy, southern summer afternoon, father and daughter enjoying an in-the-moment time of silly ecstasy. Later, when we regained our composure, Dad summed up the situation in his preacherly manner. Those cats were like two children who had just gotten caught with their fingers in the cookie jar. They had an every-man-for-himself attitude and were desperately trying to get away, to look out only for

77

themselves, neither of them interested in the welfare of the other. A life lesson for us all, especially when trouble comes.

Dad and I remained amused by this memory every time we recounted it as if we had just witnessed it for the first time. It was a wonderful father/daughter memory that brings a big smile to my face twenty-five years later.

The Incredible Shrinking Brain

By

R.S. Raniere

She wakes in a mood—dark and distant—
hissing from the crumbling corridors
of a mind she no longer commands,
like a conductor unable to raise the baton,
and so the music falters.

She strikes at me with fists of rage and
searing epithets, but soon her mind
will draw its shade and she'll forget—
and yet, will know instinctively to say
"I'm sorry" for words she cannot recall.

How stealthy the shift from healthy
to a wasteland of unkempt hair, fits
of fury, and urine stench, where
no corner of dignity is left unswept—
how helpless are we against such tyranny.

She pounds her head in frustration
at the merciless thief who thwarts each grasp
at clarity; a robber of rational thought
and remembering, who leaves behind
a tangled web of sticky strings.

Helpless tears pool behind my watching eyes
as she slumps in a chair that seems to
swallow her—this gray and formless sack—
unceasingly rifling through her empty purse,
searching for the lost part of herself.

Sorrow shadows me
As I mark her evanescence,
like rings of smoke fading
ungracefully into the void.

THE BURNING CANDLE

By

Carolyn Julien

Boom! Boom! A third boom and the door and windows in Eli's room shook with urgency. The sounds interrupted him from sleep and he ran and jumped into bed with his mother, Denise.

Living on an army base with his parents all of his six years he was accustomed to the loud thunder from soldiers playing war games in the middle of the night. However, tonight's fire practice sounded more threatening than anything the young lad could remember.

"Mom, mom," Eli shouted as he tapped her on the shoulder. "I'm afraid. I think the soldiers are going to blow up our house."

"Calm down," his mother said. "Everything is just fine. Honey, you know the soldiers are just playing War again. Now go back to sleep, you should be used to this commotion by now."

"But mom, it's really different this time. Not just the windows and door shook, but my bed shook too – that's what woke me up!"

"Alright dear, you can sleep with me tonight, but just stay on your side of the bed."

This young wife noticed that the hall nightlight was out and attempted to turn on the lamp next to her bed, but it would not come on. She looked behind her at the digital clock, but it was not working, either. She concluded that the electricity was out. However, she was not concerned, since the power on base occasionally went out for no apparent reason. Consequently, Denise not heeding her husband's warning lit a candle to read Bible verses and fell asleep with it still burning on her nightstand. While in a deep slumber, she heard someone pounding on her door so hard, it rattled the window panes. She wondered who was knocking with such insistence and forced herself out of bed, threw on a robe, and walked hastily to the door. She peeped through the curtain to find two MPs dressed in combat gear holding flashlights and M16s. She also saw her neighbors herded on to Army buses like cattle. Feeling anxious, Denise opened the door and asked, "What in God's name is going on so early in the morning?"

"Ma'am, all I can say is that this area is on high alert and we are under direct orders to evacuate everyone from this housing area immediately."

Denise assumed that she was an involuntary participant in a military practice exercise and said, "Not today, I didn't sign up to play war games this time" and assisted that the policemen (MP) go away and let her sleep! The second MP assured her that the alert was real and she had no option but to come with them. He further warned her that failure to comply could result in her being arrested. The MP abruptly said, "Ma'am, anybody else share these quarters with you?"

Finally realizing the seriousness of this situation, she said, "My son and I right now, my husband too, but he's away on an assignment in Canada – although I can't imagine why. Aren't the Canadians one of our closest allies?"

"Well, yes ma'am, but out great country has enemies everywhere – even in our very own backyard Ma'am you need to secure your son and come with us. You've got exactly five minutes to pack a small bag."

The concerned mother ran to her bedroom, gathered a few clothes, some hygiene items, and stuffed them into an overnight bag. She did the same with

Eli's backpack. She woke him, put on his jacket, grabbed his hand, and led him down the dark hallway and out the front door as they followed the MPs to the parked military bus. She and Eli sat in the vacant seat closest to the door. The boy, too sleepy to care about the situation, immediately fell asleep in his mother's arms. The housewife occupied with this shocking revelation was halfway between disbelief and the disturbing probability that her great country could be under attack by enemy forces. Was it possible she thought to herself – I mean the Armed Forces, FBI and CIA have been on alert since the Twin Towers tragedy and the bases have check points at every gate?

As the bus drove off, filled with slumbering neighbors from her street, she questioned if life would ever be the same or if she would see her warm, comfortable home again with the joyful print of Michael Jordan and Tweety Bird in her son's room; or the Mona Lisa painting that graced her hallway.

Except for faint whispers, the forty-three-minute bus ride to a secluded compound was quiet and the darkness seemed blacker than usual, almost unnatural as if anticipating something catastrophic to occur. The infants and young children even appeared unusually quiet for the duration of the ride.

The military complex did not come close to meeting her expectations. It looked more like a movie scene from a World War II prison camp where yards and yards of barbwire surrounded the monstrosity.

Two to three families were assigned to a set of sleeping quarters according to the number of children in the family. After a while nobody really cared about the assignments. Everyone just wanted somewhere to lay their weary heads.

Later that day nobody was any wiser to the events that led to their evacuation from military housing. They knew that cell phones were inoperative and electrical power remained lost to the military installation and the two surrounding towns of Fayetteville and Spring Lake. Rumor also had it that the

NBC News Studio had been taken over by ISIL who broadcasted their own version of the nightly news in Black and white. There were also more frightening rumors that communities across the country, excluding Hawaii and Alaska, had been bombed and thousands of Americans were presumed injured or dead. All the armed forces, including the National Guard and Reserve, were ordered to report to duty immediately; no exceptions.

Denise woke early on Day 2 with feelings of doom. She was overcome with grief about the future of her country and what it had in store for her young son as she gazed at his angelic face.

The civilians in the compound were woken at 0700 hours that morning, and served a simple breakfast of eggs, toast, bacon, orange juice and coffee. At 0930 hours, the adults were ordered to assemble in the icy courtyard for further instructions and an update.

Since it was in the dead of winter, most were dressed to fight off the freezing temperatures--Denise wore her favorite coat, turtleneck, sweat suit and a ski mask. During her hasty packing, she had dropped a glove, but wore the remaining one, since one warm hand was better than two cold ones.

The group flocked together to hear updates. Everyone had ideas and expectations about the future, but nobody was definite about anything. Many unanswered questions pondered their thoughts. Had power been restored to their homes and would they be returning soon? Was their great country truly under attack, or was this just some sick psychological war game devised to determine how families would respond during an actual invasion? The most pressing question was if whether or not their active duty spouses were gearing up to fight a ground war on American Soil for the first time in the 21st Century? The one detail Denise knew with certainty was that everyone was apprehensive concerning the events of the past couple days.

As the Officer in Charge addressed the group, Denise noticed that her neighbor, Captain William's wife was struggling with her large purse.

Poor young thing, Denise thought. A foreigner who has only been in the United States for about two years must really be having a difficult time dealing with this news. The woman had met Captain Williams when he was stationed in Afghanistan. To further complicate matters, Mrs. Williams was pregnant with their first child. As Denise moved closer to provide Mrs. Williams comfort and compassion, the woman pulled

away from her and grunted loudly while she released a dirty bomb! The dreadful concoction emitted a reddish-orange powder that covered a significant portion of the area. A sergeant watching from a distance instantly donned his protective mask and sounded an alarm. Soldiers already in protective gear promptly apprehended Mrs. Williams and took her inside the compound for decontamination and interrogation. She refused decontamination. The soldiers' abhorrence and displeasure for this Judas made it easy for them to honor her request. Regrettably, this proved to be poor judgment.

The crowd was shocked and enraged with this awful woman for betraying them and for the life-threatening harm she may have imposed on everyone. They were thankful though, that most of their bodies were protected with clothing and that the children had not been exposed. Furthermore, except for mild skin irritation, the chemical seemed almost harmless, and feelings of terror were replaced with concern and anxiety. Soon, everyone was under the impression that the device was probably more terrifying than destructive.

As instructed, the group assembled into the decontamination facility of the complex, undressed and showered in cool water. Initially, the cool water felt soothing and refreshing leaving them to believe that the worst of their ordeal was over.

However, as victims begin to wash further, the water reacted more like Alka-Seltzer to the areas of their body exposed to the substance. Their flesh sizzled, peeled, and burned incessantly.

Hysteria broke out by those showering as they screamed and cried out for mercy. Confusion and insecurity filled the minds of those who were preparing and waiting to enter the showers. Realizing the association between the chemical and the water, the non-commissioned officer in charge (NCOIC) shut the water off immediately.

Denise was now whimpering from the pain of her one exposed hand and thankful to God that she had chosen to wear the other glove. Still flabbergasted with what had happened, she contemplated: Who could have known that refreshing cool water would serve as a catalyst for the chemical mixture?

Still in disbelief over the events of the day, her thoughts wandered back to her neighbor, Mrs. Williams. If she had it her way, she would toss the evil women into a pool of water and watch her entire body sizzle like a french fry.

The exhausted mother returned to her bunk and found Eli napping. Still whimpering in pain from her injury, she lay beside him.

Her sniveling startled Eli who woke up screaming. "Mama, mama; your hand is melting!"

The housewife woke up to find her hand resting on the nightstand where hot candle wax had been dripping on it for minutes.

What a crazy nightmare she had had! The power had been restored to the home and she was in her own room. She blew out the candle, gave Eli a kiss, cleaned off the wax, and returned to her bed, wondering if her dream could ever become reality.

HOT CHOCOLATE

By

Cynthia Anne Cofell

Hot chocolate hot chocolate

Yes, I want some.

Hot chocolate hot chocolate best drink in the world, Delicious fun.

Hot chocolate rich chocolate

My dream in a cup.

Hot chocolate milk chocolate rich chocolatey love.

When I'm feeling down purple and blue.

I look to my left, back to my right, up on the shelf hot chocolate to brew.

Hot chocolate helps me think, relax to. when I'm drinking hot chocolate there
is nothing I can't do.

Hot chocolate has a way of making the coldest days, a little warmer.

The frigid winter nights a little hotter.

Arriving home from a hectic day. Worry frown on my face. I reach for my
fancy white cup.

Then quickly fill up the tea kettle with water and patiently wait, for that
glorious sound the steaming whistle.

What more can I say. Hot chocolate is on the way.

My cup and I smile, as I pour the hot water over the chocolate goodness.

Oh yes!

With just a touch of vanilla cream, stirring ever so carefully not to waste any
is heaven to me.

My treat.

The contrast from the white cup. Makes the rich, milk, chocolatey, velvety
smooth texture, pop' and I love it.

The funny thing is I can drink hot chocolate in the spring, summer, fall and of course winter when it's especially chilly outside.

My fuzzy robe. A scary book and my hot chocolate right beside me.

Every warm smooth sip that cascades down the back of my throat delights my heart and soul

Yummy Yum Yummie!

My hot chocolate and me inseparable.

Hot chocolate hot chocolate.

WORDS OF LOVE

By

Casey Muller

I was born into a world of chaos, silent and lightless; thus it only makes sense that my first memory, appropriately savage, is of my mother's teeth sinking into my five-day-old flesh. I can only assume that the caretakers constantly surrounding us screamed at her to stop, pleaded with her, cried for the tiny creature she was in the slow process of killing, yet the pain overpowered every other sensation, and I can't be completely certain who and what ceased it. I just recall the sudden release of pressure, and the warm arms of an attendant a few moments later, wrapping my wounds in gauze and running her fingers gently through my thin layer of hair.

I was in a fortunate position as an essential newborn and was adopted into a family and given a new mother with no desire to attempt my murder not long after my recovery, left only with small scars and a constant sense of caution. And yet, despite the prior events of my short days, the life that I was rewarded was able to considerably lift my fallen spirits. The family that was gracious enough to accept me, even in my damaged state, has been the sole reason for my survival. My parents, colorful and animated people, are perhaps the best thing to ever happen to me. Despite having two young daughters of their own, they willingly brought me into their home and embraced me with more love than I had ever imagined possible. My new mother, warm and affectionate, woke every few hours to check on my small, sleeping form in the crib— equipped with a heating pad and plenty of blankets—next to her bed.

"What are you?" she whispered, leaning over the railings, her hair falling around her face, her mind still disoriented with sleep, "This isn't real. You're not real."

But, by day, she would wrap me in small blankets and watch as I slowly learned to army crawl across the carpeted living room, eyes shining, voice elevated as she called the rest of my new family to watch the progression across the vast room.

My adoptive sisters were intrigued; they watched me, held me, and oftentimes spoke to me in quiet voices with love evident in their hazel eyes, but the youngest daughter of the family, six years old when I was accepted as one of them, was by far my favorite sibling. She spent most of her spare time by my side, dressing me in doll clothes and carrying me around the house with a wicked gleam in her bright eyes. She was a lively, energetic child with long, wild red hair, an infectious, melodic laugh, and wide eyes constantly full of wonder. Her mischievous nature was a perfect contradiction to my up-tight personality; she was, and still is, the only person who can make me fully relax.

My new family—the only people I truly belonged with—allowed me to truly see for the first time.

As I grew older, I began to exhibit serious developmental defects. I displayed obsessive compulsive tendencies at a young age—biting my hands until I bled, causing alarm among the other members of my little family—remained extremely small for my age, and, most alarmingly, seemed incapable of speech. My father would sit on the living room couch, my small body in his lap, and attempt to be my teacher.

"Okay, buddy, repeat after me,"

But I could only ever manage soft exhalations of breath, slightly pitched, but nothing close to traditional speech, and yet, he never gave up on me. He would hold these informal lessons every evening after he returned home from work, despite their seeming failure. I, still young and deeply influenced by the abuse from my biological mother, was terrified of this lack of success. No matter how much love he had shown me since the day I was accepted into their home, I was constantly worried that the adoration would turn to frustration and, eventually, to murderous rage. And so, I worked my hardest to please him. In retrospect, there was no possibility of him hurting me in any way. No one would have minded if I had remained mute for the rest of my life, but the fear motivated me to, finally, one evening, speak. And, from that day forth—much to the chagrin of my family—I have only gotten more vocal.

Those lessons evolved into a sort of home school. I was a sickly child—I was allergic to absolutely everything—and staying home was the best option in my situation. My mother spent her days with me, thus, I learned everything I know from observation or experience. Among my home-learned skills is a wide knowledge of musical scales and lyric writing. My mother, spirited and enthusiastic, liked to sing to me as I followed her around the house on the lonely days when my sisters were in school. I would sit on the carpet or the bed and watch her, my head tilted slightly to the side, and be entertained for hours. My childhood was filled with original songs and upbeat melodies, sung from the top of my mother's lungs. Luckily for me, her energy never seemed to wane when it came to singing.

Years passed, and we all evolved and grew up, morphing into different people and back, experimenting with who we wanted to be and where we wanted to go. Today, as the story of my early childhood is written, I am nine-years-old and putting my hardships behind me. I rarely think of the attack forged against me by my biological mother, and my true mother has managed to help me deal with my debilitating allergies and obsessive compulsive tendencies. My youngest sister, my best friend, once wild and bright, has matured into a young woman with slightly more controlled hair and still-devious eyes, but she still finds time in her busy, teenaged schedule to accommodate her small, damaged brother. She remains the source of much of my happiness. Being where I am today—loved and comfortable in a life that the attendants at my birth would never have imagined for me—I can only envision things will only continue to improve as I age.

Funnily, I've only just realized that I failed to open my story with an introduction, but it's better late than never.

My name is Buddy Holly, Maltese puppy.

NO ONE ASKS

By

Delores L Staton

THE WORLD FADES,

THE HEAVENS BURN,

THE WATERS SOAK UP,

THE ANIMALS FALL QUIET,

NO ONE ASKS, BUT IS IT OVER.

THE MOUNTAINS CRUMBLE,

THE DESERTS CRACK AND SPLINTER,

THE OCEANS ROLL BACK,

THE TREES INCLINE,

NO ONE ASKS, BUT IS IT OVER.

THE FOG DROOPS DOWN,

THE UGLY MIST CLOAKS THE EARTH.

THE HOT SPILL OF VOLCANOES

SEARS THE SOIL.

THE SUN BLISTERS LIKE

AN UNLANCED BOIL.

NO ONE ASKS, BUT IS IT OVER.

THE TINY SEEDLING POKES THROUGH.

THE DEEP, RICH EARTH ENFOLDS IT.

THE HEALING LIGHT STROKES IT.

THE WARM SOOTHING RAIN CARESSES IT.

NO ONE ASKS, BUT, YES,

IT IS NOT OVER.

REGRETS

By

Delores L Staton

A dark figure hobbled to the impressive home. Time had been lavished on the grounds. The lawn was manicured; the bushes and trees pruned to perfection. The man, bent and moving with measured step, inched up to the front window.

The room was very quiet, in fact, motionless. The children were studying their homework. The man stooped slightly, mysteriously, peering into the window. The dark figure was dressed in old, tattered clothes. He wore a fleece hood over his head. His physical attitude was the image of halting curiosity. His demeanor, calm, almost serene as he gazed into the window.

As he focused his eyes, a young, beautiful woman slipped into the room. She seemed to be saying," hey, you two, it's time for dinner." The kids jumped up awkwardly, scattering their books and papers. Startled by the sudden movement and noise, the dog began to bark.

The dark figure followed the family to the dining room window, there, he could watch as they sat down to dinner. Umm, he stroked his beard," where is the man of the house?"

Mom, the beautiful, slender woman sat down at the table. Almost simultaneously, without direction, the kids, bowed their heads, folded their hands and closed their eyes.

Mr. Mysterious leaned closer to the window. He wished he could hear the prayer. The family prayed and began to eat.

"Oh Lord," he murmured. "A table set for a king. Look at all that meat, potatoes, vegetables, coffee, and milk." The sight of the bounteous meal made his eyes water; his stomach ache. "Lord, I'm hungry. But where is the lucky head of the household?"

The night darkened. The air grew cold and uninviting. Mr. Mysterious pulled his rags around him. He noticed that his knees, hands and fingers ached with arthritis. "No matter, he thought. It goes with the territory. Yes, I'm getting old. But I have to try, one more scheme before I am called up there."

The solitary figure moved along the streets to the beautiful park in the square. Town squares in New England have a special place in all men's hearts. They are replicas of Norman Rockwell paintings. Our old man, walked over to the stately elms, made himself somewhat comfortable and closed his eyes.

The cold morning dawned. The near winter air seeped into one's bones. Such incongruity between the trees, glazed with light snow and the heart wrenching sight of three or four homeless individuals, slumped, in various positions, against the elegance of the trees.

David Ward Folsom opened his eyes, and took inventory of his meager belongings. He unscrambled his limbs, forcing himself not to wince at the pain. Oh well, he mused, not such a bad beginning. He had found the house. He had seen the family. He had allowed himself thoughts of what could have been. David murmured, "If I don't succeed, that vision of family harmony will sustain me until death."

DW, as he was known in his other life, had overcome huge obstacles. David had just been released from prison. A hell hole, he vows to never see again. Improbable, as his current physical condition worsens with every moment spent in the elements. Upon his release a week ago, he made his way from Boston to Ashland, small town near Framingham. He carried an old letter in his pants' pocket, horribly wrinkled, blurred, and nearly illegible. He could make out only the address, the "Dear", and " love you, Dianne." It hadn't been an easy trek. The roads were not well marked. No one picked up hitchhikers anymore. It was practically impossible to find a Samaritan to offer help.

"I sometimes marvel: have all the good people been called to Heaven? "

DW shook himself, stowed his grungy belongings in an even grungier knapsack. He made his way slowly to the local coffee shop. There is one in every town. Thank God for the monotony that is modern architecture. He approached the garbage barrel, furtively lifted the lid

"Would you look at that?" Scones, untouched. Doughnuts, undirtied. "Maybe there is a God, after all.

"Hi, Dianne. How 'r ya? Genevieve, your neighbor.

" Yes, of course. I'm fine. What about you?" It's been awfully cold, right?"

"Yes, that's why what I saw last night, troubles me so?

"What's that?"

" Well, last night, I caught a glimpse of a, what looked like an old man, leaving your front yard. I couldn't make out any features. He limped. He had to be intensely uncomfortable. It's probably nothing, but I thought I should call you."

"Absolutely, Mrs. Weinblatt. Thank you, that's a little scary. We didn't hear a single thing."

"Okay, gotta go. Have a nice day."

97

Dianne placed the phone on its base. She was shaken. Her face paled, her eyes widened. "Oh my God. I bet he is back."

The "he" Dianne referred to was her father, David Ward Folsom. Dianne had cut off all communication when her Dad, accused of being a pedophile, had been sent to prison for 8 years. It had been hard; the kids had asked so many questions. Dianne had finally settled on the story that Grandpa had been lost at sea, on one of his many damn fishing trips. The kids had been heart stricken. But, as we know, if enough time passes by, we tend to forget even the most painful events. Or at least, the pain becomes less acute. Panic struck her heart.

"Oh my god, what if he has returned? What if he is back? What do I tell the children? Will Paul and I dare trust him with the kids, his beloved grandchildren? Should I even tell Paul? Let's see, it's only eleven am, plenty of time to think about this before Paul returns from work."

Dianne began to reflect on the uneasy relationship that her husband, Paul, and her father had had. Paul was everything that David was not. David was messy, disorganized, forgetful, crazily unleashed. While, her magnificent husband was impeccable, proper, controlled, with an eye for detail.

Back at the coffee shop, David had made himself comfortable, sitting on a pile of containers, munching on breakfast, humming an old familiar spiritual.

"Nobody knows the trouble I've seen. Nobody but Jesus." I gotta figure out a way to let Dianne know that I am in town. I pray that she hasn't lost any of her loving charity for humans in distress. Above all, I pray that she will open her heart, and accept me into the family. I miss talking and hearing about them. I tried over and over again to convince the authorities of my innocence. Just dumb luck, I was the only one left in the park. I don't blame the frightened little boy. He was so scared; he would have identified Jesus himself. So there I was, no other witnesses.

Looking in on the grandkids, Paulie and Janie, David had flashed back to images of happier days. Both the kids had loved to venture out on the ocean to fish with him. Their parents had held their breath until he would drive up to the fieldstone home, returning his charges, without mishap. The kids had always seemed supremely happy with him. They laughed, they told Grandpa things they wouldn't dare mention to Dad and Mom. They shared their favorite recollections of family life.

"Yep, those were some very precious moments."

After straightening up the house, Dianne had poured herself a steaming cup of coffee. How she cherished her first coffee. She inhaled the rich, dark Colombian aroma. She closed her eyes, settled back for some serious thinking.

It was nine years ago. The phone rang late, unnerving the whole family. No one calls after eleven, unless someone is deathly ill or someone has passed on. Dianne approached the phone, every nerve vibrating. She said hello, in a very small voice. The big booming voice on the other end announced the Police chief.

"Dianne, we have your father down here. We have him in custody. It appears he has molested a little boy in the park"

"What?" Dianne had screamed into the phone? "What?"

"Sorry, Dianne, I know this is hard to hear. But, we can send him home as soon as we take his statement."

"Are you talking about my Dad, David Ward Folsom?"

99

"Yes, Ma'am. Someone needs to come and get him, he's pretty shaken. He doesn't seem to fully understand what he is charged with. You're gonna need a damn good lawyer."

"Well, what is he charged with?"

"We have him on a molestation charge. Seems pretty cut and dried."

"That's preposterous.!" My husband and I will be right down."

The trial had taken an eternity, or so it seemed. Dianne recounted every painful detail. She remembered how she had cried, sobbed. She remembered the excruciating pain of telling the kids. She remembered their expressions, as if they, themselves, had been personally molested. Then came the dull sensation of helplessness. They knew, all of them knew, Grandpa could not have been the one in the park. Grandpa could not have been, would never have been the molester.

They were never able to prove his innocence. So, off to prison he went, shackled, and now branded. "Pedophile."

Dianne continued ruminating. "Let's consider the positive side of all of this. There is real lemonade to be made here from these pretty sour lemons. Paulie and Jane would have their beloved curmudgeon of a grandpa back. I would have my dear Dad back. We would replace the missing piece in our family circle. The kids and Grandpa would once again be able to go out on their fishing sorties. Their time together always freed me up, gave me down time. Down time was always welcome. Okay, let's move on to the negatives. Paul and Dad are like oil and water. Paul won't be the least bit happy to have him back. Dad will find it impossible to keep from being the explainer-in-chief. Paul will question the additional expenses for Dad's upkeep. Lord knows, he has a lot of medical problems. Most likely, he no longer has medical insurance or access to his pension. So, that part won't be easy. All we have is the college fund. Paul will staunchly refuse to use any part of it. I may have to work part time. No biggie. I have been thinking that I need a diversion. I need to get out of the house, search for adult conversation. Mrs. Weinblatt, bless her heart, zones out when the conversation reaches intellectual level."

David had finished his "untouched scones", and his morning ablutions at the local gas station. It had occurred to him, that he should just check in at the local police station, identify himself, and ask for help in communicating with his daughter, Dianne.

"Why not, he thought. I have to make myself known eventually. May as well be now."

David made his way unhurriedly to the police station. He took time to note the beautiful sky, and the crispiness of the air. He was reasonably content, having breakfasted on "untouched and undirtied scones."

"Ah, there it is", he murmured. "Not sure it is as I remembered it. Wasn't it two story? Oh well, it's probably been modernized."

David gingerly approached the door. Adjusted his hood. Re-arranged his knapsack.

"May as well, be now." He made his way up to the desk sergeant, ensconced behind protective glass. "Good Morning. I am David Ward Folsom".

"Yeah? Whaddya need?"

"Hate to say this, but I have to register as a child molester."

The protected sergeant jumped to his feet. Called for back-up, unholstered his gun. It all seemed in one fluid motion. It also appeared that at the same time, he pushed a button, automatically closing all doors, and also preventing any mode of escape.

Uniformed officers appeared, rushed him, pulled him to the floor and handcuffed him. For DW, it was a sudden and unwelcome surprise.

Why all the rig-a-ma-roll. I'm here, aren't I?

He was summarily pushed, shoved, and marshaled into a small, windowless room.

The one in charge, spoke hoarsely. "Ok, run that by me again. Who are you?"

David could not find his voice. He was taken aback at the violence of what just happened. He looked up, imploring the officer to give him time. Let him collect himself.

The officer shook him, saying "What's the matter, you gone deaf?"

"I hear you. I need to register as a child molester. I should be on file. I am hoping that you can help me speak to my daughter, Dianne Melbourne. She lives on Chateau Lane."

"THE MELBOURNES? Impossible!" our premier Afro-American family? Hey, officer Jake, take this guy down to fingerprinting. See if he is in the system."

The work day ends, Paul Melbourne arrives home. He drives his beautifully detailed Land Rover into the garage. He sits quietly, anticipating a nice cold vodka tonic.

"What a day this has been."

He knew that Dianne and the children would be extra happy to see him. He had been away for three days, obligatory business conference. He didn't mind, usually. But this time had been excruciating. The export-import business was slacking. God knows what's next. Britain voting to leave the EU. China devaluating its currency. Oh well, he shook off the doldrums. Put a smile on his face, and opened the door to the kitchen.

Paulie and Jane ran up to their handsome Dad. They hugged him, unwilling to let him go and hug Mom.

Dianne said, "Go'on you two, wash up for supper. Let me say hello to Dad."

Paul and Dianne enjoyed a long, endearing embrace.

"It's good to have you back. How was the meeting?"

"Oh, you don't want to hear, it will only spoil dinner."

Dianne, taking her cue, understood that any talk of DW being back in town would have to wait till after dinner.

The family sat down, prayed and ate. The kids took up most of the conversation, babbling about events that had taken place in school. Mom and Dad could only nod, and agree profusely. After supper, the kids went off to their bedrooms, to watch television, and to pretend to do their homework.

Dianne poured her husband another vodka tonic.

She began tentatively, "the strangest thing happened last night?"

"Oh yeah? What was that?"

"Mrs. Weinblatt called this morning to say that she had seen someone, hunched over, leaving our yard. She called because she was concerned, and wanted to alert us. I have been doing a lot of thinking today, wondering if it's Dad."

"What, exploded Paul?" "What are you talking about, wouldn't we have been notified?"

"I don't know, but something in my heart, tells me it's Dad. We should call the police."

"I don't know about that, let's calm down. Let's wait until they call us. We may be jumping to a major incorrect conclusion."

Dianne thought to herself. I knew it. I knew he wouldn't be happy to hear that Dad is back. In fact, he will deny it until he is confronted with the physical presence of the man."

"You are probably right. You are always so sensible I am always so emotional. Of course, we should wait until the police call us. Don't know why that didn't occur to me."

At Precinct 303, things were buzzing. This was perhaps the most activity anyone had seen since The Boston Marathon, April,2013. The fingerprint officer had determined that although this broken man had declared himself to be David Folsom Ward, his fingerprints named him Robert Louis Johnson. The duty officer was frantically attempting to send and receive queries about both men. So far, no response. He certainly couldn't report to the Chief. He didn't have anything to report. He had one fact nailed down. The man in the cell was not David Folsom Ward. Beyond that fact, he had no intel about David Folson Ward nor did he have any definitive intel about Robert Louis Johnson.

The phone rang, Officer Beatty, the duty officer, thought Balls.! Chief Petty is not very forgiving when you don't have answers. Maybe I could just not answer.

The phone rang again. Officer Beatty, screwed up his courage, picked up the phone. "Duty Officer" Yep, it's Chief Petty.

"Hey Beatty, where's that report. Should I call the Melbournes or not?"

Officer Beatty cleared his throat. "Chief, I wouldn't call them just yet. The finger print lab indicates that the man in the cell is Robert Louis Johnson. He's most definitely not David Ward Folsom."

"What? Are you sure." Chief Petty closed his eyes, imagining the taut body of Mrs. Melbourne, tall, chocolate beauty. "Well, have you located David Folsom."?

"No sir, the last inventory has him at Walpole Maximum Security. But they haven't responded to my e-mail. No one appears to know Robert Louis Johnson."

"See if you can hurry them up, we gotta git to the bottom of this. I need to know who to call, who to incarcerate, or if I should incarcerate. Git this done."

Officer Beatty grunted," Yessir!" Don't know what I can do to speed up the computer, or the other officers in the other cities. Don't know what you expect me to do. God, I hope they answer soon. Wonder if the old guy has had anything to eat."

David Ward Folson or Robert Louis Johnson was nodding, his head on his chest. He seemed so peaceful. Officer Beatty didn't want to disturb him. He would then have to confront him for lying to a police officer. He heard the notification ring on the computer, and ran back to his desk. Yeah, two responses.

Officer Beatty opened up the first email, it was from the National Registry. He breathed a sigh of relief. It is now confirmed that the man in the cell is not the father of the most prominent black family in Ashland. That's just flat out good news. Didn't wanna hafta make that phone call. The Melbournes were a little touchy when it comes to family.

"Hello Chief, Officer Beatty here. It is confirmed from the National Directory, that the man in the cell is not Mrs. Melbourne's father. I'm still waiting on more intel explaining the whereabouts of Mr. Folsom, and clarification of who Mr. Johnson is? And what is he attempting to do by masquerading as Mr. Folsom. The old geezer has convinced himself that he is DW. He knows an awful lot about the family. If you ask me, we're not talking incarceration, we're talking mental institution."

Chief Petty barked a thank you, replaced the phone on its base. He thought I better go out to the Melbournes. Perfectly, legit, I get a chance to see the chocolate beauty. I can at least alert them to the investigation. Maybe they have more recent information relative to the whereabouts of Mr. Folsom.

Chief Petty opened the text, as he was getting to his car. The text read, Johnson was a former cellmate of Ward. Ward in hospice, near death.

"Well, he murmured. At least, now I can reassure the Melbourne's that their father isn't roaming around town, in tatters, scrounging for food. It will be somewhat easier to let them know about the imposter. Oh well, I will still have to deliver a sad message. Her father, DW, maligned, in my opinion, is now in hospice and dying."

Chief Petty climbed into his squad car, brushed the papers off the seat, took off his police issued cap, and started the engine. ' His thoughts wandered to the image of Mrs. Melbourne, tall, slim, taut, very chocolaty.

Chief Petty maneuvered the car easily through the narrow streets of Ashland. Not much traffic at this time of the day. Most of the Boston traffic had now returned home. I like this old sleepy town. Not too much happens here, and that is a good thing.

Chief Petty pulled up to the brownstone. He took a moment to drink in the fact, that by God, this damn house is owned by blacks. Go figure. He swaggered up to the front door, peremptorily rang the bell.

"Oh, Chief Petty, come in. Let me get my husband. Paul, Chief Petty is here."

"Must be very important for you to come personally. Please take a seat."

Chief Petty, sidled awkwardly into the room, taking in the elaborate furnishings. "Mrs. Melbourne, I am afraid I have some troubling news. We understand from Walpole Max that your Dad is near death. They have put him in hospice."

"I don't understand; why didn't they notify us?"

"Don't know, ma'am. But we discovered all of this because we have detained a drifter, claiming to be your father. No worry, we have him in custody. We will most likely recommend hospitalization for his medical problems. It's not clear, but apparently he thought he could impersonate your Dad. Maybe fool you into believing that he WAS your Dad. He believes he is your Dad. According to our information, he was your Dad's cellmate. He has convinced himself that he is David Ward Folsom. Just remember ma'am, fingerprints don't lie."

Paul, now in the room, stood quietly behind his wife. "Can you tell us, how to proceed with visitation rights."

Dianne glanced at her husband. He seemed touched that David was dying. It struck her that an awful lot of time had been spent in acrimony. David cared!

Chief Petty, glad to show off a bit, declared. "Certainly, sir, we can ease you through the process. Drop into my office in the morning. I am working this week-end. We will fix you right up with a visitation time and identification to express you through to hospice."

Paul looked at Dianne for agreement. Dianne nodded her head, in awe of her husband. Would he ever cease to amaze her?

The trip from Ashland to Walpole was quiet. Neither Paul nor Dianne could speak.

The regrets were swimming through their heads. Why did we let him slip away from us? We knew that he was innocent. What foolish pride to not stand by our father in his hour of need. Why did we just close the book on grand-pa. Now, we feel pain, now, we feel regret, now we hurt for him as he lays dying. Now, we see clearly. Now, we ache for what could have been.

RHYTHM OF LIFE

By

Barbara Scott

The rhythm of life, the nodding head
A beating heart, a deep cleansing sigh

Where does my satisfaction lie?

The tapping foot to a remembered tune
A hum or whistle or singing off key

Why does it all matter to me?

A searching mind, a seeking heart
Shortness of breath - dimness fills the eye

When will I finally die?

Take a break, think happy thoughts
Temporary pain, eternal hope.

MOON

By

Everett Smith

I am Stone.

Humans would say that I am a moon orbiting a distant planet. They would be amazed to discover that I am alive. They would be even more amazed to discover that I need them as they need me.

In the beginning, time meant nothing. I danced with my planet, we danced with our sun, all through the long night. We were alone and content, at peace.

Life began – quiet, slow – on the surface of my planet. Consumed with the dance, I overlooked this origin, this birth. Such was my first mistake.

It spread rapidly. Penetrating the crust, swimming in the seas, floating in the atmosphere – this energy permeated my planet. There were many different living forms, some larger than others. They did not live peacefully, one with another, for that is the way of organic life.

Then, one form grew strong. Minds powerful, they became dominant. Their eyes looked outward from their home, my planet. They saw me dancing in the darkness and they wished to touch me. Using machines, they leaped to my surface. And, finally, I became aware of this form, this life.

They had given themselves a name. It wasn't a human name because they were not human. I shall borrow an ancient word from Earth and call them the Nascens.

Several times, the Nascens touched me, then returned home. I examined the locations where they had been and learned much. Some of them died before returning to my planet – I looked deeply into their bodies.

I can see with the particles of myself — humans call them atoms and molecules — and I can see with an entire mountain at once, using all forms of energy. But sight is a human word; for me, sight, hearing, taste, smell, and touch are all one. Also, I have another sense: the human word 'gestalt' weakly describes what I receive from this sense. It is a summation, an empathy.

The Nascens had no secrets from me. Or so I thought.

I prepared my surface to be comfortable for them by nurturing the seeds — called DNA by humans — that the Nascens left behind. I ensured there was food available that was compatible and familiar to them. I brought clean water from deep aquifers to the surface for their use; this liquid was essential for their survival.

When the Nascens returned to me, I revealed myself as a stone, a piece of myself that spoke to them, giving it their appearance and words.

The Nascens reacted with fear and hostility, attacking the stone with their weapons. Although reduced to gravel, they couldn't damage me or even the piece of me I showed them. After all, the stone was still present, only in another form.

I tried speaking with them again and again with the same result. For the first time, I was puzzled. How could I communicate? I looked again to the Nascens.

This group was different; they came to me planning to remain. There were more this time and several were young. The minds of the young were as yet incomplete, their bodies still growing. Perhaps I could speak to them.

Now, long after, I give her a name: Prime. I spoke to her as a stone and she listened, unafraid. I gave her visions — where to find food and water, how to live on my surface. I became aware that her body was damaged, some of her internal organs were failing. The Nascens knew of her problems but lacked the skill to repair her.

She wasn't afraid. She knew her body was dying. She had dignity and grace. She gave of herself to those around her. I watched, almost too long. She slipped into a coma.

Now, at last, my knowledge of the Nascens could be used. Quietly, I entered her body, removing the dying tissue, triggering growth, healing. I felt her gathering strength. I gave her the Stone, the essence of myself, and altered her mind so we could speak directly, one to the other.

The Nascens didn't expect her to recover. When she walked again, it was beyond their understanding. They attacked her.

She didn't resist. Each blow, each cut — I healed. I blocked the pain that would have fractured her mind. She opened her eyes and laughed. The blows stopped, the Nascens drew back.

I watched over her but there were no more attacks. Instead, the Nascens began to defer to her. And, silently, we spoke, she and I.

It was the beginning. She was my first Seer.

I gave her access to my memory and knowledge. Many skills were beyond her understanding; gently, I explained. I hungered to learn about the plants and

112

animals inhabiting my planet; the Nascens willingly brought them to me. I studied these life-forms and released them undamaged to my surface when done. Thus, I populated myself and stored the information in my structure, my body.

More wished to be Seers. I welcomed all but, somehow, Prime was special. Then, I did not question why. The Nascens, led by Prime, waxed powerful. And they were noticed.

An enemy came out of the vast emptiness, the void humans call space. Focused as I was on my life-forms, I was unaware of their presence until their starships were orbiting my planet. Then fires rained down blotting out the cities of the Nascens.

This was the way of organic life but, this time, I could not condone it. I fought back.

I would change a mountain to a dust mote in a tiny sliver of time — humans might call it a near-singularity. Focused, it clawed their ships from orbit, crushing them against my surface. I aimed the light and heat of my sun with a great energy lens I held together between my planet and sun, igniting their ships, creating chained explosions.

The invaders became aware of me and attacked. It was a mistake many didn't survive to regret.

At near range, I swept through them, destroying but also gaining knowledge about this enemy. I learned about their bodies, their strengths and weaknesses. I discovered the secrets of the mechanisms controlling their starships and other devices, how they were constructed, and with what materials. Immune to their weapons, I knew all of their mysteries, all of their vulnerabilities.

I annihilated them. The few that remained alive fled. I hunted them with my energy lens until they were out of range or slain.

But, in their dying minds, I learned that these were but a tiny finger of an immense, malignant swarm – there were many more in the vastness of space. Also, I discovered that they did indeed have a powerful weapon: they could extinguish my sun, causing it to implode. It wouldn't harm me but I was far beyond that concern.

It would destroy all organic life. The Nascens. The other life-forms. Prime.

No.

I spoke to Prime. She gathered the Nascens into vast underground caverns. I provided them with food and water. I left her and made my own preparations. Then, I waited.

The enemy came again. Their great weapon took station close to my sun. Their fleet came near and, again, went into orbit around my planet. When I did not react, they landed – first on my planet, then on me.

I leaped forward through time.

Physically, we – the Nascens, life on my surface, myself – were in the same location relative to my planet but we were nine human years later. Such a mighty disjunction required immense energy. I had drawn from all nearby sources: the enemy vessels, my planet, my sun. The sun released an huge flare, immolating their weapon before it could be fired. The enemy fleet, its component atoms torn apart and stripped of all energy, ceased to exist.

When I turned to my planet, I discovered that the weapon I'd wielded so effectively was double-edged: it was coated with ice. The core had no heat at all; the human phrase 'absolute zero' was accurate. All life was dead, the seas and rivers hard-frozen to the bottom, entire mountain ranges exploded from ice expansion. It would take millennia for it to thaw, far longer before life could begin anew.

I had killed my planet.

I think, act, and sense with all particles of my mass – yet I was fumbling to comprehend what I'd done. The humans have a word for it: shock. Then, I heard a cry for help.

It was Prime. I turned inward and focused, listening to her. The Nascens had not survived the leap through time. Their bodies were too fragile. Only the Seers still lived. As their bodies deteriorated during the disjunction, the Stone imbued in each healed them.

They had seen the other Nascens die and they had seen through my mind what happened to their home, my planet. Prime spoke to my mind. When I gave of myself to each of the Seers, their bodies had changed: they could no longer reproduce.

The Seers were the last of the Nascens.

Prime asked if I could create more of their kind. It was a question I never asked of myself but, surely, this could not be beyond me. I searched my memory, all of it – nothing. I combined the chemicals that made up their bodies, infused them with energy, waited. Again, nothing. I asked Prime if the Nascens knew how their life began. They didn't know. They had legends and stories. I relentlessly pursued them.

Nothing.

Now, when it was too late, I realized my first mistake. When organic life began on my planet, I was entranced with the dance with my planet and sun. I did not see how this life began and I could not replicate that origin.

Then, Prime asked to have the Stone removed, she wanted her body to die. The other Seers whispered that they wished to follow Prime in death.

I didn't understand. Organic beings clung to life, this was a constant. I hesitated but I had always given her and the Nascens the things they needed. And, looking into her mind, I saw that she needed this.

I removed the Stone from them. It was then a matter of time. They were still unable to reproduce, my Seers accepted that. Without healing, their bodies withered and turned to dust.

Bereft – my planet dead, Prime and the other Nascens gone – I was alone again.

Alone but not at peace.

I thought again about the enemy, they had brought me to this. I turned to the life abounding on my surface. Some of the forms brought from my planet had died when I leaped through time but many others still lived. I couldn't create life but change was easily accomplished. My studies were put to use: I combined the seeds of life using a tree as a medium, infusing it with intelligence, giving it the ability to add to and alter its own DNA. This Tree would rule my surface.

I reached into the animals and plants, altering them so they were stronger, faster, more deadly. I unbalanced minds, instilling hunger and hostility. In the minds of all life-forms, I firmly fixed an image of the invaders, these were to

116

be destroyed before all else. But I was careful: I made sure all could reproduce.

Some of the invaders survived the leap through time. The altered animals and plants hunted them down, destroying and rending without mercy. When the enemy returned and touched me, they would not get an easy victory.

I knew they would come back, that is the way of organic life. They would seek to destroy me. Let them try.

I looked outward and stopped. My sun was undamaged but, if I pulled from only it to leap through time, the energy drain would be too much. My sun would nova, consuming my planet and myself. There was no energy to be had from my planet – it was frozen, lifeless.

There was no answer. My greatest weapon: I could ravage my enemy but I would then be destroyed. I could slay any of the enemy that came close but, eventually, they would target my sun. I would survive but all other life would die. Regardless of my actions, the life on my surface was doomed. While grappling with this problem, I became aware of a change.

Seven tiny sparks of light rushed out of the emptiness of space, aiming at my planet. I readied my defenses but hesitated: this was something different. I pulled them toward me; two spiraled down to my planet, the others touched me. Four fell into the life now swarming on my surface, one impacted where my body was exposed. I looked.

It was a tiny ship, dispatched from a far distant planet. A dominant form sent these into space in a desperate effort to establish themselves elsewhere in the universe. Within this machine, were the seeds of this life-form – they called themselves 'humans' – and others indigenous to their planet. Then, I found the mind.

117

It called itself a Grail, a number completed its name: 2839-11. I looked into this Grail and learned how to unlock its secrets. Using sound, I spoke the code to activate it. I did not expect the result.

The mind of this diminutive vessel controlled a crystalline matrix holding huge amounts of information: the history of these humans, tools and methods they used to survive, detailed information about their planet and solar system as well as what the Grail itself learned during its great voyage. I learned their languages, making sense of the rest took longer. It was a torrent. I encoded this knowledge in my body, scanning for anything that would help solve my dilemma.

War. The Grail paused its flood at my command. The human's world – Earth – was attacked by an enemy from space. Outmatched, the humans were nearly exterminated, then they fired a weapon into their own sun. The resultant flare destroyed much of the enemy fleet and drove the rest away, but destabilized the human's sun. The humans expected their sun to nova. They launched these Grails, twelve together at each distant planet, trying to establish themselves in the immense reaches of space.

They were the same. The descriptions of the starships, the invaders, all of it the same. Their enemy was my enemy.

I found a log, indicating speed and approximate distance between the human world and my planet. The Grail had been traveling through space for hundreds of human years. If, indeed, their sun had been about to nova, their Earth was dead. No more than a scorched rock, it would be barren of life. The Grails were all that were left of the humans.

I reached into the human gametes, learning about this new life form. Their DNA was simple, yet enormously more complex than the Nascens. The more I looked, the more puzzled I became. These humans were a jumble of contradictions. Bent on self-destruction, they were heroic and cowardly, resilient and fragile, cruel and kind, healers and murderers.

Then I saw it: each had within themselves seeds of greatness. When pushed, they could transcend, becoming greater than before. This was how the humans turned back the invaders and why they flung the Grails into the endless night of space. It was even coded into their languages – words like faith, love, and hope.

And they were flexible, mind and body – with my help, they could step through time. If they were few, I could easily supply the energy needed.

I thought again of Prime. She, too, had the ability to transcend. Although she did not have their form, Prime, too, had human traits. I was puzzled: was she human even though she did not have human form? What was human? Then I realized that simply asking these questions was why I saw her as different, special.

I altered the seeds of these humans, preparing them. The birth sequence began and I waited. When a few had developed to the point that they were capable of holding the Stone, I gave myself to them.

Outwardly, they retained human form but they became my color – humans called it 'blue'. Their bodies melded with mine uniquely, changing each in different ways. The Stone was everything: my people were powerful in combat, we could speak mind to mind, their bodies could heal themselves.

But there was a problem. The Stone was so all-encompassing, so complete, that it buried those crucial seeds of transcendence. Somehow, I was incompatible. If these altered humans expressed their innate greatness or even spoke their own names, they would be destroyed.

119

Yes, their names. In their minds, names expressed their humanity and that was foreign to the Stone. Each fled from the other within their bodies, causing cataclysm within and without, tearing them apart. But the changed humans had a hunger to find their names.

I allowed some of the humans to grow unchanged. If they had been prepared to accept the Stone, their bodies and minds remained incomplete, the seeds absent. If not prepared, they could not survive amid my own wildlife but making further changes to the plants and animals would jeopardize their ability to combat the invaders.

I could have made the humans stronger by augmenting their DNA with other genes from their world or the life brought to me by the Nascens. Such modification would have made it possible for them to live, even thrive, among the other life-forms I'd transmuted to battle the attackers. The Grail itself knew the mechanics and how to maximize the alteration. But I sensed that making such a profound change to the human's gametes could make it difficult or impossible for those elusive seeds of greatness to develop.

I remembered the other four Grails that landed on me. I discovered they survived. All now had thriving communities of augmented humans around them. Their lives were entwined with the life on my surface, they were no longer separate.

If the humans carrying the Stone could meet another whose seeds of transcendence had developed into greatness, they might learn how to balance their innate humanity and the Stone within. It was a way fraught with peril, a slender hope indeed, but I clung to it.

I gathered my people to the Grail that I pulled from the sky. The blue humans would remain few in number but would protect the other, prepared humans.

I spoke to the transformed Tree, telling it about the changed humans within the life on the surface. I explained all. The Tree began searching.

Those with the Stone would seek among the Grail communities, speaking mind to mind with any that could listen. My people would help from afar, guiding.

I have great knowledge, but have made terrible mistakes. Prime, the Nascens, my planet – all dead because of my ignorance. The misjudgments I have made with the humans might yet doom them and me. Still, I have learned.

I am no longer content to be alone.

I need you.

Come.

AT THE BRINK

By

Delores L Staton

DISASTER LOOMS,
IN NOT SO MANY MOONS.
HOW DO WE FIND STRENGTH
TO GO THE FULL EXTENT
WHERE DO WE FIND LOVE
TO RISE ABOVE.

THE SAFETY NET UNRAVELS,
DISEASE, FAMINE, INTOLERANCE, ALL TRAVEL.
WORLD THINKERS ARE CLEARLY BAFFLED.
HOW COULD OUR WORLD OF
BEAUTY NATURAL,
WITH QUIET AND CALM PASTORAL,
CRUMBLE INTO THE DARK NIGHT,
CREATING HORRIFIC IMAGES OF FRIGHT.

WE LIVE UNEASY, WE WORK INSECURE.
WE PRAY IN DISBELIEF, WE WAIT IN WANING HOPE.

WE FACE HUGE BULWARKS OF PAIN,
NOT UNDERSTANDING IN THE MAIN.

WHERE DO WE GO FROM HERE,
AS WE TEETER ON THE ROTTING PIER,
AS WE STAND AT THE BRINK,
TERRIFIED THAT WE MIGHT SINK,
INTO AN ABYSS, A BOTTOMLESS CHASM.

OUR WORLD IS IN FREE FALL.
EVIL IS SUPREME OVERALL.

LOOK UP, LOOK UP,
IMPLORE GOD'S GRACE
MAY HIS COMPASSIONATE BOUNTY
ENLIGHTEN OUR RACE.

BODIES IN THE RAIN

By

Michael McLarnon

CHARLES REYNAUD ALWAYS DREAMED OF LIVING IN MALIBU.

Growing up in the agricultural area of Oxnard, he often sat in the back seat of the family sedan as he rode down the Pacific Coast Highway on the way to Santa Monica, where his sister took baton and dance lessons, or to Venice Beach, where he met with other geeks to play video games and share computer graphic design techniques. Passing the Malibu hills, he would gaze up, starry-eyed, at the sprawling estates overlooking the ocean and dream. He made himself a promise—one day he would live up there, in luxury he could barely imagine.

Later, while studying for a degree in Cinematic Arts at the University of Southern California, he would climb into his car and program the Nav-Drive to take him along the serpentine roads of Malibu where, hidden behind stone walls and gated entrances, he caught glimpses of houses large enough to be museums.

After completing his degree in Animation and Digital Arts, he took an unpaid internship at a digital movie studio, working nights as a waiter and picking up the odd web-design job to pay his bills. One day, while watching cartoons with his two-year-old niece, as if being struck by lightning, he was hit with the idea for an animated cartoon show called *The Runaway Duckling*. That night he called in sick at the restaurant where he worked part time, toiling until dawn doing digital mockups of his idea. For the next few months he devoted all his spare time, even ditching his beloved video games, to work at a fevered pitch on the project. And work he did. Snatching a couple hours

124

sleep here and there, while designing the characters and writing the stories with eyes red from sleep deprivation.

Remembering what one of his instructors said, that there are no new stories, only rehashes of older ones, he took the stories complied by Joel Chandler Harris's Uncle Remus and the fables of Aesop and Jean de la Fontaine, and modeled them into new versions, all containing his masterpiece, the Runaway Duckling, as the protagonist. Fortunately, no children, and most adults, were familiar with those stories, so they seemed new his test audiences. And, using knowledge he picked up in a class taught by one of the psychologists from Disney on character creation psychology, he crafted his baby duck so that it would be instantly engaging to children.

Unsuccessfully shopping his idea around, he discovered what seemed to be an immutable law in Hollywood: that in order to become famous, you have to already be famous. At least that's the way it worked for him. In a quirk of fate, he was at the La Brea Tar Pits one afternoon, sketching ducks for his project, when a toddler raced by chasing one his subjects. The duck fled to the safety of the nearby pond. Heedless of the looming danger, the child fell headfirst into the water. Being close by, Charles jumped in after the youngster—the water was only knee deep and didn't pose a danger to him. He plucked the lad from the pond, waded ashore, and handed the dripping bundle to the lad's frightened nanny.

Like locusts, the local news channels descended on him and, of course, he was labeled a "hero." In every interview, he shamelessly took the opportunity to mention the work he was doing on *The Runaway Duckling*. By the end of the week, producers who hadn't given him the time of day were now badgering him at home and work, begging to "do lunch." A bidding war broke out. Weeks later, he pocketed a one million SDR advance and became one of the producers of *The Runaway Duckling* children's TV show.

125

Living in Malibu was no longer a dream.

After viewing properties with a real estate agent was when his dream came crashing down to reality. Houses with a view of the ocean started at three million SDR and skyrocketed from there. When he signed the contract to produce his show he couldn't believe how much money he was given, his hands even trembled when he deposited the check in his bank account. It was more than he ever dreamed of, more money than his dad was able to save in a lifetime of backbreaking work. However, compared to the cost of property in Malibu, the money seemed a pittance. He discovered that life is all about perspective. Standing on hot coals in bare feet for a second would seem an eternity compared to kissing his high school prom queen for an hour—not that he ever did either.

About to shelf his dream of living in Malibu, his real estate agent told him that if it was an ocean view he wanted, an ocean he shall have. She showed him a three-acre plot of undeveloped land farther up the mountainside that had a view of the ocean, if only a sliver. The area was part of an old ranch that was being subdivided.

The land was cheap, relatively speaking. However, it was on a severe and rocky slope and would require heavy equipment to excavate and prepare the site for building. When most buyers factored that cost in, it was a deal killer—land prep would cost triple what the land was being offered at. But Charles didn't think that was going to be a problem for him. His father worked for a small road construction company and the owner treated Charles and his dad like family. After Charles closed on the land, he spent the next few weekends helping his dad and his dad's boss grade a building site. A stone structure, probably a horse barn, sat on the property; they razed the building and used the stones for the exterior of the new house. His dad, having seen the results of shoddy work, insisted on sinking piers five feet deep into the bedrock upon which to build the house, telling Charles his house would withstand Noah's flood. Charles was now thankful for his father's foresight, because that's what it seemed they were into.

Within a year of closing on the property Charles moved into his dream house, a modern structure with a gourmet kitchen, and a master bedroom with panoramic windows where he could wake up each morning and look out to the ocean in the distance. And of course there was the *pièce de résistance*, the home theater, where he could play video games to his heart's content, and watch *The Runaway Duckling*, of course. Charles covered walls of the room, the ceiling, and even the attached bathroom, with PlasmaWall monitors. Like a monk holing up in his cloister, Charles retreated to that room every Saturday to watch college football, only emerging to grab food and beer from the kitchen.

Which is why he was now living alone.

Rich and the owner of a mini-mansion in Malibu, women previously out of his league were suddenly in. He no longer had to awkwardly pursue them, it was they who were on the prowl. And he was easy pickings. A girl with movie starlet looks fresh from the wilderness of Minnesota showed up on the production lot one day and batted her eyes at him. That evening, after a steamy date, he was putty in her hands. She moved in the next morning, taking over the house as if it were her own. An ex-prom queen, she was the type of girl he only dreamed about having. She was an aspiring actress, model, performance artist, dancer, singer, or whatever caught her attention that day. And she needed constant attention and approval, especially in the bedroom. At first he was more than willing to oblige. After a few months the thrill began to wear thin. Although not exactly a genius, he needed more in life than simple carnal functions. His friends, most of whom were as socially awkward as he, couldn't believe his luck. They gave him leering looks and

127

said they would willingly take her off his hands. Eventually the ex-prom queen tired of him and, as easily as she changed shoes, she left. He tried to feign anguish, but breathed a sigh of relief when she said goodbye and drove off in one of his cars.

He was glad to be rid of her.

But she did leave him with two things. First, like Judas did to his rabbi, she gave him one last kiss. Unlike Judas, however, she gave him one hell of a kiss, which ended an hour later with the sheets thrown on the floor and he on his back panting to catch his breath. When she rolled out of bed and dressed, he almost begged her to stay, at least for the night. But he didn't.

Second, she left him with three labradoodles. She purchased the dogs a week before that final kiss—he wondered if she had planned to leave him with them all along, as some sort of passive-aggressive punishment for not fulfilling her needs.

She had named the dogs Puddles, Scruffy and Shaggy. After she left, he was going to change their names to something more masculine, but their monikers seemed appropriate, as they were always shaggy messes. So he didn't. He now was stuck with the responsibility of caring for three rambunctious dogs. The creatures did have one redeeming quality: they didn't mind going out in the rain. As a matter of fact, they loved it. When he sent them outside to go to "potty," they usually wouldn't return on their own volition, forcing him to wade out into the downpour and track them down. Invariably, he would find them jumping into puddles or rolling in the mud. Even though he hosed them down in the garage before letting them back into the house, his white carpets were dabbled brown and yellow like an achromatic Jackson Pollock painting.

When the Pineapple Express roared in from Hawaii and the rains began, the rushing waters eroded the ground in the Malibu hills, causing many of the mansions he once coveted to shift, crack, and even some were washed downhill. Thanks to his father's foresight, his house was spared that ignominious fate. In his case, the rainwater was shunted around his house, carving gullies, large enough to sweep away a car, into the rocky soil. The shifting ground undermined his driveway, causing cracks so large he had to install a metal pontoon bridge, like those used in the military, so he could pull his car into the garage.

On this day, weeks into the seemingly never-ending deluge, having returned from the studio, he settled onto the leather recliner his ex-girlfriend purchased with his credit card and gazed out the picture windows. The view of the ocean he paid a premium for was hidden behind sheets of rain. Although his house was safe, he worried that as the Malibu hillside was being eroded, the surrounding roads would collapse and he would become trapped, turning his mansion into a prison.

He watched the rain mindlessly for an hour, decompressing after spending another day with screaming kid voice actors and their prima donna parents, then let out a sigh. When he arrived home and opened the door leading from his garage into the house, the dogs, like bulls being released into the rodeo ring, rushed past his legs and bolted into the rain. He let them go. They had to use the bathroom, and so did he. But now it was getting dark and he knew the dogs weren't going to come back in voluntarily. He didn't want to grope around in the dark for the mutts, nor did he want to roam the neighborhood searching for them. He contemplated leaving them out for the night, but was too kindhearted to do that.

After changing into a worn pair of jeans and a tee shirt, Charles went to the garage, pulled a rain slicker over his head, tugged on a pair of tennis shoes that were perpetually soaked and beginning to grow mold, then stepped into the downpour. The rain was so heavy he struggled to keep his head upright.

He could only see a couple feet ahead. Keeping his head down and yelling the dog's names, he edged down the driveway while trying to avoid being swept away by the water steaming downhill. He was just about on top of the dogs when he spotted them. With their sandy colored fur caked and matted down, they resembled balls of mud as they furiously clawed into the side of one of the new ravines, throwing mud high into the air. They had burrowed out a hole next to the driveway about two feet deep and three times that in diameter. When the dogs didn't respond to his yelling and continued to dig and sniff, he waded into the knee-deep mud and snapped on their leashes.

About to pull the dogs to the garage and hose them off, he paused as a shock wave raced down his spine. For a second, he thought he saw something that looked like a bone. A leg bone. Brushing rain from his eyes, he crouched and took a closer look. There were a number of bones, too hard to say how many, protruding from the mud. Some were bone white, others had leathery flesh attached. Remembering the real estate agent telling him that this land used to be part of a ranch, he thought he could have been looking at the remains of a dead horse or cow. He squinted and leaned closer, almost falling into the murky water, and noticed the flesh was devoid of hair. It looked like the dried out human skin on a mummy. He wasn't sure how cow or horse bones compared to human bones, or what animal hide looked like after being buried for years.

But the hairs on his skin stood up nevertheless. Because there was one thing of which he was sure: neither cows nor horses wore blue jeans.

INTERIM

By

Delores L Staton

the season fast approaches
the visible, tangible signs are there
the exteriors lit with lights ablaze
the streets adorned with garlands that daze
the taut, crisp air turns less inviting
the stores festooned and primped
the needful bells urgently peal
the neighbors toast high their zeal
the apples, red and green, wither and die
and I,
I wait....................

THE TREE

By

Cynthia Anne Cofell

The story comes alive in late fall.

Claireanne is a forty- five-year-old widow, dressmaker. 5'8" in height, two hundred pounds red bouncy curly hair. She lives solitary, in her two-bedroom ranch style home at 616 Timber field way.

Thirty miles east of Wisconsin. In an underpopulated spirited town titled Whishmeyers.

Claireanne relocated to the Whishmeyer community about nine months ago. To create a new life for herself after the sudden passing of her husband Dane. He died a year and a half ago from a fatal heart attack. So grief stricken, Claireanne makes a drastic decision to sell their home. Donate the entire content to charity, except some memories and a few valuable items. Threw it all in the trunk of her station wagon heading anywhere. Accidentally came across Whishmeyers. Claireanne realizes she has to move on with her life. But can't seem to shake Dane's ghost.

She sees his smile in a fresh cup of coffee, hear his familiar chuckle in the wind, his soft reflection in the window. His kind voice calling out to her from the next room, as he often did, when he required her assistance choosing the right tie. Misplaced his favorite shirt or how much longer till dinner. Which proves too much for Claireanne and ultimately propels her into deep sadness, and overwhelming depression and riding the wave of her many crying spells.

Claireanne was hoping the new found living arrangements, small town charm, fresh air and friendly atmosphere. Would somehow make her feel a little better about losing Dane.

Nine months, thirty-five days, thirteen minutes and still counting. Claireanne discovered she was terribly wrong. The desperate move did just the opposite of what she had imagined. She felt worse and lonelier.

The sweet memories of Dane, endlessly plagued her mind. Particularly how they first met. Exchanging gardening tips, quick jokes over the stale chips and not so tasty onion dip. At a mutual friend's house dinner party. They talked for hours that day. Learning they shared similar interest.

Dane liked fishing, she likes fishing. Dane like watching late night movies while eating crispy bacon, and so did Claire. Six months after that first encounter. Dane proposed to Claireanne. They were happily married for twenty-five years.

Claireanne is fourth generation gardener. She was taught at early age by her grandma Willeena how to till the ground and prepare the soil for the seed. Claireanne remembers how every Saturday, Sunday. Grandma Willeena would be awaken to the annoying screeching crow of big red. A rooster that lived next door to them on the farm. As a little curios girl peering from the doorway watching grandma tie on her flowery kitchen apron. Eggs sizzling in the pan. Buttery biscuits baking in the oven. Homemade blackberry jam. Choice of bacon or sausage. Claireanne always chose bacon, grandma preferred sausage. Claire breakfast. And after breakfast. It was gardening time. Grab the bucket, shovel, work cloves and out the door they went, out there all day in smoldering heat. Raining down gallons of water on the seeds. Dane and Claireanne loved to toil in the yard. It was one of the many things they did together. Planting squash, eggplant, yellow, green heirloom tomatoes, three kinds of peppers, okra pods, wild green beans, peas and strawberries. A tradition she is forced to carry on alone.

Saturday afternoon. The sun at its highest in the sky as the leaves lay quietly on the cool ground. Claireanne notices that in all her sadness, she has terribly neglected her garden. It was in desperate need of care. Claireanne grabs her bucket, shovel, work gloves and a hand full of seed packets. Down the hallway through her kitchen out the back door she went.

Digging up the black soil from the earth. Rolling the gritty sand between her fingers. Rich smell of fertilizer, Placing that tiny seed in the ground. She almost had forgotten how much she enjoyed planting. Witch suddenly sparked an idea to sell vegetables to the community to make ends meet. After the passing of Dane her finances have changed considerately. Dress making was slow but steady and wasn't as successful as she had envisioned. No children to fall back on. Claireanne must create an income and fast if she is to survive.

She created a sign. It read, "Fresh Vegetables By The Pound" spreading the good news every where she went, at the market, the bank, the post office." Fresh Vegetables By the Pound"

But strangely after two weeks no one had showed any interest in the vegetables. Claireanne became puzzled, confused and a little depressed. What was wrong with her vegetables? Claireanne was dumbfounded that no one came to purchase or even inquire about her three kinds of peppers, okra bushels or her huge egg plants. Claireanne concluded she needed more vegetables.

So the next morning an excited Claireanne awakes earlier than usual anxious to plant more vegetables.

She grabs her gardening bucket, shovel, work gloves this time she intended on planting, watermelon, beets and cucumbers Down the hallway through the kitchen out the back door she leaps, as she has done so many times before.

But this time things go awkwardly wrong. Somehow Claireanne's feet misses the last step on the stairs as she desperately tries to catch her balance, she fumbles and falls face down in the strawberries.

The bucket, shovel, and seeds went flying. Claireanne dust of her clothes. pluck strawberries from her mouth. Sweeps away all the dirt out of her eyes and face. How silly" she chuckles to herself.

Three weeks later. Claireanne was gazing out the kitchen window when she noticed something odd blocking her view. She scrambles for glasses. Cleanse the lenses. But the odd vision was still there. Claireanne hesitantly heads out the back door investigate what mysterious thing that was lurking in her garden. To her amazement, a tree had grown, not just any tree but a funny shaped tree made of... vegetables.

On the right side of the tree, branches hung down like fingers made of strawberries and on the tips of the strawberries were small clusters of okra. On the left side of the tree two long branch curved in an angle, with several smaller branches dangling peppers in midair. Heirloom tomatoes covered the

entire top of the tree like a big curly red wig. And a few thick branches protruded out of the front and back of the tree, slightly drooping where squash and eggplants cling to the tips. Clusters of wild green beans and cabbage heads covered the trunk of the tree Five Watermelons stood up at the base of the tree like an anchor. Stems from the beet bulb hung upside down under the branches. And there was this very long skinny twig that stuck out at the very top of the tree with one pea pond on the end pointing west.

135

After a few seconds of taking it all in. Claireanne burst into a deep hearty laugh. She laughed so hard she fell backwards in the peppers, kicking her heels in the air and Laughing hysterically. She could not stop laughing no matter how hard she tried. That one lonely pea pod at the top of the tree kept her in stiches.

A neighbor was passing by heard all the commotion and came to see what was happening. When she witnessed the funny shaped tree made of vegetables. She too started giggling, so hard in fact she fell to her knees, laughing uncontrollably. As they attempted repeatedly to catch to their breath and glanced up at that funny tree. The laughing would start all over again. The laughter was contagious and nonstop Before long, dozens of people were in the garden. Tickled pink.

Because of the way it made people crack up, Claireanne decided to have the tree glazed to last forever. Over time, the tree became a tourist attraction. People came from all over the world. Even too this day, ten years later, people are still busting a gut at the funniest tree made of vegetables.

The end.

A DATE WITH PILLOW

By

Lorraine Sullivan

A date with a pillow
leads to anticipation.
Going gently into the night
with expectation.
Looking forward to
its presentation.
Soft like gourmet whipped cream
a tasty sensation.
Enchanted inner galaxy stars twinkle
with flirtation.
Some deep yoga breaths
for relaxation.
Soft curves and valleys
give titillation.
Head cuddles into marshmallow fluff
and hot chocolate for sedation.
Counting merry go round sheep
with recitation.
To sleep, perhaps to dream,
an odd implication
Another sleepy eve
Looking for restoration.
A date with a pillow

A night vacation.

Looking for restoration

Looking for restoration.

A date with a pillow-

A night vacation.

LUNCH WITH DEATH

By

Carolyn Julien

Head usher shot to death and his alleged mistress seriously wounded by the enraged wife was the first order of business at our bi-monthly usher meeting. We were asked to pray for the bereaved family and the injured female.

A few of those bullets actually had my name written all over them. Nobody knew this part of the story but me, and I never shared it with anyone.

While a single student at Louisiana State University, I attended Faith Baptist Church. The largely populated church was located on the outskirts of Baton Rouge. After being a member for three months, I volunteered to work on the usher board.

Church members were kind to me and I appreciated their down-home southern hospitality. Every fourth Saturday, we shared a delicious potluck dinner. After awhile everyone could count on me to bring my pineapple upside-down cake and three-meat cheesy lasagna. I never ate my homemade dishes, but feasted on their Louisiana cuisine of Gumbo, Crawfish étouffée, dirty rice and other delicious entrees.

My role as an usher was very simple. I paid my monthly dues, showed up for our bi-monthly meetings and ushered on first and third Sundays. Even though I was only twenty-one, I overlooked protocol and joined the senior usher board (40 years and older).

Although later approached to consider serving with my age group, I opted to stay with the more mature ushers. In part, I believe because I enjoyed the maternal nurturing from the older women. This may have proven to be a fatal mistake. Later in life I pondered why I was permitted to join the group where I did not meet the age criteria. Was this the devil or Jesus scripting my life? In hindsight, I believe it was most likely Lucifer.

I was primarily quiet and kept to myself during church services. I wore high-collared dresses and was bent on holding on to my virginity until marriage. I didn't even wear make-up, so I figured no mature man would be interested in a timid-looking skinny girl with her hair pulled back.

The thought never entered my mind. Not even when Usher Brown asked me to have lunch with him one Saturday afternoon during our regular meeting. He said he was having some marital problems and just wanted to talk with someone. A compassionate Christian, I felt sorry for the man and thought it harmless, since my major in college was Social Work. It would be a great opportunity to put some of my newly found skills to use. If all else failed, I could at least empathize with him. That was one non-committal social work skill that I had learned well.

I barely focused during the entire meeting due to thinking about what I should do. I finally asked myself, if I had a husband would I feel comfortable with him taking another woman out to lunch? At first I said no, but then I said it would be probably be all right if it were a colleague. Technically, *I was* his co-worker since we both worked together on the same usher team. Eighteen years later, I believe I was pushing my co-worker angle a bit too much.

I was told to close us out with prayer that memorable Saturday. With scattered thoughts, I managed to run through a simple and brief one, which ended with, "And God grant us guidance when we are confused about which paths to follow, Amen."

I exited from the sanctuary immediately without waiting around to converse in idle chitchat with the members. Before I could get my key in the car door,

Mr. Brown was practically breathing on my neck asking if I was ready to go to lunch, his treat. Before I could say yes, he told me I was the prettiest girl he had ever seen. That comment sparked my intuition. He told a big fat lie. I wore a brown loosely fitting high-collared dress almost touching my ankles, black flats, hair pulled back and no make-up. I looked plain and drab as always, and didn't care.

What I cared about was the lying compliment he had just given me. Now, could I trust a man who gives women deceptive compliments? Never!

Well, there was my answer and guidance from God. I told him no because the offer did not rest well in my spirit.

The moment I declined his invitation, it felt like a heavy weight had been lifted off me. I should've have known immediately that it was wrong for me to dine with this married man. The thought had tugged negatively at my spirit for the duration of the usher meeting. My grandmother often told me, "If it doesn't feel right, it ain't right, and that's just the Holy Spirit's way of letting you know."

Thank God for my split second decision. Usher Brown found someone else to have lunch with him that day. Whether guilty or naïve, the young woman died twenty-three days later from the gunshot wounds. Mrs. Brown had stormed into the restaurant where he and the lady were just beginning to eat. She accused him of being a liar and a cheat while she unloaded her pistol on the two of them at close range. A church member said his long history of adulterous behavior, ultimately drove his wife over the deep end causing her to snap.

End

WISHFUL THOUGHT

By

Edgar Levy

What if
Personal mountains were easier to climb
And all crooked roads became straight
And for every good soul a pot of gold
Awaited at the rainbow's beginning
And not the end
If only

What if
Mother Nature didn't have an aggressive side
And cyclones and hurricanes
Were merely wisps of air
And tsunamis were a minor splash
If only

What if
The heart was incapable of hatred
And there was no malice, no need for guns
What if there was no such illusion as the upper hand
And what if freedom was actually free
And taxes were totally banned
If only

What if

There were no such maladies

As melancholy

Malcontent, depression

Torment, poverty and its parallel grief

If only

And what if birth

Marked the beginning

Of a perfect

Stay on Earth

If only

Only if

LITTLE LION

By

PJ Renfroe

Gale force winds whipped the surface of Pamlico Sound into peaks of foamy meringue and moved inland lashing trees into a furious dance. The pounding rain smoothed forest roads into mud slides, and sent people huddling inside beside a roaring fire. Larry worked late to finish the day's paperwork. He worked with his crew earlier in the day to get the concrete foundation of one building poured before the storm hit, and later, just as the storm moved in, covered it securely with plastic. If the foul weather blew over, he would only lose one day's work while waiting for the construction site to dry out.

As he ran for his truck, the downpour stung his back through the thick black poncho and soaked the seat of the truck before he could close the door. Shivering, he fired up the truck and turned on the heat. Isn't it supposed to be warm this time of the year? He thought as he pointed the nose of the truck down one of those muddy roads toward the cabin he rented for the duration of the job. A mile further along, he reached to adjust the windshield washers, while thinking, three-year-olds wander off all the time. If Teddy fell off the bluff and into the sound during this storm, who would know it wasn't a tragic accident?

From the time he met Serena he did not want to share her company with anyone; and he never wanted children. As a twelve-year-old boy, he hated his younger brother, threw him across the hall and through a door, nearly killing him, and was disappointed his brother survived with only bruises. He decided then that he would never have children of his own. So the year after their

144

marriage, when he learned his wife was pregnant, he did not know what to do. She was Catholic and would not even consider an abortion. So in due time, the boy was born. The baby was a squirmy little brat that took up all her time, leaving little for him. Everything they did, as well as most of his wife's love, now centered on the boy.

He couldn't understand why everyone thought it so great to have a son. People said Teddy was a handsome boy, just like his father, but it only annoyed him more. Not concentrating on his driving while mulling his anger he misjudged the truck's speed, took a curve too fast, and the vehicle's back wheels slid off the muddy road slamming into a ditch. His head bounced off the side window, and he cursed a blue streak. He rubbed his head but felt no blood. That was all he needed, with the truck stuck in a ditch, his well-made plans were going awry. He opened the door, was struck by a curtain of rain, and closed it again. Revving the engine, he tried to rock the truck out of the ditch but just got in deeper.

"Dammit! Now I'll be late getting back to the cabin." The only time he had Serena to himself was when the boy was sleeping. He was thinking about packing branches beneath the wheels to give the truck traction when he remembered Logan would be coming this way soon. His coworker was maybe ten minutes behind him, and could pull him out. So he waited, and as rain beat on the roof, he refined his plan to get rid of his son.

Earlier that day, Serena, who always loved storms, watched this one through the floor-to-ceiling windows facing the sound. During the day she made up games for Teddy to play, built a fire in the big stone fireplace, and let him toast marshmallow's and cook a hotdog. Later, he snuggled up in her arms and went to sleep. She carried him to the room with two single beds, tucked him in the one away from the windows, and covered him up to his chin. She kissed his forehead, and smiled. Teddy enjoyed the storm as much as she did.

145

Her husband had rented the cabin, which was in woods a mile from the warehouse he contracted to build for a Texas company. The cabin was strongly built, and set back from the edge of a bluff overlooking Pamlico Sound with an open porch that spanned the front of the cottage.

He usually worked late and today was no exception. After putting Teddy to bed, she sat in a rocking chair, reading a book and enjoying the fire.

It was around eleven o'clock when she saw movement on the porch at the base of one of the front windows. Looking in was a little black animal she first thought was a possum or a raccoon, but then noticed it was neither. She put the book down and walked toward the windows, it was a small black dog. It surprised her as the cabin was the only one on a long stretch of lonely country road. She opened the door and spoke to the dog, coaxing it to come inside, but it shied away and ran off the porch. It was raining heavily and she could not leave Teddy alone in the cabin to hunt for it in the woods. Instead, she left the door open a few inches and went back to her book. The dog would come inside if it wanted to. A few minutes later, it returned to the porch, looked in through the open door, and crept inside. It went to the fireplace, hopped up on the stone hearth before the fire, and began to groom its fur.

Serena got up, closed and locked the door, and went back to the rocking chair and her book, occasionally looking up to check on the dog. It was very small, a lap dog, its black fur looked like it was in a high wind. She wondered how such a fine little dog came to be out in the woods alone.

She spoke to it. "Hello little fellow, did you get lost in the storm? Well, you are welcome to stay until we can find your owner."

A little later, it came over to her, sniffed her feet and looked her over, and to her surprise, jumped up in her lap. When she tried to touch it, it snarled, letting her know there were rules to his affection. She lifted the book a bit

146

higher and continued reading. The dog lifted its leg to lick its stomach and that was when she saw it was injured. Its stomach was scraped raw.

"Oh you poor thing, what happened to you?" What could she do for the pup since he would not let her touch him? She slowly stood, sliding the little fellow off her lap, and searched the kitchen cabinets for something to doctor its stomach. She put a bowl of water on the floor and a saucer with bits of hot dog left over from Teddy's dinner. In a cabinet, she found a bottle of extra-virgin olive oil. Pulling off a small section of paper towel, she saturating it with the oil and went back to the feisty little dog. When it lifted its leg to lick its raw stomach, she dropped the bit of towel on its stomach, and was amazed by what it did. With its nose, the dog pushed the towel around over its stomach until the oil completely saturated the wound.

Serena checked in on Teddy, and then returned to the rocker, sat down, and picked up the novel she was reading. She expected the dog to jump back in her lap, but instead, it started sniffing around the cabin. A little later, when she looked for the dog, she couldn't find it, and assumed it was sleeping under her bed. Tired of reading, and just tired, she showered and went to bed, and with the rain pelting a rhythm on the windows, she drifted off to sleep.

Larry used a flashlight to flag the oncoming truck slowly making its way through the mud. It was his co-worker, Logan, driving a Land Rover with a front hitch. They connected the cable and pulled Larry's truck out of the ditch. Larry took some ribbing about his driving, thanked his friend, and again headed for the cabin. He was really late, tired, wet and his tall rubber boots were muddy. Serena would understand when he told her why he was late. She knew his work was important.

He pulled off his muddy boots on the porch, held them in the rain to wash them off, shook the rain off his poncho, and quietly unlocked the door, put the boots on the hearth to dry and hung the poncho on a peg beside the door. The cabin was quiet except for the sound of the wind howling around the building and rain hitting the roof and windows. He walked into the master bedroom. Serena was sound asleep. Her beautiful blonde hair spread a fan over the pillow.

Now was the time to get rid of the kid and she would never know what happened. He would pick the boy up and throw him off the bluff into the sound. He would be a sad man for all to see, and would make sure there were no more kids. It would be easy to make Serena think she had neglected the boy, that she had failed to lock the door, and pass on the blame. He would then comfort her and pledge to always be there for her.

Slipping on his flip flops, Larry went into the dark room. The hall light gave enough illumination to see the boy was sound asleep, curled up in a blanket. Now was the time. He reached down to pick the boy up, when a ferocious ball of fury flew at this arm, growling, snapping, and tearing at the sleeve of his jacket! Stumbling backward, he yelled "What the Hell!" as he hit at the dog but missed, and the snarling dog continued after him as he backed out of the child's room just as Serena, awakened by the commotion, came running.

"Larry, what's wrong?"

"I . . . I went in to check on Teddy to . . . to cover him up, and that dog almost took my arm off! Where the devil did it come from? I'll kill the little monster!"

"Did it hurt you?" Serena asked, concerned for her husband.

"It ripped my jacket sleeve, didn't get any skin, but it sure as hell tried! It just scared me half to death! What is it doing here? Whose dog is it?

Serena laughed; relieved he had not been bitten. "He came up on the porch and I let it in from the storm. Tomorrow, I will look for his owner. I'm sorry it startled you. I never expected him to be on Teddy's bed. I thought it was sleeping under our bed."

She tiptoed to Teddy's bed, amazed the boy slept through the commotion. The little dog was now back on the bed, curled up on top of the blanket at Teddy's feet. It did not growl at her, but snarled at Larry, where he stood beside Serena staring down at the dog. Serena smiled. She would sleep soundly knowing Teddy had such a good bodyguard.

Later, Larry lay awake with Serena in his arms, thinking of the unusual circumstances that had aborted his well-made plan to get rid of his son. He was a good driver, and it was unusual for him to lose control and slide into a ditch, and then, the inexplicable arrival of the dog. The only reasoning that made any sense was divine intervention, and that thought sent cold shivers down his spine. He had never been a religious man, but his wife had a strong faith in God, always in church on Sunday. The bizarre arrival of the dog that took an immediate liking for the boy sent fear to the tips of his toes. That dog was no mongrel. If he remembered dog breeds correctly, it was an Affenpincer, a very expensive dog.

As his sleepless night moved slowly on, he remembered all he had been taught about God, a myth he had never believed. But, now, for the first time in his life, the idea that there could actually be a God, sent fear shuddering through his mind. He felt real fear, not the fear one feels from an injury, but fear from deep in his soul. He realized something unnatural had happened to protect Teddy. For only a supernatural being could have sent that kind of a dog in the middle of a forest, in the fury of a storm, to stop him. He vowed never to even think of hurting the boy again, and for the first time in his life he prayed for forgiveness.

During the rest of their stay in the cabin, Serena tried to find the dog's owner. Finally, she left a description of the dog with the local vet along with her cell phone number, but no one called to claim the dog she named Little Lion. As ferocious as the dog could be, he was a very gentle playmate for Teddy, and from that day on, the Little Lion seldom left her son's side.

A GREAT FEAR

By

Barbara Scott

The artist knows,
How precious her gift
To see and understand
And not just to drift.

The eyes grow dim,
The details, they fade
They only see
What once she made.

Her mind starts to stumble
What did you say?
I can't remember
Just yesterday.

Her hands start to tremble
They want to create!
But all that she touches
Show a terrible fate.

She hears only the mumble
Of music and song
She tries to listen
The silence, a noisy gong.

Oh! To see with her soul
And hear with her heart
To savor the moment
And create her art.

MR. OZZIE'S GREEN DOOR

By

Lorraine Sullivan

One evening, I sat by the fireplace in my cozy home, pipe in hand, with my newly acquired faithful dog by my side. I had named him "Z" after the last, but not the least, letter of the alphabet.

I reviewed my good fortune in the big city. I had established a lucrative practice, and I was particularly proud of the bright orange sign that hung outside my front green door that said: "Mr. Ozzie, Counselor Extraordinaire".

There was a knock at the door. You can imagine my amazement when I saw a young girl who looked as if she had arrived from another land. She had on a simple pinafore dress and her brown hair was braided with blue bows at the end of each pigtail...." A typical farm girl", I thought.

She asked to come in, and as she threw herself down on my couch, she explained her arrival.

She had taken a walk in the nearby park that afternoon. As she meandered along the brick path, licking her purchased ice cream cone (rocky road flavor was her favorite), she saw the green door of my house. As emerald green was her favorite color, and as she saw my spectacular sign on the outside, she decided to take me up on my offered services.

She announced that her name was Dorothea. She prevailed upon my inspector instinct and told me of her dilemma. Poor Dorothea, indeed a farm girl, had come to the city hoping to break into show business, attain fame and fortune...and, as the story usually goes, hoping to find her prince charming.

I listened in my best Sherlock Holmes and Sigmund Freud manner – investigating a comment here and insighting a comment there.

She returned again and again. Each encounter gave me fresh views into her personality and subsequent tales of her dating adventures.

First, there was Tim – but, as she described him, he was "tinny" and didn't seem to have a heart. After that fling, she bought a jar of special facial oils to enhance her beauty. She also changed her name to Dorothy.

At the next session I heard about a man named Leo. She expressed that he had a lion of a personality, but that underneath he was a coward; therefore, not her type. After Leo, she took elocution lessons to help her enhance her stage presence. She also changed her name to Dorothy.

During session number three, she told me about Mr. Straw. I didn't believe that Mr. Straw was his real name, but rather his stage name. She raved about what a wonderful dancer he was. They danced together for a while. He helped her perfect her skills for music and performing. That's when she got her first Broadway role and changed her name to Dot.

Shortly afterward, she told me that I was her true Prince Charming and she moved into my house. At first she spoke again and again about how wonderful I was with my wizardly advice and fatherly concern.

Our relationship continued as I reveled in the glory of her success. Fame came to her in front of the cameras and on the stage. Further fame came to her when an author friend of mine, Mr. Baumelaire, added her as a character in his bestselling book. By this time, she had changed her name to Do.

But all this did not seem to be enough for her. She had emerged from the cute, simple, farm girl, who first knocked on my door, to a wise, sophisticated woman. Our relationship reflected the varied skies of the city – alternately bright with yellow sunshine and then gray with depression.

One day in March there were weather warnings. That was the day that she told me that she would no longer stay with me. She had met an older chorus girl named Miss Fairee who had convinced her to leave me and told her that travel was necessary in her life.

The moving gray winds of that day seemed to call -actually insist – and, indeed, she evacuated my house. Out came her suitcase. I watched her as she packed her belongings... in went the tattered blue hair bows... in went the peasant-type clothes in which I had first seen her– in went memory pictures of Mr. Tim, Mr. Leo, Mr. Straw, and ME!

I saw her slip into her pretty red dancing shoes, one by one, onto her dainty feet, and step by step, my Do clicked toward the green door. I momentarily turned way, overcome by a sense of loss. I heard the door open and close. And I believe that I could hear clicking sounds fading towards the park. (But probably it was only the tornado force winds that made the branches click against the windowpanes.)

The next morning, I called my dog, "Z". "Oh, Z, where are you?" There was no response, so I turned to my next comfort item – the newspaper.

As I turned to page six, I saw an article. The headlines read: "Local girl, Dorothea, returns after big city visit and stardom." The article continued with details, but my eye was drawn to the accompanying color picture. There she was! Red shoes! Blue ribbons! An elderly lady, identified as an aunt, stood nearby, and sitting beside her was "Z"! Do had taken my dog when I momentarily looked away as she was leaving!

I had lost two loves – Dorothea and "Z". As I looked at the welcoming, now rusted, sign that announced my profession, on the jaded green door with the crumbling paint, I realized that I was losing a third love.

I pondered to myself, "What color should I use to repaint my door?"

My inner voice responded: "Perhaps I should paint it the color of the wheat fields of Kansas."

HOPE SOWN IN SPRING

By

Edgar Levy

There'll be other skies to gawk

Other scenic roads to walk

Other days to ponder the oddities of life

Other opportunities to whisk away and talk

There'll be other winds surging

Sending dust clouds billowing over the road

There'll be other green spaces imploding

Frisky hare, wild flowers and agile deer to behold

There'll be other romantic nights

Camping out beneath a curious moon

Other occasions to bear reverence

To the Dogwood's royal blooms

There'll be other deep gasps as the hawk sweeps past

Other lyrics, other poems, other rhymes

Just keep living in the sunshine, believing in me

There shall be other times

AND JUSTICE FOR ALL

By

Carol G. Vetula

She sat in the high-backed chair facing the door, her fingers lightly stroking the small silver weapon in her lap. The room was a cheap, run-down place behind a brightly painted exterior. There was no color around her. A small bed, a chair, and a tiny dresser made up the contents of the room. However, it didn't matter. It was a suitable place for a suitable end to his dirty existence.

Again, she ran her fingers along the smooth, shiny barrel, never once daring to move her gaze from the knob of the door only five feet away. At any moment, there would be a slight, ever so slight, movement of the knob. Janice Glenn had to see that movement immediately. Her life depended on it. Possibly even her sanity. She had to finish this once and for all. To blot out this dehumanizing source that had eliminated the past sixteen months of her life. It seemed longer. It still hurt. Friends of the past no longer called. Even Tony had turned away.

"Dear Tony," she said aloud, suddenly realizing she hadn't spoken his name for quite some time. She was not sure of how long, but too long, she worried. Immediately she remembered his clear blue eyes. His eyes were usually the first feature someone noticed about him. A tiny bit of sadness stuck in her throat. She loved him so much. It would have been a good marriage. They belonged together.

She shifted slightly, continuing to bolt her eyes on the doorknob. Several times in the last few minutes, her eyes had played tricks on her. Thinking she had seen a turning of the knob, she tightened her grip on the weapon and pointed to toward the door, only to realize it was a mistake. It then took several moments to relax the tension her body had built up.

At first, she wasn't sure she'd be capable of carrying this off. She had never done anything so difficult before. However, it had to be done and apparently, no one else going to do it. In the beginning, her parents were on her side. They would have helped her then. Her parents had been so comforting.

Richard Glenn said that a rapist had no right to a trial. "Let me get my hands on him for just two minutes," he said to anyone within listening distance. "He'll never touch another woman."

Janice had seen him cry, sitting there in front of the big picture window. Her mother had held her and cried too. "It'll be all right," she promised, "Daddy will take care of it. He and Tony will see that Henry Carter pays for what he did to you." Sara Glenn was sure of their men and the law.

Tony Winters, unlike her parents, had trouble holding her. He tried. Janice knew he tried, but something had happened to him too. Tony was from a prominent Springfield family. He and Janice had known each other all of their lives. Their social circles, however, had been on different levels. It wasn't until college that they had dated each other. The chemistry between them worked perfectly. Their wedding had been announced in September. It was officially cancelled in April.

Wedding plans and Christmas plans had kept Janice busy. During December, Janice decided to spend some vacation time in California visiting her maid-of-honor. They expected to shop for wedding things. "It'll be fun," Elaine had told her over the phone.

"Please come."

California had not been fun at all. Janice returned home far from the happy, lovely woman who left a few days earlier. Being a victim of a brutal rape leaves a woman feeling alone and helpless.

158

Everyone was caring at first. Later everyone whc encountered Janice, formed their own opinion about why this woman was attacked . . . how she had been chosen. Close friends and relatives, including Janice's parents, and even her Tony, felt she had done something, no matter how innocent, to attract this evil man.

Most people didn't actually say it aloud, but Janice was able to read their eyes and thoughts. The feelings by those she loved the most, were probably the hardest part for her. Her parents said it was "such a shame this terrible thing happened to her." After a while, they didn't speak of it again, but Janice was able to feel their coolness whenever they were around. Before Janice was ready, again, to join her world, that world excluded her. Even Tony, dear Tony, had to conform to standards as he interpreted them.

Prior to their final break-up, Janice had noticed a lack of interest in Tony's attitude. He had excuses for not attending functions with her. Afterward he called it a misunderstanding on her part. Finally, he used the excuse that she needed more time to work things before they were married. She knew it was all over. Henry Carter had ruined her marriage, too.

Henry Carter had been in jail from the beginning. And, he was supposed to stay there, she hoped, for the rest of his life. He deserved worse. Henry Carter put an end to her life, as she had known it before, and he was going to pay for it. The law was good. She believed in the law and justice.

Again, she shifted her position slightly. She was beginning to ache across the shoulders, and was not sure how long she had been in that chair. Soon. It was going to be over soon.

The weapon seemed heavier than before. Continuing to stare at the door, her eyes became tired. She had to stay awake, so she forced her body to obey.

"Janice," her mother once said, "you can't stop living because of this thing. You have many good features in your life. Don't ruin the rest of it because one terrible thing happened to you."

Even her mother used the word "thing". No one said rape. Rape was such an offensive word that people had trouble saying it. They preferred saying nothing, but when necessary, they used another word. Usually they said, 'that thing that happened', or simply, 'it'. Only Doctor Kelly used the correct word. He had been the one to encourage Janice to say it. Even she had trouble with saying that word at first.

Why was rape such a hard word to say? There was no other word to use. Rape was rape. It was a fact. Janice Glenn had been raped. She wanted to forget, but could not. No one used the word, but everyone thought about it.

Janice had been used, attacked, beaten, dehumanized, dirtied, and had satisfied a sick desire of a very sick person. Then she had been outcast by her world. She had been raped, and was not able to alleviate the pain. Rape wasn't like the measles. One recovers from measles. Not so with rape.

Tony had wanted to know why she stayed in that hotel bar after Elaine had gone to bed. "What were you trying to prove?" he shouted at her. "A woman does not sit alone in bars unless she is looking for trouble." He pushed his hate and hurt out into the open and it went away for him. He got up and fixed a drink.

"Why did this happen? I loved you so much. We had everything." He shook his head in a slow motion as if trying to wish it all away.

She had said nothing. There was nothing to say. It had all been said over and over again. Janice was tired of repeating all of it. She said nothing. Several times, she heard him repeat, "I loved you so much." Just like everyone else, he was turning against her. He didn't love her now. Henry Carter had used her. Tony Winters did not want a used woman. She remembered hearing him suggest they both needed time.

They had postponed the wedding until later. He took her home. In the car, he mentioned his family. "God, Janice. Mom has been so upset with all this. Yesterday she had to see her doctor and he gave her a sedative to help her sleep. This has hit her so hard."

He paused, directed the car in a left hand turn and continued. "You know, Janice," he said looking straight ahead pretending to concentrate on the light traffic. "Dad was the first one to suggest postponing the wedding. He wants you and Mom to both be ready for the big event."

Janice heard only the part that was important to her. Suddenly, she realized it was not only Tony who was concerned about the wedding, but it was his father. The Winters' family had accepted her as their future daughter-in-law with some reservations, Janice believed, but this was changing everything. Now they were going to use this to stop the marriage. Their position in society would not permit such a stain on a family branch. Society had to be very careful. She had listened without comment. What good did it do, she decided, to argue? Tony did not understand that she was innocent. His parents did not understand. Henry Carter had ruined her marriage. He was going to pay. Janice believed in the law and justice.

The nightmare of the rape had been intensified by the trial of Henry Carter. All the questions, the lies, the crying, the repeated questions. People testifying, who did not even know Janice. Specialists, they were called. Called upon to explain details so the jury could understand. The judge had to understand. Everyone wanted to understand everything, but no one tried to understand Janice. The jury listened quietly to all of it. Janice had to describe,

161

repeatedly, the events of that hour in a hotel room in California. After telling the story for the fourth time in one day, she rushed to the restroom and vomited. Remembering it all in detail made her sick, often.

Well, the District Attorney had warned her that a rape trial was going to be difficult, but with her testimony, they were going to put Henry Carter away for a long time. At least he was not going to do the same thing to someone else.

So, she had been warned. Just the same, it had been painful to recount it all. When Henry Carter came to testify, he told a completely different story. He said he bought her a drink and invited her to come to his room for a nightcap. Also, he claimed he only did what she wanted him to do, and insisted she remover her own clothes as soon as they were together in the room. Henry Carter described the things she did to him, and said she became a tease, and continued to repeat it was all her doing . . . them being together, and all. He admitted he did get a little angry with her, and maybe he did hurt her arms, but she led him on and he did not like it one bit.

Henry Carter lied. But, he lied so well. Tony must have believed him Janice's parents must have believed him. The whole world must have believed him. Most of all . . . the jury believed him.

"Not guilty," the foreman of the jury had said. The District Attorney agreed there was not enough evidence against Henry Carter. It was only her word against his. By the end of the trial, Janice was not the innocent victim any longer. Henry Carter's lawyer had taken facts and events and turned them around to suit his client's purpose. That lawyer did not prove that Janice was as bad as he wanted the jury to believe she might be. He only had to plant seeds of doubt. That was his job. So much for law and justice.

Therefore, Henry Carter had gone free. Free, perhaps to do the same thing over again to another unsuspecting woman. Again, to ruin a life. Something had to be done about it. Someone had to stop him.

The feel of the cold, hard steel in her hands brought Janice back to the present. Her shoulders and back ached, but it did not matter. The important affair had to be dealt with. No amount of discomfort was going to stop her. Soon it was going to be finished. "Hurry," she said softly.

"Hurry," Tony had said to her on that beautiful day. "We can't be late to our own party." They both laughed as they rushed through the shopping mall. "It is only a little back yard party. You look fine. It is not necessary to change your clothes." He steered her outside and toward the car. His eyes were so beautiful.

"It will only take a minute to slip into this blouse. I want to be comfortable. Meeting all your family this afternoon isn't going to be easy for me."

"They will all love you," he breathed into her hair. She knew Tony loved her. She was so sure of his love. Nothing was ever going to change that.

That afternoon had been a success. Janice Glenn had been accepted into the family. Soon she would have it all. It was all at her fingertips. At her finger tips.

Her fingers were becoming numb, but she dared not loosen the grip on the weapon. Soon, it was all going to be over soon. If she had to wait for hours, she would wait. It was going to be worth the wait. Janice Glenn believed in justice. Others did not.

She'd take care of everything, and then she and Tony could be together again. She'd have it all again. It was worth the wait. She knew he was coming.

Henry Carter knew where she was. She had seen him watching her for some time. He had somehow found where she lived. After the trial, he had shown up several times. She had seen him watching her room from the street. Even though she had changed residences several times, he always found her. Why did no one believe her? Even though she had seen him, he was always gone by the time she got anyone's attention. She had seen him every night since moving to this new place. Once he had been outside her door trying to get in. However, Janice was smart. Since no one was going to help her, she had found it quite easy to plan and carry out this justice alone.

He was going to be at her door again tonight. She knew it. This time she was ready. Tonight Henry Carter was going to pay for what he did to her. There was no escape for him this time. Janice Glenn was going to have her justice.

The movement was ever so slight, but she saw it immediately. Her body stiffened. Both hands gripped the silver piece, holding it steady. Her right index finger came to rest in the correct place. Janice took great care so as not to do it too soon. No mistakes this time. She was surprised her palms were dry. She was not afraid or nervous. It was all as if rehearsed many, many times.

But this was not a rehearsal. Tonight was the real thing. It was time for him to pay for his crime against society. Against Janice. Especially against Janice. After tonight, Janice and Tony would return to planning for their future together. After tonight, she was going to be able to hold her head up again. Justice was about to be gained.

A light knock came from outside the door.

"Come in," she whispered, trying hard to keep her voice even and calm. "Come on in," she repeated even more softly.

The door flew all the way open. A large form was framed in the doorway. Her finger yanked at the trigger. Once, twice, three times. She screamed obscenities as the figure fell to the floor in front of her chair amid the sounds of breaking glass and falling metal. She fired again, and again, and again.

Still she fired at the downed figure, with tears streaming down her face. Her voice was hoarse and her words full of hate. All the pent-up hate finally loosing itself from the mental prison that had held her for so long. This hate spewed all over the room. It bounced off the walls and danced across the empty room. The bars on the windows could not contain all the hate. It crept out the windows and flew off on the air.

She fired repeatedly. As she lifted the silver piece to use as a bludgeon, a hand reached out and gently removed the silver hairbrush form her hands.

Janice heard sweeping near her chair, but it did not hold her attention. Something pinched her arm, and at once, she became warm and sleepy.

"I'm so sorry, doctor. She really surprised me this time. All day she was quiet, just sitting in that chair." Nurse Walsh placed the silver brush on the bent tray next to the broken glass pieces and left the room.

"Sleep for a while, Janice," the doctor said to her as he and an aid laid her on the small cot. "It has been another bad day for you, hasn't it? However, it is going to be all right now. Just rest." He patted her shoulder and both men left the room.

Janice knew it was going to be all right now. She had taken care of everything. As she closed her heavy eyes, a smile formed on her lips as she sighed, "and justice for all."

THE END

A LIFE LIVED

By

PJ Renfroe

Truth's keen blade of finest steel
Grows strong within the age of reason
Righting a multitude of wrongs.
Sincerity and Integrity, although forged
Of purest gold if ill sheathed in
Greed or Lust will rust then break
Before Vindictives cryptic thrust.
Sorely wounded, vast Kindness falls
Momentarily to press Compassion's
Healing hand to troubled breast.
Time heals, and strength renewed
Calm Courage turns her wary head
To face Sadistic Subterfuges'
Revolving stage set by
Lethiferous' evil deed to feed
Unctuosity's greedy breed.
Erudite mind now expands to battle as
Great Wisdom begins to grow
Calling on Mighty Strategy
To bend a cunning bow.

A GHOST STORY?

By

Michael McLarnon

No doubt you've heard the phrase: If I didn't have bad luck, I wouldn't have any luck at all. That phrase could be my moniker, because in the course of one day—two hours, five minutes, eighteen seconds to be exact—I lost my mother, my granddad *and* my grandmother. Unfortunately, that wasn't the end of my woes. While still adrift in the fogs of the Sea of Mourning, without truly realizing it at the time, I also lost the house I had grown up in, all my childhood friends, and Boston, the city of my birth. I even lost my favorite bed, for goodness sake.

Excuse me, but I have to stop this sad story for a minute because there goes my brother, for the godzillionth time, asking how much longer, how much longer, HOWMUCHLONGER. That question means a whole different thing to him than for me. For my not-so-precious kid brother, it means how much longer until we arrive at our new home. For me, it means how much longer until the life I once knew comes to a complete and utter end.

Why he needs to ask that silly question boggles my teenage mind, because we just passed a highway sign that said End Of Life As You Know It Ville is seven miles up the road. Truth be told, the town we're moving to isn't really called that, it actually has a much more prosaic name, but that's what I call it, when I'm not calling it Sucksyvania, Valley of Tearsburg, or other names that would cause me to blush like a Southern maiden if I actually wrote them down.

Actually, I do know why my darling brother keeps asking that question over and over and over. He *supposedly* has Asperger Syndrome. At first, the string of psychiatrists who evaluated him kicked diagnoses around like a soccer ball, until they settled on that obscure title. If you ask me, I would say he is just plain annoying. A typical little brother. But of course nobody asks the opinion of a fifteen-year-old girl.

In spite of this so-called Asperger syndrome that causes my brother to be ultra-aloof around strangers and have repetitive behaviors that, frankly, are über annoying, he is super, and I mean super, gifted, with the ability to remember numbers, whether they be addresses and phone numbers, or birthdays. Remember them perfectly. Because of that talent, he really rocks at history; it's his best subject. Remembering the date the Moors conquered Spain, or when Alexander the Great died, are a piece of cake for him. Just don't ask him when my birthday is. That's seemingly too mundane for him.

Well, back to my lugubrious story.

I laughed—something I haven't done much of lately—when I wrote that last sentence. While dad was driving us through endless corn fields in Iowa and Nebraska, I hopped on the internet and researched synonyms for "sad." I filled page after page of my notebook with them, losing count when I passed two hundred. So there you are, dear diary. I am now an expert in sadness.

How, you might ask, did I lose my mother and both her parents in such a short period of time?

To paraphrase one of my dad's favorite philosophers, Lao Tzu: The journey of a thousand miles begins with a single step. In my mother's case, it was that single step that ended her journey. Her life journey that is. Talking on the telephone with a patient—she is, or rather was, it's hard to believe she's dead,

168

a pediatric neurosurgeon—she stepped right in front of a bus. Not surprisingly, she came out on the losing end of that encounter.

I was in school at the time. My dad was at home and rushed to the Emergency Room. When the ER doc told him they couldn't save my mother's life, he called my grandparents to break the tenebrous news—tenebrous being another way of saying sad, dear diary.

My great-uncle who was there at the time said that within seconds of my granddad answering the phone, his face turned redder than a beet, the veins in his head swelled like an engorged river, and his eyes bulged like balloons about to pop. The phone slipped from his fingers and he clutched his chest, ripping at it as if to pry open his ribs to set his heart free. Then the world seemed to stop for a beat. A questioning expression creased grandpa's face. In slow motion, like a gnarled oak toppling to the ground, he began to tilt. Before his body slumped to the floor, like flipping the switch to turn the lights off in the room before going to sleep, his eyes dimmed, then became flat and glassy. My great-uncle was riveted in his seat, stunned, unaware of the news his brother just received.

When my grandma returned home from her doctor's visit, upon hearing the news of the death of her husband and her only child, she died as well. How that happened is shrouded in mystery. Grandpa died of a broken heart, the local newspapers called it the Takotsubo Syndrome. The newspapers didn't give a cause of death for my grandmother, saying the medical examiner hadn't released it at the time of publication. Dad, mincing his words as if stepping through a minefield, mumbled something about grandma also dying of a broken heart. If that's the case, I can only hope weak hearts don't run in the family.

We weren't able to attend my grandparent's funerals as we had one more pressing of our own with which to deal. In addition, we were living in Boston; my grandparent's lived, and died, clear across the country, in a beach town in Oregon—our current destination. After my mother's funeral, dad said we were moving. Both he and my mother came from the same small town where my grandparent's lived. When my mother finished her training in pediatric neurosurgery, those types of specialized positions only exist in metropolitan areas attached to one of the larger medical schools. My dad never adjusted to the big city, and now that he no longer had to live there, like a salmon returning to the river of its birth, back he came—with us in tow.

My dad is an artist: painter, sculptor, writer, actor, artistic director, and any other thing related to the arts. Nice for him, but it hardly pays the bills. It was my mother who was the breadwinner. Without her income, my dad's income, such as it is, wouldn't support us in an expensive city like Boston. With my mother being an only child, my dad and us inherited the homestead. So off we went on this cross-country trip, moving to a new city, a new house, a new life. I had been to our future abode once before, when I was lost in the mists of early childhood. I remember very little, and what I do is jaundiced by the prism of childhood. I recalled it rained. The entire time. Also, the house seemed really scary.

That's all I remember. A scary house. A cold rain. Something that perfectly matches my present mood.

So here I am, tossed about by the seas of misfortune. Don't get me wrong, I'm not religious, but one summer my parents sent me to bible camp, wanting me to be able to make up my own mind on the subject. I remember listening to the story of this unfortunate man named Job. Or perhaps it was Lot. I'll look it up later, but I think it was Job and that's what I'll call him for now. Job had everything going for him, until one day, for no apparent reason, God, they

170

say, rained horrible disasters down on his wretched soul. He lost his family. His home. Even his health. But they say he never despaired. Never gave up his love for God. One thing Job didn't have to deal with was losing his cell phone number. With our move, the carrier we had in Boston doesn't get service in The Sea of Tears Town. I would like to see how Job would have handled that.

Well, the miles have flown by, dear diary, and here we finally are, turning onto our street. In a few minutes I'm going to have to stop writing to help unpack. As my new home, three stories of gables, dormers and turrets, comes into sight, it looks just as scary as I remember. Even scarier, as two people recently died there. I'm not a superstitious person, but what if ghosts really do exist? Would they haunt their old residence? Would they be evil?

While dad pulls the car into the driveway, my eyes fly upward to a third story dormer window, drawn by what sounds like a woman's voice, pleading, wafting in the wind. Through the drizzle, I catch a glint of light off the window. From behind the pane, the drapes stir, as if caught in a gentle breeze. Then my heart drops to my knees, my face blanches, my skin prickles with clammy sweat. Partly shrouded by the gossamer drapes, for a nanosecond, I spot an elderly woman's ghostlike face peering back at me.

The face of my dead grandmother.

THE BYE-BYE KITTY

By

Lorraine Sullivan

The Hello Kitty raises s paw to say both hello and goodbye.

I have a bye-bye kitty.

I always greet him with my human hello

For my handsome cat fellow

He never follows with a meow

All I get is eyes of mellow yellow

Those honey syrup pancake eyes

Almost look like wise sighs

But instead of hellos and his

They are full of bye-byes

I try to entice his favors

with treats of special flavors

All is naught for my labor

From my unrequited love he does waver

And goes to visit an unknown neighbor

Sometimes his volcano eyes

Almost erupt with love sighs

It's only a guise

For more of his lies

I am sometimes allowed to pat

Over his imaginary hat

He poses as if on a yoga mat

My impertinent cat!

I am the Keeper of the Door for him

Whenever he has that go out whim

He walks in and out so prissy and prim

The exercise keeps us both very trim

A hello kitty his is not

No matter how much he is taught

He cannot be snack-bought

He doesn't want to be love-caught

It's such a pity

That I have a bye-bye kitty.

THE SEARCH

By

Sharon Davidson

Sarah hesitated. She looked up the old wooden attic steps with trepidation. She had climbed those stairs hundreds of times before. Why then, did she dread it this time? Was it because each step toward the attic brought her closer to her emotional anguish?

She had no idea what possessed her to try and locate what Becky wanted. Was it the sight of her daughter's pleading blue eyes, a constant reminder of Becky's father? How they cut her to her very core. Her sweet daughter didn't understand her grief? To her it was just a school project.

Sarah fished for the old rusty key from the pocket of her jeans. It fit loosely into the brass lock. She fumbled with it until she heard the snap of the bolt echo in the silence of the hallway. As the door creaked open, she stood staring into the darkness.

Gathering courage, she stepped into the attic; the smell of forgotten memories assaulted her mind. Her hand went instinctively to her nose. After a moment, her eyes adjusted to the faint light filtering through the ventilation grill at the end of the house. Dust particles floated down the light beam.

Sarah's past came into focus as she glanced around the attic. Someday she would have to muster up the gumption to clean out this mess, but now, she just wanted to find the photograph for Becky.

The box she needed was stowed away in the attic when they first moved into the house, about fourteen years ago. Yes, that was right, fourteen years. Becky had just turned two. It was her first year without her father. Those first few months were Hell for the both of them! The empty, nagging feeling never subsided. She felt alone. If she hadn't had Becky, life wouldn't have been worth living.

But she wasn't going to dwell on that, not now. She was over that pain, or so she thought; she had to find the photograph for Becky and get back downstairs to start dinner before sitting down to review her daughter's homework.

She dragged the first box to the center of the room. The silver duct tape securing it had turned sticky after all the years in the heat of the attic. In strong bold print the top and sides were labeled '1968.' Sarah hesitated before peeling back the tape.

Inside, wrapped in newspaper, were odds and ends that her mother said she would someday need to start her own home. She laughed recalling the day her mother insisted she take the silver crumb catcher with its matching miniature broom. Sarah had argued with her mother that it was old–fashioned and they didn't have the room for it in their one-bedroom apartment. Her mother's argument was that no self-respecting young lady would be caught dead without one. "What if the Pope comes to dinner?" her mother would tease. Sarah just smiled and gently wrapped the silver aardvark in newspaper and put it in the box and here it remained for all those years.

Continuing to delve deeper into the container of memories, Sarah came across a badge adorned sash from her Girl Scout years, the blue ribbon she won at her first swim meet, and the dance card from her senior prom.

She lifted the aged card from the box, carefully turning the yellowed pages. She ran her fingers down the faded names. Smiling, she formed a picture of each classmate in her mind, and wondered what had become of them. Then she saw his name: Eddie Duncan. Oh, how this brought back memories; they flooded her mind even as she tried to build a dam to hold them back.

But the dam burst and her mind catapulted back to her senior year. Clad in the typical tie-dyed shirt, bell bottoms and brown suede vest, he strutted down the hall toward her as she stood by her locker. What really caught her eye was his shoulder length brown hair and his ever present blue-tinted wire rimmed glasses.

"Hey babe, how ya doin?" He winked at her in a way only Eddie could.

So shy all she could manage to say was "Fine."

"You save me a dance tonight won't ya?" He slid his glasses down his nose to look across them, his steel blue eyes studying her hard.

"Sure Eddie," she beamed. Fumbling though her purse. "Here, sign my dance card." She thrust it toward him.

Eddie smiled taking the paper. "Sure thing." He took the pen she offered and wrote his name on the last line. "I want the last dance so I can take you home." He handed the card and pen back. With a smile and a nod, he set off down the hall again. Sarah watched him walk away. Little did she know this would be one of many times she would watch him do that.

She shook her head to refocus and closed the dance card, resumed her search and pulled more memories from the box. Next were their high school diplomas, Eddie's college diploma and his selective service draft card - "A1."

Then she spotted the object of her search: her wedding photo. She lifted the frame from the box, her fingers trembled as she ran her shirt sleeve across the glass to remove the dust.

She stared at the photograph and sighed, they made a handsome couple. After listening to her mother moan and groan about wearing traditional white, she finally gave in and agreed. They compromised with a sprig of wild flowers for her long straight blonde hair. Eddie, one of the original flower children, was persuaded to wear a tux. That day, and much later, the birth of their daughter had to be the happiest days of her life.

Sarah turned the frame over to remove the photograph. A small yellow envelope slipped out. Sarah's hand shook as she picked it up, her mind propelled into the past.

******

She had rushed home from work that day, wanting to get everything ready for Eddie's return. He had been away for almost a year this time. She was excited and wanted everything to be perfect.

The front door bell rang. She glanced at her watch -- 5:30, it must be her mother bringing Becky home. Sarah called to the door. "Come in mom, it's open."

The buzzer sounded again. Sarah ran to the door, pulling it open. Standing in front of her wearing full dress blues was Eddie's commanding officer.

"Mrs. Duncan?"

"Yes." Her voice cracked with emotion. Her heart pounded as if it would burst through her chest. The tears welled up in her eyes. She knew before he even spoke what he would say. Uncle Sam always said the same thing.

"Mrs. Edward Duncan: We regret to inform you that your husband Captain Edward…"

THE LAST TIME WE MET

By

Delores L Staton

The last time we met,
Our feelings were unknown.
The raw stirrings of unbridled passion,
muffled, unrevealed as yet.

In the absence of warm contact
We have time to reflect
We have time to envision
The road we take next.

Where are we off to?
Will the road taken be familiar, routine?
Will the road taken be uncharted, novel, new?

Will the strangeness of the journey
Unleash the rawness of unexplored feelings?
Will the purity of the journey be sullied by taint
Will we have the courage to ride the swell?
Will we have the courage to break all restraint?

For it is ultimate, however fleeting, pure freedom is chaos.
The innate need for order, the rule of the day,
The need to put "everything back"
Rears up, erupts through, forces us
Our passion to retract.

For shame, no taste of the pure unknown
As fear paralyzes us, drags us back
Binds us, crams us into the cage of freedom blown.

UNCLE FLUBBS

By

R.S. Raniere

Welcome to Brooklyn, the sign says, dredging up memories of the 18th Avenue El clacking overhead, the corner pastry shop that made the best cannoli in all of New York, and, of course, street stickball. It was a "boys only club." But I had a singular talent: a wicked curveball that would invariably strike out Billy (The Bull) Murphy. And so I became the only girl on the 83rd Street Bobcats stickball team. These are the images strolling nostalgically through my mind as I exit the Belt Parkway.

I was born here, in my grandmother's two-family row house on Bay 11th Street. My mother was traumatized by the merest thought of a hospital. It was futile trying to get her to leave the house. She had locked herself in the bathroom, and were it not for Doctor Petrulli, who made house calls at that time, I might not have made it into this world ... an event that, at times, I had regretted. And now I've come home. Although the reason has not quite crystalized, I suspect it has something to do with "closure," the intractable process of resolving, forgiving, and moving on. This seems a reasonable explanation as to why I'm standing over his grave on a cold, dank morning in late March, inhaling the effluvium of wet leaves and musty earth while holding a dozen Easter lilies. Decades have passed. I feel like an alien who has just landed on planet earth, yet is oddly at home. He once told me, "you can take the girl out of Brooklyn, but you can't take Brooklyn out of the girl." Not at all an original adage, but he was so right. The smell of it, the feel of it, the street corner patois. And, of course, the memories, once manifested in bad dreams, cold sweats, and nervous tics. Now all that remains of the story is the last paragraph of the final chapter in a book that will be closed and put on an unreachable shelf to gather dust. I've come home to do this. Apparently driven by some existential need to formalize, I've forgiven you, moved on, and goodbye with a grave-site visit and a bouquet of his favorite flowers.

It was my tenth birthday, and I was in the midst of sucking in my breath for the big candle blowout when THWACK! He slapped her. Hard. I could see the blood rising red to the surface of her skin, gradually filling in the whiteness of his hand print. I felt her stinging embarrassment as if it were my cheek. My eyelids slammed shut against the scene, like the spring action of a screen door. But the image continued—frame by frame—behind my eyes. I scrunched down in my seat, silently repeating some inane incantation that might make me invisible. Only moments earlier, the room swelled with shouts of "Happy Birthday" and the requisite Birthday Song as I prepared to empty my lungs over ten candles on a strawberry ice cream cake topped with pink and blue Smurfs. The whirring crackle left a deafening hush in the room that no one dared penetrate. The air filled with soundless gasps and unspoken sympathy for Aunt Kate. This was the first of many times I would witness his temper. It was this … initiation … that struck my child's sense of invincibility, like a stone pinging off a windshield, leaving that tiny star-like crack that would eventually grow wider and deeper.

Aunt Kate was a pretty woman with a slim figure accented by a generous bosom. She had many *corteggiatori*, as my beloved Nana, would say. Her final choice of a husband, however, was not well received by the family. In fact, there had been a thumbs-down consensus. Sadly, no one could prevent Aunt Kate from screwing up her life. And mine.

They had just been married. I was not invited. Aunt Kate thought it inappropriate for children to attend certain functions, particularly her wedding. My mother, as was her custom, disagreed with her sister.

Vehemently. Nonetheless, the "no children" ruling stood. As for me, I could not have been more delighted. It meant a babysitter, all the chocolate chip cookies I could eat, and staying up as late as I wanted.

He was a large man—Aunt Kate's new husband—with a round, plump face and deep, pleasing dimples that belied his volatile nature. He was not what you'd call handsome, but neither was he hard to look at. As far as I was concerned, though, an ever-expanding beer belly that flopped contentedly over his belt canceled out any appeal he might have otherwise had. Apparently not for Kate. She seemed to have missed a plethora of character flaws. But children, in their inherent guilelessness, have a way of seeing through the brume; a gift dulled by time and various self-deceptions. I did not like him—this boisterous, oversize adult. He frightened me. It was his hands, though, that chilled me to the bone. They were large, and thick, and stubby. My throat went dry whenever I looked at them. And he was loud. Thunderously loud, billowing and bellowing like the mile-long freight train that rumbled the length of Emmons Street. I dubbed him, Flubbs—as in flabby and loud. It gave me a measure of satisfaction to think of him as Flubbs. I could say it over again in my head whenever his threatening demeanor loomed. Flubbs, Flubbs, Flubbs. Somehow it diminished him; made him seem less of an ogre. Of course, I could never call him "Flubbs" to his face. That would have made him very angry. And when he got angry his entire head expanded, his eyes bulged, and his face became a cartoon shade of scarlet. So I simply called him, Uncle. He seemed to like that.

We lived in Nana's house—all of us. She and her two unmarried daughters (referred to as the twins, as though they were not given names) occupied the main level. Aunt Kate and Uncle Flubbs were on the "lower level" (his euphemism for basement), and Mama, dad, and I were "upstairs." Three families in a two-family house. We gave new meaning to the term "closely knit." The house was an impressive brick and stucco structure. The only one on the block with two stone lions sitting innocuously on either side of cobbled steps that led up to a double-hung, solid oak entrance door with the Italian flag chiseled into it. An indelible image.

Nana was a snip of a woman with salt-and-pepper hair and perfect skin. She said it was a gift from God, but I knew all that garlic and olive oil had something to do with it. Her searing dark eyes flashed a captivating mix of mischief and wisdom. Nana's world was bound up in home and family, a ligature unavoidably loosened by the vagaries of life. While she was alive, Nana made Sundays special. A sort of celebratory cap on the week: pancakes the size of Frisbees for breakfast, twelve o'clock Mass at St. Bartholomew's, then back home for dinner where Nana prepared a five-course feast with faerie dust and a wave of her magic spoon. One could almost levitate on the aromas of Italian cooking that floated on the air like herbal cumulus clouds. The entire house overflowed with a cacophony of voices. Aunts, uncles, cousins, and lots of friends from the "old country." Nana wallowed happily in the joyful noise that filled the rooms on Sundays—a cheery resonance regularly disrupted by Flubbs' raucous behavior between the antipasto and dessert, his minacious tone increasing with each swig of Chianti. And they were countless.

I did not like living on the top floor. Getting up there was spooky. The hallway was a long, dim stretch from the entrance door to Nana's apartment, with the stairway to the second floor smack in the middle. Each time I entered the house, I'd make a mad dash for the stairs envisioning the bogey man crouching in the darkened stairwell, waiting to pounce—a childish chimera that materialized in the person of Uncle Flubbs soon after my eleventh birthday.

182

"Stop it!" I squealed when he pulled me under the stairs as I came out of Nana's apartment, spilling her garden-grown tomatoes down the hall. He put his hand over my mouth and pushed me against the wall, pressing his flabby body into mine.

"If you're quiet, I'll take my hand away, and we'll play a game," he whispered. "Ok?"

I shook my head with such force I thought it would break off. I knew I wouldn't like this game.

"Leave me alone," I begged as quietly as I could. "I'll tell. I'll run away," I said, groping for words I thought might persuade him to release me.

"Which will it be my little angel?"

I hated it when he called me that.

"B … both." I managed to squeak.

"Even if you run away, you'll be back," he said. "You can take the girl out of Brooklyn, but you can't take Brooklyn out of the girl." Immortal words.

I tried desperately to wiggle out of his grip, but he was not yet done with me.

"You know, Mandy, you are my sweetie."

"Amanda," I corrected. For some quirky reason it seemed important he use my given name.

"Shhhh. This is how you greet your uncle." He towed me deeper into the stairwell and kissed me on my mouth. I'd never been kissed on my mouth. I swiped my lips with my sleeve.

"Pucker," he instructed, "like this." He kissed me again. "You're not puckering. You have to pucker, like you're whistling."

I slid down and out of his grip and ran straight for Nana's door, not at all concerned about the stream of urine running down my leg. In my mad dash, I tripped over the threshold, willing myself not to fall. I sped through the rooms—hitched together like railroad cars—living room, dining room, and finally the kitchen. I pushed through the back door where Nana was planting basil in her garden.

"*Cara cuore*." She put her arm around me and received my bear hug. "Looka you faccia. *E cosi rosso*."

"I know, Nana," I said, breathlessly. "I was running."

"*Andare*," she said, shooing me toward the house. "Go. *Bere un po d'acqua*."

"No, Nana. I don't want any water." I felt myself starting to cry, but raging fear plugged my tear ducts before I had time to think about it. "I want to stay here with you. Help you plant the basil." I did not leave Nana's side until my mother returned from her part time job at Rainbow's.

I neither ate nor slept that night. Mama and dad took turns keeping vigil; looking in on me every few hours, wondering what had caused my sudden vomiting.

"Amanda." Mama's tone was as furrowed as her brow. "You didn't eat the berries without washing them, did you?"

"No, Mama." I closed my eyes and feigned sleep. Please don't ask me any more questions. I had no further contact with Uncle Flubbs until the following Sunday. Sundays became our "date night." I avoided Flubbs like a field mouse avoids a snake, but he'd somehow find ways to slither in my direction.

He'd grab me and hold me so close I could not breathe, rub his chest against mine, and try to find my lips as I kept turning my head to avoid being kissed. This depravity continued through my fourteenth year, when at last we left my grandmother's house.

II

On a blistering summer night, Millie Caruso, Nana's next door neighbor—a woman never seen without a cigarette dangling from her lips—fell asleep while smoking in bed. It was Friday; the night Loews gave away free dinnerware. It didn't much matter what the film was, Mama, Nana, and Aunt Kate were completing a thirty-six-piece set, so Friday was movie night. This was not my favorite activity. No one was home on Fridays. I'd have the entire house to myself. But, as usual, my preferences and protestations were completely ignored.

"I can't. Homework." I'd tried that excuse before to no avail, but that did not stop me.

"What homework?"

"Math."

"Who you kiddin'? You nevva have homework on a Friday."

"I do, Auntie—fractions, and I'm behind."

"You're lying," Mama chimed in. "Go put your shoes on before you get smacked." And so I was dragged along. As it happened, being "dragged along" was an unexpected blessing.

We spotted the fire trucks two blocks away as we walked back from the theater. The fire marshal stopped us just short of the street corner where we lived. Except for smoldering stacks of bricks and cinder block, there was little left of Millie's house and most of the houses on either side. Nana had to be sedated. There were several casualties. One fatality: Millie. The entire neighborhood mourned for months, and my life on Bay 11th Street became a surreal memory. The Sunday feasts, the lush, scented garden, that familiar and special atmosphere of family holidays; these were completely restructured. The spirited, passionate grandmother I knew and loved folded into herself as everyone branched out and settled in their respective nests. Dad bought a lovely house for us several miles away, even while bemoaning the fact that it was "mortgaged to the hilt." Aunt Kate and Uncle Flubbs moved to an apartment in Bay Ridge, and Nana and "the twins" rental a small house near the by, where she would take long, quiet walks along the always breezy, fish-scented boardwalk. Although an excruciating transition, there were two prayed-for benefits for me: One, I would have my own room—at long last! Two, I would no longer be living under the same roof as Uncle Flubbs.

It made little difference that our family had been dismantled. Flubbs maintained his self-appointed patriarchal role. And no one questioned him. I'd always attributed this family-wide acquiescence to the .38 side arm he carried. When he decided to play matchmaker, I'd assumed he was ready to "turn me over" to someone else since I had left the building, as it were, and was beyond his grasping hands. Or perhaps I had simply become too old for him.

It was Wednesday night. He and Aunt Kate were getting ready to leave our house after their weekly poker game. "Mandy," he grabbed my arm on his way to the front door. "I have the perfect guy for you." Flubbs was not one to belabor a point. I told him no thanks, I had a boyfriend. I lied. He said, "Fuhggedaboud it!" He knew a real nice guy—a Rookie at the precinct where he was currently working the seven-to-three shift.

186

"But I have a boyfriend." Somehow I knew he wasn't buying it. My stomach began churning hot coals. "Fuhggedaboud it!" he repeated, his voice rising a full octave. "This guy's perfect for you. End of story."

I could always tell when Flubbs was getting dangerously close to his scarlet hydrocephalic look. So I forgot about it. But I marveled at the irony. He did not like cops, and he absolutely hated being one. He defined his job as "playin' cops n' robbers," and disparaged his poor career choice at every turn. His sole objective was to put in twenty years, collect his pension, and move on to the "Big Time" (wherever that was remained a mystery). His eagerness to introduce me to a cop surprised me.

The Rookie's name was Tommy Fisher. He picked me up on a Friday afternoon straight from his shift. He was darkly handsome with steel blue eyes that played mischievously off his indigo uniform. I expected someone younger. He was twenty-four and pure Brooklyn; rough around the edges, slicked back hair, a la "The Fonz," and an attempt at a John Wayne swagger that did not work for him. He looked to be about five-nine, with clean-shaven olive skin. How bad can this be, I thought. After all, he is an officer of the law. Still, I was wary. Flubbs was the only cop I had ever known, and he was not exactly a stellar example.

Tommy opened the car door for me. A gentleman, was my first erroneous impression.

"What would you like to do?" he asked.

"I don't care," I said, shyly.

"Okay." And that was all he said. For the next long ten minutes we drove around in silence. The farther we drove, the closer I snuggled up to the door.

187

"Come over here," Tommy suddenly blurted.

I jolted. He said, "Don't be so shy. Move any closer to that door and you may as well be riding in a side car."

I thought he was trying to be funny, so I laughed, then sidled ever so slightly to my left—easily intimidated child that I was—feet together, knees touching, hands clasped tightly in my lap.

"Relax, will you. I'm no serial killer … promise." This did not comfort me one bit. We continued the drive, exchanging small talk. "What's your favorite song?" "What kind of movies do you like?" "Do you dance?" Blah, blah, blah. He made a quick right onto a gravel driveway next to a long ago closed down Stewart's, but the ramshackle structure remained. Tommy turned up the radio and pulled me roughly to him. A surge of adrenalin amped me up for the "fight or flight" response.

"Your uncle was not kidding when he said you were 'some dish.'" He gave me a sinister smile that reminded me of the villain in a Charlie Chaplin movie; the one where he ties the girl to the railroad tracks. I loved silent movies. I had a collection of them—people who didn't speak—how wonderful.

I inched toward the door again. I hadn't yet dated—unless you count the A & P stock boy who walked me home a couple of times—but I was not unaware of my attraction to boys. I spent enough time in front of the mirror for confirmation. Beauty is a double-edged sword. At once a blessing and a curse. It may open doors closed to the uncomely, but not without cost. So much to live up to. It became clear that Tommy's patience was wearing thin. He again pulled me to him.

"What are you doing," I screeched.

"What do you think I'm doing?"

My thoughts were flitting about like sparks from a cyclone fence struck by lightning. I so want out of this car was what I was thinking. When I found my voice, it sounded weak and unconvincing. "I want to go home."

Tommy flashed an incredulous look at me while exhaling noisily through his nose. I tried being a bit more assertive.

"I want to go home right now!" I demanded. This had little impact.

"Oh, come on." He did his hair slick thing again. "Shit. I just want to kiss you." He pulled me to him again and cupped his hand over my breast. His tongue searched for my mouth, but found my eye as I turned my head down and away. I pushed him as forcefully as I could. Then, Oh, God, I began to cry. "Take me home right now!" I wiped my teary face with my sleeve, feeling like a runny-nosed first-grader after spilling juice all over her best-effort artwork.

"Okay, okay. Jesus, what a fucking drag." He threw the stick shift into reverse, skidded on the turn-around, and streaked off the gravel like a deer skittering from a rifle boom.

"Jesus Christ!" Flubbs was apoplectic. He came by our house the next morning to "wring my neck," as he put it. Dad was at a convention in the city so did not get to participate in the "fireworks." Not that it would have mattered. My father was a good, but rather quiescent man. And not a fan of Uncle Flubbs. To be completely accurate, when Flubbs walked in, my father walked out.

"What the hell's wrong with you?" Flubbs continued his growling. "Here I set you up with a solid guy and you blow it. What the hell is wrong with you? Redundancy was his means of emphasis. His head increased in size. Uh-Oh!

"You made a freakin' fool out of me. And you're gonna apologize. Not just to me, but to Tommy, too. Right now!"

I could feel the tears burning their way out. "I didn't do anything wrong," I screamed, and raced to my room pursued by the tail end of his roar. I slammed the door behind me fully expecting him to barge in to continue the harangue. Surprisingly, he did not.

"Calm down, Jimmy," I heard my mother's cooing voice. "Sit. I'll put on a pot of coffee." Flubbs had a soft spot for my mother. It was she who cooled the fires of his inflamed pride with a slice of homemade cheesecake. And it was she who assured him that I would apologize. And I did. I did not speak to my mother for three weeks.

III

Flubbs grew larger and louder following his retirement from the NYPD. His behavior see-sawed from looming ogre to Falstaffian clown, ever-enlarging his persona as a barroom braggadocio, cemented in fantasies and repeating, ad nauseam, an unlived past of underworld figures and hookers, barking and blustering and stomping his feet if you did not maintain rapt attention. For a long while, I remained introverted and passive; fearful of arousing his anger, pasting on a rictus smile, and keeping a low profile. My quest to transcend this agonizing part of my youth and live my life outside an asphyxiating, Old World patriarchy proved daunting. I managed to get through college and grad school while working part-time, and ultimately landed an enviable position at an eminent financial institution, and while I functioned at a relatively high level, my childhood baggage continued to follow me, snapping at my heels like a mangy pit bull.

Following an impulsive marriage and quick divorce, I sparred with a bout of depression that threw me to the mat and left me shaky and disoriented. Therapy was helpful and Xanax took the edge off—primarily by putting me to sleep. I realized that I was beginning to rely on both a bit too frequently. On the same day I flushed the pills down the commode, I decided to get a tattoo. It was more a means of distraction rather than any serious intent. The tattoo was a brilliantly imbued Painted Lady that adorned the length of my upper arm. What made this butterfly unique was that it was attached to a leash. The implications for Freudian analysis were

vast. My big mistake was wearing a sleeveless dress to Aunt Kate's fiftieth birthday celebration.

"What the hell is that?" Flubbs' head began its slow but inevitable expansion. Oh, God, here it comes.

"You get that crap off right now!"

I stood mute, temples pulsing, as I absorbed his tyrannical outburst.

"Right now!" he repeated, "Or I'll take it off myself with a Brillo pad!"

Somewhere deep down I knew those colorful cat scratches just beneath my skin would not be well-received by Flubbs, but I did not expect the donnybrook it caused. I suddenly had an epiphany, as if I had died and were engulfed in that warm, bright light. I was thirty-two years old, divorced, and fixed in a world ruled too long by a bullying male. It was high time I stepped out of this unacceptable tableau. Although a waste of good vodka, in one swift motion I tossed every last drop of my drink in his face. Then I left. I may not have fully grasped the import of my impulsive action at the time, but I knew I had rounded a sharp corner.

I had little contact with Flubbs following the tattoo incident. My attendance at family functions became few and infrequent. Not that I purposely avoided them—well, perhaps that's not entirely true. When I did show up on occasion, the man would not leave me alone. As if it were not enough he had crawled into my psyche, leaving behind his pernicious larvae to guttle what little self-esteem I'd managed to salvage, he circumvented every avoidance device I'd try, including the one refuge I was certain he would not invade.

"Why are you running away from me?" he grumbled. "I need to talk to you."

 We were at the wedding reception of a close family friend.

"What's wrong with you?" I was astounded he had actually followed me into the Women's Restroom. "Get out of here!"

Two elderly ladies were powdering their noses … literally. They made a quick, head-shaking exit the moment they saw him.

"I know you're avoiding me, Mandy."

"Brilliant deduction, if a twisted understatement."

"Don't be such a wise ass with your fancy talk," he said, voice rising incrementally.

I will not cave, I will not cave. While the forgiving phase was a long way off, I saw an opportunity to address the resolving phase. "Here's another one for you: "OBTUSE." I was shouting now. And it was freeing. "Don't you get it?" I pressed, clinging to my righteous indignation. "I don't want you around me. Not in my sight, not in my presence, not in my life!" That ugly pustule known as repression had erupted. And there was no stopping its projectile.

"Don't you talk to me like that!"

I was beyond caring that Flubbs' face had turned crimson. "Haven't you done enough damage?" I said, my voice beginning to crack. "Get out," I managed. "Just get out."

He took a step forward, his hand reaching out to me in a kind of pleading gesture. He opened his mouth to say something, but not a word came out. This was new. The mournful look on his face spoke volumes. There was nothing more I could or wished to say. I turned, went into the stall, and slammed the door. If he dares try to come in here, I thought wildly, I will kick him fiercely in the balls. I heard the door to the Women's room open, and softly close.

IV

That was the last I saw of Uncle Flubbs. He passed several years later. I did not attend his funeral. I was, as they say, in process; still working on the last of the three ings: moving on. I expected to feel nothing. I wanted to feel nothing, as though his death was of no consequence. A variety of emotions, however, filtered through. Anger, regret, hatred, guilt and, perhaps even some form of love … or whatever shape such inexplicable connections take on. I gave each its space, understanding that there could never be a rational explanation for the phenomenon that is the familial bond.

I pry myself loose from the past, and place the flowers in a metal cylinder before the marble stone that reads: Jimmy Castelone, 1946 – 2013, Loving Husband, Devoted Family Man. I cannot help but smile as the sun begins to push through the clouds, warming my face. Georgia is calling me back, and I remind myself that I have a plane to catch. It feels good to be leaving Brooklyn … finally.

THRU THE WINTER

By

Edgar Levy

It was the summer of no regrets…

The morning sun was a blur over the fields

Birds sang, trees swayed

And the Bermuda grass with dew was wet

I sat in the car

Waving good-bye

Hoping that you wouldn't notice

The water in my eyes

Once it has been touched by love

No heart is ever empty

No touch is ever strange

It was the summer of no regrets

And a winter of the same

TRY TO FORGET

By

Carol G. Vetula

Elaine tried to forget, alas, she could not. In spite of all the methods she had tried, and as hard as she had worked to substitute something in its place, she could not forget. Why was it so hard to forget? It had been a long period of agony and nightmares. Even with the help of doctors, she was seeing at least three of them who thought they could help her; she knew they were not that clever. She could not forget Jeffery or the place she was! On the other hand, why had she allowed him to place her here? Being here for several months, she discovered, sometimes it was easier to find relief in her memory. Now, she was not supposed to try to remember all the details of why she was here. That's what everyone said. You will remember someday, they all told her. Oh, she remembered all right. She remembered why Jeffery came every week.

Yes, she knew more than they thought she knew. It was time to get out of this place and find a new life for herself.

Life was good to her when her parents were there to care for her… when they were alive, but her brother, Wayne loved her, but he lived and worked in Italy now. In spite of his letters and phone calls, the pain and fear were still there with every waking hour. Jeffery. Dear, sweet Jeffery. Why Jeffery? Why did you do these things to me? She had asked herself the same questions many times since she came here. Knowing he was due to arrive for his weekly visit soon, her plans came to the front of her troubled mind.

Recently, she decided she would have to save herself because no one was going to help. She was on her own.

It was not long until they brought her meal. They placed a red paper plate holding some unidentifiable fare on the little table beside her chair. These villains thought she would eat it, but she was smarter than that. She knew all the ways they were trying to deceive her. They were not as smart and clever as she was. Had she not suffered enough? Why won't people leave her alone? She knew what was going on. There was no one to help her, or no one she could get in touch with to save her. Knowing she was able to beat all of them, and get out of this place soon, kept her going. Jeffery came to see her about once a week. She knew it was not because he cared. She had hoped he forgot about her and her special possessions he had been looking for. That thought brought tears to her eyes. She wiped them away with her tissue. "Dear Jeffery. Why did you did do this?

These doctors, or so they called themselves were clever. They put sedatives in her food and even in her water bottles. She knew it, but they did not suspect she knew. Usually she went into the bathroom, drank out of the sink faucet, and emptied her food into the toilet, always remembered to flush it a way. They had not thought to change the water in her bathroom, yet. Sometimes when no one was looking, she crept down the hall to the room next door and borrowed food from that room. These people were not trying to drug that young girl, so her food was safe. She could tell this girl was someone special to them.

Elaine's sister used to come often in the beginning, but she had not seen Meg for months. Meg had her own selfish reasons for not coming to see her. Elaine understood it all too well. Perhaps others had moved on with their lives, but Meg, she knew, was going to hang in there.

Her husband and sister wanted her money and jewelry, but she was not going to tell them where it was. She was smarter than they were. It was about time to put her plan into action. Jeffery and Meg were going on a trip, so he had told the nurse a couple weeks ago. He did not think she had heard or understood him. He was to leave today, but he would come by to see if she were any better.

Aware that someone was hiding in her room at various times of the day and night, she felt like a child who knew there were monsters around. Oh, yes, she knew they were there, but if she let on, who knows what they might do to her. They were trying to do away with her in a way that was to look as if she left this hotel for unknown reasons.

She was aware of many things they did not want her to know, but if she let on she knew they were watching her most of the time... what project could they come up with for her. Oh, dear, she had to gather her information and equipment as soon as it was bedtime. It had to be tonight.

Watching and waiting for the right time had filled most of her days. Now that time was here. She knew, just what she was going to do. She had figured everything out, and worked on her plan each day. Only she knew what she was capable of doing. Her plan was to escape out the window and run for safety. They could not see into her mind. That was for sure. But, it wouldn't be long before they found a way to do that, too. Oh, they were clever, but she was smarter. And her valuables were not going to be found. No sir. She was much too smart for them.

Once she could get outside and get to her money and jewelry, she would go to some foreign country and be safe. They'd never find her. Her plans were solid.

She sat at her mirror and brushed her hair, loving the feel of the brush through her long flowing hair. Still beautiful, she mused. Still beautiful and still young she said to the mirror. Why would anyone try to keep her here? The answer was simple. Jeffery had put her there, and she had consented, knowing the time could keep her safe from them and give her an opportunity to put her life back together, again. Her life had been ordinary, at least by her estimation. Why did he want to make her life so miserable? Sometimes she did not know all the facts, and sometimes the facts seemed misty and unreachable. However, on her clear days, she worked on her escape plan. Today was a clear day for her.

A knock on the door brought her to the present. "What?" she said to the closed door as it opened. "Sure," she said aloud, "Come on in," as if she had any choice but to allow someone in or not.

"Miss Elaine, you have a visitor." He set a glass of water on her tray and waited for her reply.

"Who is my visitor?" she inquired, playing the expected game. "I really do not want to see any of your people." She sat in chair and pulled a blanket over her head.

"This is a special guest," he told her, pulling the blanket from her face. "Someone you have been expecting. Shall I show him in?" Without her permission, he went to the door.

"Hello, Elaine." Jeffery said. "I hope you don't mind if I came a day early without prior notice?"

"Who are you?" she asks politely. "I have very few guests these days. Shall I order tea," she tried to pretend to return to the days gone by, doing the polite thing with guests. This ruse was expected so she provided the entertainment.

"No, darling, I have come to spend some time with you, today. Would you like to go out into the garden? We can talk there." He began to push her wheelchair that she insisted on when going outside her room.

"I don't know who you are," she spat at him. He stopped pushing her chair and remained quiet and still. "Why are you here? Are you looking for my treasures?" Sometimes it was such fun to make him feel useless. He had done it to her, and now, returning the favor was fun.

"Sweetheart, I do not want your treasures. I only want to visit with you and see how you are doing." His sparkling, blue eyes portrayed a memory she had of someone, sometime, somewhere. She had loved someone so much that it still hurt.

"Who are you?" She demanded. At this point, she pretended fright. She wanted to ring for the security guard and have him ejected. Where was her button?

He wheeled her out onto the sunny porch, out the screened door, and into the courtyard.

"Are you going to tell me who you are and what you want, or do I have to call security?" she asked in not a polite tone. She was having so much fun at his expense.

"Sweetheart, I know you do not remember me now, or any time I come to see you. But it's okay, dear. I need to know you are safe and are receiving good care. He bent down and kissed her smooth cheek.

She pushed him away. "You have some nerve. You do not take advantage of me because I am in this chair." She brushed her cheek to remove any trace of that kiss. "I have been nice to you, but I am getting darn tired of being nice. Who are you and what do you want?" She pulled her blanket up over her chest.

"Elaine, I am Jeffery. I am your husband. Please try to remember. It is so very important that you do." He sat across from her wheelchair on a bench, and tried to smooth back her beautiful red hair from her face.

Suddenly she became outraged. "You are not Jeffery. You were never my husband. Do you think I can't remember my life? If I had a husband, why would I be living here? Why would he not take me home? How could I have a husband? You are trying to get my jewelry and money. I know what you are trying to do. You are working with those so-called doctors and you all expect to share my possessions. Don't expect me to change my mind. I will not tell you where my treasures are. So there!" She looked off in the opposite direction and refused to look or speak to him.

He wheeled her back inside. It was the same old story. She was too stubborn to understand the truth, or to give him the information he needed. Maybe she never would! Perhaps his hopes of a new life were gone. Her treasures were all she wanted to talk about. Her treasures! However, she never spoke of where she had hidden them. There was a substantial amount of money and some very expensive jewelry given to her through the years by her parents.

Jeffery was her husband and had been driving when the wreck happened. He had not been hurt, but it had confused her mind and their marriage. How had she survived? She had received so many serious medical injuries that no one thought she would live. A roll down a steep embankment followed the car wreck. Elaine had lain there for several hours. Jeffery claimed he was unconscious. Yet his medical condition was never of prime interest. He had some bruises and abrasions, but nothing serious. Doctors told him that she might never remember him. Maybe her treasures, the medical people thought, meant her two grown children who, along with Jeffery were suffering with her condition.

Doctors had tried everything available to take her back to that day. All had failed. She could not remember. Maybe she did not want to relive that time. Jeffery had been devastated.

Everyone had said he was devastated, and everyone the couple had known showered blessings and casseroles on him.

After several months of her hospitalization, Jeffery began dating Meg openly. Elaine had learned about their affair the day before the accident. He suspected she might have known much earlier and had said nothing. Elaine had been the quiet and shy type. She had learned to suffer in silence from her upbringing. What did she know? What might she remember? So he made sure to visit her regularly to check on her progress…or lack of it.

"Tell me about your money and jewelry?" he finally asked. "Where did we keep those special things that were so precious to you and me?" He had tried before, but with no success. "I could get them out and bring them to you. You always looked so beautiful with your special jewelry pieces on. Please tell me where they are and I will bring them to you tomorrow.

"I do not know what you are talking about." She said. "Please go. I want to go to sleep.

Take me back to my room."

"As you wish," he replied, angry she did not remember the things that were most important to her, and to him. He wheeled her back and put her in her room. "I will see you next week," he told her.

"Whoever you are, you do not need to come back here. I don't know you and I don't want to talk to you…ever." She turned her chair from him. Again, he tried to kiss her cheek. "Go away and leave me alone," she screamed. "Go!"

Elaine knew he was leaving town…with her… for a vacation in the sun. Good for Meg. She deserved the kind of man he had become.

Jeffery walked out the door and closed it behind him.

When he was gone, Elaine rose from her chair, made her way to the window, and looked out. "It's either tonight or never," she said softly.

After dinner, they brought her medications, which, as usual, she did not take and being ready to depart, she was so excited that she was giddy. "Yes," she said, "tonight's the night". Tonight I will be on my way to a brand new life." Looking around her room, she made sure no one had heard her. Finally, when the room lights dimmed, and her door closed, that was the signal for everyone to go to sleep. Everyone was to sleep except Elaine.

She reached under her bed and pulled out a long coil of bed sheets tied together making a rope. She changed into a pair or old jeans, a tee shirt, and put on her old sneakers. "He is not going to make a fool out of me," she said to no one in particular.

Opening her window, she threw out the sheet rope, and climbed onto the sill. It was only one floor to the ground from her room. "Now or never," she said as she put her feet over the sill and slid down the rope. Elaine had always been a bit athletic and it was going to pay off now.

"She watched Jeffery from the bushes in front of their house. When he drove away, she found the extra key hidden under a rock in the back yard. Letting herself into the house, she went, directly, to the large piece of art on the living room wall. Pulling back the artwork, revealed a safe. When she entered the correct code, the door swung open. She clapped her hands in glee.

There is was. All her expensive jewelry, most of which her parents had given her when they were alive. "And all my money!" she exclaimed. Not being sure how much she had put away before their marriage, she knew it was enough to make him crazy to find it. Especially since, she was, supposed to have a serious case of memory loss. "I'll teach him to cheat on me with my sister."

Closing the door and readjusting the frame, she ran to the office safe and retrieved her current passport. Everything was ready for her flight to Italy. Jeffery could never imagine she was capable of leaving the mental hospital, let along the country. Nevertheless, she could, and she did.

As the Italian airliner left the gate with Elaine onboard, she sat back in First Class, ordered a glass of champagne, and began to enjoy the rest of her life.

"So long Jeffery. I never did like you or my sister, Meg. Both of you were lovers behind my back for the three years we were married. Now try to find my treasures! And don't forget to look behind the picture of your parents." She laughed aloud and settled back for the long flight to her new life. "It had all been worth the stay in that crazy place. Oh, so very well worth it!"

Elaine closed her eyes and leaned back in her seat holding a glass of French champagne in her hand. "Good bye, my dear Jeffery," she mused, smiling from the luxury seat of First Class. She sailed into tomorrow when she expected to be in Rome.

"Breakfast, Ms. Elaine." Freddie came in, placed her breakfast tray on the mobile table, and moved it over to the bed, adjusting her bed in an upright position. "Did you sleep well, my dear?"

END

I'M AN AMERICAN CITIZEN

By

Cynthia Anne Cofell

I say that loudly, with strong convictions.

I understand a price was paid, for my existence.

Blood was shed, for my freedom.

Pain endured for my survival.

I understand that American history is forever stained with blood, cruelty,

sabotage and hatred.

The sins of our fore fathers landed on our shoulders. Their voices cry out from

the highest mountains. For forgiveness, healing and restitution. A debt still

owed.

We must not look back on the past with criticizing eyes, judging

conversations and a hatred mentality. From the comfort of our modern,

technical reality.

Only forward on with hope, compassion and unity. Erasing the color barrier,

tearing down the money wall that continues to divide us.

Any small contribution I may offer to society, seems tiny in comparison to the

suffering mothers of yesteryears their hearts bleed from beyond the grave.

I answer their call with my footprint planted firmly in the sand.

My place in the world, where I stand. To promote change. My torch lit.

While racing against the clock to get it right.

As humans we are supernaturally linked together like puzzle pieces, strategically moved around on the same board game. Every piece relevant. Every piece purposed. For the bigger picture. A complete image we may or may not ever witness.

I choose to believe in something greater then my own thoughts.

I choose to trust even when in doubt

I choose to seek happiness. Never waiver from the truth. That I'm a powerful creature with limitless possibilities.

I recognize we all have a part to play in sustaining humanity, and the world at large.

Keeping the line drawn in the sand, regarding family and moral valves.

To live, to learn to love and alive is a gift.

We must be readily open for change. Often smell the roses by the side of the road.

As human's accountability is the cure.

As human's sustainability requires more.

From birth to grave we must be willing vessels with open arms, not only receiving but constantly giving back to the universe where needed.

My pledge, duties and obligations as an American citizen are clear to never retreat, never point fingers. Reframe from blame. But boldly march on to the inward beat. Run bravely threw the forest, even when I'm tired, hungry, out gunned outnumbered and judged.

To set the path ablaze like so many before us. In spite of our dark past, hidden secrets, bazaar occurrences, unfair justice practices, senseless killings in the streets, unexplained mysteries and the evil minds that walk among us.

I'm still honored to be an American citizen.

For the following reasons. Were a proud country, courageous, were resilient, creative, inventive, resourceful, brilliant and above all survivors.

I call America my home. I was born here, born free to believe in what's possible.

My hope for the future. Preservation of the whole family. My hope for Americas recovery, economically or otherwise. No Mather what walk of life were from. There is one common thread we all share. This instinctual need to take care of our own. And somehow survive this ruff, jagged, hilly, evil, dangerous, but beautiful terrain we call life in one piece.

I'm an American citizen I say that proudly.

ROSIE

By

Moira Fisher

The telephone rang. Rosie closed her book, using her glasses as her place marker.

"Hello?"

"Mom, it's me. Noah's coming tonight to help you with your bath."

"Ah, my sweet grandson drew the short straw did he?" Rosie twirled the telephone cord with her free hand.

"Mom, stop it. I cooked too much stew at lunch, so I'm sending some for your dinner."

"I can still cook darling."

"I know, but it's nourishing and you like my stew. Got to go. Love you!"

Yes, she reflected, she did like her daughter's cooking. Among her daughter's many skills, it was one that she could take no credit for. Cooking had never been Rosie's strong point. And now she cooked less and less and her clothes showed it, hanging on her bony frame. She shuffled to get a glass of almond milk. Perhaps she should do better and make the effort to eat more. Maybe she'd have more energy.

The doorbell rang promptly at 6:00p.m.

With a smile that reached eyes that shone down at her like the summer sky, Noah held out a bowl of freshly picked green peas.

She smelled their crisp aroma as he exclaimed, "Fresh from my garden."

"So how is horticulture treating you, Noah?"

"As good as I treat the earth, Grandma. But you know I never learned that in college."

He set the basket his mom had sent on Rosie's kitchen table, turned and gave her a bear hug. She inhaled his cologne.

"I can heat this up while you bathe," he said, gazing outside at his grandma's window boxes spilling petunias, foxgloves, phlox and ivy and on to the untended garden, now overgrown with long grass and weeds. He knew if he walked back there that he would smell the fragrance of moth balls—his grandma's way of keeping the snakes away.

Turning from the window, he set a single plate at the table. One fork, one knife, and a spoon—just in case. And he wouldn't stay to watch her eat unless invited. If she was particularly shaky today, she'd be embarrassed, so he set his books on the coffee table in the living room where an armchair had its back to the table.

"Are you doing okay, Grandma?" he called out.

"Just fine, Noah. Thank you. Won't be long. How are your mom's many projects going? She's always too busy to keep me updated."

They talked through the closed bathroom door, Noah standing nearby.

"She's doing well. Busy with her volunteer work and practicing for the Easter pageant. She is performing some of her own compositions on the piano. Did she tell you?"

"Yes. You know how proud I am of her. I can't wait to hear her play. And Emily? How's her math?"

"Yikes! That part of her brain just doesn't fire on all cylinders. All those extra lessons have done nothing for her. She's still limping along."

"Oh my! Just like me. I could add and subtract and do the times tables, but all that calculus and higher math I never got. I guess she got my genes, poor thing."

Noah heard her splash as she got out of the tub. This was when he always held his breath.

"Grandma, you've got to stop blaming yourself for every bad thing that happens to us."

He wasn't sure she heard because the hairdryer started up before he finished talking.

"Noah. I'm ready." She cracked the bathroom door. Noah walked into a cloud of steam and took the proffered jar.

"My miracle cream." She turned with her exposed back, in her pajama bottoms, modestly clutching her towel to the front of her body.

"Load it on, Noah. It makes my muscles relax and helps me sleep through the night."

"I know, Grandma. I'm so glad mom found this blend for you. Did I get you good?"

"Yes, that feels good." She put on her pajama top while Noah looked behind the bathroom door, reached for her robe and helped her shrug it on. She tied the sash as they walked to the kitchen.

"Hmmm…. smells good." Rosie saw the setting for one. "Not eating with me, Noah?"

Noah spooned the stew into a bowl for her and set it on the table.

"I ate before I came."

"Well, sit with me, will you?" she patted the seat next to her.

Rosie wiped her mouth with her napkin after just a few bites.

"I have something for you!"

"What Grandma?"

Shuffling in slippered feet, she reached in the broom cupboard, pulled out a shovel and a pick, then stumbled under their weight.

"Oh, let me get that," Noah steadied Rosie with one hand as he took the tools with the other.

"I want you to have these. I'm not going to be doing yard work anymore. I've decided to go with the natural look out there. I'll just keep my pots and window boxes looking pretty. I'm still feeding the wild birds every day. I've made my peace with the weeds."

Leaning the tools against the fridge, Noah guided Rosie to her seat at the table, "When I get time…."

"No, Noah," she cut him off, "don't worry about me. You need to focus on your studies. And these times we share are so precious to me."

"I appreciate the tools but you don't have to feel like you have to give me something every time I come."

"I know. But I want to." She squeezed his hand, then pulled a black scrapbook out from under a stack of mail and papers at her elbow. She slid it towards him.

"It's from our trip on the Orient Express." Noah looked from the book to her, then turned the pages very gently.

"You were only twelve. Look how cute you were, struggling with our luggage. And all those curls! Where have they gone?"

"They're still there, Grandma. I just keep my hair shorter these days." He leaned in, examining the pages intently. "Our tickets! You kept them."

It had been a magical vacation, just him and his grandma, dining extravagantly every night on 5-star cuisine, the luxurious sleeping compartment they had shared on the train, the sights they had seen.

"Good times," Rosie whispered, "Do you still have the miniature train set, Noah?"

"Yes, Grandma. Still have it."

"Well one day when you have a son maybe he will enjoy it too,"

Noah nodded solemnly, knowing his grandma had paid a small fortune for that train set with all its extended track.

"Well, this is for you. Memories to keep."

"It must have taken forever to make," Noah paged backwards now, examining each photo again. All the memories neatly mounted on board. He touched a napkin from a restaurant where they had dined, pressed flowers from the gardens they had visited, museum maps and opera programs and ticket stubs. She had saved every piece, bringing every memory alive again for him.

"I love you, Grandma," he kissed her forehead.

"I know, Noah," she said as she watched him close the scrapbook. "Well, your mom has excelled again, the stew was delicious. Tell her for me. I'm going to read in bed for a while. Thanks for coming tonight. Will you lock the door on your way out?"

They embraced.

Noah knew the history. His mom had told him many times that when he was four years of age, Rosie had told her that she was saving to take him on the Orient Express. It was her plan for just the two of them. Grandma loved trains—as an artist she had painted trains, had a train set with an elaborate village under her Christmas tree every year and had bought him his first train. Rosie would tell people how she had noticed his passion for trains when he sat at her Christmas tree at the age of three, having to be pulled away to eat. Laughing with delight, she would tell how he would crawl under the tree while watching the train go round the track and fall asleep. She'd tell how they would put him to bed only to find him sitting at the same spot when they woke in the morning. She had waited all those years to be able to take him on that journey of a lifetime on the Orient Express. And now she had ensured that every memory would be kept alive by this beautiful scrapbook she had lovingly made for him. He tucked it under his arm; too moved to even talk. He drew her to him and held her tight. Then he reached behind her, picked up the garden tools and picnic basket his mom had sent.

He looked down once more at this woman who was growing old too quickly. His throat closed, filling with tears. He simply nodded and turned to go.

᠄᠄ ᠄᠄

Rosie picked the phone up on the first ring.

212

"Waiting for your call, Mom?"

"I was dusting my telephone table," Rosie said cheerily.

"Emily is coming tonight to help you with your bath time," she said. "Is there anything you need from the grocery store? I'm going this afternoon."

"No, I'm good," Rosie smiled at the photo of her daughter with her family.

"Okay. Emily will be there at about 6 this evening."

Emily arrived in her usual flurry of bouncy blond curls, excited voice and colorful combination of clothing, toting bags that looked too big for her petite frame.

"Hi, Grandma. Your fairy garden pots look lovely by the front door with those daffodils all blooming."

"Thanks, they were growing wild in the backyard, so I just transplanted small clumps of them to the pots. I think they add a nice pop of color. Actually I fixed the pots for you to take home with you."

Emily hugged her Grandma.

"You're shrinking, Grandma," she said, holding her at arm's length.

"Well, if you'd quit growing like a weed, darling." They both laughed.

"I hear your bath water running," said Emily.

"Oh, yes, yes, let me check on that."

When she returned, Emily had her head in the refrigerator.

"Oh, Grandma. If it's okay, I'm going to spend the night so I brought some salad ingredients and I was looking for a tomato. Or did you plan to have something else for dinner?"

"That's perfect, darling. I'd love you to stay over and I have some of Noah's peas too. Tomatoes in the bottom drawer. There are some veggie patties you can fry in a little olive oil to go with the salad. Same drawer as the tomatoes. See you after my bath."

"Okay," Emily washed lettuce. "Call me when you want your lotion."

Rosie, lotioned up, in her robe and slippers, settled herself at the table where Emily had set two places. She fingered the fresh tablecloth, her eyes resting on the neat stacks of her papers.

"You know, Emily, I left the mail piling up on purpose," her voice filled with tears, "hoping he'll come through the door and sort it all, just like before."

"I know, Grandma, but it's just you now." Emily gently stroked Rosie's hand. "That water bill has to be paid. I made three stacks--unopened mail that looks like junk, bills that have to be paid, and places Grandpa used to contribute to. I'll help you write checks after dinner. It won't take long and then I want you to help me with a couple of paintings I'm doing for your children's book. I just can't seem to get the colors right."

"Okay." Emily noticed how Rosie brightened when she mentioned the paintings. She should enlist her grandma's help more often. She knew that Rosie loved telling people that she was collaborating with her granddaughter on her books.

After dinner, Emily quickly cleared the dishes away, put the kettle on for tea, and they settled down to write checks, making short work of the piles. Only a stack of to-be-mailed envelopes were left on the table.

"I'll drop these in the mailbox on my way to class in the morning," Emily said cheerfully.

"Thanks my love. Now let's look at your paintings."

"Aren't you tired, Grandma. We can do it another time."

"No, no, I'm good. I want to see what you've done."

Emily pulled out two small canvases she'd been working on. Rosie turned on a side lamp and, holding the canvas close to the light, examined the painting.

"Are you doing your breathing like I showed you, Grandma? Remember, seventy percent of toxins are released through breathing. Nice full exhales," Emily demonstrated.

"Yes, yes, and I'm still in the top ten in my yoga class. I do better than those young things in their fancy tight outfits. I'm more limber than they are."

"Good for you, Grandma!"

"Ahhh—it's the roof of the barn that needs more shadows. See where your light source would be?" She pointed to show Emily. "Paint some dappled shadows here on the barn and it will give it the atmosphere you need. Don't be afraid of using dark—it will make the light colors pop. And this one needs a deeper sky. Paint it over, dot in the clouds and then redo the trees."

Emily sighed. "Ugh, I know, Grandma, I've been staring at it for days and could see that the sky was wrong, but I thought you'd have a quick fix. Redoing it will take forever!"

215

"It won't take long once you just start. It's sitting there staring at it that paralyses you."

"Like the bills and the unopened mail, right?" They both laughed.

"Come, Emily." Rosie carried Emily's painting. "Let me mix up that blue for you."

Emily followed Rosie to the enclosed porch Rosie used as her studio. It had been Rosie's dream when she and her late husband, Henry, had moved in almost fifteen years earlier.

Rosie remembered how they had planned the shelving to accommodate her art supplies and he had built it all. The natural lighting in the morning was perfect for painting but now it was night and she flipped on the lights which immediately lit up the unfinished works on the easels around the room.

"Ahhh…always a reminder." Rosie sighed. "So much to do."

"Grandma, don't be so hard on yourself. You're in your writing season now. If it bothers you, take the canvases down and stack them. Label them, 'waiting for inspiration to arrive' or 'back burner'."

"You're right, my sweet, I'll do it tomorrow." Rosie reached into her paint drawer and pulled out a couple of tubes and blended the paint for Emily who was selecting the perfect tool from her grandma's vast collection of brushes.

Rosie settled into an armchair and watched as Emily painted, giving pointers. Soon the sky was perfect. Emily mixed the greens the way her grandma had taught her, using black and yellow, and soon her trees were done and the painting was complete. Quickly her brush flitted to the second canvas, her strokes sure.

"I'm going to make us some chamomile tea, Emily. When you're done with that roof we'll be two paintings closer to publication."

"Have you decided which painting will be the cover, Grandma?" Emily used the back of her hand to brush her curls off her face.

"No, think about it while I make tea."

Emily painted the shadows on the roof and walls. Then she took all of Rosie's paintings off the easels around the room, stacking them neatly on an open shelf. She set her paintings for their book on the easels. And she was washing her brushes when Rosie came back with their tea tray.

"Oh my, Emily your paintings look wonderful. This is the first time I've seen them all at once. What a beautifully illustrated book this is going to be!"

"I thought that while we're drinking tea we can look at them and maybe decide on the cover."

"Okay." Rosie set the tray down, her eyes not leaving the paintings. She handed Emily her teacup, took her own, and settled into a cozy chair. Sipping the warm liquid slowly, she finally set the cup down and closed her eyes, laying her head back. She smiled.

"What are you thinking, Grandma?"

"I've made my choice. I'm just visualizing the title on the cover.

"Tell me, which one?"

Rosie stood up and walked over to the painting of a little girl lying on her tummy, looking up at a starry sky. Picking it up, she held it in front of her. "This one."

"I love it too. It is the whole story, isn't it? And I can't believe that I painted it like ten years ago." Emily said.

"It was inspired. Some painting just is, my darling."

They sipped the rest of their tea together and then trudged off to bed—their evening's work well done.

When Rosie woke up the next morning, a note lay where her pile of mail had been the night before. In Emily's hurried script, Rosie read her expression of deep love for her grandma and that she should call her publisher and get the book rolling. Emily had proofed it yet again and thought it was perfect. The manuscript lay next to the phone.

After a hurried breakfast and with a pot of coffee brewing, Rosie settled by the phone. She dialed the publisher's number.

&❥ &❥

She had just hung up the phone when there was a knock at the door. She squinted through the peep hole to see her daughter on the step, chewing at her thumb nail.

"Mom, I couldn't get through on your phone. I kept getting the busy signal. So I had to drive over to see if you were okay."

"Oh, I'm fine, darling. I was just on the phone with my publisher. He had me read the whole manuscript."

"I wish you'd get call waiting or a cell phone. This isn't working. I'm a wreck worrying about you if you've fallen or something."

"Sorry darling," Rosie stroked her daughter's arm.

"Well, did you get it?"

"What?"

"The book—is it a go?"

"Oh, yes! Written by me. Illustrated by Emily. I'm so happy. I can't wait to tell her. I've got to ship the paintings to him. He had me email the manuscript while we were on the phone."

"I'll take you to the UPS store tomorrow if you like. And congratulations, Mom. Oh, Eli's coming tonight to help you with your bathing. And we're having a yard sale at the church to raise funds for those missionaries that Dad used to support in Ecuador. Perhaps you could go through your closets. Pick out some shoes you don't wear anymore, clothes. This might be a good time to donate Dad's stuff. It's a good cause and you know how he was about missions."

Rosie looked away, "I'll see."

"I brought some cardboard boxes. Eli could help you. He has to leave at 8:00 because he's teaching a youth meditation class at 8:30 tonight."

Her cell phone rang. "Got to take this, Mom. Love you." With a kiss on the cheek, she turned and was out the door.

Rosie noticed the cardboard boxes and packing tape neatly stacked on the bench beside her front door. She picked them up, set them on her dining room table, and suddenly she was terribly tired. Sinking into the couch she allowed the sadness to envelop her. Somehow she felt that her resistance to clearing out her late husband's closet, allowing mail to pile up, pretending he might walk through the front door smelling like the outdoors, kept him alive. Sometimes she would open his closet and bury her head in the loosely hanging fabric of his shirts, longing to smell him. In recent years his fragrance had left the closet and only old clothes hung there. With legs of lead she trudged to the bedroom and opened the closet, inhaling deeply. Nothing. She reached in and touched the fabric. Soft and limp. No substance of the man.

Her daughter had once told her that she should use his shirts to make a quilt, but she just didn't have that kind of energy anymore. Quilting had frustrated her on her better days in her youth. It was not something she wanted to attempt and be frustrated with. Not with her failing eyesight and trembling hands.

She hugged the fabrics in a big embrace. No romantic memories. No electricity. No Henry. A sob escaped her tight throat. She looked for the flannel shirt he was wearing in the photo she kept next to her bed and couldn't find it. It had been so long, she realized, that she had probably ripped it up for rags when he had torn it. She simply couldn't remember.

She picked up the photo of Henry in that shirt and sat on the chair at the open window in her bedroom.

"Henry, dear. I've kept your clothes for so long, hoping you'd come back to me. But I suppose that is just silliness and I have to move on. Now they're having this yard sale for missions and I know your heart was always to help so I'm doing this for you. To honor you. And I'm going to give away some furniture I don't use too. Might as well, right?"

The wind blew the curtain into her face and she laughed, reaching for a tissue when she realized she was crying.

"Henry, my love, I was looking for you in the smell of old clothes and yet here you are in the warm breeze of a beautiful day! I will always love you."

She kissed his photo, put it back next to her bed. She stood strong and steady, suddenly filled with energy and purpose for the task at hand. Shoes went in one box, shirts neatly folded in another, many boxes of suits, then trousers and casual pants. Rosie marked each box she filled. All the boxes were packed and she was making more piles, some of her own clothes, some small appliances, lamps, books. She filled flower pots and laundry baskets, trash cans and plastic tubs.

Delighted with her progress, she forgot the time and was surprised by the knock at the door.

"Oh, Eli," she embraced her grandson, "I'm so glad to see you."

"Hi, Grandma. Mom said I was to try to encourage you to part with Grandpa's stuff, but if you're not ready, I understand."

"Oh, no. I'm ready. Come and see."

Eli was wide-eyed at the array of boxes and piles of clutter all over the bedroom, kitchen and hallway.

"Wow, Grandma! You have been busy. Good thing I brought my pickup truck." He said with a laugh.

"Your Grandpa would be happy to be giving to this mission project, so I'm happy to be uncluttering too."

"This is fantastic."

"And I have these pieces of furniture too." She indicated two large pieces. "Now if you or someone in the family wants them, fine. But otherwise, donate them."

"I'm going to call my friend, Jonathan. He can swing by on his way to the meditation class tonight. We can load everything on our pickup trucks and take it to the church. That's where my class is. This is great, Grandma."

"My pleasure. I'll run my bath. You make your call. I don't want to make you late. And I want to hear all about that class you are teaching."

"More space. In my bathroom." Rosie said when she came out. She handed Eli a bag filled with toiletries. "Man stuff. Shaving foam, after shave, razors. You boys can see if you can use any of it. Otherwise toss it if it is too old."

"Do you need me to do your lotion, Grandma?"

"You know, Eli, I don't know if it is the simple act of giving, or the encounter I had today with what I'm interpreting as the presence of your Grandpa, or the publication of Emily and my book," she rotated her head, checking her neck, "but I feel fantastic!"

"Whooh…slow down, Grandma. Explain."

Rosie told Eli in detail about her day, while she cooked them dinner.

They ate together and then Rosie stretched out on the couch.

"Leave those dishes, Eli. I'll get to them later. Come and tell me about the meditation class you're teaching."

"Well, Grandma, you know how I've struggled with focus and the label they gave me at three. Asperger's Syndrome?" Rosie nodded. She had thanked God daily that Eli was born into her daughter's family, with two older siblings to emulate and two parents who were patient and willing to do whatever was necessary to bring up a child in the nurture and admonition of the Lord. She knew Eli would succeed. It had not been without challenges for them all, especially for precious Eli. She squeezed his hand.

"You remember the classes I took when I was three, Grandma?"

Rosie nodded. She recalled how she had called him the pterodactyl, because his outbursts of hissing. even at her, had become so intense that his mom had sought intervention. When the diagnosis had come, Rosie had regretted her naming him a flying dinosaur. Her daughter had never let it go.

She remembered how Eli had said that Grandma and one little girl his own age were his only friends, and she regretted the pterodactyl label even more.

Eli told how his classes helped him to embrace his feelings, acknowledge his emotions and express verbally what was going on inside of him. Rosie simply nodded, encouraging him to speak, knowing that he was simplifying something that had been a mountain of a task for him. She squeezed his hand when he came to difficult parts, acknowledging his pain and struggles. The months and years of doing the same thing over and over, until he could just do it. And now he was teaching it. To those who would become strong and overcome the way he had. Her heart swelled inside her.

There was a soft tap on the door.

Eli rose, "Oh, that will be Jonathan," he glanced at his cell phone to see the time, "We better get loaded and down to the church. Thanks for listening, Grandma."

"Oh, darling," Rosie hugged him and started gathering overfilled baskets she could carry out to the trucks.

She stood waving goodbye to the two young men with her heart so full of love for her grandson and in awe of the battle he had fought and won. She picked up the broom and swept away the circles left by the pots she'd given Emily. The little alcove by the front door seemed bare and lacking character. She dragged a few pots from her collection around the bird feeder, added a small bench and stood back to admire her new arrangement. The evening breeze blew and she inhaled deeply, smiling, remembering Henry in the breeze, she turned to go indoors, firmly locking the door behind her. She washed her hands at the kitchen sink.

The phone was ringing. She lifted it with the kitchen towel still in her hand.

"Mom? Eli, called me. He was on his was to church. What happened exactly?"

Rosie gave her daughter a quick synopsis of her day.

"Is it too late to come over? Are you up for a visit, just me and Dan?"

Rosie looked around her kitchen with the dishes still not done, "Oh, that would be lovely, darling. I don't have anything but some gingerbread cookies, though. I can make some tea or decaf, what would Dan prefer?"

"Decaf would be great, see you in a few."

Hurriedly, Rosie put on the coffee, packed the dishwasher, lit a few candles, tidied up the magazines on the coffee table and set out a tray with her homemade cookies. She saw the car's lights coming down the drive and hurried to the door, thinking she was glad she had arranged things at the front door so it would look welcoming.

They all hugged and walked through the kitchen to the living room with Dan carrying the tray to the coffee table.

"Mom, we'll get right down to the reason we are here," Rosie noticed how much her daughter looked like she had at her age, her thick, brown hair swept back from her face, "I am so impressed with the way you have cleaned out and given to the cause. And I know Dad would be proud of you for moving on."

Rosie just nodded, glancing at Dan who was chomping away on a cookie. Dan nodded back, enthusiastically, brushing away crumbs from his chin. She loved Dan. He was the son she had never had. The perfect man to complete her daughter. He brought humor to her sometimes too intense way of looking at life, he calmed her down, and loved her deeply. When she was on a tangent about this or that, he would gently, yet level headedly, bring her back to her family and things that matter most.

"And we, Dan and I, want you to move in with us." Rosie raised her eyebrows. "This is not a sudden whim of mine, Mom. We have been planning for months. You know how I have been doing renovations and always talking to the builders? Well, it is for the addition we were building for you!"

"You did this without consulting me?" Rosie asked.

"Yes," Dan said, clearing his throat. Rosie noticed how he touched her daughter, gently, yet firmly—a sort of signal like he was taking over the conversation. "We know that the children come over every night. They love coming over and spending time with you. But we," he waved his hand over his wife and himself, "miss out. So we figured the best solution would be to simply move you over with us. Wanna come and see what we have done so far? Then you can make modifications before the builders leave completely!"

"Well, Dan, since you put it that way," Rosie smiled a slow smile. What a day of surprises it had been!

225

They drove over to the house. Rosie smiled as she saw her own private entrance to her suite. A hand painted sign with an arrow said, "Grandma's Place." Even in the dark she recognized Noah's landscaping and her own pots that she had given Emily a couple of days ago stood by her new front door. As she entered she inhaled the fragrance of fresh paint and wood.

"Ahhh…heaven," she moaned. "You know I'm a sucker for fresh timber smell, Dan,"

Everything looked perfect. An entire room, well lit, for painting and writing, a small yet well laid out kitchen, and when she reached the bedroom, Rosie's hand flew to her mouth. There, on the bed, lay a homemade quilt with fabric she recognized, "Henry," she whispered. And she knelt to touch the quilt, fingering each block, so carefully cut and stitched.

She turned with tears running down her cheeks, "Who?" was all she got out.

Her daughter nodded and came to kneel next to her mother, hugging her gently. "I've been busy stitching this for you, Mom. But now the quilt is done, the house is done. And if you agree, we can be together. What do you say?"

"I say it's perfect, and thank you!"

"Then, welcome home."

Rosie's Miracle Lotion

RECIPE:

Ingredients:

1 cup filtered water
1 cup magnesium chloride crystals (Epsom Salts)
(you can use any quantity just use equal quantities of each)

Method:

Bring water to boil in a non-aluminum pot or pan. Stir in crystals and blend until fully dissolved.

Pour into a spray bottle or wide mouthed jar so you can get your hand in to take out the liquid.

Apply to back, shoulders, back of neck, legs, preferably after a bath or shower. Never apply to genitals or face. Wash hands very well after application of your product. Touching eyes with this product will cause discomfort.

Sensitivity will occur if you are lacking magnesium. You will experience tingling. This will minimize over time. Start by treating a small area first to see how your skin reacts and avoid the crease of the elbows and knees (back of knee joints). And do not ever apply to freshly shaved legs.

CROSSOVER

By

Delores L Staton

the suffering has been put by
the dying is done.
the pain is dimmed,
the crossover complete.

the end was peaceful,
not long in coming,
the day before
a false warning.

of Death, there are many visions.
however painful is the ultimate decision,
there are many consoling metaphors.
Death is the definition of Life.
Death ends all strife.
Death brings release.

Yet, in the quiet of my lonely room,
I feel anguished, undernourished, impoverished
By the departure of my beloved Mom.

TRADING PLACES

By

Michael McLarnon

BEHIND EVERY SILVER LINING LIES A DARK CLOUD.

Those were Moreland O'Telo's thoughts as he pulled back the glittery bedroom drapes his wife asked him to install the night before. He expected to see the sky socked in with the thunder clouds that rumbled overhead all night long, letting off thunderous explosions, lighting up the sky with fingers of lightening, and dumping so much rain Noah would have been sent scurrying to the nearest Home Depot for supplies to build an ark. Instead, he was surprised to see those same clouds, like cowards fleeing the battlefield, racing west, away from the sun rising above the neighboring brownstones.

In a way it was a pity. It was Sunday, his one day off work that week, and he was hoping to have an excuse to stay in, put his feet up, and swill a six-pack or two in front of the TV while watching anything sports related. Little did he know at the time, had those clouds mustered the courage to stand up to the sun and linger over his Brooklyn neighborhood, his life wouldn't have been rocked to the core.

But the clouds did depart, leaving in their wake what was setting up to be a beautiful summer day, and in some bizarre solution to Heisenberg's uncertainty equations, setting the wheels in motion for what was to change Moreland's life. However, as he stood in his boxers and gazed at the wakening Prospect Park neighborhood, he didn't know those things, and even if he did, it probably isn't possible to avoid Fate.

A few feet outside the window, a robin alit in the branches of the twin maples guarding the entrance of their renovated brownstone and began feeding her peeping babies. Three stories below, emerging from the corner coffee shop door, was a familiar sight—a man, looking beaten down by the mediocrity of life, holding two coffees, a bag of pastries, and a newspaper crammed under his arm as he shuffled along the sidewalk with his head down. The man passed a homeless person of indeterminate sex, wrapped up in a full-length wool coat more charred black than green, rummaging through garbage cans. They crossed paths, neither looking up, as if they were living in different universes.

Moreland was amazed at the regular rhythms the neighborhood fell into. He couldn't exempt himself from that circadian dance, because here he was, like most Sunday mornings, at the same precise instant, waiting with bated breath for a specific runner to materialize around the corner.

Biding his time, he studied the mother robin. She had constructed a nest made of yarn and twigs, all held together by flecks of shredded newspaper. He wondered what newspaper he would choose if he were that bird. The Wall Street Journal? Hoping his children would grow up to be commodity traders like himself. The Times? Well-rounded liberals working for a nonprofit out to save the whale and the world. No, he would choose the sports page from the New York Post. His children could become happy and productive members of society working as bartenders or barbers.

A neighbor who lived on the second floor, and her yappy Shih Tzu, emerged from under the building canopy, both on arthritic joints, they hobbled down the sidewalk in the direction of the park. The woman glanced up at the chirping birds and Moreland stepped back a foot to avoid being spotted. His shoulders slumped, about to step back and close the drapes, when she appeared. The female jogger. The woman he called "Heavenly Angel."

One snowy November morning, less than a week after he and his wife moved into the converted brownstone, he peeked out through this same window at this exact hour and day to check the weather and spotted her, Heavenly Angel, clad in a lime green windbreaker and black spandex running pants. Moreland felt his wife's eyes on him as if it were a physical presence, so, using a skill he learned in the military, without moving his head, he followed the jogger with his eyes as she jiggled down the sidewalk and disappeared into the park.

By chance, or maybe design, he searched through the window the next week, at the same time, and there she was again. And almost every Sunday since. Like clockwork, she passed below at around the same time each week. On the occasional Sunday when he didn't spot her, he allowed his imagination to go wild. Sometimes he fancied her to be a world-renowned surgeon at the nearby New York Methodist Hospital, away on assignment for Doctors without Borders, saving lives and taking names. Other times, he imagined she was a paleontologist on staff at the Brooklyn Museum across the park, dressed in khaki shorts that showed off her shapely legs while doing a dig in a dusty desert in Ethiopia or Outer Mongolia. Other times she was an architect, designing office towers in Santiago, Chile. Admiring her from afar over the months he thought about taking up running so he could get a closer look, but what precious little time he had off work he wanted to spend sleeping.

On the sidewalk below, Heavenly Angel shimmied and swayed in all the right places as she dodged the homeless person, ran by Mediocrity Man, and passed directly under Moreland's building. He tried to use his mind to will her to look up, but she kept chugging along. And he felt the pleasant stirring beginning.

"Up so early?"

His attention was broken by his wife's voice burbling in over his shoulder. He smiled. She was using her sensuous voice, her bedroom voice, which always reminded him of water babbling over pebbles in a brook. He tore his eyes away from the window and turned.

Dusty, his wife, smiled coyly, her eyes tracking from his face down to his silk boxers, lingering there a second, then back. Moreland hoped she didn't guess the reason he was up so early. Her eyes twinkled in the light filtering in from outside. "I thought we'd have time to snuggle," she said in a husky voice.

"I was thinking about work."

"This should help get your mind off the office." Dusty pushed the covers down to her ankles, then kicked them off her feet. Her purple silk negligee ended just below her hips, her tanned skin glowed in the morning sun. Her blonde hair, hazel eyes, and freckled cheeks a contrast to his own dusky skin and brown eyes.

She arched her back and threw her hands over her head as if reaching for the sky, hiking the negligee over her hips and elevating her breasts into a perky position. The pose, as always, elicited the reaction she desired.

She gave him that smile that made him putty in her hands while her eyes tracked back down to his boxers. "You've already risen," she waved him over with her finger, "come to bed and play."

He let go of the drapes; they fell together, shrouding the room in semi-darkness. Rolling onto the bed, he threw his arms around his wife's waist, planting his lips against hers. She let out a soft moan. Then her moans were replaced by ones coming through the baby monitor on the nightstand.

Moreland let out a moan of his own. "The babies. I hear them stirring."

Dusty lie on her back, her arms around his neck and pulled him to her. "They can wait," she whispered against his neck. "I can't."

He reached over and flicked the monitor off.

Dusty pulled him on top of her. "Hurry, before they start crying."

He nibbled her neck, ran his hands over her silky skin, thinking it ironic that before he was married he worked to prolong his performance; now that he should have all the time in the world, he had to act like a rushed teenager in the back seat of a car. Losing himself in his wife's caresses, he forgot all about Heavenly Angel.

Minutes later, he rolled on his back, catching his breath. Dusty kissed his cheek, then brushed her hair back and climbed out of bed. From the chair in the corner she grabbed a knee-length kimono, cinching the obi as she went to tend to the babies.

When she was gone, Moreland wondered why Dusty had chosen him from all her pursuing suitors. And she had many. She was a definite find. A woman who turned men's heads. Whatever it was she saw in him, he was grateful. He chastised himself for watching the jogger, when he had such a beautiful woman sleeping next to him every night. His friends all told him how lucky he was. And he did consider himself fortunate; but there wasn't anything wrong in looking. To make it up to Dusty, he was going to devote the entire day to her and the children. She was right: today was his only day off and it was no time to be thinking about work.

Moreland stumbled to the kitchen and started the coffeepot. Telling Dusty she could get ready, he took the twins from her and fed them their bottles while he lounged on the couch watching SportsNexxus, a national sports news show. The twins finished eating and were babbling on Moreland's lap when Dusty returned, radiant in a flowery sun dress. She took the twins from him and dressing them in matching jumpers. The forecast called for sun with temperatures in the eighties, so after showering, Moreland threw on cargo shorts and a polo shirt. While Dusty packed the diaper bag, Moreland strapped the twins in the tandem stroller, then they caught the elevator to the lobby.

"Let's walk to the park." Dusty said once they reached the sidewalk.

Moreland gestured with his head in the opposite direction. "We have all day. How about we take the train and go to Central Park. We can take the twins to the zoo."

"There's a zoo right here in Prospect Park."

"Let's go into the city. You've been cooped up in Brooklyn all week."

Dusty worked as an editor for a number of magazines and did all her work in the apartment in front of a computer monitor.

She playfully grabbed his arm and looked up into his eyes, giving him a look that melted him inside. "Only if we can get pastrami sandwiches at Carnegie Deli and have a picnic."

How could he refuse? "It's a deal."

They caught the subway into Manhattan and exited at Rockefeller Center where they raced across the street to catch the tail end of mass at St. Patrick's Cathedral. Then, hand-in-hand, they strolled across town to Seventh Avenue and the Carnegie Deli. The place was packed, the line snaking down the sidewalk.

"I'll wait in line," Moreland said, knowing his wife was craving pastrami. He briefly wondered if that was a sign she was pregnant. But if that were the case, what was the explanation for the rest of the people in line?

Dusty crouched down by the children and shook her head. "The twins will get antsy."

"Take them down to Times Square and back. This place is the best."

Dusty eyed a deli two doors down with no waiting. "Pastrami's pastrami," she said. "Let's grab a sandwich and get going."

While Dusty waited outside, Moreland entered the neighboring deli, remarkably like Carnegie's but without the line, and ordered an overstuffed sandwich, again remarkable like Carnegie's but half the price.

"Two pickles," Moreland said to the man taking his order, knowing his wife was a big fan of the pickle. At least that's what she always told him when they snuggled in bed.

Moreland stashed the sandwich under the stroller and took the stroller, pushing the children to the park. On the way to the zoo, they stopped at one of the lakes and watched the remote control sail boats. The twins wanted out of the stroller and toddled around, almost falling into the water. They had a season pass to the city's zoos, as Dusty took the twins to the Prospect Park Zoo at least three times a week. So they put the twins back into the stroller and Moreland led the way to the Central Park Zoo. The twins didn't seem to enjoy the penguin house. In the petting zoo, Bertha tried to grab the horns of one of the goats and was knocked on her back when the animal had enough and butted her in the chest.

The children began yawning when there was an announcement that it was feeding time for the sea lions. The sea lion enclosure was located in the heart of the zoo, an octagonal-shaped pool with a jumble of rocks about two stories tall rising in the middle. Even sea lions had to live in high rises in Manhattan. They made their way in time to see five trainers, wearing knee high waders, emerge from behind a fence, each carrying buckets of fish. The sea lions seemed as excited as the crowd, jumping out of the water to sit on the rocks, their eyes riveted on the gate where the trainers walked through, clapping their flippers along with the human visitors. Each trainer paired up with one of the sea lions. The animals did tricks, including shooting high out of the water, giving their trainer a high five, bouncing a ball on their nose, even slashing some of the people sitting in the front row. After each trick, the twins clapped while the trainers threw their charges a fish or two.

When the show was over, the twins began crying, which meant it was time for their feeding. Moreland glanced at his watch, thinking that those kids had an amazing sense of timing—it was noon, his stomach was growling, it was his feeding time as well.

They exited the zoo and found a sunny spot in an open field near West Drive. While Dusty started feeding the children mashed peas and carrots, Moreland bought two bottles of ice tea from a pushcart. When he returned, Dusty had a child in each arm, feeding them from a bottle, while their eyes drooped closed. When the children were fast asleep, Moreland helped his wife lay them on a blanket and positioned an umbrella to protect them from the sun.

Moreland pulled out the sandwich, piled so high with shredded pastrami the pieces kept falling out. He handed half the sandwich and a bottle of iced tea to Dusty and they ate their lunch while around them scores of people were throwing Frisbees, playing fetch with their dogs, or flying kites. Along the road, people streamed by on rollerbladers, bikes, or on foot. Moreland's eyes naturally migrated to the young women bouncing by in skimpy running outfits.

As he surveyed the scene, his eyes gravitated to a woman who had stopped to get a drink from a nearby fountain. She must have been looking at him for a while, because when his eyes moved from her legs, to her chest, then up to her face, and when their eyes met, she didn't look away. She didn't smile, but had a look of longing in her eyes. It seemed as if time ground to a halt. The woman wiped her mouth with a certain seductive grace, then pushed her bangs from her forehead. She broke eye contact, panned over Dusty and the sleeping babies, then her eyes returned to him. A smile, so faint Moreland wasn't sure if he imagined it or not, crawled across her lips. She bent down and took two more sips, not breaking eye contact with him. She straightened up and wiped her lips with the back of her hand. Moreland felt uncomfortable as the woman continued to eye him as she pulled a towelette from her fanny pack and wiped her hands. Finally, pushing her hair back, she gave him a smile and broke eye contact, then turned and merged with the crowd running down the road.

Moreland continued to follow her with his eyes as she ran steadily south, eventually disappearing behind a stand of trees. He had never seen Heavenly Angel from eye level, always looking down at her from three stories above, but he was amazed at the resemblance, unable to shake the idea that they might be the same woman, as unlikely as that would be. The woman at the water fountain had the same legs and jiggly bottom. And a face he imagined Heavenly Angel would have.

Moreland glanced over at his wife, who, thankfully, was watching a couple playing fetch with their yellow lab. The man, who had been throwing the ball, handed it to his wife, who reared back and hurled it. The ball slipped from the side of her hand and bounced their way, settling between the babies. Dusty had supernatural reflexes and tackled the dog before it could pounce on the ball. Moreland reached over and handed the drool-covered ball to the dog as the couple ran up and apologized profusely for throwing the ball their way.

One crisis averted, Moreland and Dusty snuggled together and pulled part of the blanket over themselves. With Dusty in his arms, he closed his eyes and fell asleep, dreaming of the dark-haired woman at the water fountain wearing a gossamer gown as he chased her through fields covered in flowers.

The babies stirred, waking Moreland. As he opened his eyes, he was looking directly at the water fountain. He caught his breath when he realized the dark-haired woman, or someone looking just like her, was bent over taking a drink. The sun was just going down over the skyscrapers to the west and the air took a chill when he realized the woman was looking directly at him. He didn't remember what the woman he saw earlier was wearing, but was sure they were one in the same. He gave her an embarrassed smile and a nod. She seemed to narrow her eyes but didn't look at all embarrassed. Taking two more sips of water, she wiped her hands with a sanitary towelette, then spun on her heel and joined the runners streaming south.

The babies were whining, ready to eat. After they finished a jar of baby food and drank juice, Moreland and Dusty took the twins to a toy store on Fifth Avenue and let them do their thing. It was after five when they caught the subway back to Brooklyn. Dusty said she wasn't in the mood to cook, so Moreland went to the corner deli and picked up an order of fettuccini Alfredo and garlic bread. While he carried the bags of food to their brownstone he couldn't shake the feeling that someone had been following him all afternoon. He didn't want to be paranoid—that was for crazy people—and he didn't believe in conspiracies, so he didn't look over his shoulder, and didn't see a dark-haired woman in running clothes across the street tracking his movements.

ALL THIS FACE

By

Eunice L. Sykes

All this face all over the place
Straight from God's amazing grace
Cheeks galore, whatever for
Nose ye wide, could be a door.
All this face all over the place
Straight from God's amazing grace
Perky "just right" upper and bottom lip
Keeps a silent prayer always at the tip.
All this face all over the place
Straight from God's amazing grace
Wide, high forehead attempts to hide
My well-used brain that lives inside.
All this face all over the place
Straight from God's amazing grace
Eyes wide set, shiny with brows too
Two nostrils centered—What God can do.
All this face all over the place
Straight from God's amazing grace
And then, at the end, a well placed chin
He's got it right, from dust it all begins.
All this face all over the place
Thank you God for saving grace
Who could have done it better?
Detailed precision, down to the letter.

CHRISTMAS JOY

By

C. J. F. Mobley

Christmas! Just the word brings a giddy rush of emotions to body and mind alike often before the Thanksgiving turkey is pulled from the oven. From excited squeals of youngsters to bah humbugs of apathetic Scrooges, I generally find myself somewhere in the middle of the spectrum of emotions during the holiday season-- but not this year. For the first time in a long while, I felt not the joy of the Christmas Spirit.

Instead of anticipation and excitement, I felt like Dickens' famed character wanting no part of the traditional festivities that mark the month of December. I didn't want to shop for gifts for friends or family finding it a rather bothersome chore. I lamented the stores crowded with holiday shoppers, long lines at the check-out registers and my ever-shrinking bank account. I grumbled at paying for gifts for people that I saw only once or twice per year wondering how a twenty-five-dollar gift card or cotton sweater could translate into, "I care about you" when little else was shared the remaining three-hundred sixty-four days of the year. I wondered why we even bothered exchanging gifts at all.

The traditional holiday decorations fared no better. No wreath graced the front door, no stockings hung from the mantle. Christmas lights sat in their boxes stacked in the corner of the basement to continue their hiatus for yet another year. Nativities, angles, sleigh bells and snowmen slumbered on in their cardboard domiciles instead of gracing every nook and cranny of our home. All I managed was an evergreen tree sparsely decorated with a few of my prized ornaments crafted by my children or collected from students over the years. Poor Santa didn't get his usual fair of homemade shortbread and mocha cookies.

Nor did I want to be bothered with driving two hours to see my husband's family or going to my niece's house for Christmas morning breakfast. Rifling through my somber mood, I could not find a reason for this lack of interest in Christmas. My disinterest must have shown at work also as a co-worker gave me the book, The Christmas Shoes. Reading the book with a box of tissues handy only seemed to make me even more despondent about Christmas. I just simply wanted the entire season to be over so I could get back to my normal routine.

Then came Christmas morning. My teen-aged children no longer woke my husband and me at twilight anxious to see what Santa had delivered while they slept. I had to shout up the stairs to rouse them. I made coffee and waited for them to lumber down the stairs to open their gifts. As I stood with my steaming mug of coffee, gazing at the lighted tree, surrounded with beautifully wrapped presents, I realized at that moment the cause for my unenthusiastic welcome to this year's holiday season. My children were now grown up. No longer did their innocent faces with dimpled cheeks fill with mirth and impatience as Mom and Papa emerged from bed far too slowly for their liking. It was I that now waited.

I moved to the sofa fighting back tears wondering if I would ever feel the joy of Christmas again the way I had for so many years past when my precious children's excitement made the holiday a magical time of year. My children gradually made their way to the tree to dig for their Christmas bounty while my husband snapped photos to grace yet another memory album. As I listened to squeals of delight from my daughter over some diamond earrings and saw the Cheshire cat grin on my son's face over a Led Zeppelin sweatshirt, I began to feel the joy of Christmas morning.

I realized Christmas isn't the gifts we exchange with family and friends or the decorations with which we adorn our homes, but our hopes for the future and love for our cherished family which resides in our hearts. If we keep this in mind, we can feel the joy of Christmas any day of the year.

A STAR PERFORMS

By

Lorraine Sullivan

(an octopoem – 8 lines, 8 syllables in each line)

The Atlantis stage is ready

Steadily ocean drum rolls beat.

The mermaids sing a bubbly song.

And Neptune performs his magic.

Encouraged forward by the breeze,

Beckoned by sandy beach applause,

Crowned by the rainbow ocean mist,

I brightly dance on water's stage.

MAZIE

By

Delores L Staton

It's a lovely fall morning, a typical fall morning in Georgia, when suddenly the front door of a modest frame home, flies open, and Rose Earland steps out on to the porch.

"Mazie, Mazie! I declare where has that chile gotten to? Mazie, Mazie. Mazie is that you there under the porch? What on earth are you doin under there?"

"I'm listening to the bugs talk, Mom."

"Look at you! I just got you ready for school. I had you so pretty. Now there's dirt on your dress."

"It's okay, Mom. It's only the dress that's dirty, not me."

I stared, stunned, sometimes, my chile of 10 just amazes me. "Well, never mind, come on, let's see if we can fix it."

Rose pulled her daughter to the kitchen sink, and attempted to wash out the dirt.

"Okay, where is your school bag. We have to leave; we may already be late."

"Sorry, Mom. I just wanted to hear the bugs talk."

"Well, what were they saying? Why on earth would you want to know?"

"I don't know that's why I was listening. God told me that all of his creatures have a language. That all of God's creatures have something to say. So, I wanted to see if I could understand."

"Buckle your seat belt. Tell me about your homework for the day." The engine of the old Chevrolet proved it was still alive. Rose Earland pulled out of the driveway.

"Well, today we're goin on a field trip. I had to go on-line and look up The Aquarium. It was fun. So many different species of fishes."

"Don't say fishes. It's fish."

"Mrs. England told us to learn as many facts as possible about the aquarium. I know quite a few. I know that there are whales and dolphins. I know that it was the dream of a business man. But, I forgot his name."

"Good, sounds like you did your homework. Remember sit up, be quiet and listen. Remember you already have two strikes against you. Do not, I repeat, do not, get the third strike.

"Okay, Mom." This was her plea every day. God knows, I don't want that third strike.

"Have a good day, baby."

"Okay, Mom. Mrs. England said we might be late gettin back."

Mrs. Earland watched as her little woman opened the car door, stepped out and made her way into the school building. Mrs. England welcomed her into the building.

"Now, what, I said to myself. I have so much to do before I go to work. I need to stop and pick up a few groceries. I don't like this town much, but one good thing, everything is close by."

Upland. Georgia. My, me. Not sure what would happen to this dusty, provincial town, if Atlanta wasn't close by. It barely exists, quiet, unexceptional, but most of all, just plain unexciting. Then again, I have to remind myself, unexciting can be a good thing.

Every night, on the local news. 'Breaking news.' 'We are following breaking news' which usually means there has been a shooting somewhere. I don't get it, how are so many people able to live in the midst of so much violence, hate, ignorance and pain.

"Hi, Mr. Cyrus, how you today?"

"Hi yourself, Mrs. Earland. Drove Mazie to school, did ya?"

"Yes. So far, this has been an uneventful morning."

'What do you need? I got in some very special vegetables and fruit. Go'on take a

look."

Mr. Cyrus, the local grocer. Nicest man, ever. Always so helpful.

"Thanks Mr. Cyrus. I need a few vegetables and some fruit. Maybe a piece of meat for tonight's supper."

"Mrs. Earland, seems to me that we might start calling each other by our first names. What do you think? I'm Matthew. You can call me Matt. What about you?"

"Well, okay, I don't see anything wrong with that. My name is Rose."

"Rose, huh? suits you, a pretty name for a pretty lady."

"Ah go'on, Mr..... I mean Matt. Well, let me get to my shopping."

"We got some new potatoes, and some lovely apples from Cobb County."

"Okay. I will take a pound of potatoes, and a dozen apples. Do you have any grapes? Mazie loves grapes."

"I sure do. What color does she prefer? green, purple, or red?"

"Mazie? don't matter. She loves all kinds."

"Fine, I recommend the purple, they're the sweetest."

"Let's see, four, six-fifty plus three. Oh, wait we forgot the meat."

"I prefer chicken or fish."

"Well, I do have tilapia. I am waiting on a fresh delivery of chicken."

"No problem, may I have a pound of tilapia?"

"Sure nuf, that will come to seventeen dollars and fifty cents. Let me bag it all for you."

"Thanks Matt, you have a nice day. See you agin, later in the week."

"Bye now, Rose. Give that young'un of yours a big hello."

Rose looked at her watch. "Whew, I gotta hurry. It's almost 9:30, I want to be at work by 9:45. My Boss has been riding me something fierce."

"Bye now."

"Bye now."

Mrs. Rose Earland rushed home, deposited the groceries. Checked her appearance in the mirror. Satisfied that she was still intact, she left for work. Every time she got into her 8yr old Chevrolet, she prayed that it would start, and that she wouldn't hear any strange noises. As she drove to work, Rose

Earland, liked to think about her day; make plans; dream; sing; and pray that God would watch over her as she tried to do her best.

Mrs. Rose Earland worked in a factory, picking and sorting beans to be bagged. Totally, mind boggling work, but it paid enough to help provide a passable living for her and Mazie.

Mr. John Earland, God rest his soul, had died about 5 years ago. He hadn't been well for the last 10 years of his life. Rose had been truly sad to see him die; but truth be told, she was glad that he had been called home to glory. His extended illness had taken a lot out of her; it had been difficult to provide a calm, reassuring atmosphere for Mazie. In her heart, Rose believed that the time she had had to spend away from Mazie, explained the strange fantasies of her daughter.

Mazie spent most of her time, detached from the reality of her surrounding world. She could sit for hours, tracking the movements of a spider, or of an ant.

Rose worried, that one day, Mazie would come Mazie face to face with the world, and would be overwhelmed. It worried her, that she would not be able to cope.

Oh well, enough mind wandering for this morning. Time to work.

"Good Morning, Mr. Thomas, how we doin today?"

"Just Fine, Mrs. Earland. We have a new shipment we need to sort and get ready

for distribution. We gotta be careful, there appear to be some earwigs in the shipment. We don't want to mix 'em up with our beans."

"No worry, Mr. Thomas I will be extra careful. Are the others in?"

"Yes, Mrs. Cooper and Mrs. Robinson are already at their stations. Lunch will be at noon."

Okay, here goes, two hours of boring sorting and selecting. God, just, give me enough strength to get through the day. 'Keep your eye on the prize,' thank you, Martin Luther King.

Rose had moved to Upland, Georgia about three years ago. She had been living in Massachusetts, but the cost of living had pushed her to make a very difficult decision.

In Massachusetts, she had been somebody. She had been a highly respected teacher and a beloved member of a small community. She had gained a lot of friends, associates through various endeavors for a period of 20 years, she had owned and run her own real estate office. It had been an excruciating decision to leave. Now, that she was in Georgia, she was reflecting on that decision.

Georgia, red state, certainly wasn't Massachusetts, a very blue, a very liberal state.

Rose, with her very sunny personality, had begun to carve out an existence for herself and her precocious daughter. She prayed every day, that time spent working at this bean factory would be short lived.

In reality, given a different set of cards, or a different hand to play, Rose would have been very successful in her life pursuits. Rose, a talented singer, speaks three languages, and has a Master's Degree in French Literature from the prestigious University of Michigan. Her adjustment to Upland, Georgia, was proving to be illusive and downright difficult.

Having to understand and care for Mazie in an intolerant atmosphere made her doubly anxious. Rose hadn't experienced any overt discrimination, but she sensed that every time, she entered a new situation, she was on probation. She suspected that it was the same, or more so, for her daughter. That's why she was so keen on ridding her child of those fantasy ideas, and weird playtime activities. I declare, 'listening to the bugs talk.'

Rose was very grateful for this menial job of soybean sorting. Lord Knows, she had tried mightily to find a job more suited to her background. She had endured an arduous application process for substitute teacher in Tyler County. In the end, she had given up, concluding that perhaps she was just too old to cope with high school students again. She had obtained a part time job in a private afterschool program. She remembered how she had been rebuffed, when she had offered to help students, with their homework. She was totally blindsided by the narrow thinking she heard and saw in many students. Most distressing, the narrow-minded thinking, the innate intolerance, she viewed, was most prevalent in Afro-American students. Rose wanted to scream, wake up, you are being subtly boxed in. You are being programmed. WAKE UP. It was clear to Rose that the students she saw were being brainwashed into accepting an engineered atmosphere. She watched, helpless, as students moved confidently all the while ignorant that they were puppeteered. Little manikins, dancing as they were pulled and tugged.

The students, Rose observed, were constantly being patted on the shoulder, and constantly being complimented for mediocre performances. Rose, in her inner self, screamed for truth, for honesty and integrity. She could see clearly that in many cases, students were being passed on, although, unprepared for the next level.

So, at least, here at Thomas Beanery, she didn't have to confront hypocrisy, and dishonesty. She, and the other two workers in her department, sat quietly at their stations, and just did their jobs. Occasionally, they would exchange pleasantries, or family news. But, mostly, they just ground out their days, hunched over their stations, sorting, sorting, sorting.

Whew! Finally, time to check out. Rose pulled of the gloves, washed her hands, took off her industrial weight apron, and left. No use in trying to say good-bye. No one really cared.

She drove to the middle school, the Patrick Henry Middle School, to pick up Mazie. Rose rang the outdoor bell seeking entrance. Mrs. England opened the door.

"Hi, Mrs. Earland, Good to see you. Have you a couple of minutes, the Principal and I have some questions. We would like to talk to you about Mazie."

Mrs. Earland put on her mask, always ready for these occasions. I won't let them believe that I am intimidated. I can hold my ground. I have to be strong, to do anything else, would leave Mazie floundering.

"Yes, of course. Good Afternoon, Mr. Johnson, how are you today?"

"Just fine, Mrs. Earland. Don't be worried, we aren't terribly concerned. We had difficulty getting Mazie to come in after recess. She wanted to stay out in the courtyard. She kept repeating, that she wasn't done listening to the bugs, and insects. She kept saying, they have something important to say, and she has to hear it. Mrs. England says that she has noticed this peculiarity before. So, our question is, have you dealt with this?"

"Yes, I have noticed this behavior. But, in all honesty, I believe that it's Mazie's attempt to get more attention, to be noticed. She started this strange behavior after her father died. I am still trying to understand what she thinks the bugs have to say. I have been trying to spend more time with her."

"Well, we, here, at school, wanted to be sure that you were aware. If we can be of any help, please let us know. On our end, we will keep you apprised of any behavior, we observe. For now, we will just watch closely. We appreciate your taking time to talk with us. We all have the same goal, that is to nurture our children, to give them confidence and above all, to give them a first rate education."

"Thank-you, Mr. Johnson, and you too, Mrs. England. I appreciate your help. It isn't always easy, being a single Mom."

"Understood, Good-bye, and take care. Don't hesitate to communicate with us."

"Thank-you Mr. Johnson and you too, Mrs. England. Where can I find Mazie?"

Mazie's homeroom teacher pointed to the room next door. Rose entered, and saw Mazie, sitting quietly, reading a book. "Hey Mazie, ready to go home? Come along now."

"So, do you know what we were talking about, the Principal, Mrs. England and I?"

"Yep, I know that you are worried about me and my listening to the bugs. Don't worry, Mom. I'm okay. I know, in my heart, that God is leading me, and He won't lead me astray."

"I trust you, Mazie. But, promise me that you will share any lessons you learn, or any new information that comes to you?"

"Fine, what's for dinner."

"Not sure, you should get anything to eat, after gettin everybody up in an uproar."

"Not my uproar, theirs."

"Okay, Miss Smarty. Go change your clothes. Then, come and help me set the table."

Mazie dropped her book bag, and ran up the stairs to her bedroom.

Not going to worry about her, I agree completely, if she is listening to animals, bugs, insects because she is being led by God. Not going to put myself between my child and God.

Mrs. Earland had a fairly accurate picture of the south, treatment of minorities, and above all, the conservatism evolving into protectionism and nationalism.

She thought, I'm going to work very hard to shield my daughter from this narrow thinking.

Mother and daughter sat down to a supper of tilapia, mashed potatoes, carrots and a salad. "Mazie, do you want a glass of milk?"

"No, Mom, I think milk makes me sick."

"Oh, what kind of sick?"

"Well, it hurts my tummy."

"Ok, no milk, have a glass of ice tea. We will ask the doctor. You could be lactose intolerant."

"What's that, Mom? Am I goin to die?"

"Gracious no, it's that milk, cheese, yogurt, and other milk products may be hard for you to digest. We will see. Do you have a lot of homework?"

"Yes, but it's easy. I can do it quick."

"Good. I am going to put a load of wash in the washer. Bring out your dirty clothes, before you begin your study."

"Okay. Mom, do you think I could have a puppy?"

"Oh, sure, that's just what we need, another mouth to feed."

Weeks droned by. Nothing exciting to report in the life of Mazie and Mrs. Earland. Then, one day, May 20, 1975 to be exact. Mazie, rushed over to the car, after school. She was breathless. She was so excited, she kept tugging on the door handle, without much success.

"Mom, Mom! You won't believe it! Wait till I tell you what happened today in school."

"Well, get in the car. Catch your breath. Then tell me, what has you so fired up."

"Well, I want to tell you. But, maybe I should wait until, we are at home. I want you to be comfortable in your favorite chair, when I tell you."

Well. that's pretty extraordinary. Mazie, wanting me to be comfortable in my favorite chair. This has got to be huge.

"Okay, your news, tell me when you wanna."

After dinner, Rose was comfortably settled in her oversized armchair. Mazie, sat down in front of her, on the three-legged stool.

The ten-year-old, in a very shaky voice, said. " Mom, the test results came back today. I placed first in my school, Mom. Not just my grade, Mom. First in the school, better than the high school kids. Mrs. England said, that the test results mean something very special. She wants to know if you can come to school, next week for a conference."

"Wow, Mazie, good for you. I have always told you that hard work pays off. See, what can happen, when you study hard and when you focus. I am very proud of you, and yes, I will be glad to go to school for a conference. Do you know what the conference is for?"

"Yes, Mom. Mr. Johnson and Mrs. England said that it is about my future."

"Your future? What did they mean?"

"I don't know, but they seemed pretty excited."

Later that night, Mazie had gone to bed. Rose Earland, strong willed, and of strong character reviewed the events of the day. She lingered over the news of her daughter placing first in her school. She pondered, what it could mean for the future. She cautioned herself, must not get too excited.

I've been here before. I've been at the door of success, only to get dragged back, knocked down, and ground into the dirt.

The day of the all-important conference, Rose had left work early, and had gone home to primp for the meeting with Mr. Johnson, the Principal and Mrs. England, Mazie's homeroom teacher. She was ready for anything, yes, she had her mask ready, if need be.

Mrs. England ushered Mrs. Earland into the Principal's conference room.

The meeting had been swift. Mazie was being offered a special path to college.

Mr. Johnson had explained, that Mazie had qualified for the state program for the gifted.

Cautiously, Rose asked what would be required of her and her daughter.

"Yes, I am thrilled to have my child recognized in this manner. But, realistically, we may not be able to participate without financial support."

Mr. Johnson stated, "that's the beauty of this offer. Mazie has a sponsor, willing to pay tuition, books, and lodging."

"What" asked Rose, incredulity resounding in her quavering voice."

"Yes," boomed, Mr. Johnson, you only have to agree. This is a marvelous opportunity for Mazie. She will be able to attend a private school, study with other children of like intellect. This program could fashion her future, and set her on a path of exemplary excellence. What do you think?"

Rose, still stunned, hadn't yet grasped the full parameters of the offer being set before her and her daughter. She folded her hands quietly in her lap. She bowed her head, took a moment to ask God.

"Have you said anything to Mazie.?"

Mrs. England, interjected, "no, we needed to talk with you first."

Mr. Johnson took her hand and said very calmly, "Mrs. Earland, we, here, at Patrick Henry School, are very proud of your daughter and the acclaim she may bring to our school. But, the decision is yours. You need to be confident that it is the right decision for Mazie and for you at this moment in your lives."

Rose nodded, taking her hand back. "Thank you. Thank you, Mrs. England. It's a lot to consider. Let me take some time to think about it, and some time to see how my ten-year-old likes the idea of living away from home."

Mrs. England moved closer to Mrs. Earland, and whispered," our school psychologist has done a thorough evaluation. She is confident that our little Mazie is ready for prime time. We have started the application process, so we will need a firm commitment by the end of next week. If you need more time to confer with anyone else, just let us know."

Rose held her hand out to Mrs. England. She really seemed to be one of the good ones. She seemed genuinely interested in Mazie. I will still have to stay on guard, and be very deliberate in my consideration. Not sure I'm ready for Mazie to live in Atlanta in some private school. Don't care how prestigious.

"Oh well, she said quietly, we'll see."

Rose retrieved Mazie from the library. As she approached, she noticed that Mazie was talking to another student. She read pain in her daughter's face. She stepped up her pace.

"Hi Mazie, how are ya doin?"

"Hi Mom, fine. I took out this book on Selma, Alabama. Not sure I can finish it. It's too painful to read all the horrible things people did to each other. Where was God in all of this?"

"Don't know Mazie. We have some serious talking to do. It concerns today and tomorrow. Let's go home and get some dinner."

Mazie packed up her belongings, grabbed her jacket and left with Rose.

Outside the building, Rose stopped, caught her daughter by the shoulders, and said, "What were you and that kid talking about? You seemed unhappy."

"Susan, oh nothing. She wanted to know why on earth I was trying to read an ole, dusty book like Selma. I couldn't really explain so it bothered me."

"Listen, you read the book. Then you will have an answer for, "what's her name?"

Dinner was a quiet affair. Both Rose and Mazie were immersed in their own thoughts. They talked only when passing the potatoes or the salad. Mazie got up to begin cleaning up the kitchen. Rose interrupted her.

"Never mind that. Come here and sit with me. We have to talk about your marvelous accomplishment."

"Okay, some of the kids have congratulated me at school. But, some of the kids have been cruel. Some of them have actually yelled mean things. Like," there goes the teacher's pet. One even called me pick-a-ninny, asking me if I knew my place. Not sure what she meant by that."

Rose closed her eyes, took a few minutes to reflect. Yes, I am sure they did. Sadly, this is only the beginning. Once they see that you are trying to rise above, that's when they come out in force to push you back and worse to push you down. Crabs in the barrel.

"Mazie, you know, you and I have talked about a lot of things. We have talked about your behavior, your presence, and above all we have discussed your color. We have talked endlessly about how some people will treat you differently; how some people will dislike you, even before you open your mouth. I have tried to prepare and shield you. But, you are about to be tested."

"Tested, Mom? Are you goin to give me a test?"

"No, I mean, that if we take the opportunity offered by the school".

"I don't understand."

"Well, you have excelled in your exams. You have been offered a place in a private school for the gifted because of this success. We have to be very sure that you are ready. We have to be very sure that you can stand up to the insults, the hurts, the obstacles which will be placed in your way."

"Mom, don't worry. I have already heard rumors, that this would happen. I'm ready. I want to do this. Going to a private school will give me a chance to learn a lot of new things. This will just be awesome."

"Are you sure that you will be okay, living away from home nine months out of the year? I know that you will be able to come home holidays and vacations. But there will still be a lot of time that you will have to spend alone. There will also be a lot of hard work. I want you to be realistic. It won't be easy. This is a very good opportunity. But it may be very painful, especially, if you run into a lot of 'Susans.'"

"Got it. Already had a chat with God. He told me to go for it."

"Hey, Mom, do you think we can go shopping? I would like something new."

"umm, you know I think that's a good idea. Why not, you have earned a reward."

"yeah! When can we go?"

"We'll go tomorrow morning."

Saturday mornings are usually fun for Rose and Mazie. The two love getting up a little later. Rose always fixes a generous breakfast of bacon, eggs, and sweet rolls. Breakfast gives them time to chat randomly about everything that has gone on during the week. But, this morning was extra special.

"Mom, do you think I will fit in with all those rich kids?"

"Well, I suspect that not all of them will be rich. There will be students like you, there on scholarship. You will have a lot in common."

"Really, what?"

"Well, all of you want to learn. All of you will be smart. All of you have parents who love you dearly, and want you to succeed."

"Umm." "Mom, do you really believe I can do this?"

"No doubt in my mind. You are bright, funny and very cute. Now go along, get dressed for shopping."

"Okay, Mom. Wow, what a day this is going to be."

Mazie jumped up from the table, put her dishes in the sink, and sprinted up to the bedroom. The excitement in the air was palpable. Rose began to clean the kitchen. The phone rang.

Oh gosh, who could this be? I really don't have time to talk. Not with Mazie about to jump out of her skin.

" Hello, Rose Earland."

"Good Morning, Mrs. Earland. This is Principal Johnson. Sorry to call you so early, but this is very important."

A lump leaped into her throat, Rose caught her breath. She could hear pain in Mr. Johnson's voice. She was afraid to ask what he wanted. Mask time, hear no evil, see no evil, speak no evil.

"Yes, Mr. Johnson. How are you doin?"

"Well, I wish I could say that I am doing better. I have some not so good news.

Mazie has been denied a place in the State's gifted program. I'm so sorry."

"What? I thought that it had been decided. I don't understand."

"Well, frankly, neither do we. We're all stunned. The letter came yesterday. I didn't want to call you until I had had an opportunity to speak with the Director of the program. Her response was that she thought Mazie would not fit it, and that the adjustment would be too difficult for the other students."

Wouldn't fit it? There it is, that's code for we don't want your kind here.

Rose groped for the edge of the phone table, "Mr. Johnson, are you saying what I think I'm hearing." Oh, Lord, don't let this happen.

Rose dropped her chin to her chest. Suddenly, this happy Saturday morning was veiled in images of water hoses, beatings, burly policeman, blocking the way.

"Yes, Mrs. Earland, unfortunately, it seems that Mazie has been dropped from the program because of her color. As a matter of fact, my school district will fight this for you if you agree. We are convinced that we are talking racial discrimination, here. We had been assured that Mazie was in. We had been congratulated by the state board in our selection. We would have never discussed this with you and Mazie, if we had not been assured of her place in the program."

"Thank you, Sir. I really appreciate what you, Mrs. England, and the school district have done for my daughter, but to fight it, would only expose her to more hurt. I don't think so. We will just have to chalk it up to a painful lesson learned. I need to hang up now. This won't be easy to tell Mazie."

Rose covered her eyes, briefly.

It just won't be easy. No, it won't be easy at all."

"Mrs. Earland, I hope you believe me when I tell you, that none of us here at Patrick Henry share these outdated attitudes. We are as devastated as you are. Let us go to bat for her. We will support your appeal. We believe in our student and we believe in her Mother. Your call."

"Thank you, Mr. Johnson. No, we'll deal with this in our own way. Disappointments like these give us strength, build character. She's young, so much better to have had this first obstacle now. Bye, now, thank you for letting us know."

Rose slowly hung up the phone. She sighed, took a deep breath, turned around, and collided with Mazie. A tear rolled down her soft cheek.

"You heard, didn't you?"

"Yeah. Why wouldn't they let me in? What did they say? I promise I won't talk to the bugs anymore. Tell them, tell them, I'll be really good, Mom. Please, Mom, call 'em back."

Rose took her beautiful, bright, and funny daughter into her arms. She held her tightly as she softly hummed. "We will overcome. We will overcome."

262

OLE'

By

Lorraine Sullivan

"Ole'"

Perhaps a strange dying gasp from the man I had just killed,

But not for him.

He was probably hearing and repeating the cheers

From his female admirers.

He had given so many red roses to his adoring ones.

At one time I was his chosen.

I used my knife to slash a tassel from his vest,

A lasting memory to attach to my flamingo dancing dress.

Then I did my frenzied, fire-y dance of revenge

Around his lifeless body.

Castanets were draped, hanging and clicking everywhere.

The red sequins of my dress flashed

Like unbalanced Chinese lanterns.

My nostrils flared, my hair flowed and my tassel danced.

My own, now wilted, rose was clenched between my teeth

As I twirled around and around.

I let the rose fall from my lipsticked lips.

I softly whispered "OLE'".

And I smiled my Spanish smile.

THE PUTT

By

Michael McLarnon

THE SILENCE WAS DEAFENING. The tension thicker than the pollen on this bright, spring Georgia afternoon. And the cursed headaches won't stop. Chewy Wan messaged his temples, hoping to ease the pounding. It didn't.

He scanned the area from under the bill of his cap. Tens of thousands of eyes followed his every move. The crowd was riveted in anticipation. Even though fifty thousand people circled around him, the quiet was eerie. It was Sunday afternoon, the crowd in hushed reverence as if in church. Not a murmur. Even the chirping birds and droning insects seemed to have gone silent. Waiting to see history made.

The silence wasn't only deafening, it was maddening.

Chewy closed his eyes and could swear he was alone. He strained his hearing. Barely audible—perhaps it was his imagination—a pair of holovision announcers were whispering. They were breaking down his upcoming putt. How a playoff would work if he missed; the historical significance if the ball found the bottom of the cup.

Chewy tuned out the announcers. The throbbing pain drowned out everything. It was as if an entire army of construction workers were inside his skull, using jackhammers to burrow their way out. His eyeballs felt inflated like balloons, about to pop from his head, as if a circus clown was pumping them full of helium.

He rubbed his temples. What the hell was wrong? Could it be the pollen? Everything was covered in a patina of yellow powder. When he pulled onto Magnolia Lane—was it only six hours earlier? —a radio announcer with an almost incomprehensible southern drawl said the pollen count was over eight thousand. Chewy never had problems with allergies before. But then again, eight thousand? That seemed really high.

Chewy opened his eyes and inched his way to the cup, peering down. The damn thing looked so small, like he was staring through the eye of a needle. With his head tilted downward, it pounded even worse. The hole seemed to shrink smaller and smaller; reminding him of Lewis Carroll's rabbit hole. He wished he could jump inside and be magically transported to another world, a world where headaches didn't exist. He swore under his breath, hopefully quiet enough so those furry animal-looking, high-powered microphones didn't pick up what he said—don't want to piss off the sponsors.

He backed off and paced the green. Surveyed the contour. The grain. Used his feet to feel the slope. Futilely searched for imperfections: the bentgrass green was almost perfect, like a felt-covered billiard table—and his golf ball would roll just as fast and true. He took a breath. He'd dreamt about this moment from the first time he picked up a golf club. Who didn't? Now, after almost twenty years and countless hours of practice, it all came down to this.

One putt.

One tricky, side-hill putt.

He'd seen this putt hundreds of times on television. The hole was cut in its usual Sunday position: mid-left, on a flattish part of the green, just beyond the front bunker. The putt would break to the right.

Not a bad location, considering what happened earlier. Distracted by the pounding in his head and another slow play warning, his tee shot hit one of those damn holly trees, leaving him in horrible position for his second shot. The best he could do was hit an approach shot to the front apron of the green. Fighting the distraction from the hammering in his head, he hit what was not his best chip of the day to here, twenty-five feet from history.

He willed himself to forget about all that, the tournament was in his hands now. One putt. He caught a quick glimpse of his caddy, who gave him an almost imperceptible nod, his lips pursed. Chewy knew the man was trying not to look nervous. He wasn't doing a good job of it.

Chewy approached his ball and grimaced, preparing himself for the fact the headache was only going to reach stroke-level when he squatted to assess the putt. It had been that way all day long. Maybe it was stress. Perhaps information overload. There were so many factors to take into account, no wonder his head was killing him.

He let his eyes take over as they measured the putt: Twenty-five feet, three and three-eight inches to the hole—definitely not his best chip by a long margin; Five and one-sixteenth inches uphill—a plus, always better to have an uphill putt; Slope gradient four degrees, fifty-seven minutes from his right to left, not so good; Estimated Stimpmeter reading 12, the sun had been out all day and the greens had gotten firm and fast, it would be like putting on a sheet of ice, get the ball moving on the right line and there was little chance of leaving the putt short.

Calculations over, his mind flashed back. He was amazed at how much had happened in so short a time. He'd gotten his tour card less than twelve months earlier, in May, after winning a tournament as a Monday qualifier. And that was less than three years after suffering a near fatal stroke, leaving him all but blind. Then, in early June, playing in only his second pro event, he won the US Open at Torrey Pines. His putting accuracy was out of this world: he averaged less than 24 putts per round. He went on to win the British Open at Carnoustie on a blustery and rainy weekend. Then, in August, he blew the field away at the PGA Championship at Whistling Straights, winning by thirteen shots over his closest competitor. He even won the FedEx Championship in September, needing only nineteen putts on his Friday round.

All those had been relatively easy victories. Double-digit wins. Now he was hanging on to a one stroke lead. But, if he made this putt, he'd join an elite group, holding all four major titles at the same time.

If he holed the putt.

And if he didn't collapse first. He had to drain the putt. Or three putt and get it over. It had to end now. Then he could take a handful of opiate painkillers, lie down in a cool, dark room, and throw an icy towel over his head. A playoff was out of the question, he'd never survive.

It had to end here.

He tried to block out the pain.

In seconds, his mind calculated thousands of potential launch speed-angle vectors from the data his eyes collected. He let his mind superimpose potential vector lines on the green, different paths the ball could take to the hole depending on the speed of the ball as it left the putter. He had to squint and grit his teeth to drown out the searing pain so he could concentrate and choose one of the potential lines. The optimal vector-angle had a ninety-three percent make probability. Other lines had percentages ranging from eighty-eight to forty-five percent. He chose the optimal line, why not? In his mind, he erased the other lines and kept the chosen one, the one he labeled "Tao," superimposed on the green. He stood and walked along the line, looking one last time for imperfections in the grass that might throw the ball offline. The course had the best maintained greens he'd ever seen, and the optimal line was the one he'd been taking during the entire tournament. This time, the optimal line went directly over a repaired divot mark, impossible to predict how the ball would react when it passed over that area. Even though he didn't want to, he pulled his divot repair tool from his back pocket, stooped down, and loosened the grass with the tines. He stood up, patted the area with his putter and took a good look. It would have to do. The line was almost perfect, more than he could ask for.

Chewy walked the line back to his ball, making a final, obsessive check. He breathed slowly and deeply. This putt could fulfill a dream, didn't every person who ever picked up a golf club dream of this?

To hole a tricky putt to win a tournament?

To win the Masters.

When he approached the ball, some sort of insect with diaphanous wings landed on it. The creature didn't seem to know it was being broadcast on holovision around the world. As much as he wanted to, he couldn't squash the bug on public television, some save-the-insect organization would protest and he'd lose half his endorsements. He shooed the insect away as gently as possible. He marked his ball and tossed it to his caddy to clean it off one more time. Chewy studied the rapt crowd, they were so still he could have been looking at a painting.

Certainly the officials wouldn't assess another delay of play penalty now. If it weren't for those two earlier penalties, he could have three-putted from here and still won the tournament. But the rules are the rules. Even though he was playing in the last group and wasn't holding anyone up, the damn rules were the damn rules. If anything, he should get a medal for playing slow; he was sure the TV network was able to air tons more ads geared toward the coveted older, white male crowd: Cadillac, Rolex, and of course the ever popular Viagra and Cialis advertisements.

He could have asked for a medical excuse—the headaches—to avoid the penalties. But that would have raised even more questions, as if there aren't enough already. How did a previously middle-of-the-road college golfer, coming off a three-year golfing hiatus, burst onto the tour and win just about every tournament he played in? And in record fashion?

His caddy dropped the ball back into his hand, patted him on the shoulder, and gave him a reassuring smile.

Chewy placed the ball on the green. Meticulously, he lined the arrows on the ball with the line he intended to use. He removed the lucky buffalo nickel, the token he'd used to mark his ball in every major, and pocketed it right next to his lucky divot repair tool and lucky green tee.

He stood behind the side of the ball.

He superimposed the vector line.

He recalculated the launch speed: 3.12 meters per second.

He took practice swings, until he was able to get his swing speed within a deviation of five percent of optimal.

He shuffled his feet forward and looked directly down at the white dimpled ball. Out of the corner of his eye he spotted his playing partner, jaw tight and arms crossed, hoping, Chewy imagined, for a chance to get in a playoff if the putt were to miss. Just beyond him stood a mobile cameraman, lens pointed at his opponent's wife and young daughter, both with fingers crossed and eyes closed. Chewy felt a pang of emotion—there was no wife or girlfriend pulling for him, just tens of millions of anonymous fans wanting to see history being made. Not to mention the fifty thousand people surrounded the green.

He placed the blade of the putter behind the ball and focused on the beginning of the glowing vector-line. He took a deep breath—the entire crowd seemed to do the same—and tried to keep his knees from knocking together. The silence deepened, so profound he could hear his heart beating like a kettle drum. Time seemed to grind to a halt.

He centered himself and repeated a mantra, his special golfing mantra, under his breath: *Om mani padme hum, devagolf.* He chuckled inwardly and relaxed, sending the headache to a faraway land, if only for a moment.

He drew the putter back the practiced amount.

With perfect rhythm, he followed through.

Connected with the ball.

The ball took off on the *Tao*—the chosen path.

He closed his eyes, matters now out of his hands. He would let the crowd's reaction tell him what happened next.

A RIME FOR MR. POSSUM

By

Edgar Levy

martin put the garbage out

and let me have my peace

martin put the garbage out

and let me have my sleep

martin put the garbage out

and then you'll have your peace

MARTIN! MARTIN! MARTIN MILLER!

that man done fell asleep

i guess I'll put the garbage out

i guess he needs his peace

MEMORIALS ALONG THE SIDE OF THE ROAD

By

Carolyn Julien

Traffic moved at a snail's pace as cars, trucks, and other vehicles lined up for miles on the Georgia interstate. Blue lights flashed and sirens blasted while onlookers anxiously glared with curiosity and disbelief at the unfolding scene. Some of the people rolled up their windows to stifle the stench of burning flesh—the flesh of an eleven-year-old boy, his four-year-old sister, his loving parents, and his pet Beagle.

What happened and how it transpired bombarded the thoughts of onlookers as they crept along and were afforded the opportunity to view the misfortune in their paths. The cause of this catastrophe was as common as it was tragic: fifty-nine-year old Harry, Sr., a veteran truck driver, swerved and slammed his rig into the back of the family's Corolla while trying to retrieve a dropped cigarette from the floor of his vehicle.

Thirty-five-year old Lucy Campbell was one of the many spectators. Whenever this freelance journalist took a road trip on an assignment, she was always intrigued by the memorials placed on the side of the road by bereaved loved ones. During this drive, Lucy observed several such monuments and wondered about the people's lives prior to their fatal calamity. She was finally an eyewitness to deaths on the highway and wondered if the bereaved loved ones of this deceased family would also leave behind a monument.

As Lucy mused, she hoped the victims had crossed over peacefully. She was doubtful though, since the sudden flash of imminent danger shocks and traumatizes one's soul. Her grandmother, Beulah, often said when souls die brutally, their spirits have a difficult time accepting their passing and won't crossover to the realm of the dead. Lucy exited the interstate, still deep in her thoughts, remembered a heartfelt story frequently told by her senile grandmother regarding her youngest son, Frank. He was only five years old when he died in a house blast that leveled the structure. This was not just any house fire, but a crime of arson committed by both her grandmother and great-uncle. Their intent for starting the blaze was to collect insurance money. They saw it as an easy way out of debt brought on when Grandpa Hank, her grandmother's husband, went fishing and never returned home.

Initially, Lucy's grandma worried and speculated that he probably drowned. However, when all her checks bounced, she figured out the rest of the story.

Penniless and pregnant, Beulah was uncertain how she would make ends meet with three children and another one due in four months. This occurred in 1956, in a rural community where there was no public assistance and jobs for a homely, middle-aged, pregnant woman were limited.

On the advice of her criminally minded brother, and against her better judgement, she allowed him to torch her home. The plan was for her brother, Raymond, to come to their home at 1:00 AM, enter through the kitchen door, turn on the gas stove, and leave it on long enough for the kitchen to fill with fumes. He would then bang on the

door three times as a warning to alert her that she had ten minutes to get herself and the children out.

Restless and awake, Beulah lay on the living room sofa while anticipating the arrival of the arsonist. Finally, she heard Raymond slip through the back door. After what felt like hours, she heard the three knocks. Beulah woke the children, told them she smelled fumes, and they rushed from the house across to a dirt patch out of harm's way. With the dwelling visible where everyone stood, Beulah anticipated the explosion at any moment.

Unfortunately, the eruption did not occur immediately. Raymond was still in the house laboring over what should have been a simple blast. The children and their mom could see him from the kitchen window working busily. Frank, the youngest, thought their father had returned home and ran back into the house undetected in the midst of the commotion.

By the time his mother realized he had returned to the dwelling, it was too late to go after him. Raymond ran out of the front door as Frank ran in through the back, calling for his daddy at the onset of the explosion. The kitchen windowpanes blew out and the force of the blast slammed Frank against the wall. The impact was more than his tiny body could withstand. Grandma said she stood there numb and dumbfounded over the death of her precious child. Frank died, but grandma said his spirit didn't die with him. She was certain of this because, during the early hours of the morning in their rebuilt home, she often heard the faint cry of a small boy's voice calling out, "Daddy, daddy."

Lucy's grandmother often retold the story when she became old and less inhibited by family secrets. She never forgave herself for little Frankie's death. The child deserved better than this awful ending.

Tears swelled as Lucy replayed the tragedy in her mind. Enveloped in thoughts, she missed her GPS prompting to turn.

"Damn," she yelled, knowing she would have to drive another few miles to turn around. With this setback, and the fifty-minute delay experienced earlier in traffic, the GPS estimated she would arrive thirty minutes behind schedule. Lucy had never been late for an assignment and did not desire to be tardy for this one, either.

With the accident miles behind her and blessed with clear roads and beautiful countryside views, Lucy accelerated in a last-ditch effort to redeem some lost time. Realizing she would not make it precisely on time, she attempted to dial the interviewee on her cell.

Unfortunately, she looked down briefly at her phone and did not have enough reaction time to respond to a deer crossing her path. Lucy wasn't wearing a seatbelt, and the deceleration of slamming on her brakes threw her from her convertible into the base of a large tree. Without a soul around to assist, she was destined for a fatal demise. Too frail to render cries for help even if someone could hear her, Lisa felt her spirit drift from its body, leaving her weak and powerless. She fought with everything in her inner being to hold on to her last breath, but the unwelcomed supernatural force was too much to endure--she succumbed to the will of the overpowering energy.

However, on the contrary what she was taught to believe, Lisa did not see bright lights or deceased family members coming to greet her soul. What she saw frightened her as much as it intrigued her journalistic curiosity. The story of a lifetime was unveiled right before her, and she wasn't even alive enough to write about it. Lucy looked up from the tree and spotted a monument by the side of the road. It was a memorial with a silk rose and a white wreath attached to a wooden cross. Less than three feet from the tribute, she saw the ghost of a young woman walking smoothly toward her, almost if sashaying. The woman looked to be about twenty-three-years old and was wearing a rose-colored jogging suit.

"Hello," the energetic-looking blonde called out to Lucy. "My name is Halle Montgomery from Alpharetta, Georgia. I was named after a celebrity; you know, the famous older actress, Halle Barry. All my life I was told that my charismatic personality and great looks would make me an instant star. I really never wanted to be an actress, but figured it must be my destiny since I heard it from people all the time. Yea, I did a few commercials and appeared as an extra in movies, but nothing really big."

Lucy was dumbfounded watching this character all wound-up as if programmed to give this rehearsed speech. She was adapting to her own new transformation and listened patiently.

"The day I of my fatal car crash," the woman went on, "was supposed to have been the day I landed my big break—I had my big break all right. One of the paramedics who came to my rescue said I must have been broken in about eleven places! Who'd thought this 99- pound body would've had so many places to break?"

The writer less frightened and still captivated by this figure continued to listen attentively. Lucy thought to herself, "A Life before the Monument," story was babbling away at her, and she would never be able to share it. Lucy looked down at her watch and interestingly, it was the exact time of the scheduled interview.

Her weakened spirit felt stronger, her journalistic persona took over, and she interviewed Halle.

"So Halle, was that," pointing at the wreath, cross, and rose, "shrine constructed in your memory?"

"Oh, yea, that. My mom and younger sister came by shortly following my departure and mounted this masterpiece in my honor. I guess this location makes sense, since this is the area where my car crashed. My passing really hurt them. I felt awful seeing them in so much pain, especially my mom since we had argued right before I left. She carried guilt for my stupidity. I disrespected her and acted like a 'B'. I just hope my mom knew how much I really loved her."

"I'm sure she did, Halle. I'm sure she did. What exactly happened to cause your mishap?"

"Well, as I guess with most accidents, I was rushing. I had this important audition and didn't wanna be late. My agent assured me that I would finally get a speaking role. In trying to save time, I put my makeup on in the car. I was finished, but decided to change lip colors. If I would've just stuck with the ruby red, maybe I would still be alive. I only took my eyes off the road for a split second to remove the lid from my fuchsia lipstick. And in a blink of my eye, some idiot jetted in front of me. I didn't have time to react and smashed my little Bug into his big 700 series Mercedes. The rear end of his car ended up in my chest and abdomen. He survived, but I didn't stand a chance. The paramedics and police figured out what happened when they detected the bright smudge cemented into my windshield."

"How heartbreaking. Now, if you were in the world of the living, what advice would you give to the public?"

She chuckled and said, "I'd say, if you ever decide to smash into a car, make sure yours is bigger. No. Just kidding; I would probably tell them that distractions destroy, and to disregard them all by any means necessary, while driving.

"Yep, I learned that one too. Anything else?"

"Yea. As hard as it might be for some, I would plead with everyone t to cherish every living moment by always being kind to one another, especially family. You never know when you'll take your last breath."

Yes, (nodding her head) I can see why you would say that. "Hal," Lisa slurred as she found herself weakening again. She was too fragile to utter another syllable of the girl's name and found that she could no longer exist in the spirit world. Feeling faint, she forced her hand to wave at the girl, and the apparition waved back while watching her guest respond to the soul returning to its body.

Paramedics worked vigorously to restore life to Lisa. She was a wreck, but by God's mercy would survive her injuries. Her outlook on mortality was changed too, and she vowed to never take risks again. In her line of work, she now knew if she missed one story, another one would be waiting somewhere along the side of a road.

RED NAILS LEGACY

By

Eunice L. Sykes

At ten years of age, my lovely diva-in-training granddaughter, Kira Vivian,
remarked

"Love your red nails, Nana! " Memories from Second Street she immediately
sparked

Of a time in another place with a favorite woman, I called Ma

Her class oozed from such a sassy, vivacious spirit—I held her in awe

Your great granddaughter has many ways like you; read on

You would be pleased, love her dearly, and engage her in fun.

Your memories are numerous and vivid, one I will share…

Of your pretty fingernails, aaaaahhh, yes those nails!

Bright, bright red, never anything that pales

Colored hues at the end of each long narrow finger

I see them as if you are here, memories still linger

At the tips of long café au lait digits, like those I have

Only wedding rings adorn them, I stifle a laugh

Half moons at each base showing—never to cover

Not sure why I don't see that anymore.

But red nails…..yes ma'am, they are everywhere

Painted, no they are polished, I patiently share

And with assorted other delights meant to layer

Not simply red, but red nail art, unique to a serious player

With shades and hues that delight, excite and amaze

Colors of a bejeweled burgundy sort, like risky risque

And foxy broadway frost, with glitter to boot!

Brickhouse red, truest red, really red, raspberry hoot

Red roses, sparkly red, sprinkles, also poppy dream

Bright berry, roses are red, then there's infrared cream

You could shop all day and never tire for days

And still see assorted and varied reds in a star struck haze!

Even so, there are other colors too…. You'd be delighted

Purple passion, blue glitter, champagne cocktail….I get excited!

Apple coral berry, frosts, creams, dark midnight blue

There are also numbers: 201, 173, 89, and 402

Black lacquer adds dots, stripes; it's called "nail trends"

No telling what's going to land on you finger's ends

Enamel nail tips with white, called French manicure

Or in reverse, nail tips colored blend to neutral sheer.

Then there's toe art. Designs are "off the chain"

That means really cool, Ma. Let me make it plain!

Imagine a ring on your toe? I'd never wear one!

But your granddaughters sport them like foxes on the run

Kira paints her nails, I polish mine….an endless time to converse

We compromise: sometimes she paints mine and I polish hers

Not really sure how she got that notion in her pretty little head

Even with all the variety, your baby girl—me--still prefers bright red.

Thanks for the girly memories, Ma, It's my honest opinion

Your red nails legacy lives on in great granddaughter Kira Vivian

THE RESCUE

By

PJ Renfroe

Max left the airport headed for long term parking where he retrieved his old Jeep Wrangler. He did a quick check for any awkward surprises, found none, and pitched his satchel onto the passenger seat. With a sigh, his entire physiology relaxed as he eased into the known comfort of the brown leather seat. Home again, and this time with only a few nicks for Henry, the doctor, to attend. However, this time, he is determined not to take on any more dangerous assignments. At forty, and financially secure, still on his game, it was time to plan a different future, but to what? He had no idea.

The road leading to his property was through green forests, with a view of the ocean from an occasional rocky cliff. There were only two other houses on that lonely stretch of road. One he knew, and had been friends with for years, the other sold this past year to a stranger, only because his offer to buy the property had not arrived in time.

He used a remote to open the decorative iron gates, and drove through on the fake brick driveway which meandered through tall firs to the stone and timber house. He clicked open the garage doors. The Beamer was gone, so Henry was not home. He drove in and closed the doors. Picking up his bag, he unlocked the mud room door, shut off the alarm, nudged his shoes off and left them on the rack, and walked into the kitchen, spotless as usual. There was a lingering odor of beef stew in the air.

Wherever Henry had gone, he had taken Woolfie. He missed the little brown and white mongrel's enthusiastic welcome home.

He skipped up the stairs to his bedroom, took off his Ralph Lauren gray suit, left it on the chair to send to the cleaners, and checked himself in the full length mirror. Six three still toned, his curly brown hair needed a cut, bandages in at least five places on his back and chest, satisfied none was bleeding, he turned on the shower as hot as he could stand. He stood there letting the pulsing water massage and relax his muscles from the rough action and the long flight. He had not expected to get physical on this job. It had been a necessary reaction.

Stepping out of the shower, as he checked the cuts on his chest and arm, doctoring what he could reach, he suddenly felt uneasy. It was a feeling he only got when starting a new investigation. He quickly pulled on a thick brown cotton sweat shirt, old faded jeans, and a pair of light weight walking shoes. He felt closed in with almost a desperate need to get into the open air. He selected a small pistol and slipped it along with a cell phone into a waist pack, wrapped it loosely around the outside of his clothes and pressed the Velcro closed. On his way out, he took a bottle of water from the refrigerator and chugged it down. adding another to his hiking pack along with a house key.

Now, which way should he go? He decided to check on the new neighbor. Without Henry to tell him, he didn't know what to expect

He took the path along the cliff's edge which meandered uphill and down before reaching the next property line. He still felt uneasy yet no sharp threat of danger. Danger had its own cat's claws that would rake his mind, now they were sheathed. Standing on an outcrop, sharp wind in his face, he smelled the rain in the dark clouds overhead. This would be a short hike or he would be walking in a rain storm.

Stepping over some low growing plants, he followed a narrow path he knew well until he came to a point where he could see the back of his neighbor's house. The landscape there was overgrown, neglected. Normally the garden was well tended and designed to follow the seasons. It had a curving stone path down to a pool set in a depression well back from the cliff. As he turned to go, his outline lost in shadow, a woman came from the house clutching the hand of a little boy, so, he waited. She was carrying a child's backpack, and practically dragging the child along the path ... Hmm, he thought she's a little brutal. Are they going for a hike?

He did not have long to wait. As soon as they reached the swimming pool, the woman, wearing a wide brimmed hat and loose red cardigan, looked up from under the brim of the hat and scanned the forests. She was young and attractive with brown hair that swung to points along her jaw line. Satisfied with her perusal of the forest, she walked the child to the deep end of the pool. The day was crisp and cold yet the boy wore no jacket. She looked up at the sky, now overcast with dark clouds, lowered her gaze furtively scanning her surroundings, but did not see Max in the shadowy thicket. And then, in one smooth motion, she picked up the child and threw him into the pool. She waited long enough to see him sink to the bottom, turned and ran back up the path to the house.

Max instantly loosed the waist pack and was pulling off his sweat shirt dropping them as he slid down the incline struggling through rough brush to get to the pool. The boy could not swim or she would not have thrown him in the pool. The child was desperately pulling at the water trying to get to the surface and making a bad job of it. As Max neared the pool he heard the roar of an engine and the screeching of tires as a car wheeled out onto the road.

In the pool, the boy was losing the fight. Running all out Max dived in, grabbed the boy and pulled him to the surface, and blew air in his lungs as he kicked his way to the side, where he hefted the boy onto the pool surround, and lifted his own body up by the pool's edge. The boy was limp, he cleared his airways and started a gentle artificial respiration, stopping only when the boy took a deep breath and vomited water. Holding him in a sitting position, he listened as the boy coughed and vomited more water, his eyes wide open, a panicked expression on his face. As their eyes met, he whispered, "Thank . . . you . . . sir, she . . . she threw me in . . .

"Who was she?"

Tears came from the lad's eyes when he said "My Mother."

"Your mother? Why would she want to kill you?"

"Too . . . much trouble," He whispered.

Max lifted the boy, and climbed back up through the rough brush. He picked up his sweat shirt, wrapped it around the boy, and snagged his waist pack. Not sure what to do, knowing the woman had left, he strode the narrow path, back to the main trail, and still carrying the boy, ran all the way back to his house.

He stood the boy on a bench in the kitchen, removed his wet clothes, and wrapped him in a large beach towel, drying his hair. He hugged the child and assured him he was now safe. He really wanted to tell him it would be all right. But it would not be all right, not for him, not ever! Instead, he sat him on the padded seat of the breakfast nook, and to make sure he was warm enough, wrapped him in a wool blanket. All the while, thinking, what the heck am I going to do for the child? He removed his own dripping jeans, slipped into a dry pair of walking shorts, and a loose blue wool sweater. He was taking cups down to make hot chocolate when Henry and Woolfie came home. The little dog had such an excited fit it would not settle down until Max had given it his full attention. Then the dog followed the smell of the boy to the table and started barking. Henry picked up the dog and asked "Do we have a guest, Max?"

"Do you know him, Henry?"

"No, never seen him before. However, our new neighbor has a son, I have been told, but I have not met her or her son."

Max nodded, "The good neighbor threw him in the pool, and then left. So I plucked him out and brought him home. I need time to decide what to do."

An expression of horror skewed Henry's face. "She what?"

Max nodded, and repeated "She threw him in the pool and left and from the sound of the engine; I would say she is driving a Porsche 360.

The first time Max met Henry was in Paris. Henry was a homeless alcoholic when he found Max unconscious in an alley behind a night club. He had pulled Max into a deep doorway, and poured the last of his whiskey into the wound on Max's back, which brought him screaming back to consciousness. He wrapped the shaking man in his own overcoat. When two men came looking for their drunk friend, an American, they said, Henry told them the man had staggered into the street and a taxi picked him up.

When he was sure they well out of sight, he said "You are much trouble American. Now I will have to move. You have money, yes?" Max had only

nodded. "I take you to healer. Can you stand?"

"Help me up, I will try." His old coat hid the blood on Max's back, and they staggered down the street like two old drunks holding each other up, until they reached the steps of a townhouse where Henry slammed the brass knocker against the lion's head, and a servant opened the door.

"We need the physician."

"I saw the jeep when I opened the garage, so knew you were here. Step aside, I will do that, you will make a mess of my kitchen. What is the boy's name?"

"Have you met your new neighbor?"

"Observed them on the road, not people I want to know."

The boy looked up at Henry, and said, "She threw me in the pool." There was a puzzled expression on his little face.

"I believe you boy, but you will be safe here with us. Are you warm enough?"

"The boy nodded.

"Max, he is still in shock."

"I was making hot chocolate for him when you came in."

Henry put a cup into the automatic pod coffee maker and soon hot chocolate flowed into the mug he placed under the spout. He put a big marshmallow on top and poured cold cream in to cool it some and put it down in front of the boy. Drink that young man, and you will feel much better. How old are you and what is your name?

"Benjie Renning. I am four years old. My Daddy is dead."

"How long ago did your Dad die?"

"I was two years old and now I am four and have a nanny." And then, he concentrated on drinking the warm chocolate.

"Thank you."

"Henry, the blue room, do you think?"

"Yes! Anyone would have to pass both of our rooms to get to him."

"Benjie, I think you should stay with us until we find out why your mother did such a thing. I will go check on your nanny. You stay here with Henry and Woolfie. Henry is a doctor so if you don't feel well let him know, and if you get hungry tell him. He is a great cook. Try to sleep. You are safe here, believe me no one will hurt you while you are with us. Okay?'

Benjie just nodded, and Max picked him up and carried him up the stairs, showed him where the adjoining bathroom was and tucked the boy into bed in what they called the Blue Room.

"Will you tell her where I am?" Benjie asked real fear reflected in his eyes.

"No Benjie No one will know you are here unless you want them to know, or I decide to tell them. Even then, I will ask you first. Do you have any grandparents?"

The boy thought a second or two, "No."

"Max smiled, you have two very strong uncles now to protect you. So sleep

well and tomorrow will be a better day, I promise."

Benjie attempted a smile as he snuggled down under the covers.

Back downstairs, Max said, "Henry, Benjie swallowed some pool water and threw up twice. I pumped him pretty good but some may have gotten into his lungs. What do you think?"

"I checked his eyes, and I'll go up in a few minutes and listen to his lungs. Don't worry; I'll check him during the night to make sure his lungs are clear. He will have my complete attention. Go! Find out what that evil bitch is up to."

Max changed into dark clothes and slipped the Browning into the back band of his jeans. He took the path back toward the neighbor's house, this time he took the main path from the bluff down to the pool and followed the walkway up to the house. Toys were strewn along the path, a stage set. The back door was standing open. He found a woman probably in her forties, passed out in a chair, the nanny he assumed. The wide brimmed hat and red sweater casually thrown on the sofa, were obviously hers. He checked her heart beat. It was strong and steady, she smelled of whiskey. Either drunk or drugged or both. He thought and figured she would wake up before long. He decided to let her make the report on the missing boy. He checked for cameras, found three but they were turned off. Of course the mother would not want her dirty deed recorded. He left as silently as he entered.

It was the next morning when the police rang the doorbell. Henry answered as Max and Benjie sat watching cartoons upstairs. Max turned the sound down and shushed Benjie.

"We're looking for a little boy, Benjie Renning. He lives down the road from you. He wandered away from his nanny. Have you seen him? He is four years old with blue eyes and brown hair."

"Was no one watching him?" Henry asked. "This is a dangerous area for a child, considering the cliffs and woods.'

"His nanny put him down for a nap and fell asleep herself. When she woke he was gone, the back door was open, and toys were on the walkway that leads to the pool, but the boy has disappeared, his mother is frantic."

Listening on the intercom, Max, thought Yeah I'll bet she is, wondering who saw her try to murder her son, and wondering when she will get the blackmail letter. Henry walked outside with the policemen, and asked, "Have you checked below the cliffs?"

288

"Yeah, there's a search group down there now. If he fell, the high tide would have washed him out to sea. However, they are looking for any sign he fell.

 Did you hear anything late yesterday?"

"Sorry" Henry said, "I was in town shopping, returned around five. Mr. Max came in from the airport about the same time. What time did the boy go missing?"

"We aren't sure. The nanny said she put him down for his nap at two. She fell asleep, and didn't wake up until the boy's mother and a friend came home at six."

"Can I speak with Mr. MacArley? I'm Detective Brown and have met him before. Is he here?"

"Sure, I'll call him down." Henry stepped over to the intercom and said, "Max, can you hear me?'

"A minute later they all heard a "Yeah, I can hear you, what's up.'

"The police are here; a neighbor's child is missing. They want to know if

you noticed anything when you came home yesterday. Can you come down and talk with them?"

"Be right there." He turned off the intercom and whispered to Ben. "If they

find you are here, they will take you back to your mother. Do you want that?"

Ben shook his head vigorously no.

"Then stay here and be very quiet."

After the police left, Max, knew why he lied. Due to his line of work, he could not afford to have his picture plastered on the front page of the newspapers. He would have to find another way to solve this crisis. Without his witness they would just return Benjie to his mother giving her another chance to kill him. Why would a mother want to kill a child? Only an evil woman would do such a thing. So it must be a case of inherited money she would get once he was dead and it would have to be accidental. She had set the nanny up to take the fall. Simplicity in itself, or was it? Nothing, he thought, was ever simple. He went to his computer and looked up Benjamin Renning. What he found was very interesting. Benjie's dad was killed in a car accident. His wife was at a meeting at lodge where they were staying on vacation in Ireland. The information continued. His first wife had died from complications during childbirth. Benjie was two years old when his Dad married. So the brunette was not really Benjie's birth mother.

He called his office, a woman answered, "Select Investigations."

"Hello Molly, anything interesting happening?"

Molly squealed, "Max! You're back! Are you all right? We have been worried sick, reading the news."

"Yep, I'm back and in one piece. You can send the bill and add 40 percent hazard pay, plus the expenses I have already emailed to you. They did not tell us the true nature of the job. Now I want you to do something for me. Look up all the information you can find on a Benjamin Renning. He was killed three years ago while on vacation in Ireland. What happened to his wife and who got custody of their son? Get everything you can, even if it seems irrelevant, and get back to me ASAP."

"Max that is the name of a missing boy. It came in this morning on the police report."

"Yes, but if anyone wants to know why you are inquiring, just tell them you are following up on the report should we be retained to find the boy. Do not mention my name or my interest in the case. Okay?"

"Got it! Are you coming into the office today?"

"Not for a while. I'm taking a vacation."

"Damn, Max, you're hurt aren't you?"

"A few scratches, is all. Now get on that report and let me know as soon as you can. I'll call back later today, don't call me."

"I got your report yesterday. And, John is working a new a new job around the corner. So business is good."

"Okay, talk with you later today." He called down to Henry, "Henry, do you have plans for tonight?"

"Just a date with my lady friend, dinner at Harry's, if you need me I can cancel."

"No, Tillie would wring my neck. When are you two going to get married?'

"When you retire."

"Well, I am seriously considering retirement after that last job. So make your plans."

"Not until you find someone to take care of you. By the way I told the realtor if the house where Benjie lived comes on the market, I want you to buy it for me."

"You have certainly earned it, Henry, and more. I couldn't have a better friend."

"Can't bring yourself to say Butler, can you."

"Henry, doctors are not butlers."

"Humph, right now I'm a chef, lunch is ready."

It was three o'clock before Molly called back with the information on Benjie. "Max, that little boy has had a lot of bad luck. His mother died when he was born. His father married his secretary two years later, her name is Mancy Trent. Of course, I did a check on her and did not find out much. Her background proved normal; although, she was not well liked by her co-workers, but no one could say why. According to the police report, the nanny said she seemed very devoted to the little boy and never abused him in any way. That could be because he inherited a fortune from his father and grandfather. Other than the businesses the rest is in trust funds, the investments overseen by a law firm. There was a pre-nup Trent just inherited the house, car, and a yearly allowance, which should be enough for anyone after a two-year marriage. I checked her credit cards and she has debt but nothing her income won't cover. She likes jewelry and has bought quite a bit this past year. The trust fund pays the nanny and all the boy's expenses, so Trent only has her own expenses. Unless there is something not showing up in my inquiry, she does not seem to be in enough debt to want to do the boy harm."

"What happens to all the money if the boy accidentally dies?"

"We need a copy of the father's will."

"Max, you might talk with the nanny. She is under suspicion and may say more to clear her name. Perhaps she held back when the police questioned her.

I'll keep looking; see what I can dig up on Trent's childhood."

"Do that. I know she is guilty. Don't ask me how. So there must be something there to find."

"I'll stay on it and let you know if I find anything of interest. "

"Molly, did the police report say how long the nanny had worked for her and if there were other nannies before. Get any and all names and addresses etc. I want to know where she went to school. Talk with people Mancy worked with her before the marriage, those who socialized with her, who still know her. Who does she see, does she have a boyfriend, etc. Were there any questions about Benjie's father's accident? You know the drill, go for it now."

Jock devised the perfect plan, but now something has gone wrong. He was the only one who knew the day and time of the planned accident. Did Jock double cross her? Her mind raced through all the possibilities. Tuesdays, the neighbor's butler went into town to shop, or to see his girlfriend. So he would not a suspect in the boy's disappearance.

Did someone see her throw the boy into the pool? She had scanned the forest with binoculars before taking the boy to the pool, and waited for the sky to become overcast. There she had looked carefully all around. She walked the floor pulling at her hair, almost hysterical wondering what happened to the boy's body? He was as good as dead when she went back to the house and he could not swim.

She made sure he did not learn to swim, so he could not have got out of that pool by himself. This had been in the planning for two years, and someone had cut out a link in her chain. If there was no body, the nanny would still be blamed for neglect if not for murder. Everything had gone like clockwork, until the boy's body disappeared. Someone, somehow, had taken the boy's

293

body. Could it have floated to the surface and a bear or cougar drug it out? Or, perhaps, someone was waiting for her to inherit the fortune due her, and would then contact her and demand money. There was nothing she could do but wait, and the tension of not knowing was wearing her down. She couldn't call Jock again, by now, her phone would be tapped by the police. It would look bad if she started asking about the inheritance at this point. Besides, she already knew, she would get it all.

As worried as she was, Jock was much more worried. Stealing fifty-billion, seemed so easy when he planned it three years ago. Now someone had thrown a wrench in the well-oiled machinery. Was Mancy Trent trying to double cross him? She seemed sincerely scared earlier when they discussed the boy's disappearance. She had done what they planned, and her alibi was tight. However; if she cracked would she give him up? Of course she would, he well understood human nature, and she was the only weak link in his plan. He had always known a time would come when she would have to be eliminated. Perhaps now was that time. Whoever took the child would see how useless blackmail would be if she were dead. He had made plans for any contingency, except for a disappearing boy's body.

Detective Andy Brown pulled his Taurus to a stop behind a pickup truck at the red light at Willow and Main. He was in the turn lane so was shocked when a

car pulled around him driving on the sidewalk. He caught a glimpse of a pretty brunette before the car passed the pickup truck and bounced off the curb and into the busy intersection. He gritted his teeth, as he heard the crash and the pickup slammed back into the grill of his Taurus. He turned off the ignition, and pushed at the door thumbing his cell for 911.

Max turned on the news before sitting down to steak and eggs Henry had prepared for breakfast. Henry almost dropped the carafe of coffee when the news flashed to a story of an accident at the intersection of Willow and Main. Benjie was still sleeping. Both men sat riveted watching the news as the story unfolded.

Last night, the widow of billionaire Benjamin Renning was killed when she drove her Porsche into traffic at the intersection of Willow and Main. The accident was witnessed by Detective Andy Brown who was waiting for the light to change. She drove past him on the sidewalk and out into the intersection. It happened so fast no one could have stopped her. Her car was broadsided by a dump truck which skidded into a pickup truck in front of Detective Brown sending it back into the Detective's Taurus.

Trying to remember the expression on the woman's face, Brown said she seemed calm, he only got a glimpse of the side of her face, so could not say for sure what her expression or emotions could have been. Her stepson recently went missing from the family home on Torkay Bluff when Mrs. Renning was not home. The child's nanny is being charged with neglect. No reason has yet been found for Mrs. Renning's odd behavior. Perhaps losing her husband and stepson was a factor in her death. An autopsy has been ordered. More news as it is released by the police.

Max sat stunned for a moment, thinking whoever planned this job, was clever, and cleaning house. He leaned back and said, "I have a theory, Henry, and want your advice.

"I can't tell the police what I saw without my picture being splashed on the news. So, I've been thinking what if . . ..

"What if an attorney handling a rich man's will, and knowing all the man owned, thought wow, what I could do with that much money! When he visits the man's office, he meets the rich man's secretary and on a whim asks her out. He gets to know her, and learns she is a greedy little bitch. He suggests she could do well to marry the lonely widower and become a rich wife. So she comes on to the man and he falls for her and marries her, but he isn't dumb. He has another lawyer draw up a pre-nup. She agrees to it as she had been advised by first lawyer, because that lawyer now has a plan. Once the greedy bitch has married the lonely widower, he will set up an accident and although the greedy bitch won't inherit all the man's money and estate, his son will. She will be fixed for life with a yearly allowance and get custody of his two-year-old son. After two years of marriage, rich man has an accident in his auto and makes the big jump. Wife only inherits the house, car, and a generous yearly allowance. Son inherits all which is in trust funds and businesses, etc. With no other living relatives, if son dies all goes to stepmom. But that is a sticky wicket. If anything happens to the boy the stepmom will be suspect and get nothing, so she hires a nanny she discovers has a secret drinking problem. Stepmom and lawyer decide after two years, to set up an accidental demise for son and lay the blame on the nanny's neglect. All goes as planned except the boy disappears from the pool. Now, there is a big rip in the fabric of their scheme. Where is the boy or the body? Did he actually drown, or did someone save him, is the boy dead or alive? Not knowing what happened to the boy gets stickier each day for the planners, and the police start looking not only at the nanny but the stepmom as well. Will her alibi hold up? You with me so far?"

"Yeah, Max I'm getting the drift."

"Okay, no body, and a missing boy, this sends fear through the lawyer's well laid plan. A fear of discovery reflecting on him sends his mind seeking all possibilities. Did someone see the widow throw the boy in the pool? Did they save him? Is he dead? Where is his body? Off the cliff and washed out to sea?

296

What happened to the little boy and where is he? That someone has deliberately ripped a big hole in his well laid plan causes the greedy lawyer look for a way out. Will the widow hold the fort or will she break and point a finger at him? Now he needs to cover his tracks. No one knows his affiliation with the widow is anything but business, except the widow, so she has to go, but how? With her out of the way, his law firm will take over the missing boy's estate and administer it to the best of their ability. He only has to take care of that one small rip."

Max stops to eat some breakfast, sips his coffee, and continues.

"Henry, I can't go to the police with my hypothesis as I can't take the publicity. However, I hope you won't mind, I have invited Agent Loren for dinner tonight. The boy's inheritance spans three continents, so I think his advice on the subject and his subsequent closing of the case will get him a raise and me off the hook. So Henry, what do you think of my hypothesis?"

"My only question is who will get custody of Benjie. He will be a full time job for someone. Maybe for a man who wants to retire and do a lot of fishing?"

That night, Max and Agent Loren talked for a long time. Max took him upstairs to look in on Benjie. Then Loren made some calls and set up a quiet investigation. The first thing Agent Loren did was talk with members of the law firm who handled the Renning account.

That was only a few days before the accident at Willow and Main. And for Benjie's sake Max agreed to give a statement of what he had seen happen. The hardest thing for him to do was turn the boy over to the court. His reputation was considered, and the damage the publicity would do to his livelihood was considered. Since Mrs. Renning was dead, no charges were filed and the boy to be placed in a good home where he would be protected.

297

An oversight group was appointed by the court to take care of his inheritance until he came of age 21.

Returning home Max was not happy. However, the court had handled Benjie's situation in the legal manner that would be to the boy's benefit.

As he and Henry sat before the fire, already missing Benjie, Max said.

"Well, Henry, this has been an unusual homecoming. I sometimes wonder about my decision to go for a walk, as tired and sore as I was. Occasionally, in my line of work, a miracle does occur, which surprises this jaded warrior. This time, someone up there was looking out for Benjie, maybe his real mother and father were doing all their spiritual bodies could to protect their son. Although Benjie is now safe and protected, I surprised myself by asking the judge for a twice yearly visit from the boy. I want to be sure he is being well cared for in every way. And I have been doing some soul searching. People talk about women when getting older realize their reproductive clock is ticking. Do we men also go through a time when we want to leave something of ourselves behind? Do we ache for a son or daughter? With Benjie, I realized what was missing from my life. I wasn't seeking a new future; I think I am really yearning for a family."

"Max, you do need a family. You just need to get out more and meet women. What about Molly, she knows you well and as you have said, she is a beautiful woman."

"I can't say I have not been attracted to her, but we don't really know each other. I'm getting maudlin, let's change the subject."

"Did they autopsy show the Trent woman was drugged?"

"I'm still waiting for the autopsy report. They are checking for any drugs since I don't think she was the kind to commit suicide. As jaded as I have become, it still amazes me when people decide to do evil. When I take on a new job, I first check my mental recipe file of evil, try to find which recipe this particular perp's are using. After years in this business, I could write the book. Very seldom do I conduct an investigation that brings out a new or unusual recipe. The trick would be to catch them before they kill. Since no one has that kind of foresight, I can only see they pay for their crime, and that keeps me working."

"Molly called, said to ask if you are ready for another job. I invited her to dinner on Sunday."

"You did! Did she accept?"

"She said she would be delighted."

Well that should be an interesting interlude. What are you serving?"

"Does it matter?"

"Probably not, everything you cook is great."

"A detective Brown called, said to call him back before noon tomorrow."

"Detective Brown found Mancy's cell phone in her crushed car. There were several calls made to one of the lawyers of the firm handling the family's account. He could be the planner, the one who set up a hit on Benjie's Father. Brown plans to quietly investigate that particular man. If he was the planner in this sick farce, he may never be charged. It will be hard to find solid evidence.

"Sunday, huh! That should be interesting."

SIR SALSA

By

Lorraine Sullivan

poetic proverb: into each life some salsa must fall
Therefore, appear, Sir Salsa,
my flavorful friend,
my gourmet guru.
Cajole with your seasoned serendipity.
Come capriciously
With your palatable poems.
I open your jar
of hot jelly bean juices
spoons of savory salsa
filled with spicy similes
and multicolored metaphors.
Sometimes your words spill
like hurtful hugs
or tempestuous tears
or intimate images
or dangerous dances.
Always they pleasantly provide
flavorful word confetti to my mind
and surprising spicy sauce
to satiate my senses.
As I close your poetic container,
lingering lines rest with me,
still tempting my cerebral tongue.
I relish the remembrances
and tastes of your mind.
So stay, my succulent Sir Salsa,

EFFIE

By

Margaret Chester

Hi, my name is Effie I was born in 1888 in Milton County Georgia and lived until I was seventy-three years old. The world changed quite a bit from the time I was born until my time on earth ended in 1961. My mother, Mary, was a proud and strong woman who, despite raising nine children, milked the cows and fed the hogs. Life, in the time I was born, was simple but required hard work. I loved watching my mother cook the meals early in the morning and keeping them warm on the pot belly stove. I learned to cook, sew, farm and take care of the farm animals. We would go to my grandfather's church every Sunday without fail. This is where I met my husband to be, Chelsey, as well as, friends who I kept in touch with for the rest of my life. I married in 1910 and with his love and support bore ten children, eight of who lived to reach adulthood. My husband was able to find work in Atlanta at the newly constructed Ft. McPherson under the government program, WPA, which supplied jobs for the unemployed during the great depression.

We felt very lucky to live and have him work in Atlanta, where we felt prosperous with our family. Unfortunately, he died when he touched a live wire with a metal spade. I was heartbroken, and was left with children, still in their teens, to support on my own. My brother-in-law offered me a house next door to where my beloved husband and I had lived. I was faced with a choice that I had never thought about before, how to support a family without the financial support of my husband. The only job I could think of at the time was taking in laundry from around our community to make ends meet. It was not easy, but somehow we managed to make it without starving.

I was able to manage raising a family during the Great Depression, when the world as we knew it was very poor. Everyone struggled to provide enough food to feed their families. Living in Atlanta, the world did not seem as poverty stricken as the rest of the country because the city had learned to diversify into such areas as paper mills, pencil factories, military bases, and auto factories. People in the more rural areas were forced to send their children to textile factories where they worked six hours a day while also attending school. As a general rule, these children wore no shoes and worked in very dusty and dirty conditions. Often they would develop brown lung, from the fibers in the factories and die horrible deaths

Yes, I felt very lucky to be living in Atlanta, where my husband and I helped to build a church a block away from our house. We loved to share our lives with our church members in good times and in bad. I don't know what I would have done without my church family when my husband died.

When WWII was declared, after Japan bombed Pearl Harbor, most of my children were grown but the country felt the pressure to help in the war effort. I was proud that one of my daughters decided to work for Western Union, a company vital during that time, helping the war effort in communications.

Although things began to change after WWII was over, I remained the same. I still used a two-eyed stove that ran off of coal that not only cooked but served as the heat that I used in my two-story-house. My only constant reading was the Bible, that I read every day and shared with my church friends. My son-in-law and I would argue viewpoints of religion whenever we got together. I really enjoyed our debates. When my granddaughter, Evelyn, came over and stayed a few days I enjoyed cooking her favorite foods and talking to her in the kitchen. She would tell me how loved and comfortable she felt with me in my kitchen.

Now I look back on my life and how things have changed during my seventy-three years. Starting off we lived a comfortable life in a farming area with my grandfather as a minister and eating all the food we grew. My life was very structured. Each family member knew what was expected of them, everyone simply did what they were supposed to do. I marvel at the technology that has made my children's lives much easier and better. I washed clothes by hand, then hung them on a clothes line. My children have automatic washers and dryers. I listened to my stories every day on the radio. I enjoyed meeting with my women friends to work on different quilts and catch up on all of the current news. I canned fresh vegetables from the garden and went to the small stores near me for all my staple supplies. My children watch television and travel to grocery stores to buy their food. I walked everywhere I wanted to go; my children drive their shiny new cars. The doctor who treated me lived two blocks away and even did house calls. As I grew older and had more problems, my children would take me, in their shiny new cars, to different doctors and hospitals in the area. I am really glad I was born in a rural area where people helped and stuck by each other, not like the later years when people were more concerned about material things. I had a good and fulfilling life surrounded by my children, grandchildren and great grandchildren.

REVELATIONS

By

Eunice L. Sykes

Tieing a tie to a man

Is like putting on makeup to a woman

It begins at a young age

And you're always trying to get it right.

MUSINGS FOR YOUTH

By

Eunice L. Sykes

On excellence: Set your expectations high

Don't settle for mediocrity.

In the school of life, strive to be an "A" student

You have to be!

"C" players sit the bench.

What's great about being African American?

You can dance both ways.

Child of mine calls it "toggling."

Don't fall prey… know!

WHERE DID ALL THE JUNK COME FROM?

By

Carol G. Vetula

Have you ever wondered where all your household junk really comes from? Or, why you had to saved it? When you get right down to it, probably half of the stuff sitting in your house, in the closets, pushed back into drawers, and of course, the "good" things packed away for the future in the shed or garage, all could be eliminated with very little damage done to your lifestyle now, or in the near future.

This enlightening fact fell upon me, recently, when we found it necessary to pay for a household move across the country. Always before, our precious belongings were packed and moved by a company at the expense of my husband's employer. And they allowed us to take it all. I did clean out a few drawers and managed to have a garage sale, thus eliminating from our lives, a few unnecessary items, but with these few exceptions everything else went along to the new homes … until now.

When it became evident we were going to be paying the bill for this move, we quickly decided we could live without a lot of the precious junk linked to our lives. So we had a garage sale! And this sale would surpass any twelve-family garage sale ever held. It was amazing what we found we had not been able to live without.

The piano, I suppose, was the hardest thing to let go. This dear member of our family had been with us for over twenty years, dragged around from city to city, crossing the country at least twice, had been in storage more than once, and had put up with more than five sets of hands learning to make fingers, brains and piano keys all come together at the same time with some reasonable sound. But this piano, in spite of everything, was nearly in perfect condition. And it should have been. I took very good care of it. Also, no one played it any more, at least, not for the past twelve years after our daughter, Diana, moved away. It was, however, assured a good future. The young woman who bought it played beautifully in her trial of it, and almost cried for joy when we agreed on a price.

Besides all the "like new" furniture we sold, I shed only a few tears over most items I had to sort, classify and price. There seemed to be about a thousand other goodies I placed in our garage sale. Well, it seemed like that many at the time.

And only I was capable to make these dreaded decisions. My dear husband, always asked the same type of questions. "Do we really need three sets of round cake pans?" Or, "What is this thing, and do we still need it?"

It was hard to admit to him that I hadn't baked a real cake in years, and as it was quite doubtful we would ever again own a square tub Maytag wringer washing machine, it was probably safe to throw away the knob from the old lid of the last one.

As we dig deeper into our belongings, and into our hearts, we found we could possibly live without six cartons of books, some of which never had been opened in fifteen years. The faded copies of well-used Golden Books, the complete years and years of monthly Reader's Digest magazines, and several volumes of books on raising tropical fish. Can you believe I hadn't any idea where half of the stuff came from? And I swear, some of it I never saw before.

My sweet, generous, mother, who was always giving things to us, has contributed a lot, as well as the rest of my family. Have I have been doing the same thing to our kids? I do enjoy picking up small items I'm sure they will love and try and use. Like this flower pot I bought for our daughter, Kelly. It is sort of a ceramic sneaker pot formed to look old and with frayed laces. I thought it was really her. After all, she was into jogging.

Now, however, I have been granted a new start. All the old junk has been sold, given away, or trashed, and I will never, never allow this fate to happen again. I will just have to stay from the flea markets, department stores, and my mother.

END

LOVE'S WONDER

By

Delores L Staton

she sat by the window quiet like,
Her demeanor calm, unlaced.
She looked into the deep, blue night.
Her hands in her lap, gently placed.

Her lips moved in serene worship,
Her eyes closed in simple piety.
Her breath came and went, lyrically.
The gentle, long, slow rise and fall of her bosom
revealed a painful schism.

As I watched, I asked myself
Should I offer compassion to this beautiful one, candidly bereft.
As I hesitated, insecure in my assumption.
the beautiful one turned in my direction.
She held out her hand, inviting my embrace.
I leaned over, lifted her up, touched my lips to her face.

I looked down as I felt her sway.
Emboldened by the warmth of our closeness,
I closed my eyes
and kissed her
up-turned smile.

SUMMERS PAST

By

C. J. F. Mobley

Ah, summer! Every child loves that glorious time of year when school doors close to welcome those long hours of sunshine that linger until bedtime. I can remember those summer mornings when I could sleep late, the yellow school bus on hiatus in the bus barn, but I never wanted to lounge in bed past sunrise. There was too much to see and do!

My ten-speed bike, the best transportation for a twelve-year-old, waited patiently for my arrival in the garage for our daily neighborhood jaunts. Up the street I'd peddle, as fast as my feet could move me to meet with the other kids that lived on my street. Such grand adventures awaited us in the woods behind my house or the creek that ran behind the houses opposite mine. There were numerous trees to climb or turtles to catch.

My mama did not like for me to go to the creek. Not because she feared I'd fall in, but because of the water moccasins that lived close by. I would always skip that part of my day when hunger forced me to return home for lunch, my mom asking what I'd been doing as she fixed me a tomato sandwich. Belly full and rested, I'd head back out the door to go watch the water striders glide across the surface of the creek or snatch up a frog.

Summer was always a marvelous time, even when Mama would pack a suitcase for my sister, Linda and I before shipping us off to my grandmother's house for three weeks during the summer. My granny, as we called her, lived in Savannah, Georgia, a good 300 miles from our home in the Atlanta suburbs. I loved spending time with my Granny, for it was a true vacation from the rules my mother enforced as proper behavior for Southern girls—no shoes, no baths, and no bedtime! Granny only enforced such horrid rituals if we were going out in public.

My Grandmother lived on a fixed income so we did not visit the tourist spots along River Street or Tybee Island. Long before the days of computers, satellite television, and video games that eat away the hours of today's youth, my sister and I were expected to create our own entertainment on those long summer days when classes were suspended. There were myriad ways to enjoy the summer hours away from our closest friends. Outdoors, we played kickball, dodge ball, or hide and seek with other children in the neighborhood. Hauling our bikes to Savannah was out of the question, but Linda and I sported wheels in the form of shiny metal skates that strapped onto our shoes.

Jacks, Chinese checkers, and paper dolls were all standard entertainment paraphernalia for when typical afternoon thundershowers sprang up from the ever-present humidity of the American South. In the evening, we could be found relocating lightning bugs to a new home in a mason jar, which we promised to release come morning. Afterwards, the three of us spent hours playing gin rummy while we sipped coffee or rather the original café lattes my grandmother made. When we tired of cards, we scrutinizing jigsaw puzzle pieces until every piece fit into place.

My granny didn't drive so we had to walk everywhere we went, but she lived close enough to all the modern day conveniences like the IGA, a produce market, and Woolworth's Drugs. She would insist we walked to the grocery store in the morning, "Before it gets too hot," she'd say. Linda and I never noticed the summer heat as we followed behind our granny. We were too busy looking for a coin on the sidewalk or a soda bottle carelessly tossed from a car window. A returned pop bottle would get us a nickel, all we needed for the five and dime store. It's amazing to think back on how little money one needed to buy a treasure. Linda and I usually sported a

lovely new ring made from the finest pink or red plastic for which we spent five whole cents each, a sacrificial splurge for the sake of fashion.

Candy was an even better deal. Bazooka bubblegum, BB bats, Mary Jane's, Now or Later's, and pixie sticks went for the whopping price of a penny each. Finding a quarter was as good as robbing a bank. Of course, Granny had a piggy bank she kept especially for our visits. She would give us a fifty-cent piece before walking with us to the corner store. Emerging from the store, pockets and mouths crammed with candy, Granny would make us put the rest of our stash away until after dinner.

I remember how Granny loved to cook for us. She had an aluminum cookware set with lids which had a circular vent on top. The little vent flap would vibrate up and down as steam rose from whatever dish she was cooking. The tinkling sound let us know she was busy in the kitchen.

I had so many favorite dishes that she would prepare. One I recall vividly is creamed corn. She would lead my sister and me down to the local farmer's market where she would pick out a dozen or so ears of fresh, yellow corn. Once home, Linda and I would help shuck the corn while she fried bacon. She would cut the corn kernels off the cob, dump them in a little bacon grease, and then add a little water. While the corn simmered, she would stew tomatoes and cook a pot of rice. Linda and I would snitch a slice of bacon when Granny wasn't looking. Most of the time, she would shoo us out of the kitchen to play cards while she tended to her pots and pans. Later, Linda and I watched expectantly as she added heavy cream to the corn. Granny let us "help" her cook by assigning the task of crumbling the fried bacon. We would drop the crumbled pork belly into the corn. It had a glorious summer smell, like those

311

of fresh cut grass and afternoon rain which, can only be appreciated on a hot summer day.

My Granny did not send us to bed by the hour stated on the clock rather Linda and I could stay awake as long as we could keep our eyes open. After dinner, Granny would sit on the front porch while Linda and I played in the yard in the evening twilight. When we tired of that, we would go inside and play cards. It didn't take long for my eyes to start drooping and my mind to start wandering in the direction of "La La Land", always falling asleep before my sister did.

I always hated the day when we had to leave and head back home. Leaving signaled the fast-approaching end of our carefree summer days and the coming regiment dictated by the local school board. A new school year was just around the corner.

Now, I am grown and for different reasons, summer is still the best time of year. My Granny is long gone from me, and now I sit on the front porch watching my children catch lightning bugs in the evening twilight, the scent of fresh cut grass lingering in the warm air. Small hands help me in the kitchen, crumbling bacon into the fresh creamed corn that simmers in my Granny's aluminum pan, the little lid plays its tinkling tune as we play cards.

NOW LISTEN! WHIMSY, WIT AND WISDOM FOR THE AGES

By

Eunice L. Sykes

Nonagenarians—people who are ninety years old and up—are an ever increasing segment of our population. Many are active, charming, engaging vibrant, enthusiastic, upright, thriving, and spry! They have wisdom to share and stories to tell; their slice of history. My willing role models who don't want to take their whimsy, wit, and wisdom with them when they leave earth are Essie Mae Lynch, Worthy Coe Hamling, and Ruby Sims Brown. Now listen!

~~~~~~~~~

Essie Mae Jones Lynch wasn't my first interviewee, but she was the oldest. Mrs. Lynch was the centenarian, turning one hundred years old in November, 2014. We found each other via Facebook. To my amazement, she had a lucid, bright mind, was extremely independent, and had a positive, sassy spirit. I had not seen nor talked to Mrs. Lynch, who was one of my favorite "church moms" when I was a youth, in more than thirty years. She was a woman who knew me before I even knew myself. I connected with her daughter and only child, Marian, on that popular social media internet site. Marian was a former high school business student of mine. Once I explained my project to her, we set up the interview with her mother on her mother's terms: No Facebook, no skype, no face-to-face encounters, no pictures, no face time. A telephone interview was her choice.

Sitting on my kitchen bar stool, with an outdated landline phone in speaker mode, I learned from Marian that "Momma" moved in with her five years ago. Marian warned that her mother was recovering from pneumonia and might have to occasionally stop—even end—our conversation, if necessary. I happily agreed to those terms. Marian informed me that "Momma" uses a wheelchair and a walker and remains upstairs most of the day. As Marian put it: "She is her own advocate."

"OK, let's do it!"

When I heard her mother's voice, I was awestruck at its clarity, like a finely-tuned piano. She must have read my mind.

"It's not my voice that's old; it's the body."

We laughed like old friends sharing a secret. Before we started and after squealing with delight at the sound of each other's voices, Mrs. Lynch told me, "I would not do this for anyone but you."

I was honored and blessed into momentary silence.

We began by reminiscing about our shared history, in a place called St. Peter's AME Church, on County Road, in Weirton, West Virginia. I remember Mrs. Lynch as a tall, slim, and beautiful woman, with a sweet disposition. I imagined her the same as we began our telephone conversation. She later told me she was skin and bones…Still slim, I thought. I've never known her to be heavy, slightly heavy, or anything other than tall and slim. Mrs. Lynch was still a widow, having lost her husband, Reuben, in 1967.

Born November 19, 1914, the oldest of ten siblings to Eula Broxton Jones and Lovie Jones, Mrs. Lynch willingly began our interview and, within minutes, she uttered the command "Now listen!" And she never stopped talking, nor did I sense any discomfort on her part. She was having fun; I loved her spirit.

"Now listen!" A phrase I remembered hearing these words in conversations from my youth some sixty years ago, as if the decades had not passed.

Obedient, I sat back and prepared to do so, taking copious shorthand notes. She began her story of leaving the rural south, specifically Elba, Alabama, in the 1940s at the impressionable age of twenty-eight and migrating to the burgeoning northern steel manufacturing town of Weirton, West Virginia, the hometown where I grew up. Then, she was Miss Jones, a single, fine, and sassy young adult. Other family members, including her sister, Irene, had already moved north. Most of her remaining siblings eventually trekked north and settled in the "jobs-a-plenty Ohio Valley." Her mother, Eula, died when she was twenty.

It was in Weirton that Ms. Jones met a handsome lad who also migrated there, from Lynchburg, Virginia, to find work in the burgeoning steel mills. His name was Reuben Lynch. As they began their courtship, he proudly told her, "You don't need to do anything but cook and keep house."

I laughed loudly, knowing that statement would not sit well in today's culture. They married shortly thereafter, and she loved being a housewife—cooking and keeping house.

Mrs. Lynch was nearly forty-five when she had her one and only child, Marian, born fourteen and one half years after marrying Reuben. As her body grew to accommodate the baby, she was unable to do much of anything. Her next door neighbors on Fifth Street, Willie & Lucille Salter, brought food over and placed it in the oven; Mrs. Lynch was on the couch during much of her pregnancy, exhausted. In today's terms, she endured a "high risk" pregnancy.

I moved us along to my next question, "If you knew you were going to live this long, would you do anything differently?"

"That's a good question!" she said with a laugh. "No one knows how long they are going to live. God blessed me to live this long." She paused a second. "I would travel more and see more of the world."

"What do you appreciate most?" I asked.

"All of it. I took care of my brothers. Since my mother died when I was young, as the oldest of ten children, I babysat my siblings. I didn't mind."

"How were you affected by racism and segregation?"

"My family didn't have to mix with white people.... Dad owned his own property. I knew about it (racism), but never experienced it. "

"What are two of your life's greatest moments?"

"Meeting my husband Reuben and having my daughter, Marian. She now takes care of me in my senior years. Marian's in charge. I was her mother; now she's mine!"

To my question: "What do you want people to remember about you?" She teased, "How would you answer that?"

We enjoyed another moment of laughter before she answered "That I was a do-good person and haven't hurt anyone along the way. That I have been a good example to my daughter and my two granddaughters."

"What gives you hope?"

"Living until God gets ready for me. I've never been a party person, so I don't feel like I missed out on anything much. I don't have any hobbies. These days there is not much I can do anymore. I have to hold on to the walls to get around when I'm not in wheelchair or using a walker. I guess I'm getting old! I've lost a lot of weight—I'm skin and bones now."

Then, without prodding and out of the blue, she offered this astute observation: "Policemen years ago were about protecting you. Now, they are killing you. It's not safe anymore. Not in church, not in school."

She was still a member of St. Peter's AME Church. When I mentioned her great sense of humor, she remarked that her pastor, Rev. McDaniel, told her the same thing several summers ago. Currently, she does not have any boyfriends or romantic suitors. She recently saw someone on TV sitting in a wheelchair romancing or being romanced!

"Gives me hope!"

We laugh heartily.

"I am reminded of your mom when you laugh, Eunice."

I was delighted to hear such a personal note about my mother, who passed away over forty years ago. Before ending the call, we reminisced on one more thing—her husband singing in the church's senior choir. My mother was the pianist/organist, today's version of a minister of music. "He sang duets with Odessa Schaeffer." fondly remembered early worship services.

She offered a final nugget: Marian Anderson's mother told Mrs. Lynch that Reuben was her baby sister's baby boy. For those of you who don't know, Marian Anderson is the great American contralto and a celebrated singer of the twentieth-century who was the first African American to perform at the White House. Marian Anderson and Mr. Lynch were first cousins. Hearing Mrs. Lynch recall something Marian Anderson's mother said about a generation before her was heartwarming; it brought history to life for me.

"Any regrets?" was my last question for this woman of wisdom.

"I could probably go back and find something. BUT, if I have to go back that far, it doesn't matter 'cause I couldn't help it." That was good wisdom and advice for us all.

We wrapped up and once again, before we hang up, she said, "You laugh like your mother!"

I smiled from ear to ear. "I love you."

"I love you too."

Thank you, Mrs. Lynch, for that trip down memory lane. It's been a long time!

Author note: Subsequent to this interview, Mrs. Essie Mae Lynch celebrated her 100th birthday with a surprise (well, not really) birthday celebration in her honor at her daughter's home on November 29, 2014. She passed January 5, 2015. I am blessed to have spent time with her.

~~~~~~~~~~

Worthy Coe Hamling, ninety-six, is the lone male in this story. He is dapper as a participant in the Forget Me Not Luncheon series sponsored by the Atlanta, Georgia Alzheimer's Association. We met at a monthly gathering of early memory loss people and their care providers at Chili's Restaurant. He was seated on the opposite end of our long narrow table, set for twenty. Coe (rhymes like row) grabs my attention because he was standing and singing loudly to the group, but to no one in particular.

"I want a girl, just like the girl, that married dear old dad."

"He carries a tune well; he's a reasonably good singer." I said to the lady on my right, who has apparently been in his company before, "He's quite the entertainer and loves that song," she replies. Coe surveys the room. When he spots Lucretia, one of the staffers, he shouts "Hey pretty girl!"

Laughter breaks out all around.

An amusing, charming, handsome man of German descent standing about five feet, eight inches tall, Coe—he wants me to call him that—is impeccably dressed in a tweed blue-grey silk sports coat with a pocket square tossed neatly into the chest pocket, cotton linen blend tan slacks, brown alligator belt around his trim waist, a blue stripped shirt, and brown tasseled loafers. Coe, I find out, has been with his companions Brian and Jamie for eight years. My husband Don is intrigued too by this man! They strike up a conversation.

"Where you from?" Coe inquires.

"Kansas City, Kansas."

Coe chuckles. "That's where all the rich people live."

Coe turns to me with a twinkle in his eye. "He's wealthy!"

"Well," I said, "if he is, I sure don't know it!"

Lunch arrives. Coe's choice was hamburger sliders ad potato cheese soup. We eat, continue enjoying the group, and towards the end, Brian spotted a free booth away from the crowd for our interview. After we settle, Coe began by talking about having half siblings that he did not know well. He was born August 5, 1918 in South Dakota to Sadie and Albert Hamling.

" I'm a southerner!" he bragged.

As a kid (his word), he shoveled snow off the sidewalks. He also sold newspapers on the street corner, making twenty-five cents a day. He later worked in a speakeasy and had a feed business for chickens. His entrepreneurial spirit and Midwest work ethic were apparent. He always had plenty of responsibility and had been self-sufficient from an early age.

When recalling riding a horse to high school, Coe mimics the movement of riding. He was very agile, even with a cane. Betty, Coe's wife of sixty-four years, was "a wonderful person." She died recently at age ninety of Alzheimer's Disease. She spent her last few years in memory care and Coe was her primary caregiver.

Coe was known to have an occasional after-five adult drink; A vodka tonic was his drink of choice. He got plenty of exercise, including walking. He exercised all his life. He loved butter pecan ice cream. In fact, he ate it several times during the night. His favorite foods were soup and ice cream. He had few complaints, and considered himself a "lucky guy, no, a blessed one." Actually, at his core, Coe was a very humble person.

"It's quiet when he's not here," remarked one of his neighbors

"Ichabod" and "iskcabibble" are his favorite words, I call them Coeisms. His care provider, Brian, interprets them for me.

"Who cares, whatever."

One of Coe's remembrances of racism includes a local KKK burning a cross in his yard.

When speaking of a valley experience, he gets serious. "That's a good question!"

He remembers and mentions his good friend Julian McDonald.

In high school, he played football and basketball. He recalls their helmets did not have straps. He considers it a blessing that he attended Hamline University. After college, he sold flour.

"What's the role of romance at your age?" I asked him.

"It's still important. I've had quite a few girlfriends. All the women love me. I like girls better than boys."

Coe is a salesman and a singer at heart. Over the years, he's had many odd jobs. Once he was visiting travelers on a train so engrossed in selling his wares that the train left the station and he had to get off at the next stop. He obviously had the gift of gab. He spoke of his experiences at his church. He's upbeat and positive and has a sense of humor. A prankster also, in his youth he tipped over a privy (outhouse) during one Halloween night.

In his prime, he was a wholesale furniture salesman, a manufacturer's rep, selling from his car. He's always bought big cars. He still prepares his own breakfast (cheerios and sliced bananas), and says a prayer every day at noon. He willingly shared this value: "If someone is hungry, give them food."

"We (my family and I) are blessed. The Lord has taken care of us."

"Any regrets?"

"I'm a hard worker.... but that's not really a regret. I still do. Would do it again."

Coe rambled, letting me in deeper. "I have lots of cousins. I once ran over a cow. I felt obligated and paid the farmer for it."

"What's the best thing you've done?"

He ponders. "That's a good question!" His response is that he's "nurtured his family, friends, and relationships."

Coe's upbringing shaped his family closeness. His family loves him. He loves his family. He has a newborn, great grandchild. He passed on this advice to his grandchildren. "Feel responsible for yourselves, help your parents. We were poor. We had to earn money. It's important to make a contribution."

He ends our conversation with this tune: "When your hair is turned to silver, I love you just the same." I was delighted to have spent time with him.

Author's note: Worthy Coe Hamling passed October 29, 2014, months after our conversation. Our paths crossed just in time. Rest well Coe. Sing for the angels.

~~~~~~~~~

Mrs. Ruby Sims Brown, a feisty ninety-year-old, was born April 20, 1924 in Locust Grove, Georgia, to Iona Glover and William Sims. She had a clear, bright mind, was very independent, energetic, and had a vibrant spirit. I visited with her at her home in McDonough during the summer of 2014. A church mother at my place of worship, Wesley Chapel United Methodist Church, down the street from her family home, Mrs. Brown has been an usher at Wesley for more than forty-four years. Indeed, she was the organizer of the Usher Board.

Mrs. Brown married James Brown, her husband, in August, 1943, at her grandmother's home in Locust Grove. He went into the service in 1944. Her firstborn, whom she calls Junior, and whose real name was Randy, came along in 1945. When I inquired about being married to the same spouse for seventy-one years, her reply was, "I kept my mouth shut. Left the room. It

322

takes two people to argue." Wise counsel. She got her attitude from her momma. She couldn't stay mad long.

In her prime. Mrs. Brown was a homemaker. She always lived on the same piece of land: The Brown homestead. The house where her seven children were born or raised is still on the property. Midwives assisted in all their births, except her youngest. Two of her children have passed away.

The Brown family is very fruitful: Mrs. Brown is the oldest of fifteen children, nine of whom are still living. One of her sisters is in her eighties and has ten children. Growing up working in the cotton fields, Mrs. Brown, the family matriarch, shared "at the end of hoeing a row of cotton in the woods, there was another baby." Her sense of humor is intact.

Mrs. Brown regretted not getting better schooling, perhaps nurses training. Her grandma and granddad were farmers and were not able to send her to college, though she graduated high school with honors. Despite receiving scholarship awards, they were not enough to pay for college. Still, Mrs. Brown taught one year in Locust Grove. A forgiving woman, she believed in doing the right thing, treating people right, and asking for forgiveness.

Regarding her valley experiences, she had two sons who were killed, both during the 1970s.

She said she is still here because: "The Lord kept me here. I wanted to see all my children grown and did not want them to be raised by a step mom. But I asked that the Lord's will be done."

She lives for her children and her grandchildren and their families, trying to help people every day, including her husband and extended family.

Some of Mrs. Brown's greatest moments include quilting. She "pieces quilts," making her own patterns. Though her eyesight is poor, all the children and their children have quilts she made and was completing. She and her deceased daughter Christine did one together called "star." It was made of black and gold stars.

She has won prizes for food canning at local fairs. She wanted to be remembered for her smile, humility, her giving nature and for helping others.

When I asked Mrs. Brown what's important in life, her answer was simple, but profound: "Being able to move on my own. I am blessed with good health. My priorities have changed over the years and are not at the same level of importance as they were when I was thirty. Then, it was living, getting that next paycheck. Also, my church work and raising money for ministries is a priority."

When asked the role of romance, Mrs. Brown blushed, providing no answer. Then smilingly said, "It's a military secret!" She kiddingly frowned at the thought of holding Mr. Brown's hand. With seventy-three years of marriage under her belt, she offered this insight: "It's not been a bed of roses." Her legacy is absolutely family, with seven children, nine grandchildren and twelve great grandchildren.

Her final admonishment? "Smile, even when you are down. Someone cares for you.... smile."

I am smiling! I hope you are too.

WRITE FLIGHT

By

Eunice L. Sykes

When I write, I soar and take flight

It's a sojourn in which I thoroughly delight

Words spin off my head to fill the paper

If I don't write fast enough, the muse begins to taper.

Thoughts are like airplanes whizzing quickly by

Headed for destinations unknown in the sky

Eager to get to the next one before I pen

Take it to the laptop or iphone before they're in the wind

 Writer's block? No, often thoughts break seed

Just a clear, relaxed mind-- that's usually all I need

Of nothing to write, I know of no such thing

As God blesses me, to you new insights I bring

Middle Man Steal

By

Carol G. Vetula

Wayne woke suddenly, but did not move. He raised his head slowly from the sand, watching, listening, ready to fight or run for his life. The ocean sounds beyond the wall were almost a comfort. However, he could not allow himself any comforts, not just yet. The past few hours had been the hardest part of his life so far. He shifted slightly and peered around the end of the low rock wall, staring into the early morning sunrise. He saw nothing that seemed unusual.

Cautiously pulling himself up, he rubbed at the soreness in his arms and legs, and moved forward as leisurely as he could toward the street, away from the beach. Not wanting to draw attention to himself, he slipped into the movements of the early morning exercisers and achingly jogged north on highway A1A.

As he jogged, the tension and soreness began to vanish. In his well-worn tee shirt and shorts, he blended with others on the street. Even his unshaven face was not particularly out of place. At thirty-two, a man should not feel old, but the last twenty-four hours had made Wayne feel very old. He suddenly discovered time to be a precious commodity in life. Especially his life. His life was hanging by a few delicate threads. Threads that could be snipped away at any moment, if he became careless.

He continued his pace, finally turning into the industrial part of town. Having reached the mini storage warehouse he found the bin he had rented earlier that week. Inserting a key, he unlocked the metal door and pushed it up revealing the much used, dusty, once red, Camaro purchased two days ago for cash.

The Camaro trunk held typical fishing gear. A well-worn, fourteen-foot rowboat was tied securely to the rusty luggage rack on top. Perched on the back seat, was a 5-horse outboard, and the rear floor held two 5-gallon cans of gasoline. A chipped plastic picnic cooler occupied the front passenger seat. A wave of apprehension swept over him. It was almost over.

Opening the driver side door, he found the compass had fallen to the floor of the front seat. He got in, shoving the compass into his shirt pocket.

The drive through Miami and south to the Keys was slow and easy. This was not the time to be stopped by cops for any reason. The Camaro was not slick and shiny. Nor was it fast or noisy. Best of all, it could not be traced back to Wayne.

"Keep it slow," he mumbled as he maneuvered the car southward. Everything seemed in order. The trip of less than a hundred miles was going to take about two and a half hours. Slow and easy drive for the first hour, after that, an hour on the water to rendezvous with his friend in crime, Jim and their money.

Wayne had met Jim Hamar six years ago. Both men had sat in a Fort Lauderdale diner reading the same Miami Herald classifieds for rental apartments. After talking about the shortage of apartments and jobs, they decided to pool their efforts and money. It would benefit them both, they decided. And it had!

Both men had arrived in South Florida looking for the good life they had heard so much about. The good life, however, was not so easy to find. They learned this fact early. Everyone seemed to be divided into one of two categories … those with very little money (and little chance of finding any), and those who found money extremely plentiful, with more of it waiting to drop into our-stretched wallets. The two men learned quickly that it was nice to have money. It was not so nice to have none.

327

At first, construction work was easy to find. In addition, it paid well. However, with over-building, the chances of steady work and good money quickly ran out. So they took what work they could find, asked few questions, kept their mouths shut and their wallets open. And their wallets got fatter.

They worked for Roberto Delgado long before they actually met him. His was not the sort of work you filled out an application for. Delgado had several business ventures going, but the most profitable was drugs. He bought large quantities from boats off shore, brought the merchandise into Florida, and quickly distributed it to eager local buyers. It was into one of these buying runs that Wayne and Jim were now involved. It was not their first time. It was, however, their biggest, and as it turned out, their most profitable employment.

Delgado had arranged for last night's buy off the Grand Bahamas. Wayne and Jim were to deliver the money and return with the merchandise. Simple. But the two men made a calculated change of plans. Keeping all the money seemed like a better idea. One million dollars in untraceable cash! After this one, they'd be able to retire. It was risky, but extremely worth the risk for that kind of money.

Last night, four of them, with the million dollars stashed inside a large briefcase, left Fort Lauderdale on Delgado's yacht. It took a lot of guts for them to even consider the steal. More so, to pull it off.

The two crewmen had struggled briefly when they were tied, and shoved below. All these men were seasoned to the ways of South Florida waters and the drug traffic that covered it. All knew the pleasures and the dangers. In spite of, or perhaps because of these elements, they chose to work this kind of life. If it wasn't today, it would be tomorrow, or next month, but violent death came with the business.

After securing the crew below deck, the two now-pirates loaded themselves and the briefcase into a sturdy lifeboat and raced away from the yacht. Within minutes of their departure, the yacht exploded with a violent force, rocking that part of the ocean. Their lifeboat moved slightly with the vibration, then continued on its journey. The explosives did a nearly total job. Nothing would remain except for small bits of debris blown beyond the explosion. Pieces found later would identify the yacht and, hopefully, would lead to the assumption that all aboard had been killed. All details had been thought through very carefully.

After the expensive yacht exploded, both men had breathed a little easier. The hard part was over. Now it was going to be all patience and finishing details. They had to dispose of the lifeboat and replace it with another boat. If the lifeboat existed at all, Delgado would find it … and then them. However, they expected to steer toward the Grand Turk islands. That seemed far enough away for a safe life.

Jim had stayed aboard the lifeboat with the money last night. He was to head south and meet Wayne in a few hours after dawn this morning. Dragging the money through the water in a night swim was impossible. To take Delgado's lifeboat anywhere near shore was a foolish thought. As a result, Wayne had slipped into a wet suit and headed for shore to secure the replacement boat and a few supplies.

Jim had offered few suggestions during the planning of the steal. He left the important decisions to Wayne and seemed to be comfortable with what Wayne organized. Jim's knowledge of the sea, however, was another matter. His was far superior to that of Wayne, and he proved it in the quick, careful planning of this early afternoon's rendezvous. Jim had calculated it all and explained it to Wayne as best he could. What Wayne did not understand, he accepted as gospel. Jim explained how, when, and where this meeting was to take place on the water. He instructed Wayne with diagrams, and gave exact instruction about using the compass and the boat. Wayne handled the physical things. Swimming, blowing up the yacht, and getting all the gear they needed transported.

The night swim had been a long one, and several times Wayne had the feeling a boat was following him. Eventually, the boats all veered off to another direction. Wayne reached land about three o'clock in the morning to discover an all-night beach party going on near the only part of the shore not occupied by high rise condos or hotels. He was not going to risk being seen by some party drunk or condo dweller who spent the night in nocturnal activity.

Crawling into the corner of an L-shaped rock wall surrounding the edge of a park he waited for the party to end. Stripping to a brief pair of cut-offs, he hurriedly buried the wet suit in a shallow sandy grave. Exhausted from the swim, he fell asleep.

Their meeting was planned for about ten in the morning, an hour plus south of where the small boat was to be launched. The boat was old, but seemed reliable. He made a brief stop at a 7-Eleven store and picked up a couple six packs of Michelob Dark, and some deli sandwiches. He bought ice and packed it around the beer and sandwiches in the cooler. He had plenty of time so he did not hurry.

Wayne drove the Camaro into Miami and then south. June was hot and sticky. After two minutes on the road, his clothes stuck to his body. He hadn't bothered with the A/C. There was some sense of freedom and peace driving they highway, windows open, the hot, salty ocean air rushing past, leaving traces of itself on the skin. Glancing at the rearview mirror several times, he determined he was not being followed.

Buying or selling drugs was dangerous enough, but to steal from the middle was an altogether different game. This time both sides were going to want them. And both sides would want them dead.

On one of the tiny Keys, halfway between Key Largo and Key West, Wayne unloaded the small boat, locked the motor in place, and stashed the fishing gear beneath the center seat.

The full cooler was also put aboard. Typical supplies for a typical day of fishing.

Dragging the boat into the water, he gave a shove, climbed aboard and rowed out a good distance before trying to start the motor. He was wound up and tense. Today was the biggest day of his life. It was a do-it-right or die day. The next couple of hours were going to be biggies.

A few small boats drifted nearby, lazy sailors and fishermen held lifeless poles pointed at the horizon, caring about nothing or no one, it seemed. Wayne worked at looking lazy and uncaring, too. At least until he was well out in the ocean. Until the broken chain of coastline that formed these Florida Keys no longer seemed a threat to his life.

It had taken three pulls of the starter cord before the motor came alive. The motor coughed, then coughed again, vibrating the small craft, and at the same time, overwhelming Wayne's structured calmness and quiet.

He glanced back along the fading shoreline with darting eyes and tried to swallow the panic rising in his throat. Slowly, he turned his back to the open ocean, sitting stiff and straight, waiting for that fatal blow. Or, would he hear the gun before he felt its message?

With the motor wide open and roaring, he glanced at the compass, and pointed the bow of the boat to correspond.

Finally, unable to contain his excitement any longer, he said it softly at first. "One million dollars!" Then louder. "One million dollars!" A broad smile cut across his face. The blood in his veins was racing. His entire body felt like it was on fire. It was going to be all right now.

Everything was going to work. He and Jim were going to split one million dollars. Soon.

He checked the compass and continued toward the meeting place. In this little fishing boat, the pair would track a course beyond the tip of South Florida and into the Caribbean. It would take time, but they had time now. They planned to keep just within sight of land as much as possible, but far enough away to stay undetected. Keeping it slow and easy, but keeping it moving. Away from South Florida. Away from Delgado.

He checked the compass again, pricking his index finger on a jagged piece of metal somewhere on the case. He sucked the drop of blood away and returned to searching the area for signs of Jim and the lifeboat. Somewhere nearby the boat was waiting. He checked the compass again.

Wayne circled the boat several times within the planned meeting area. He checked the compass, again. Something was wrong. Somehow, he had missed Jim. His little boat was where it was supposed to be. He was sure. His calculations were correct. He had done it right. It had to be at this spot. Right here.

A nagging in the pit of his stomach started to erupt. He surveyed the entire area, trying not to give in to reality. Again and again he circled the planned area. The sun was hot and his lips were parched. He didn't think about the beer. He thought about the million dollars, and of where he might go to get out of the hot sun. He knew he could not go back to the shore. It wasn't safe for him any longer. He thought of Jim. And … he thought about the money.

If he were lost, he was sure Jim would find him. Jim would never leave him. They had talked about going to Jamaica. Maybe Jim had gotten confused and started for the Caribbean.

Maybe a lot of things. Wayne refused to think about the most logical.

After giving some thought to his situation, he checked the compass again and steered the tiny boat in another wide circle. Jim was going to be just ahead, and then off to the beautiful Turk islands.

He emptied the last can of gasoline into the motor and slipped into the bottom of the boat for some rest. He held the boat on a circular course. His eyes were heavy and soon he closed them to dream of his million dollars. Jim was just ahead. He knew it.

As he lay in the bottom of the gently rocking boat, lips parched and skin seared by the constant burning sun, his mind wandered from where he was to where he wanted to be. Sitting in the shade of a very large palm tree with a soft April rain pattering around him. He combed his fingers through the mound of loose paper money beside him on the ground. The bills felt cool and yet, electrifying. He smiled.

The smile and the pain of his cracked and bleeding lips brought him back to the boat. His hand found an object. Small, round, smooth. As he closed his fingers around it and brought it toward his face, his finger was again, pricked by something sharp around the edge of the compass. Through squinted, swollen eyes, he surveyed the damaged to his finger and then looked at the sharp culprit. Vaguely, he remembered doing the same thing before. He looked closer. A small metal needle had been partially implanted into the strip around the edge of the compass.

As close as Wayne could make out, it was protruding from the North indicator position. As he juggled the instrument, he noticed something else he had not been aware of before. The directional needle of the compass did not move around the dial, regardless of how he held it.

It jiggled a little, but always hovered around the North direction.

This thinking and looking made him very tired. He closed his eyes again. This time he saw the same palm tree, the same pile of money, the same cool rain, but it was Jim he saw sitting, playing with the money. Jim was laughing, while holding a compass, pointing to the magnetic needle that pointed north.

Suddenly the laughter faded, Jim's face faded. The pile of money faded, and all sounds faded, except for the gentle splashing of the immense ocean against the wooden sides of the little boat. Soon, that, too, disappeared. Wayne Duke never heard the clatter of the compass as it fell from his limp hand back into the bottom of the boat. The needle still hovered near the North indicator.

END

ALL THIS ME

By

Eunice L. Sykes

When I look around, time has moved

All this me and I'm in this groove

Waistline larger, boobs I never had

Chin down to here, it's not wonder I'm sad.

Over 50 eyes, can't read a report

Sometimes my arms are far too short

The printed word seems to be much smaller

As for distance reading, can you make it taller?

Undergarments meant to contour binds

My hourglass figure is no longer kind

Mercy, mercy, all this me

Whatever happened to the way I used to be?

Smiles and frown lines like birds called crow

Lotion on dry skin before I head out and go

Lordy, Lordy, how can this be?

All this me, all over me!

His Final Farewell

By

Sharon Davidson

"It's time. You know what I mean."

His words cut through her like icy daggers. She forced a smile in acknowledgement. She studied his face. His eyes still twinkled as they had for over 37 years, despite the fact that the disease ravaged his body leaving it weak and drained. His slightly crooked nose was framed by a strong face, a face she longed to keep forever in her life. Running her fingers through his full head of salt and pepper hair, she marveled at how, despite months of chemo, he had not lost it.

She snuggled closer to him drawing in his scent, trying for one last memory. She inhaled his Old Spice aftershave deeper; smell had always been a way for her to remember things.

"What am I going to do without you?" She tried to keep the tears at bay as they snuggled one last time.

"Live your life," he replied calmly smiling at her from his pillow. Those were the last coherent words he spoke to her.

Tears flowed quietly down her face and into the pillow. Crying was not allowed. His body continued to function for four more days. However, his spirit had given up and he slowly drifted away.

She tried to stay awake to be with him as he drew his last breath, but in his wisdom, he waited until she passed out from exhaustion. At 6:47AM she felt something soft brush against her neck. It reminded her of her childhood bunny, Thumper. His fur was soft just like what she felt now. Then the edge of the bed moved as if someone had sat down.

She sat up expecting to see one of her well-meaning family members, but the room was empty. She knew it was him. He was saying his final farewell.

HAIKU TIME

By

Eunice L. Sykes

Take flight with rhythm,
Always in sync together,
Stirs my soul all night

~~~~~~~~~~

No longer with us
Sassy and fine, she loved life
Still in our hearts true!

~~~~~~~~~~

Some grands don't know her
The look, style, that certain "it"
Inherent for sure

~~~~~~~~~~

Mommy, it's alright
Turmoil does not lasts always!
Of the three, she knew

~~~~~~~~~~

Because they endured
We can be strong together
Let's do it right now

~~~~~~~~~~

Michael Brown is dead
Eighteen years old and he's gone
Can't understand why

BEING A HOOKER, AND OTHER HOBBIES.

By

Carol G. Vetula

During the years when my children were small, in school, and not too interested in my life in general, I occupied my leisure hours with hobbies. Hobbies that enlisted the help of our five children, various pets, neighbors, friends, relatives and on a few occasions, my husband even consented to participate in one of my wild flings. There have been times when the hobby of the day included only myself. Regardless of the number of players, most of these leisure time activities of mine resulted in the same short-lived, non-productive end.

To best explain why I became a hobby freak is simply to say that when my husband and I were married, we blended together a brood of five young children, all within three years of the same age. After the first couple of years, the novelty of our family situation passed and reality set in. Close on the heels of reality arrived confusion, disorganization, and a mother who seemed to be tired all the time.

"You need a hobby," my thoughtful husband suggested.

"Yes," I agreed. "I do need a hobby. Something that would be interesting to do on my own time, and maybe even earn a little extra money, which would certainly come in quite handy. Maybe I could even become famous." The name of several world famous women came to mind. Why not me? I spent several afternoons that week lying on the sofa thinking about it.

It was at this point I discovered my first two hobbies; afternoon naps and soap operas. With the kids in school all day, finally, and the house quiet and peaceful, I learned to relax. At first my delightful naps were of a brief duration and usually concluded with a delicious cup of coffee. With these few minutes to myself, I was ready for the after school rush.

But hobbies are addictive and soon my short naps were replaced with afternoon sleeps. I'll never know just how long this hobby would have continued because then I discovered the afternoon soaps.

Perhaps feeling a little guilty about my sleep periods I decided to preform useful chores while watching TV. This worked well for a short time until it became necessary to do all my daily work in the TV room. It was then that I discovered knitting.

Knitting is a good hobby. It is creative and useful. I plunged in and created four pair of slippers. The fifth pair was not as much fun. I was bored and the kids were't crazy about wearing knitted slippers with large wooly balls on the fronts. My husband threatened to leave me if I presented him with a pair. I hid the ball of brown yarn. Then I met Pat.

Pat was a neighbor. She loved music and could play a great assortment of stringed instruments plus the piano. She suggested I learn the guitar and loaned me one of hers. This seemed like a marvelous and very creative idea. I pictured myself astride a high stool, guitar slung across my body, plucking tune after tune to the delight of friends and family. I even recall a bit of fantasy about fame and fortune. Working hard to master my new hobby, Pat and I practiced almost daily. I listened to all the Peter, Paul and Mary and the Kingston Trio music I was able to find. Pat accompanied me on guitar, piano and banjo. It was wonderful and I was impresses with our new musical career. At my suggestion, we invited our husbands and kids to our first concert. This affair took place in my living room. Perching on a stool, guitar slung across my chest, I played my heart out. During the second song the kids drifted off to play elsewhere. Our husbands were polite and stayed to the bitter end when Pat's husband reminded her that he had to get up early for work. They left.

Then I asked the burning question. "Well, honey, what did you think?"

He was tactful. "It was good. Very … good." It was the same tone he used when informed the neighbor's nephew was now potty trained. So much for fame and fortune and my guitar.

The holiday season was approaching anyway, so I gave the guitar back to Pat, and my sister-in-law and I started making Christmas tree decorations with Styrofoam balls, sequins, glass beads and tiny bits of ribbon. That hobby died after the dog ate a half bag of sequins. The dog lived, but that hobby died.

From there I tried sports. Skating was too difficult and fishing gave me a bad sunburn. Jogging made me sweat, which I was not keen on doing. Exercise was boring even when friends participated with me. Nothing but the weeds survived in my first garden and the kids did not appreciate my French cooking.

Suddenly, I found a new hobby. I became a hooker. I hooked rugs and wall hangings for my parents, my in-laws, my brothers, and their wives. I hooked a large eagle rug for my husband's office. I hooked seat covers and toilet paper covers. I covered paper baskets, flower pots and wine bottles. I even hooked rugs for each of the kids. That was probably my longest lasting hobby. So far I hadn't earned a dime. I worked so hard at hooking I burned myself out on that project. But it was wonderful while it lasted. To this day, nearly everyone I know has at least one reminder of my years as a hooker.

As a family project we tried our hands at raising tropical fish. We had reasonably good luck with this, but tiny fish have a way of expiring, unexpectedly, and the wails and tears of broken-hearted daughters finally got to me.

Next, I took up sewing and made two skirts and an eight piece set of yellow terry cloth seat covers for my pool furniture. My mother had to come to my rescue with the covers, and one of the skirts made me look awfully fat. There had to be something I was good at and could enjoy.

For my birthday that year, my dear, patient husband gave me an electric typewriter and fixed up a small room just for me. Now I had a real hobby. I am going to be a famous writer. I know I can do this. It's what I always wanted to do. The money I make will surely come in handy and I have lots of spare time now. Somewhere between the afternoon naps and the yellow pool furniture covers, the kids all grew up. I don't think I need a hobby any more. What I want now, is a career and I can devote a lot of time to my new career of writing. This time I will become famous.

END

RANDALL EARL

By

Edgar Levy

The last time Randall Earl felt loved

He was in his mother's womb

After which, all of life

Became a glaciered tomb

Never a sunny day

Never anything

But buzzard luck

Floated Randall's way

Randall was standing by the gate

Where dreams came and went

Was when the woman with the hazel eyes

Looking up…noticed the scowling gent

When he saw those electric eyes looking

A wondrous enchantment on Randall fell

And whether he was flying or floating

Old Randall could not tell

His eyes began fluttering in disbelief

Was this his bold new start?

The next time Randall Earl felt loved

Was when hazel eyes smiled warmly

When sunshine entered his heart

DEAR KORY

By

Eunice L. Sykes

Where in the world did the time go?
It's been over 21 years since I first imagined you
Started when my oldest announced "Mommy, I'm pregnant!"
My reaction? "Wow! You are! I love it; I'm quite content."

Yes, you were my induction into that land of grandmother hood
It was time, I was ready, on top of the world I proudly stood
The guessing began: Will it be a diva girl or a man's boy?
Delighted with either; I was filled with unspeakable joy.

Your journey to here was filled with memories galore
Presents, parties, shopping in your honor, for sure
Your arrival was hasty, the usual--without incident
When I looked at you, love blossomed, indeed you were heaven sent.

Yes, I met and fell in love with a beautiful, healthy 6 pound, 8 ounce boy
Your parents named you Kory, to them you were their new toy
At seven months, you had your first piece of candy, couldn't wait
A strawberry Twizzler, a family favorite, you greedily took the bait.

I so wanted to be called something exotic, like nana or Momma E
At the appropriate age, it was you who decided it was not going to be Gigi
For you stood on my porch, knocked on my door, and in your loudest yell
"GGGGGRRRRRAAAAANNNNNMMMMMMAAAA!" Dang! What the hell?!

That sentiment has morphed into Grammy, Grandma, most often Gram
That, to you, is lovingly who I am
Today you are a tower—standing boldly as a 6 foot 2inch young man
Tall, dark, and handsome, experiencing everything you can.
You're kind, sweet, gentle, spirited, and very smart
Ambitious, still a boy! I've loved you from the start

My blood flows through you, the offspring of the offspring
I am blessed to witness this precious life and all that it will bring
Child of my child, bone of my bones
You're now a young adult, so very grown

Paving the way for the others: Kira and Nicholas
A role model, barely, you're sometimes ridiculous!
Nearly twenty-one, though, you're the first of three
Our precious baby boy Kory, part of my legacy.

Gram

Margaret Chester

Margaret Chester lives in Henry County Georgia with her husband of 29 years, three grown children and five grandchildren. Retired Federal Employee from the VA Medical Center.

I wrote about my great- grandmother, Effie for my mother who adored her grandmother. The determination of a woman during the hard times of the Great Depression and WWII. Technology had advanced tremendously from her birth until her death.

Born July 24th 1969 / Detroit Michigan. Year of the Hippies, Riots, Bell Bottoms and Go Go boots. Hated school dropped in the 9th grade. 2001 Went back earned my high school diploma.

Dream: Script writer, Home Decorator, Novelist. Currently developing 2' books (Good Morning Violet / One Million Vote). Creating stories is something I can remember doing as a child. Developing characters and concepts. Engaging my imagination. But nothing beats the feeling of finding that perfect word to complete a plot.

Father: Obie Boyd Sr. 85, Vietnam Veteran, Purple Heart Holder. Currently Resides in L.A Mother: Eva Catherine Boyd Peterson. Hairdresser, seamstress and vocalist. Nick names flanchie doll. People would come from miles, to hear her beautiful voice. Passed away from breast cancer. 91' 10 siblings:

Moved to Atlanta in 1999. Raised 4 wonderful children. Happy grandmother of three precious Grand babies including a set of fraternal twins a girl & boy.

My greatest accomplishment to date are my children.

Hobbies: Antique Shopping, Karaoke Bars, Theater & writing short stories.

Background: 97' I played the wicked witch Evileen in musical play. The Wizard Of Oz standing ovation all 3 night of performance. 98' played screaming fan at a basketball game, in the movie. He got game staring Denzel Washington. 2012' Americas got talent & Sundays Best. 2013' Apollo Theater. Selected) Extra work until present.

Home: Atlanta, GA.

My Mantra: Never give up. Use what you have on hand.

When I held my first book, *Emily's Locket*, in my hand it sealed my fate. After many years in the corporate world, accumulating information and characters, I had no idea retirement would set me on a new adventure.

After a whirlwind courtship of twenty-one days I became engaged to my soul mate and married him a few months later. Four years later a daughter arrived on the scene. From my home in Connecticut, to marriage, to Florida and then to Georgia I traveled around absorbing the people and places I encountered. The best way to people watch and learn about the world was when I traveled around the country as a software trainer instrumental in the Y2K conversion of a major financial institution. After 9/11 and the downsizing of my department my husband and I moved to Florida to take care of aging parents. With the devastating loss of my husband of 37 years to cancer I returned to Georgia to be close to my daughter.

My first book *Emily's Locket*, is a suspenseful murder mystery. A sequel, *The Traveling Corpse*, is in the works. My second published book, *Innocence Island*, is a historical romance. Both books are available on Amazon.com in print or Kindle.

I am a member of The Heritage Writers in McDonough, Georgia, where I served as president 2013 - 2015. I am also a member of Gwinnett County writers in Lilburn, Georgia. When not reading or writing I enjoys spending time with my family and Daisy, my Chihuahua.

Moira Fisher was born and raised in the sunny city of Durban, South Africa, and has always esteemed the art of writing. Her English teacher was her superhero, and she would rather have sat listening to her talk about the origin of words than run on the sports field.

In 1993 Moira, her husband, and their young daughter came to the USA. It was while homeschooling that she realized there were certain books her daughter always went back to for comfort in times of sickness, loneliness and distress. These are the types of books she longs to write for children.

She firmly believes that if you teach a child to read you give them the best gift. And by encouraging a child to read and write you ensure that he or she will never be lonely or bored and will always have something to talk about.

The main character in her first book, *Bruce the Spruce*© 2008, is a tree who wants to be important in the world. When he discovers that his brother, Patrick, was the town square's Christmas tree he is sure that fame and fortune is in his future too. Bernice Bunny tells him that he will be chopped down and left to die. Ignoring the warnings of the disillusioned bunny, Bruce grows and flourishes, dreaming of being a Christmas tree until Bob the Squirrel shows him the stump that was Patrick and tells what B.C. Chickadee had reported. When fall gives way to winter, Bruce shrinks down, trying to look lopsided so he won't be picked as a Christmas tree. A conservation minded family chooses him, has him potted, and takes him home to decorate. Bruce the Spruce has his time to shine. After Christmas he is put outside next to the garbage where his companions are icy winds, feelings of rejection, and the ominous chomping sounds of the chipper on its weekly rounds. Can Bruce find a new life and purpose? What will happen to him? Is there life after Christmas for Bruce? (Available on Amazon.com and Kindle. Also available for check out at all five Henry County Libraries: McDonough, Locust Grove, Stockbridge, Hampton and Fairview.)

It is Moira's hope that children will keep Bruce in their hearts as they mature and a whole generation of tree planters will grow from her writing. Like Bruce the Spruce she hopes young eyes will see the wisdom one can glean through diverse friendships and the knowledge of nature.

Moira continues to work on her next book, collaborating with her daughter and granddaughter—avid readers and writers themselves. Her daughter—a song writer—has written a song for Moira's next book while she is happily painting to illustrate her book.

Moira and her husband reside in McDonough, Georgia.

348

Author and Army Veteran, Carolyn D. Julien, a native of Arkansas, currently maintains a home in the Atlanta area. She grew up on a farm there with five siblings where she collected arrowheads found in the wide-opened fields and read every child's book that came across her path. Her childhood favorites included *The Little Red Hen*, *The Gingerbread Man*, and *Hansel and Greta*. During her adolescent years in North Carolina, she fell in love with the *Merlin" Novels*, and was captivated by the mystical undertone. Her most read book now is the Holy Bible, and her favorite writers are the Apostle James, Apostle Paul and King David. She is the wife of Chief Warrant Officer, Pierre Julien, a retired career Army Veteran, and they share three children, Cynthia, 1SG Brenov, and 2LT Joshua Eli. A member of Zeta Phi Beta Sorority, Inc., she earned her Bachelor's degrees from Southern University in LA and Master's from East Carolina University in NC. Carolyn currently does Missionary work with her husband in Haiti and has lived in both Asia and Europe.

She has loved creating stories all of her life and currently has two published books: *Parables from the Heart*, and *Trudy – My Sunday Morning Dilemma*. Her upcoming children's book is *Carlos Birthday – Frankie's Big Inspiration*. Her stories in this book were written when she was in her thirties and are based on life experiences occurring while in her late twenties and thirties. Her favorite quote is: You can do all things through Christ who strengthens you.

Edgar Levy

Edgar Levy spent most of his life in New Orleans, La. before moving to Georgia in 2005. He is a graduate of the Southern University System of Louisiana. After 35 enjoyable and memorable years serving as a Physical Education Instructor, Athletic Coach and Athletic Director, he retired from the public education sector in December of 2015.

Writing has always intrigued Edgar. It became for him a curious hobby, something to do in quiet times. Upon retiring, early in 2016, he joined the Heritage Writers Group.

Michael McLarnon

After retiring as a clinical psychiatrist, Michael McLarnon became frustrated with his golf game and decided to switch gears. He is now spending his retirement years in a new career, that of a novelist. He brings decades of knowledge dealing with the human psyche to craft unique mystery/thrillers.

Michael McLarnon has three books in print, *L'Orange Fire, Books One* through Three. Taking place in a near-future Los Angeles, they follow medical examiner Jennifer Singh and homicide detective Race Griffin, thrust together as they solve murder cases. He is working on sequels to the L'Orange series, as well as a number of stand-alone novels. His books are available at Amazon.com.

351

C. J. F. Mobley

Jane Mobley is a retired middle and elementary school teacher and librarian. She currently lives in McDonough, Georgia with her husband, two rescued dogs and a recued cat. She graduated from Georgia Southern University with a B. S. in Education and the University of West Georgia with a M.Ed. and Education Specialist degree in school library media. She has two grown children and anxiously awaits grandchildren, to which she has been told, she will have to wait quite some time.

Jane loves to read, write and journal. Now that she has retired from a career in education, she has time to work on the multiple projects in her writing folder. She enjoys spending time with her family.

Casey Muller is an eighteen-year-old junior at Clayton State University, studying Accounting and Criminal Justice. She became infatuated with reading and writing at a very young age and has been producing short stories and novellas for most of her life. At the age of thirteen, Muller completed her first (unpublished) novel, Adam's Heart, and at fifteen, published an article in The Henry Herald, detailing the psychological harm that media can inflict upon those with poor body image. Currently, she is in the process of writing a momentarily nameless novel about the fall of Vaudeville theater and the ruined lives of the actors left in the wake. Looking forward, Muller hopes to lead a successful career as a Forensic Accountant while leaving plenty of time to nurture her life-long passion for writing.

R.S. Raniere

I write fiction and poetry, and teach composition and American literature at Georgia Military College. I received my master's degree from Rutgers University in New Jersey, where I lived most of my life until moving to Georgia several years ago. I wrote my first poem when I was ten. I am currently working on a novel, a poetry chap book, and two short stories. One of my poems, First Kiss, was recently published in Atlanta Review. I love writing poetry. I've always been intrigued by how words can be used, in and out of rhyme, to convey meaning, produce imagery, evoke emotion; break a heart or incite a riot. This is the power of poetry.

Barbara Scott, a Hampton, Georgia resident for over 30 years, has enjoyed writing since she was a teenager. Her career began as news writer for a Christian newspaper and then a staff photographer for the local hometown weekly newspaper. For over 18 years, she self-published and edited a Christian tabloid, the SonBurst News, and often included her own relevant articles. Her poetry has been published in the annual Gordon College poetry book (Driftwood 1989), as well as in a published, collection of poetry (Forever Spoken, 2007). Currently, she is working on a fiction, to be self-published. As always, during intense times, poetry is her release. In 2009, she graduated from the New York Institute of Photography and in 2013, she earned a degree in Communications from Gordon College. Barbara and her husband, Gary, have been married for over 28 years, and are parents to 3 sons and a daughter. They have a granddaughter, Kyleigh, and a grandson, Jaxson, who are the center of their joy. She is active in both church and community and enjoys a wide variety of creative arts, playing in the church orchestra (clarinet), and is an avid photographer.

Everett Smith lives in Georgia, USA. He was born in Illinois but, being an "Air Force brat", has lived in or visited most of the states in the United States. He has two Bachelor degrees (Biology and Electrical Engineering) and has served in the U.S. Army. His career in industrial maintenance has spanned over thirty years and continues to this day.

Smith is currently working on his first book, Genesis, which will be book one of a trilogy — The Grail Chronicles. His first publication, the short story Moon, is also associated with this trilogy.

Delores L Staton currently resides in McDonough, GA. Her young formative years were spent in Ann Arbor, Michigan. She obtained a Master of French Literature at the University of Michigan. As a scholar of languages and linguistics, Ms. Staton feeds and excites her creative soul through writing and painting. Ms. Staton loves the intrigue of weaving an intellectual web. Her ultimate objective is to present images that impel the reader to personal reflection.

Eunice L. Sykes

A writer all her life, Eunice L. Sykes is a full time author, poet, public speaker, and editor. Her fourth book, Mashed Potatoes in My Salad: An Alzheimer's Caregiver Memoir, tells the poignant story of a woman, who after several unsuccessful, toxic and abusive relationships, finally finds the man of her dreams under unlikely, risky and daring circumstances, only to end up in caregiver roles time and time again as he endures serious illnesses--including the ultimate, life taking disease Alzheimer's. This is a complex, multilayered story of ambition, drive, love, romance, endurance, resilience, loyalty, survival, love, and joy. The reflective lessons learned will inspire and motivate to be all that you can be and to live your best life better.

She has written and published three other books: My Own Story; From Kibler's Bridge to Miller Road: 65 Years of Christian Service in the African Methodist Episcopal Church; and Instant Church: My Millennium Musings (selected poems). She has also edited an inspirational book, Mothers of Hope.

In her spare time, Eunice chases that elusive little white ball, honing her golf skills. You can also find her leading Ebony Eyes Red Hatters, a group of lively, energetic, fun-loving women. Eunice lives with her husband and soul mate Don near Atlanta, Georgia. She has three children and three grandchildren and is a member of Alpha Kappa Alpha Sorority.

Prior to retirement, Eunice was a five-time award winning supplier diversity officer at a Fortune 500 company, leading diversity strategies in both purchasing and workforce environments.

Her work can be viewed on www.eunicelsykes.com; her email address is el123sykes@comcast.net

Carol earned her first writing award for a mystery short story. She has received several awards since for mystery and suspense pieces, and has short articles printed in newspapers.

Her current novel, To Love And Protect, is a romance novel, published as an E-Book and can be found on Amazon. Nearly all of her writings are connected, in some way, to cruise adventures, or water experiences, as cruising is what she does for fun, and to gain additional personal inspirations to add to what she knows intimately inside the cruising world. A new novel should be out later this year.

Carol and her husband, David, reside in Georgia and cruise several times a year, mostly to and around the Mediterranean, especially with stays and trips into Italy.

www.ingramcontent.com/pod-product-compliance
Lightning Source LLC
Chambersburg PA
CBHW071211250626
47159CB00001B/286